ABOUT THE AUTHOR

O'Neill is one of a very close knit family of eleven brought up on a farm in County Carlow. His working life started in science teacher training in impoverished schools in South Africa and he is currently involved in computer based education and running a farm in Kilkenny. Recently restoring the ancient Killahara castle in Tipperary and helping his father publish a social history reconnected him to stories and beliefs that were still vibrant in his own childhood and prompted him to pull together the Fionn tales he had made up to entertain his own children en route to school.

OLD FRIENDS

The Lost Tales of Fionn Mac Cumhaill

Tom O'Neill

Little Island

First published 2010
by Little Island
an imprint of New Island
2 Brookside
Dundrum Road
Dublin 14

www.littleisland.ie

ISBN 978-1-84840-941-5

Little Island received financial assistance from
The Arts Council (An Chomhairle Ealaíon), Dublin, Ireland.

Book Cover design by Inka Hagen
Printed in Ireland by Colourbooks.
10 9 8 7 6 5 4 3 2 1

For Paula, Aisling, Amy, Christie, Maurice,
Kate and Uncle Billy

ACKNOWLEDGMENTS

Thanks to the wonderful Siobhán Parkinson of Little Island for guiding me patiently and insightfully to this point. Thank you Paula for the faith and tireless encouragement.

Thanks to Máire Uí Mhaicín for shining a scholarly light but also for kind and encouraging words; to Marian Oliver and Elaina O'Neill for the painstaking detailed scrutiny; to Bernard Voges and Inka Hagen for a great deal of work on graphics; and to Edwin and everyone at Little Island for the hard work of bringing it all together.

Good people from our past revealed themselves to me during the process of creating this book. People of my own family and neighbours who are gone but whose words and ways of thinking came back to me as I worked. There were also reverberations of voices from other parts and times whose words were recorded by the generations of dedicated folklorists who have created a National record second to none. I feel richer for having been immersed in their world. I have tried to engage with the spirit of their storytelling rather than reproducing their words. In that, I hope that I have done them some credit.

And mostly I hope that I manage to bring to your life a share of the great entertainment and wonder I have experienced in the writing of this book.

CONTENTS

1
A PLACE BEST LEFT ALONE

Stormy clouds blacked out the quarter moon. A screech momentarily paralysed Dark. Maybe a disturbed snipe. He was already close to the forbidden place.

His LED torch failed. With another mis-step into a soft spot, water seeped into his boot and the toxic spring thorns of a hawthorn branch made painful contact with his face. *Shite!* Feckit! His mother didn't like it, but recently, Dark had found that cursing helped to beat back tears of frustration. He sucked in his breath. His courage was rapidly draining away into the cold bog-water. What kind of foolishness was it that had landed him, all alone, in this dark and desolate marsh in the middle of the night?

There was a time, about three years ago now, when Dark's only worries had been the release date of the next Playstation console and whether he'd get picked for the under-twelves football team. Then, one Sunday afternoon, his father went and drove his BSA M20 into a tree and everything changed.

1

They buried him deep in the ground.

The house in Glanmire Heights had to be sold. Someone else was in Dark's room now, with the secret compartment his dad had made for them to hide the BB gun from his mam, and Dark and his mother had come to live in a converted cowshed in the middle of nowhere with no channels on the TV and awful, dark, cold silence every night from nine.

His mam 'wasn't coping very well', people said. When his father's half-mad brother Connie had insisted that they come to live in the converted 'extension' to his house, she seemingly hadn't many other offers on the table. So Dark hadn't said anything when she asked what he thought.

Dark had never met Connie before – he'd been away somewhere. He was a huge fecker with a great black mop of hair and beard. Dark had been a bit afraid of him that first day they'd arrived in the white van Connie had sent to collect them and all their things. When he talked and laughed with the van driver he could surely be heard all across the valley.

Dark hadn't liked this place of Connie's very much, but he still didn't say anything. There wasn't anything much to say anymore. That was how he felt about things anyway. That's how he'd got the name The Dark when he started at the local community school. He didn't mind the name. The names he used less often now were McLean from his father and Arthur from his mother.

At first they'd tried to get him to talk. They got some

kind of counsellor person into the school to talk to him. He could still picture her very clearly. *How does this make you feel, Arthur?* she would ask, with nowhere for him to look, no escape from her big watery eyes all surrounded in blue make-up. How does that make you feel, Arthur? It's OK to miss someone. Do you feel angry, Arthur? *It's OK if you ever want to cry, Arthur.* But he hadn't given in to any of it. He didn't have any desire to 'explore emotions' or do any of that stuff. That wasn't his kind of thing.

His mam would wait until they were in the car so that he couldn't wander off. She would switch off Beat FM and then ask him, worriedly, *How are things going, Arthur?* He loved her and was worried about her too. But this talking business didn't serve any purpose that he could see. It just made him uncomfortable. *Fine,* was all he could say. He didn't know what the feck they wanted from him.

One evening, when she was home from work earlier than usual and the three of them were in the kitchen, her on her laptop, him sitting on the armchair next to the Aga playing with the collies, and Connie mixing milk formula for calves, she said to him, 'Arthur, you should ask your Uncle Connie to show you how to play the drums. He used to be in a metal band once. Let out everything you're feeling on them.'

Dark said nothing. But he kind of wished his mam didn't think she had to be all 'with it', talking about metal and stuff.

Connie turned away from the sink and laughed.

'You can hammer the shite out of the drums any time

3

you like, Art. But maybe, Helen, you're watching a bit too much Oprah.'

His mam looked like she was going to cry, but then she just shook her head and laughed too.

That was when Dark had started to like Connie. Gloom never got much chance to settle on the house when he was around.

Dark didn't mind working with the animals. He had started to do some feeding and watering and other jobs around the yard. Connie had given him two white-headed heifer calves of his own. He also gave him a key for the quad bike on the condition that he didn't tell his mam.

Back when Connie was around, the place always had visitors. Neighbours generally called in if they were passing. They'd stand at the Aga and relay news or look for Connie's opinions, which he was never slow to offer, on anything from problems with the bank manager to scabby sheep. Dark wasn't sure whether they were mainly there for the advice and mystery poultices or for the company and the entertainment.

Then there were the others who called at night. Others of all shapes and sizes. Some talked with strange accents and most were a bit more peculiar than Dark ever remembered meeting in Cork city. Or anywhere. There was the purple-cheeked lad who had driven them from Cork in the white van. He always brought boxes of stale USA biscuits. Dark also remembered a short, red-haired man who smoked a pipe nearly as big as his head. And there was a very fat woman with a brown leather coat down to her ankles and a voice that boomed nearly as loudly as Connie's. Those people would come in and sit nursing a mug of tea or a can of beer at the oilcloth-covered kitchen table, talking, playing cards and laughing.

Connie never toned things down just because Dark was there. Dark would sit on the sofa under the stairs at the back of the room reading or playing his DS, only picking up on bits of the conversations. Connie wouldn't care how long a caller stayed or what farm work he had planned to do that day.

'Once the animals are fed, Arthur,' he said, 'there's no work that can't wait while there's good company and diversion to be had.'

Dark remembered asking Connie back then about the forbidden place. He had heard lads in school telling hushed stories of terrible things. A place best left alone, they said. Once, a tractor that pulled a grass topper too close to the McLean rath had apparently turned over and killed the driver. Another man who had collected firewood there saw his wife die of a mystery illness within minutes of him putting the sticks into the range.

'Gnarly, useless old yew and oak,' Connie said. 'Hardly worth taking a saw to them. What class of an eejit would bring yew boughs home to burn anyway?'

Dark understood even then that it was fear that had protected this ground from clearing for centuries.

Connie was usually as blunt as a sledgehammer, but he was very vague when talking about the rath.

'The people believe they'd be better off not disturbing

that place even with thinking too much about it, Art.'

'Are the stories true, then?' Dark asked.

Connie paused.

'It was always said around here,' he said eventually, 'that the *sí* are good people only as long as they are left alone.'

'The *sí*?' Dark asked. He was younger then, and didn't know much.

'The little people, I mean,' said Connie. 'Not that I believe in them. Or the little *fear dearg*, the red man. Oh no. Not at all!' He burst out laughing for some reason.

And then, about a year ago, Connie had gone away too. Not dead, though. Taken by the *gardaí*. His mother just said, 'Don't worry, Arty, he's not gone forever.'

Dark heard in school that Connie had been done for 'assault and obstruction' of a government official in the course of his duties. Dark knew there must have been more to it than that. Connie might have made big noises, but Dark had never seen him being hard on anyone.

Dark didn't know when Connie would be coming out. He didn't let on to his mam that he knew or cared anything about it.

So then it was just him and his mother alone again. She got a new job and was working very long hours, so mostly it was just him. She had quietly gone back to looking sad and worried.

He was doing a lot on the farm now, before and after school. It helped him to not think too much. A friend of Connie's, Brian, was coming in for the morning and evening milkings and getting in contractors for spreading slurry and making silage. Dark was taking care of the feeding and herding and fencing. He was tall for his age, and nearly able now to lift the bags of fertiliser or pull a calf on his own. He was trying to make sure everything kept running smoothly till Connie got back. And trying not to let farm worries pile on top of the other things that were weighing his mam down so much. He reckoned he was going along pretty OK, considering.

Except at school. Not going along too well there at all. But he was planning to be done with that problem soon.

Then two days ago this thing started.

He had been out wandering the back fields as usual, after school. Counting the yearlings. Checking the water troughs. Talking to the donkey. Thinking his own thoughts. As he was walking towards the hedge of the bog field, he saw and heard a movement. At first he thought it was a fox. Or maybe a winged pheasant unable to rise and get away. Definitely something fairly big. And close. Yet he couldn't see what it was – although the hedge was a gappy blackthorn. It seemed to move on as he walked towards it and then stop again a little way off. He kept following. About halfway along, he heard it run down from the ditch on the other side. He ran ahead to a gap and climbed over a bit of barbed wire tied between two *sceach* bushes – Connie's idea of fencing. He looked back along to where the creature had come out and could see a movement continuing through the rushes and long grass of the bog. It was again very noticeable. Like a big creature, but unhurried and still not showing itself. Too slow for a pheasant legging it. Too careless for a fox.

It was as if the creature was calling him. Leading him. He had nothing better to do than to follow. It quickly became very plain where he was going. The creature was beating a path straight to the rath that was in the middle of the bog field. Dark had had no real interest in the rath since Connie's advice not to go near it, a while back. But suddenly he was excited by it. The movement stopped a few metres from the edge of the rath. He went very cautiously to the place it had stopped. He pulled the grasses apart carefully at first. He didn't know what he expected to see. But it didn't matter because there was nothing there. Nothing he could see, anyway. And then, somewhere in the middle of the rath, he was certain he heard a strange sound. It was a high-pitched male voice, and it was laughing. From that moment, Dark began to understand that what was in front of him was no ordinary place.

He stood there, seeing properly, for the first time, the dense bushes towered over by dark, peculiar trees. He was beginning to understand that he was on the edge of another world that somehow wasn't alien to him. He knew that it was calling him into it. Indeed, he was overcome by a desire to enter it.

He found a way through to the centre, where so little light penetrated that not even brambles grew. At first, all he could detect was a louder rustle in the leaves. Then he became aware of someone near him. It didn't scare Dark at all.

'Who's there?' he called.

Then an echoing, musical voice: 'It's grey now, but my mane was as black as your darkest night. They called me The Fair One as a joke.'

A deep, quiet laugh followed and Dark caught his first glimpse of the Old Man, sitting momentarily beneath the biggest yew tree. The tree seemed to rearrange its branches to make him comfortable. Though ancient and bent, he was more massive than any human Dark had ever seen. He was wider than the trunk of the old tree. His hair and beard flowed down past his yellow and blue tunic.

The Old Man talked in a rambling way, telling a story. Most of it, Dark didn't understand. The Old Man reeled off names as though Dark should know them.

After talking a while, he said, 'Arthur, *a mhic*,' – somehow he knew Dark's name – 'I know what it feels like having the happiness crushed out of you by suddenly losing everything. It happened to Fionn Mac Cumhaill himself. His father was cut down not long after he was born. They thought Fionn didn't understand and didn't feel anything, because he couldn't talk yet. But he knew exactly what had happened. He might not have had words, but he understood how total his loss was. He knew nothing would be the same again.

'And when they took him off to the mountains to hide him from his father's enemies, Fionn Mac Cumhaill spent a very long time immersed in a black pool of anger and emptiness. The old *straoil*s who were his guardians and tutors had to try every trick they knew just to get him to eat.

Mac Cumhaill never tried to forget or to let go. Never. Over time he just began to fill the deep hollow in his life with the knowledge he was gaining of his lost father, his hero, Cumhall. Gradually, this made him strong. In time, he became stronger than most others his age. He allowed the voice of Cumhall to guide him wisely through most of the rest of his days. Never forgetting and never letting go.'

The Old Man turned his eyes away towards the tree-tops, distracted. He started whistling a beautiful tune that Dark had never heard before. But he was fading.

He stood and said, 'Yes, well, the daylight is not the right time for old souls to walk their lands freely, spinning yarns and *raiméis*. Arthur, now that you know where we are, next time you want to visit, come down here after the blanket of night has made ordinary people retreat and set the lands free.'

Dark must have looked worried. He didn't mean to, as he wasn't really all that afraid of the night.

'Don't fear. You'll be among old friends,' said the Old Man.

Then he disappeared.

That night, Dark had been sitting in his armchair as usual, avoiding homework. He had borrowed his mother's laptop, supposedly to research something about rivers in Germany for geography homework, but he was playing *Fallout* instead. There was only one thought in his mind. He kept glancing at the window. He hadn't closed the curtains. Georgina, Connie's older collie going about her own mad business in the yard, kept triggering the halogen lamp.

She had never been right since Connie went. Even with that on, the yard light faded away at the gate into the top field. There were two other dark fields from there to the bog field; two strong hedges and the stream to cross, if he went the direct way.

He got up, opened the window, and hung out. Georgina came over to sniff up at him and then went back to walking in circles around the yard. He wanted to just do it. He wanted to just climb out the window and go check out whatever there was to be seen. What had he to lose? But he also wanted to stay in the safe comfort of his room. And he knew that maybe it wasn't very sensible to trust the assurance of the Old Man, whoever or whatever he was, that he would be among friends.

One of the many seemingly random pieces of advice Connie used to give him suddenly came loudly into his head: 'There is no other creature out there on the blackest night for a decent human to be afraid of. The human himself is the wickedest creature there is.'

Without allowing himself to think too much more about it, he pulled on his parka jacket, made sure the torch was in the pocket and climbed out the window. He went quickly across the yard while Georgina was scratching after a possible rat up near the calf sheds. He didn't want her to follow.

The land at night was very different. It reverted to the ownership of the rabbits, foxes, badgers and other creatures. He kept his eyes on the small pathway of light that the torch cleared for him. Everything was very different.

A pair of yellow eyes stopped to assess him intermittently as their owner moved across the field in front of him. He made his way quickly so as not to let his courage slip away.

Dark covered the ground and got through the hedges and across the stream without too much bother. He surprised himself with how well he knew the ground. Crossing the bog was harder in the dark, though. Finding the tufts of rushes that gave sure footing in the marshy bits wasn't so easy with only the pale, white light of the torch to distinguish them. He kept going.

The screech of the snipe and the thorns tearing his cheek, not to mention his torch giving out, might have been bearable if he hadn't already been getting near the edge of how far his courage could take him. He stood and looked at the dark mass in front of him. Uninviting as it was in the daylight, it was unambiguously forbidding now. Though it had been full of peculiar whispers during the day it was deadly quiet now. Dark hadn't the slightest doubt that he was being watched. He shouldn't have stopped, because with every second he hesitated, his paralysis grew. There was no longer any way he was going to be able to talk his limbs into moving forward into this dark, unknown place.

He was turning to pick his steps back through the bog, trying to avoid the outlying hawthorn bushes this time, when something grabbed his arm hard and locked on it fast. He couldn't see anything. He tried to get away but couldn't budge. Then a whiny whisper, 'May the gods curse you. Or bless you. Whichever they fancy. What is your work here?'

Dark couldn't even speak.

Again, 'What pleasure or business have you here?'

'None,' said Dark.

'You have the whole world and you still want to enter that small place where you do not belong. You come here to pry into the affairs of others who have done you no harm. Is that not so? I have you there, haven't I? Isn't that a fact as true as the night is long?'

'No,' said Dark to the very strong being he still couldn't see. 'I ... I came. I was asked to come.'

'Asked? Asked by whom, you big lanky donkey shite? May the gods forgive me. If the blackguards exist at all.' The voice sounded a little bit deranged.

'I was asked by … by old friends,' Dark tried.

The tone changed slightly, became slightly doubtful, slightly less paranoid. 'The gods between us and all harm, and were you indeed?'

Then there came a bigger voice from somewhere inside: 'Bal, what are you at out there, you thundering *stuachán*? Will you escort that young man in like I asked you and don't be annoying him.'

'Ah, the bitter word for a little man only trying to do his job.'

The complaining voice was now pulling Dark by the arm and there was no longer any option of turning back for home.

He was pulled through a very thick clump of briars that would certainly not have been his own ideal choice of entry point. As they made their way in, the vice-like hand

13

that was gripping him and the runty body attached to it became visible. He was being pulled by the smallest man he had ever seen. A man with a mop of red hair plastered over one of the ugliest heads on earth. Dark was so shocked by the sight of him that he truly wasn't able to find words to respond to the continuing barrage of unrelated questions.

Inside was completely different to when Dark had seen it before. There was a blazing fire where there had been an old bed of pine needles during the daytime. There was great light and smoke from it, though he had neither seen nor smelt even the slightest hint of this from a few metres away, on the outside of the rath.

The ferocious man still wouldn't let go of his arm till he was warned again by the voice from the fire. Then he let go suddenly and Dark fell over. The little red runt laughed and said, 'Always shouting and roaring at the small man as if he got pleasure from his job.' Then, extending the same hand, he said, 'You are most excruciatingly welcome, by the way.'

Dark thanked him quietly without accepting the handshake.

'Come on over here, *a mhic,*' called the voice from the fire.

The Old Man was standing there. Dark's fear evaporated. He went over to him. On the other side of the huge fire was another old man, sitting on a bench. He too was enormous and with a lion's mane of hair, still black. He grinned widely at Dark when the Old Man said, 'That blackguard over there is my oldest friend, Conán Mac Liath.'

Then the Old Man said, 'Come and sit over here next to me. Will you have something to drink?'

Dark was suddenly more thirsty than he could describe. It must have been the fear and the flames.

'Only soft drinks.'

'Is this soft enough?' said a voice from right next to Dark.

There was a girl, fully grown but hardly as high as his knee. She was holding a golden chalice but Dark hardly noticed it. She had jet-black hair, large greenish eyes, and a smile that made him feel overwhelmingly shy.

From high in the trees, Bal laughed down to the young woman, *'A chroí,* don't think you are the first one to stun the lad with your looks. I nearly knocked him out myself.'

Dark was embarrassed. He took the cup and the woman stepped back amongst the trees where Dark now realised there might be many other little eyes watching his every move.

'Drink up, Arthur,' said the Old Man. 'We are the guests of the *sí* here in this great rath and they are a people who pride themselves on their hospitality towards welcome guests.'

Dark wondered how he would know whether he was a welcome guest.

Seeing his hesitation, Bal shouted down, 'And with unwelcome guests, the little goblet of poison would knock a horse on his back roaring, before he could sing a verse of "As I Roved Out".'

'Don't mind him,' said the Old Man.

Dark put the tiny cup to his mouth. Though no more than a teaspoon of liquid filled the cup, it seemed plenty and it tasted sweeter than a chocolate malt. He suddenly felt quite relaxed and sure of himself. He came and sat on a log next to the Old Man and put his hands out to be warmed by the fire, as though he had been doing it all his life. Though nobody seemed to be adding sticks to it, the fire stayed blazing and crackling heartily.

The Old Man was talking across the fire to Conán, recalling various people Dark had never heard of.

A woman with long, plaited, red hair and shiny robes appeared. She sat next to the Old Man, on the other side. Dark wasn't introduced to her.

After some time, the Old Man turned to Dark and the mellow words started. 'Have you any interest at all in passing the time with old men telling stories about times past?'

Dark nodded. He was so comfortable sitting there, he didn't care what talk was in the air.

His heart contracted as he stared into the fire and felt himself start to float on the magical story voice. Right in the centre he could clearly make out the figure of a tall old woman in a long black shawl standing at the banks of a river.

The others had settled around the fire now too: the red-haired lady, Bal and three or four other little people whom Dark hadn't noticed venturing forth from the trees. They

16

were all staring into the flames, encouraging the Old Man. To help get him started they were murmuring things like, 'Aye, indeed, and it's true for you, those were the days indeed.'

Soon they too were moving through the heavens on a carpet of mellow words. This was the story the Old Man told that night.

Calling the banshee

One dark winter's evening, Fionn Mac Cumhaill was travelling silently by chariot with three other men on the carriageway between Tara and Emhain Macha. It was truly one of those nights when, for no earthly reason, every human heart is on edge. That *Samhain* was only a day past was on every man's mind. Some of those who visited from other worlds on *Samhain* night were known to stay a day or two longer before retreating to where they had come from.

The mission they were about was not one that excited them. Mac Cumhaill had been sent by King Cormac yet again to try to dissuade Tíreach, the man in charge up in Uladh, from starting another war with the people in the west of the country.

As the chariots approached the crossing point on the moody Boann river, there appeared, from nowhere, an old woman dressed entirely in black. The men only saw her barely in time but they needn't have worried about running over her, as the horses had already stopped dead in front of her.

It was a peculiar sight. There was no cabin or habitation

anywhere near this spot, as far as Mac Cumhaill knew. And here was this old lady all alone in the spills of rain, smiling at them.

'Daghda save you all,' she said when they stopped. 'Fionn Mac Cumhaill, isn't it?'

For a moment Mac Cumhaill thought he saw an unusual light in her eyes.

'I don't think I've ever seen your beautiful face before, good woman, but if I have and have forgotten your name, I beg your forgiveness,' he said. 'Is there any help we can offer you? We have some fresh bread and cheese and you would be more than welcome to share it with us. Would you allow us to run you to your home on one of the chariots, to get you in out of the rain on this desolate night?

'No, you may not have met me yet,' she said peculiarly, 'and I'm not in need of transport at all. Where are you off to, then, on this bad night?'

'Well to tell the truth, we are about a task no one of us has any appetite for,' Mac Cumhaill told the old woman. 'Above in Emhain Macha.'

'That man up there would fight over a patch of bad grass or a scrawny cow,' said the woman. 'And the others over beyond in the west are not a whole lot better, always tormenting him. You'd be as well off resting here by the river bank for the night and resume your journey in the morning when the rain has cleared and some light has fallen on matters.'

Fionn didn't know what to say. He had told the woman nothing of his business. Yet she spoke about it as if she had

18

been privy to all his own thoughts on the matter. In fact, on this occasion, the exact nature of the complaint about which Tíreach was threatening war had to do with precisely one scrawny cow. He said nothing.

The old woman continued: 'A scabby head bleeds easy. Whether you go there tonight or tomorrow will make no difference. Nothing will stop that man eventually finding an offence that causes him to fight.'

Mac Cumhaill looked around to see what Conán made of this. When he looked back to question the woman, she was gone. He never saw her again.

Even if Fionn had wanted to continue, he would have had to do so alone. Frightened as they were of stopping here in the dark, none of the other three men were going to take the risk of going onwards against advice from a source like this.

On top of that, the going was foggy and dangerous for the animals, so they pulled the horses and chariots upriver a distance to a place where there was a wide strip of grazing on the bank and protection provided by a steep incline above it.

Fionn took Conán on foot with him to visit a friend of his, Murtagh by name, leaving the other two men to rest for the night.

Like many of Mac Cumhaill's friends around the country, Murtagh lived in a hill-top camp, cut off from the comforts of life, far from the trading and the scheming that went on in the lowlands. Murtagh and his clan contented themselves with working a steep strip of cold ground and

doing the odd bit of hunting as their way of keeping death at bay. Mac Cumhaill had an understanding of the good people of the hills and their plain, honest ways, since his childhood upbringing in Sliabh Bladma.

He didn't usually take other members of the Fianna to such places in case they might prattle about it to King Cormac when they got back, for Cormac didn't approve of Mac Cumhaill's association with the hill people. But Conán also liked the hills and the quiet ways and was not so afraid of the dark or of the spirits that inhabited its wild corners.

They had an hour to go, mostly through heavy bog and across three rivers, and then came the climb up the hill. Mac Cumhaill, impatient, strode straight up, while Conán zigzagged along a sheep track to make the slope more gradual.

A black-and-white dog came down part of the way to bark at them. At the barking, a boy appeared on the bank of the fort above them, saying nervously into the dark, 'Who is it? Is there someone there? Who's there?'

'Don't worry son,' shouted Fionn, 'it's Mac Cumhaill and a friend. Tell Murtagh we're here to see how he's getting on.'

They were led by the boy into the camp and then into the biggest hut where most of the adults of the clan were sitting around a fire, settled in for the long winter evening full of yarns and gallery.

Murtagh stood up and said, 'Come on in; isn't it grand to see you!'

'It's grand to see you all too,' said Conán. *'Daghda dhaoibh go léir,* blessings be on everyone here.'

'What has you out on such a miserable night?' asked

Murtagh. 'You're not bringing us any sort of bad news, are you?'

'Not at all,' said Mac Cumhaill.

'Well, come and sit next to the fire and we'll get you something to keep the walls of your belly apart,' said Murtagh.

Soon Mac Cumhaill and Conán were being helped to bowls of barley broth, green apples, boiled eggs and large lumps of boiled sheep meat. Mac Cumhaill knew only too well that this food had been set aside for the next day's meal. But he also knew that the hurt Murtagh would feel if his guests failed to eat their fill would be greater than the sacrifice of scarce food the next day.

Murtagh went to call the children from their sleep. He insisted they'd be disappointed not to have met Mac Cumhaill. He introduced his own three daughters and a baby son to Mac Cumhaill and Conán, his face burning with pride and affection.

People here rarely had visitors. They were hoping the famous travellers would have interesting tales that could be retold with some decoration, during many fireside gatherings in the future. But they would wait, leaving the two big men to eat in peace.

While the guests ate, the hosts continued to dispute among themselves about whether the signs from the trees and the grasses were for a harsh winter or a mild one, and when they were done with that, a *Seanachaí* in the corner started to tell a yarn that you could see was even older than himself, about a marvellous dog that knew when a cow was about to calve and would bring her home from the bog. It was a story they'd all heard before, but, like many a good teller, the old man could still hold everyone's attention with the addition of new twists to each telling.

Everyone except Murtagh, that is, who apparently was still thinking about the weather predictions, and said, 'To tell you all the truth, I don't believe in old *pisreógs*. It doesn't matter which tree lost its leaves first or what colour the grass on the south slope of the grazing land was the day before *Samhain*, the winter will still come whatever way it wants to come.'

'That's surprising talk,' said an old man sharply. 'All the plants have stories to tell and it is foolish to disregard them.'

'If they were good predictors,' said Murtagh, 'why, then, do we get surprised by the weather every year?'

'Just because we are not good at reading the signs,' said the old man, 'doesn't mean the signs aren't there.'

Everyone else seemed to agree with the old man, and Murtagh went quiet.

Because Murtagh was such a kind and gentle man, Mac Cumhaill decided to jump in on his side of the argument. 'I don't know, I think maybe Murtagh is right. Is it not the case that half the time, when the weather coincides with our predictions, we say that proves the signs are right and then the other half the time when the weather does the opposite, we say that it is just a rare exception or that we didn't take all the signs into account?'

'Hmmm,' came the murmured reply. The clan were prepared to listen to this argument when it came from an outsider, whereas they wouldn't countenance it from one of their own.

But then Mac Cumhaill's support had a surprising effect on Murtagh. He stood up and said, 'And while we are at it, that's not all. There's a lot of other things we believe in that are pure nonsense and *raiméis*.'

'Like what?' asked the same old man, concerned.

'Like the banshee,' said Murtagh.

Silence fell on the assembly. This was not something anyone wanted to hear Murtagh saying. Nobody wanted to talk about this subject. That included the visitors. And most certainly, nobody wanted to dare her to appear, as Murtagh was about to do.

'There is no such thing and if there was, I defy her to come here for me now.'

People sucked in their breaths in shock.

'Fionn agrees with me,' said Murtagh, looking for more support.

'Murtagh, dear friend,' said Mac Cumhaill quietly, 'I know that what you say comes from a lot of thinking and wisdom. I agree that we are sometimes misled by superstitions. And I would love to agree with you on this too, but I cannot, for the simple reason that I know you are wrong. I have heard that same good lady more times than I ever wanted, when she came to warn of the deaths of dear comrades who headed out with me in battle. I would plead with you to take back what you just said.'

Murtagh looked a little shaken, but he continued. 'I don't believe she exists any more than I believe in the salmon of knowledge. I think you got your exceptional knowledge from the fact that your father and mother had exceptional cleverness, the same as the rest of us got what great or little brains we may have from our own fathers and mothers. And as for the banshee, I think the sounds that people think are hers are only the sounds of vixens in heat. Again, if I am wrong, I defy the banshee to present herself.'

The mood of the gathering had changed completely. People whispered urgently to each other and started to get ready to make their way back to their own huts. But there was no time. A minute later, still a distance away, they heard a sound. It was eerie and sad to those who had never heard it before. It was unmistakable and terrifying to those who had. It held the sounds of a north wind cutting through a gap, the misery of an eternal *Oíche Shamhna*, and the shrieks of grief of a woman mourning her most beloved.

The silence that it brought to that home made the fire itself go down. In the cold and dark, the people sat and waited.

The sounds got closer until it seemed she was just over the mound of the outside cattle fence. And there was no mistaking what she was saying. She was calling the name of Murtagh. Murtagh turned white and started trembling like an aspen leaf. Not a person in the place could doubt the facts now. There was no escape. Murtagh would be dead within hours. When the banshee tired of her *olagón* and *caoining* and went off to torment some other poor souls, people didn't know what way to look. A death in the air always fills people with thoughts of *sí* and fear.

Every adult present had lived long enough already to understand how quickly death steals our friends and dear ones. They started to leave the hut quietly with their heads bowed, as though Murtagh was already gone. They didn't look directly at Murtagh as they didn't know what to say to him.

But his children didn't leave. They started hugging him and crying and sobbing to an extent that could have melted the very rocks. They had already lost their mother at the time she was giving birth to the young boy.

Mac Cumhaill and Conán would rather have been any-where else than to be seeing this.

'Maybe we should leave them to their great trouble,' said Conán quietly to Mac Cumhaill.

Mac Cumhaill cleared his throat and stood up. 'I think it's best we leave you to be together.'

Murtagh stood up too. Mac Cumhaill expected him to be angry or incoherent. But he wasn't. He was just the same polite Murtagh.

'Please, Fionn,' he said. 'I ask you a favour. Not for my-self. For my children. Can you talk to the banshee or get some of your powerful druids to reverse her spell?'

'Many have tried,' said Mac Cumhaill. 'I am sorry.'

'Tell her if she can just give me enough time to get the four little ones better started in life, then I'll gladly go with her.'

'Kings have tried,' said Conán, putting his hand on Murtagh's shaking shoulder, 'and failed. Her word can't be unspoken. All I can say to you is to make every minute from now until tomorrow stretch until each lasts as long as a day itself.'

Fionn and Conán left the children with their father. The only one other person still in the room with them was the old man who had argued about the weather signs. He stared into the red embers of ash branches as though he had been struck by a club. Mac Cumhaill now realised that he was Murtagh's father.

They went outside without saying anything further. As they headed down the hill, the devastation they were leaving behind in a friend's house was a weight too heavy for them. They sat down on some boulders and stared silently into the dense, cold night.

'It's pointless thinking about it,' said Mac Cumhaill. 'Our torment is not going to make their night one bit easier.'

'I can't tell my head what to think about and what to not think about,' said Conán. 'Even when thoughts are making me insane, I can't banish them.'

'Well, there's still nothing you can do, so let us go back to the other men and get some rest before starting our journey in the morning again.'

Conán didn't stir. 'Did you see the biggest girl, can't be more than eight, trying to settle the other two down but hugging the father tight at the same time, thinking maybe she could hold onto him when death comes looking for him.'

'I did,' said Mac Cumhaill, sitting back down. 'I was trying to forget it.'

'What did we do to deserve this?' said Conán. 'Going

along about our business with no great worries and then to get stabbed in the heart like that.'

'You are right, my friend. Curses on her and on fate,' said Mac Cumhaill. 'I don't want to leave the situation like this any more than you do. Let us ride back to Tara tonight and see what Dreoilín has to say.'

'There's no point in going back. It will just use up time. And you know what Dreoilín is going to say.'

'That I do,' said Mac Cumhaill , 'because I suppose it isn't the first time he's told me – there's no interfering with the banshee.'

'Well, then what?'

'Well, then we have to go and interfere with the banshee.'

Mac Cumhaill wanted to know what kind of creature exactly the banshee is. It's a funny thing, but people wanted so little truck with her, that nobody really knew anything much about her.

He headed to a fairy fort only a short distance from the base of Murtagh's hill, to see if the little people in there knew anything about her. They didn't, but one of them said to him, 'Why don't you suck that ould thumb of yours since you have it, rather than fluttering around asking everyone else for knowledge you have stored up inside your own self?'

Mac Cumhaill wasn't much in the habit of using his thumb of knowledge. He didn't like knowledge rushing un-controlled through his head, because he was likely to see more that he didn't want to know than that knowledge which he did desire. But time was running out and there was no normal course open to him, so he put the thumb in his mouth.

Conán looked at him impatiently. 'Well? any news?'

'It seems she's half ghost', said Mac Cumhaill.

'What good is that to us?' said Conán.

'It's the other half that's interesting. Half sí. I'm off to the place of the Lugda clan.'

'To Baile Lugdach in the very northwest? Well, you'll find me here,' said Conán.

With only a few hours left for a long journey to places that no chariots could go, Mac Cumhaill would have to run there. And run as fast as the wind. This was not a mission Conán could accompany him on.

When he got to the fort of Luan, the high king of all the fairies in these parts and beyond, in his hurry, he marched straight in through the trees and headed down into the stone entrance. Suddenly, that's exactly how he was entering – head first. His approach was too quick for the guards to recognise him. Grass snares had caught his feet and he fell on his face and slid down another twenty paces dragging the two fairy men who were trying to hold the snares, along with him. He ended up right inside the main chamber where Luan was in the middle of a grand midnight meal.

There was shock at first, when the large, bloodied head slid into these refined surroundings. Small spears were drawn and pointed. Then Luan started to laugh.

'Now, that's a fine way to introduce yourself, my good man, with your big wild head on you as red as if you've run the whole world to get here, and blood streaming out of your forehead as if you had to open the door with your nut.'

'And that's a fine way to welcome me, having your lads here string me up like fowl for your table,' said Mac Cumhaill.

Luan nodded to the guards, who were already trying to untangle their snares. Mac Cumhaill stood up, dusted himself off, using the corner of his tunic to mop the blood from the cut on his head. He bowed and said, 'Luan, Your Highness, excuse my bad manners.'

Luan also bowed, smiling. 'Fionn, old rogue, you can enter here any way you like; you are always welcome here. Accept my apologies for my guards' overprotective behaviour.'

'Thank you,' said Mac Cumhaill.

Mac Cumhaill and Luan were not close friends. It was hard to have complete trust in a relationship between a big person and the little people, when all that had gone before for a thousand generations had been caution. Two peoples who had tried to avoid war with each other but yet had never been fully at peace. But Mac Cumhaill and Luan had met many times and they had come to understand each other well. Mac Cumhaill was always the one sent to talk to Luan when the danger of war arose due to some renegade *púca* who was making trouble with the big people or when there was an errant human who was damaging the property of the little people.

'As long as you bring gifts, of course,' said Luan, laughing. 'What gift have you brought me?'

'An invisible gift, Your Holiness,' said Mac Cumhaill, mocking.

'Ah, the usual kind,' said Luan. He turned to his people and said, 'Give this foul human some food and drink and bathe that wound of his in frog piss.'

'I can't eat. No time. But maybe I do actually have a gift for you this time, other than the gift of my great company,' said Mac Cumhaill.

'What is that?'

'The gift of entertainment.'

'How is that? I've never known you to make an idle errand, so I know you didn't come barging in here tonight to make small talk or to entertain me.'

'Well, how right you are good sir! But maybe you'll be entertained when you hear my business.'

'Tell me.'

'I want to get the banshee to undo some bad work she has done this night.'

'Ah ha ha.' The fairy king laughed very loudly and heartily for such a small pair of lungs. 'As you promised, entertainment. You are surely the only person, big or small, in this land or any other, who would take on such a hopeless task.'

'You are probably right. A big fool is what I am, I know,' said Mac Cumhaill, 'but I have to do this. I have set my heart on it.'

'No fool, sir,' said Luan, serious now, 'you are no fool. That I know. I don't need to know why you want to try this impossible task, as I know by the very fact you have taken it on, you must have a burning reason. What do you think I can do for you?'

'Well…' said Mac Cumhaill, almost embarrassed at hoping for such a long shot, 'I have come to believe that the banshee is part sí, and I thought maybe you might know some of her people.'

'You know, Mac Cumhaill,' said Luan, 'she is not of our realm, as she is not of yours, and we can't reach her any more than you can.'

'That I know,' said Mac Cumhaill.

'Right enough, though,' continued Luan, 'I did hear it said long, long ago that there was a connection of the sort you mention. I heard when I was a child that Salach, who even then was the most ancient woman in our world, had the same mother as the banshee. But that while Salach's father was an ordinary humble man of the little people, the banshee's father was a ghost.'

'Where is Salach, Your Highness?' asked Mac Cumhaill. 'Maybe she'll know how to talk to the banshee.'

'Not to my knowledge. The story was that the banshee had been whipped away from her mother and Salach at birth and nobody had contact with her since. Besides, poor old Salach talks no sense anymore. She is gone very doddery.'

'Do you mind if I talk to her anyway?' asked Mac Cumhaill.

'As long as you talk gently and do not upset her. We love her very much.'

'You have my word that I will respect that request faithfully,' said Mac Cumhaill. He knew that no matter how great the respect his own people had for their old, the little people had even more. They understood that if you listened attentively enough to what the elderly had to say, you might not have to repeat every mistake that was made before. And in the case of an elderly fairy, the wisdom would be of a thousand years rather than a hundred.

A helper appeared. It seemed he had been standing invisibly right beside Mac Cumhaill all along.

'Come along,' he said.

Mac Cumhaill travelled with the little man through many corridors, pink and yellow, some short, some long, all now changing size to accommodate him as he went.

Eventually they got to a rose-coloured wooden door and the little man knocked very gently. He clearly expected no reply, as he proceeded immediately to open the door slowly. He peered inside and said, 'A visitor for you, Mother.'

Still no reply.

He opened the door fully and they went in. The room was like something from a dream. Even though burrowed deep in the earth, it was filled with sunlight. The curtains were flapping gently in a breeze. The walls were sky blue. Climbing roses draped the wooden bedposts. In the middle of it the poor little old person lay all curled up, her eyes shut. She had a kind face and seemed to be blessed with good dreams, though her face had the cracks and hollows of her thousand years.

The little man called her.

'Mother Salach, there's someone to see you.'

She didn't stir.

They turned to go. Fionn Mac Cumhaill was despondent. He knew the little man wouldn't disturb her further, as waking her might frighten her.

Then, crystal clear, from behind them, she spoke.

'Fionn Mac Cumhaill, I have heard of you. What is it you want?'

They turned back to look at her. She was sitting up with her eyes opened wide in an unnatural way. Her lips didn't move when she spoke.

'I want you to tell your sister that Murtagh made a foolish mistake. He is soft-headed. But he respectfully begs not to have his children orphaned when they are so young.'

The old woman laughed strangely. But no – it was another voice. A shiver ran through the whole room. Mac Cumhaill realised that the fairies weren't the only ones minding old Salach. The other woman, her sister, was there in the room with them, though the fairy man couldn't see her any more than Mac Cumhaill could. He was just as frightened by the coldness in her voice. She must have been taking care of her older sister all this time, without the fairies knowing anything about it.

Mac Cumhaill got down on his knees and begged. The fairy man looked at him in horror, thinking he had gone off his head.

The voice that still appeared to be coming from the old woman just laughed again. But Mac Cumhaill was blind now with determination. The more he thought about Murtagh, the more determined he became.

'I say to you with respect, this is wrong.'

The laughing stopped.

'You are long enough around to know there is no right and wrong in who gets taken and who gets left behind.'

'I normally accept that. But may I respectfully say that it seems to me this man would not have been marked by you tonight were it not for a few foolish words. That doesn't seem like random bad luck as much as it seems like you showing your power. It seems to me that if it weren't for your pride being injured, he would not have been chosen tonight.'

'That is rude, son of Cumhall', she said.

'Grant me this request then,' said Mac Cumhaill. 'Take me instead of Murtagh.'

The little fairy man grabbed Mac Cumhaill. Even though he didn't know him at all, he tried to tug him out of the room and out of his foolishness.

'She'll take you *and* your friend if you're not careful,' he whispered.

But Mac Cumhaill pulled away from him.

'I'm a man who's lived long and seen much. I've done plenty of things I regret. I've cut down people I had no personal quarrel with in battles. I am lucky to have escaped your attention so many times. Leave this harmless farming man with his children and take me now in his place.'

There was silence. Clearly the banshee was thinking about this.

Then Mac Cumhaill saw her shimmer into view above the old woman for a few instants. She had a sad face. Maybe her fear for the life of her sister had made her heart slightly softer than usual.

She said, 'You must love this Murtagh. You are brave, if foolish. I hope not to cry for you for many's a long day. For your devotion to your friend, I will also grant your request. Murtagh must stay home tomorrow to avoid the falling tree that would have killed him.'

Then she was gone. The old woman's voice was back and she was rambling, forgetting who the strangers in her room were. She fell back to sleep and Mac Cumhaill pulled the multicoloured quilt back up to her chin, saying, 'Rest well, Mother'.

He and the little man quietly closed the door behind them.

Mac Cumhaill had to leave hastily, as he needed to make it back to Murtagh before daybreak so that he could warn him. As he was fleeing, Luan was looking out the door after him laughing.

'As short of manners in your departure as in your entrance,' he called. 'It's lucky I know you well enough not to take offence.'

Mac Cumhaill found Conán still sitting on the same rock, half asleep. Only Conán could do that.

They went together back up the hill. Murtagh was given the warning. Only the little girl who was still wide awake and still holding onto her father, fully understood the news immediately and jumped up screaming 'Buíochas le Daghda, Buíochas le Fionn, thank you, thank you, thank you, thank you…'

To be sure that his work was not squandered, Mac Cumhaill stayed with Murtagh the entire day, keeping him inside the compound at all times, but also resting and talking, with a pleasure you can only enjoy in times of enormous relief.

As they were leaving that night, they overheard Murtagh saying to one of his neighbours, 'See, it's just what I said all along. Just a *pisreóg*. She doesn't exist. My friend Fionn Mac Cumhaill was just trying to get a rise out of us all for the entertainment.'

'Call her again then,' the neighbour said to him. Mac Cumhaill had to hold Conán back from going in to physically silence Murtagh.

But Murtagh hesitated. 'Well, maybe I won't, because…I don't want to frighten the children again.'

Mac Cumhaill laughed.

Fionn and Conán headed back down the hill, again in the dark. They had to take a detour around a giant pine tree that had fallen across their path. The tree that was supposed to have been meant for Murtagh.

'*Daghda is Mhorrigu orainn!*' exclaimed Conán, calling on the gods, when he saw where it had fallen, square on the rocks where he and Mac Cumhaill had sat the previous night.

Something caught Mac Cumhaill's eye. He looked up and he thought he heard an echo of thin laughter flitting away across the treetops.

When they got back to the river bank, the men minding the chariots had gone off beating the countryside looking

36

for them. When they found them, they all set off again on the thankless task of making people who wanted to talk war, talk peace instead.

The voice faded. A chilly wind cut across Dark's shoulders. He looked around him and he was completely alone. No trace remained of the fire on the bed of pine needles and twigs. A glimmer of dawn was peeping through the tops of the trees. As he looked around, he thought he heard a soft voice whispering to him from the bushes. But it wasn't repeated.

He stood up from the massive base of the yew tree and made his way home in a daze.

Back in the yard, all was peaceful. As if nothing had happened. Georgina must have finally gone to sleep. He used a broken pallet to help him climb in the window and he had about two hours of very sound sleep before the alarm went off for him to go and feed the calves and get ready for school.

2
ARTHUR'S GHOST

'You're looking very pale, Arty,' Dark's mother said in the car on the way to school. 'Are you OK?'

'I'm fine, Mam,' said Dark. He was. Though his mind was full of what he'd seen last night.

All day in school it was the same. He was turning things over and trying to make sense of them. He must have been looking a bit dazed because Sullivan zoned in on him again. Sullivan taught maths and geography and had them for the first three lessons every morning.

She came over to his desk and said, 'Well, I see our Mr McLean sent in his ghost to take his place today.' She paused for dramatic effect, as always when she had a good putdown prepared. 'But I see he sent the lanky ghost out with the pants still six inches too short.'

Dark felt himself blushing. He had outgrown his uniform so many times in the past two years, he didn't want to ask his mam again, as he knew things weren't going so well with her and she seemed to be ignoring some of the farm bills. They stayed on the table, unopened, for months.

That night, Dark had no hesitation. He could hardly wait for it to get dark and for his mam to come into his room to say good night. She stopped to talk a bit, about nothing in particular. She was distracted and was looking at her shoes. She was saying something about her sister going on a holiday or a honeymoon or something. Then she looked at him and got irritated because she said he wasn't listening to her. To tell the truth, he wasn't.

She was hardly out of the room when he had the window open and was climbing out. He had a piece of bacon rind to keep Georgina amused while he headed across the yard.

The fire was already blazing and the three big people were sitting around it. The Old Man came over to Dark.

'Is everything OK?' Dark ventured.

'Whisht,' said the Old Man. 'Listen.'

There they stood at the edge of the rath, saying nothing for a length of time Dark could not have measured, short or long. They stood while the sounds of the fire faded and the sounds of the fields grew louder. Every breath of the slight breeze became a rhythm. The blackbird was watching his back. He could even hear woodlice scurrying along the bark of the trunk at his back. He had never felt anything like it before, and for a moment he felt like he was lifting out of his body and floating.

Then there was a tiny crack. A broken twig that sounded as clear as a rifle shot. He looked at the Old Man.

'You are a good boy, Arthur,' said the Old Man.

'But what was that?' Dark was not sure that he was pleased to have the symphony of sounds broken. 'A fox or a badger? Or one of the *sí*?' he ventured.

'You won't hear the *sí* unless they want you to,' said the Old Man. 'It's a wolf.'

'There are no wolves left, they killed the last one in Fenagh in 1860,' said Dark, repeating from the store of facts that Connie used to entertain him with on his first days in this place. 'It had to be a fox.'

'You're wrong about that, *a mhic*. They're still with us. But the poor creatures have to keep to themselves. During the daytime, they keep very well hidden from the view of modern people. It is a terrible curse for them that their very appearance, something they can do nothing at all about, is enough to make sensible people shiver with fear and a desire to kill them.'

They were quiet for a while longer. Then the Old Man said, 'Tell me how things stand with you, Arthur.'

'Nothing much to say,' said Dark. 'The usual. I got in trouble for forgetting to do homework yesterday, so I'm supposed to do double today.'

'Art,' said the Old Man, looking slightly puzzled at the word homework, 'time is your own to use.'

'Homework means extra learning they give us after school has ended.'

Dark still didn't ask how the Old Man knew his name.

'I see. Well, all learning from books I'm sure has its good. Maybe it means you won't have to fight for everything. But they have to leave you time for all the other learning that comes from gallivanting and climbing and smelling and getting soaked and bruised and investigating snails and watching how the blackbird watches your back and staring at the clouds or the stars and listening to all the wonderful sounds that are to be heard when people know how to be quiet.'

'Yes. But they'll give me a bollocking if I don't do the stuff. And I don't enjoy that much.'

'If you don't learn these things as a young person, you are cut off forever from everything in the world that you are part of and that is inside you,' said the Old Man, as if Dark hadn't spoken. 'You would grow up as a shell, making the movements and sounds of a person, but empty of humanity. I cannot think of anything worse to happen to a young man.'

'Yes, but I'll get in trouble and it seems I am always the one who is in trouble. I really don't like it much.'

'That's very sensible, *a mhic*,' said the Old Man, looking straight at him as if he could see inside him. After a while he said, 'Right, tomorrow, bring whatever extra work this teacher gives you and I'll get one of my lads to fix it up for you.'

Dark had no idea who the lads might be, but this certainly sounded like a plan with promise.

The Old Man then led him back to the fireside. Conán and the red-haired woman nodded to him. He was looking around before he sat down.

Conán noticed and grinned. 'Don't worry, *garsún*, I don't think little Etain has forgotten you.'

41

The tiny slender girl with the goblet came forward and smiled at Dark. He drank. She stayed longer this time, and more of the others of her people also came out in front of the fire to listen to the yarn the Old Man was starting into.

The Old Man looked at Dark again and said, 'You have an interest in swords?'

He did. Dark actually knew quite a lot about them. There was a claymore that he was saving for and he was hoping it would not be gone off eBay before he had figured out how he could get a PayPal account set up.

'Well, there was a young woman who lived not far from here who was possibly the finest sword-maker the world has ever known.'

As his gaze settled on the flames, Dark could picture clearly the hill which was the first place the Old Man's gentle words took him to. It was only a few miles from Connie's farm. It was different though. There was a little wooden hut. And a tall woman with a hard face, feeding what looked like fish heads to a cat. She was not a young woman and Dark couldn't imagine her making swords.

Weapons Woman and the Wolf Beo

In her later years, Eibhlín Rua Ní Fhógartaigh was rarely to be found in a good temper. Even her cat, the only companion that stuck with her, was undernourished. The bad opinion she had developed of people had evolved into a dislike of all living creatures, and she kept the cat as thin as a blade of grass in case it might get notions above its station.

But she had not always been such a miserable soul. In fact, at one time, she had been considered by everyone to be one of the finest people the country ever produced. She had been a brilliant child. She invented all kinds of things for making life easier. She invented a stabiliser bar to hold pots steady over the hearth as they boiled. She invented a special harness that stopped wild heifers from kicking when they were first milked. She calculated the exact height of the mountain at the back of her parents' settlement and she discovered that the seeds of oats, when boiled, made a very good morning feed for man and beast.

As she grew into an adult, her advice was sought on matters by people from all around the country and abroad. And many young men, as well as many who were no spring chickens, tried to impress her, thinking that they could do worse than found their families upon such a rock of beauty and resourcefulness.

As she grew, her attitude became less warm. Her father was a hard, cold man who boasted about her successes and drove her hard to achieve more. Her mother never interfered with the father-daughter team, so she learnt no warmth at home. Or maybe it was that she was really just like her father and didn't have any warmth in her in the first place.

He had never allowed her time for things he considered silly, like wandering around with other girls and boys having sport. So she didn't have any close friends that she liked or trusted. And it was said that she grew bored of the men who kept coming to try to impress her. She started to think that everyone was as transparent and as useless as these visitors. She lost her liking for people and developed a cynicism about life, thinking that there was very little good to be said about any of the rest of humankind.

Whatever the cause, her own interests turned to inventing weapons and traps. After her twentieth birthday she stopped all other experimenting and discovery. For three years, she produced nothing. But all day long she would have great fires lit in a furnace her father had built for her in the Fógartaigh chief's compound. In the roasting embers at night she would be working with iron, tin and copper, dropping red hot metal into troughs of water. Crucible, hammer and tongs were the focus of her tender attentions while other people her age were marrying and building families. Then, in the early mornings, while servants were refuelling the fire for her, the air would be filled with the swishes and sighs of stone on metal. She would be perfecting different strokes that the most expert blade-sharpeners in the country had taught her. Each had their own patient, soothing rhythm which whispered to the passerby that ancient secrets were being expressed; that the angle of the stone on the edge of a new blade was perfect and the return stroke was absolutely smooth.

For some time, this was not seen as a problem, because Eibhlín remained dedicated to doing this work in the service of the Fianna's defence of the people. Not a week went by that she did not have some improved weapon sent for Mac Cumhaill to try. One week it would be a spear with a longer, narrower head that she said would more easily slide through a chest and find the most elusive heart. The next it would be spikes on hazel rods that would spring up when horsemen went through long grass, and impale the unlucky horses.

When less vigorous humours were upon her, she would produce bugles. Some were the longest and slenderest in the world, to show the fineness of her mastery of metal-work. Others were designed to terrify the enemy before ever a blow was struck, stout in the shape of ferocious unearthly boar or wolf heads and with a woeful sound you would not think could come from the land of the living.

If the truth be told, war and defence was our business and we had to take note of these ideas even if we didn't like her approach or the pleasure she seemed to get from developing the foulest weapons. We had to test them in case there was a chance they might improve our ability to save our people from falling victim to enemy marauders.

Some were used. Others weren't. That was the start of things going wrong. She would be happy enough when an invention was used. Her greatest success was with the sword. She developed one that still had the old wide slash-ing body like the older ones of us were used to, but that also had a long narrowing tip that would pierce any protection if the man behind it had the strength and will to drive it. What was even more important, she came up with a way of moulding these swords so they could be produced quickly in great numbers. This weapon became widely used by many of the Fianna. Mac Cumhaill himself never used one. He would never part with the sword that had been passed through seven generations, carrying all of the ornamental engravings that transferred the blessings and craft of ancestors into the hand of the man who clasped it and which brought him luck if his purpose was fair. Mac Cumhaill believed the new ones, made mostly of iron, would not carry recollections through to his grandchildren, but would rot away with their owners.

Nevertheless, Eibhlín was rightly celebrated for this, and maybe all the praise went to her head. On a side matter, we should mention here that all advantage that these swords gave was soon lost as they were copied in many foreign lands. Eibhlín was partly to blame for this, but the king, Cormac, had to take most of the blame. He took such pride in his people's achievements that he was not able to keep any secrets. Visiting dignitaries would be introduced to Eibhlín, who would offer each of them a sword with their royal insignia etched alongside her own special spiral signature on the handle. Despite the best advice and polite warnings from Mac Cumhaill and others, the king encouraged her to do this.

The real trouble, though, was that when Mac Cumhaill or the Fianna didn't adopt one of her creations, she didn't take it well. As time went on, she showed this more and more openly.

She would grumble, 'Useless stumps of Fianna men! They wouldn't know a good weapon if it jumped up and prodded them. If it wasn't for me, they'd still be fighting with sticks and stones.'

Once, she developed a new cap for chariot horses. It was a silvery, plain thing. Mac Cumhaill didn't like it because he knew that the bronze helmets with the old engravings gave the charioteers luck and courage. She was very angry when Mac Cumhaill returned the new thing to her with a message of thanks. She came immediately over to the caves near the summer training fields, where Mac Cumhaill and his men rested in the evenings. She stormed in, waving one of her shiny pony helmets and saying, 'What exactly is it you don't like about this?'

'It's not that I don't like it,' said Mac Cumhaill.

'It's lighter, only half the weight of the old caps you make those poor useless nags of yours wear.'

'That may be so, and it is very clever, but the difference in weight is not going to make much difference to a horse that is able to carry the likes of myself or Conán there, at a gallop,' said Mac Cumhaill, laughing. 'Sure, wouldn't the hair on Conán's hands alone weigh more than old and new pony helmets together?'

She knew Mac Cumhaill was right about this. All the Fianna's horses were very big and wide-chested, renowned the world over for being as strong as five normal horses, as calm as an old man who has seen it all and whom nothing can surprise, and as well suited to ploughing a field in quiet times as facing an enemy or storming through huge thorny thickets in pursuit of a boar.

'And because it is smooth and curved outwards, it's more likely to deflect an arrow,' she shouted.

'I'll allow you that, but I've never seen an arrow pierce the old helmets,' said Mac Cumhaill politely.

'Well, you should take them if you believe what you are

often quoted as saying: that the difference between terrible defeat and glorious victory is often just leaf thin,' she said.

'It is my decision that we won't be using the cap. But thank you for bringing it,' said Mac Cumhaill.

'Curses on you; I'm doing all that I can to help you bar going out to do the fighting myself. Maybe that's what I should do. Then I'd show you. Great lazy beasts.'

'What you maybe don't realise, Eibhlín, is that the thing that makes the best soldiers is fierce reluctance followed by blind courage. A good person is always slow to fight and will look for every other option. Only if he is finally left with no other resort, he will fight with a purpose and intensity that no ordinary paid soldier can match. At that stage it is more important for him to be surrounded by instruments that he trusts and that fill him with the pride of generations lost. These fortify his spirit.' Mac Cumhaill spoke patiently, because he realised she was still young and allowed to sometimes speak wildly.

'I think that is just *raiméis*. Just excuses for the fact that you've become weak-hearted.'

The soldiers around Mac Cumhaill bristled, but she continued, 'And with our supposed defenders as weak as noble girls, it won't take long for some foreign army to realise and to come and overrun this country.'

'That's enough now,' said Mac Cumhaill, laughing. 'Take your invention away and maybe the next one will be something we can agree on.'

That is what she did. From that point on she took away all her inventions. She decided that the Fianna were backward and that Mac Cumhaill was stuck in the past. She had done all she could for them. Now she was going to show her wares to a wider audience.

When the king heard of her decision, he was worried. He called her to Tara. He met with her in private and called her out into his vegetable gardens where he often went for peace. There he spoke to her like a daughter. He pleaded with her to continue bringing her work only to the Fianna.

'Fionn Mac Cumhaill insulted me,' she said. 'When he apologises I will reconsider.'

'Well, I will ask Fionn to do that. And then you will be happy?'

'And he should be forced to take on whatever inventions I bring to him.'

'No, little one,' said Cormac patiently, 'that would be a harder thing.'

'Why? You are the king. He serves you.'

Cormac could see he was not making any progress.

'His king indeed. And his servant. And yours too. I cannot ask a skilled tradesman to do a job and then tie his hand by telling him what tools he must use.'

'I can see you are just too soft and you are allowing that overgrown elk to push you around.'

'You are of course allowed not to bring your inventions to us,' said Cormac more imperiously, stepping back into the main hall where his advisers awaited. 'But I am sorry that I can't allow you to take your fearsome inventions to the hands of our foreign enemies.'

Eibhlín turned her back on Cormac and walked out. She

knew, as everyone present did, that Cormac, in his own quiet way, had just given her a command. And that it would be unwise to disobey. But she noted that the king hadn't explicitly forbidden her from trading her inventions with foreign forces that were not the enemies of Éirinn, even if they were not exactly friends either.

She packed up sacks and boxes of gadgets and weapons, some finished, some not. She gathered a small stash of gold rings and bracelets she had been given as rewards for some of her work. She went north and hired passage on a trading boat that took her and her wares on a long journey. She was destined for the land of the Angledanes. She had heard the fables of great dragon-slaying warrior kings who lived there and she was determined that was where she wanted to go.

But Eibhlín had little idea of what lay behind these fables or what she was getting herself involved with. Her anger and injured pride prevented her from asking for any advice.

If she had asked, she might have learned that in Angledane country there was a downtrodden people, entrapped forever by their own fears. And she would have learned that their revered king was nothing but the spineless pawn of a demon queen. This queen, the cold, ruthless power of Angledaneland, was unknown to the people of that place. She only showed herself to outsiders. All the people there ever saw were the cruel, lowly men she tricked them into accepting as their glorious monarchs.

This demon queen picked a new king every twenty

years. She amused herself by always picking rogues who would make life as hard as possible for the people of Angledaneland. When it was coming time for a change, foul men would come from every part to try to win her favour. They were robbers, pirates, murderers, disgraced soldiers, men who had either fled or been chased away from their own people. All of them were braggarts, boasting of great military feats.

Once she had picked her new man, she would initially smother him in her charms and conceive a child with him. She would allow him to ride into the castle of the outgoing king and tell the people what a great warrior he was. She would have him 'heroically' slay the terrible beast of their dark imaginations.

In horrible reality, the 'beast' that the new man was slaying was nothing more than a harmless nineteen-year-old boy, whose only offence was horrendous ugliness. In each case, the nineteen-year-old was the queen's own son, born of her previous relationship with the old king, whose time was now up.

These unfortunate boys had never harmed anyone. As they grew into young men, she would send each one out, in turn, to wander the hills at night. Without the lad's knowing it, she was sending him out to scare the people in the settlements below and to make him the object of their terror and loathing. That way, she could ensure that when it came to his slaying by her new king, there would be an aura of heroism about her new man, who was apparently saving the people from the horrendous beast that prowled around at night, terrifying the children and the horses.

But in fact, this slaying was no act of heroism. A seven-year-old, after his first week of sword training, would have been able to slay the unfortunate 'beast'.

Soon another child would be born of the love of the new sleeveen for the queen. This child, as always, would be a miniature of the teenager just killed. The reason the queen's children were all so horrific-looking was that they showed on the outside the ugly betrayal that their father bore in his heart. But on the inside, unlike him, they were pure of heart.

Before sealing the deal and allowing the new 'hero' to seize the throne and extinguish the life of the old king, she would make sure he understood all of this. She would show him his own baby. She would tell him that despite the warts, scars and deformities, this was a good child. Just like the son of the old king whom he had just murdered. She would make him curse his own child and say that he was happy that this child too would be killed by a new man in nineteen years' time. Once the 'hero' agreed to her conditions, he would be allowed to drag the corpse of the dead 'beast' down to show the people and he would be declared the glorious defender of the people of Angledaneland, and it would be several years before his own reign started to become insecure.

What was in this for the demon queen is not certain. Having a son killed every twenty years seemed to cause her no distress. It seemed that the pleasure of her life lay in revealing to humans that for all their talk of defending the good and the right, most were no better than she was herself. And there was no shortage of men ready to prove her right. To prove, in fact, that they were even worse than she was. At least she told no lies. She kept her wicked word down to the last detail, without mercy. She didn't pretend to be anything better than she was.

As it happened, the man in charge in Angledaneland at the time of Eibhlín's misadventure was known in Fionn's part of the world. He had originally departed in disgrace from an island near Éirinn. His family name was Sionnach, meaning fox, and indeed he had earned his first name – Glic, meaning cunning – though he did not like it. He thought the fox was too lowly an association for him, so once he became king in Angledaneland, he had changed his name to 'Wolf Beo' meaning live wolf. But he was always known only as Glic in these parts.

This King Glic was currently the supposed great warrior king of Angledaneland. He liked to keep absolute power. He took more than his share of everything his people produced, and left them always near starvation. He boasted that when they were hungry, it made them meaner. And when they were meaner, they showed no mercy when he led them in raids on neighbouring lands, plundering anywhere he heard of good fortune or wealth.

Under the careful tutoring of the demon queen, Glic kept power over his people by keeping alive their ancient fear that if they were not obedient to him, he might allow the dreaded beast to return again. It wasn't that they were a particularly dull people. Their folk stories told them that after more than ten years in power, every leader becomes weakened and the beast then somehow starts to come back to life. They had no reason to think otherwise, since each horrendous teenager that was sent loping across the hill looked the same as the previous one to them. After fifteen years, as the unfortunate teenager grew, the sightings would become more regular. And it wasn't just sightings. The queen and her king would give them every reason to believe that the beast was a cruel killer.

The 'beast' would always be sent out at night time. A terrifying shadow, a horrendous gangly black and purple deformity, moving across the hillsides from the disused caverns where people long ago had made stone axes. Glic, like the previous kings, had persuaded the people that he alone could protect them from this horrible beast and that once it appeared, they should all go to their huts and extinguish all lights and pray for his success. Sure enough, Glic was the only one with the courage to go out looking for it. But instead of killing any monster, it was Glic himself who killed a cow here and a goat there, and any stray people he came across.

It was easy enough for the sly king to perform this butchery. Glic was certainly not the glorious warrior that the Angledane praise-singers bellyached about. He was barely able to lift a sword. His weapon of choice in conflict was an arrow fired into the back of an unsuspecting adversary. All of his subjects had been warned to kneel facing the ground when they saw the king's white horse approach. This made short work of disposing of those unfortunates who hadn't heard the warning to go indoors on the night of a beast appearance. As the white horse appeared, they would kneel and bow to the ground, and they would receive a blow from his axe in return for their obedience.

Glic would drag the dead off to the queen's den and then return to the people, covered in blood, claiming that after a ferocious fight, the beast had fled, seriously wounded.

The people and animals discovered to be missing the next morning would be considered proof of the foul deeds of the monster.

Much of this was known or suspected outside of Angledaneland, and if Eibhlín had not been too proud to ask, Dreoilín or Mac Cumhaill could have warned her.

The problem Glic was facing at the time that Eibhlín was preparing for her trip was that he had already been many years in power. He remembered only too well the deal he had agreed with the queen. At the time he was making the deal, twenty years of absolute power seemed like forever. Now, it seemed like most of it had flown past in a blur. He had been especially loyal to her and had done more killing and looting for her than any previous king he had heard of – and there had been plenty of bad ones in the past. So he hoped maybe she would let him run on for longer. Some other kings had lasted for maybe twenty-two years before she had settled on a suitably worse replacement. Though some had only made seventeen years before she got fed up of them.

He had been to talk to her a few times recently. He would say, 'My lovely mistress, you don't have to keep doing this forever.'

'What silliness is on your mind now, little man?' she said.

He never knew whether her smile was close to violence or affection.

'Well, O lovely one, why keep changing every twenty years?'

'You know I like a fresh man,' she crooned, 'and a new baby. That's how it's always been.'

'But you could get fresh blood by expanding into new territories. I could do that for you. I could build an army for you and take over a new country every year for you.'

'You could?'

'And we could strike terror in each place.'

'Yes?'

'And you could install a new prince in each place and make each of these your lovers as pleased you. I wouldn't mind.'

'You wouldn't? That's generous of you.'

'No, I'd just oversee the army and, well, I suppose, all of these princes in each area would answer to me?'

'So you'd be, we might say, king of all these expanded territories?'

'Serving you, of course.'

'So you could have expanded my territory widely, and you say you could have added a new country every year of your reign. But you didn't?'

'Well, I was getting ready to.'

'You've had sixteen years.'

It was now easy to see which kind of smile she was wearing. A violent lash was only one more wrong word away from Glic's back.

'And then there's the problem of this great oaf of a son of yours. Funny, I've had a slight fondness for some of them, but not for yours. When he is twenty we'll have to have someone get rid of him, won't we? I think I'll have him chopped like a bush and then skewered like a pig. What do you think of that?'

Glic didn't wince.

He replied, 'I could do that myself. I've done it with handsomer men. And then we could have another child together and I could carry on for another twenty years pretending to the fools below that I'd slain another monster.' Glic knew he was babbling now.

The lash of her whip cut his breast plate in ribbons and stripped flesh from his belly.

'I don't doubt that you would rip the very heart out of your own son if I offered you one extra minute on the throne. Do you think I don't know that much about you, after all these sixteen years? Quiet now,' she said, as he curled in cries of pain on the floor. 'You have another few years and be glad of them.'

'Thank...thank you, mistress,' said Glic, as he crawled out of her cavern.

From that day onwards, the sightings of the 'beast' became ever more regular. The queen would send her son out almost every evening, unkindly telling the doomed lad that if he roamed around he might soon meet a companion his own age, someone like himself. Her real intention was to amuse herself at the sight of Glic squirming in her ever tightening claw.

Glic could see the trap closing on him. Every time the 'beast' appeared, he had to set out and kill more. If he didn't bring any kill to the queen, she would have his own life instantly. All would be over. But the more people and animals that disappeared at night, the more his subjects started to feel that their king was getting old and weak and that the beast was getting the better of him now.

By the time he reached year eighteen of his reign, there were beast sightings followed by killings every second night. The people were in terror. They were beginning to murmur that their king was no longer able to keep the beast at bay, and praying for the day that a new warrior would arrive.

Three days before Eibhlín arrived, Glic had already decided to try to kill the demon queen and to reign forever himself. Of course, he wasn't the first king to have decided to try this approach. She herself had told him that much, without giving him any details.

'Terrible how little respect some men have for their honour and how easily they try to break a deal with a queen who has been so good to them and given them such good fortune,' she said one day, reading his thoughts.

'Well, you know I am a man of honour, and I keep my deals,' he said, without enquiring about the details of any of the previous kings' attempts. He didn't want to heighten her suspicions.

'All men of honour, of course, just like yourself. High honour. Men who have sold me their souls and agreed to have their own sons sacrificed like, well . . . like beasts. Just so they can have a few short years of absolute power. It would hardly be a major bridge to cross for such an *honourable* man to consider breaking a deal with a wicked old queen, now would it?'

When she asked questions like this, Glic felt her eyes could look right through him and he thought there was no way he could ever have a moment of courage against her.

However, in the daytime, away from her den, when the sun was shining in his castle yard, he felt braver. Brave enough to think the unthinkable. Although he didn't know the details, Glic knew that some of the previous kings who had challenged her had been quite passable swordsmen, unlike himself; most of them were stronger than he was, which wouldn't have been hard; and a few of them even more sneaky, wicked and bloody than him. He would need something special.

It was in the middle of these thoughts that Eibhlín arrived. She was after twenty hard days on the sea. The boatmen skirted the ribcage of the boat around the cruel seas to the north of Cornobha, sometimes with four men rowing, other times using two small sails to catch the wind. They managed her skilfully through storm and calm, all the time trying to keep land in sight. During the journey, Eibhlín stood all day at the front of the boat with her legs slightly apart for balance, holding onto the head of the wolf that was carved into the oak nose of the boat when the sea was rolling badly, staring straight ahead as if she could will the boat to reach new land quicker. She was stern and unfriendly. They wanted her to sit safely down on the floor of the boat, but she wouldn't, except when she had to sleep. She only spoke to them when she felt the need to criticise the way they were calculating their directions from the stars and the sun.

When they eventually made anchor and sent two men in a small *currach* to take Eibhlín and her wares ashore, the other boatmen were very glad to see the back of her. Yet, when she put foot on shore, her attitude changed completely. She was suddenly all smiles and pleasantness to the poor half-starving Angledanes that came down to meet her.

'So pleased to finally be in a land of sophisticated people,' she said in their language. Being such a clever person, she had managed to learn a good amount of this language merely from a few conversations with an Angledane man who was traveling on the same boat.

'Take me to your glorious king. I've heard such great things about him,' she continued. 'Finally, someone who will appreciate fine war crafts.'

When news of this strange arrival was brought to Glic, all he heard was the part about 'fine war crafts'. Though he wasn't a religious man, he began to hope that maybe a merciful god of some kind was sending him a solution to his problem. He sent for the foreign woman to be brought to his palace immediately. He also ordered that no further mention of her arrival be made anywhere. He hoped the demon queen would not hear anything until he got a chance to look at what kind of lucky cards he had been dealt.

Eibhlín approached the castle, escorted by two castle workers to whom she payed no attention. Had she looked, she would have noticed that they were mere skin and bone. Five more followed, carrying her caskets and sacks of wares. People working on their knees in the rows of crops at the side of the pathway didn't look up at the curious clanging and tinkling sounds the objects made as they were carried.

She also didn't take much note of the fact that the castle wasn't as grand as she had heard of in the great tales of Angledaneland. The circular structure had walls of reeds and mud with a straw roof, not very much taller than the roofs on some of the huts they had passed along the way. The guards at the entrance were snoozing in the sunshine. She was able to walk right into the building without anyone checking who she was or what her business was. She assumed this was because the king had summoned her and told his fine guards not to bother her on the way in.

There weren't many people about inside the entrance chamber of the castle either. There were some hens that had come in and were picking through the sand on the floor, looking for crumbs. She didn't notice any of this. She was standing waiting to be taken through to the main chamber. There were a few women fussing over a small pot. There was one tall man picking his teeth looking vacantly at the women and talking in a kind of deranged verse.

'A Thane of Higalic heard of a man of valour.
Nægling, Wolf Beo's own sword, was shivered in pieces;
It was not granted to him that the edges of steel blades
might help him in the fight;
The champion of the Scyldings smote the fiendish
monster...'

Eibhlín was warmed to see that the great king gave shelter to such an unfortunate raving lunatic, probably a hero who had lost his mind in some gallant battle.

There was another man lying on a pile of straw eating an apple. None of them moved very much, even to look at her. By now, her impatience was starting to return.

'Can you go and tell your glorious king that Eibhlín has arrived, my good man,' she said, settling her gaze on the insolent, lazy git lying on the pile of straw.

She stepped closer to him and realised that the foul smell she had thought was coming from the cooking pot actually seemed to be coming off this loutish guard on the straw. The king's staff obviously didn't have a great fondness for water. To make things worse, he appeared to have his body smeared in some kind of pig lard, such as she used on the blades of new swords to keep them from rusting. She wondered how any king could keep such people in his service. She thought to herself, *If the poor man is taken advantage of by such slack servants it must only mean that his heart is too kind.*

The man sat up and brushed some straw off his food-stained cape. Then he stood. He was so short that the top of his perfectly bald and lard-covered head barely reached Eibhlín's shoulder. He was so fat, she was calculating that if you needed to get to the other side of him, it would probably take less energy to jump over him than to walk around him. This dirty little man was, of course, Glic himself.

When he said, 'At your service missus', Eibhlín nearly fell in a heap.

'You're looking a bit pale, my dear; I suppose it was a long journey,' said the king in his politest voice, and screamed over his shoulder, 'Get this one something to drink, you lazy trollops.'

The water in the earthenware pot they brought her had a foul smell. But she was so thirsty she drank it anyway. That was all she was offered. No mention of a place to rest after her long journey. No mention of a meal.

'Now,' said the king, after a few minutes, 'let's talk business.'

He sat back down on his pile of straw. He pointed for her to sit too, but there was nothing to sit on except the ground. She sat there in the sand. She said nothing.

'What have you brought for me, woman?' said the king in a much sharper tone.

For the first time, she noticed a leather whip that hung by his side where most warriors kept swords. He touched its stem with his short fingers.

Tough and hard though she was, sheer cold panic was starting to spread through Eibhlín's body. What on earth had she got herself into? What was going to happen next? What could she do to get home? Home! All of a sudden, it seemed so nice. Even the simplest hut in her clan's enclosure was nicer than this. Even with all her sharpness, her own king had treated her properly. And why could she not just have swallowed her pride and listened to the tall, pale boy that Mac Cumhaill had sent to shout at the departing boat, warning her to turn back, as this was not a good place? She needed to keep a cool head now if she was ever to come out of this situation, but she was finding it very hard not to cry.

'I came, Your Highness, to offer for sale some new military inventions,' she said bravely.

'Sale?' the king laughed. 'Where do you think you are?'

He nodded to the other man in the room, who continued mumbling his verses as he went to move rough-hewn boughs of a tree across the main entranceway.

'Yes. That's what I do,' she continued. 'I make special weapons and defences and sell them to, eh, noble warriors and kings.'

'Show us what you have.'

Before she could even respond, he was wedging open her caskets by driving a flint axe head into the locks, grunting, sweating, and cursing as he did so.

Eventually, with all the caskets broken, sacks cut and things thrown everywhere in the sand, he stood up in a rage and said, 'What is all this rubbish? Are you trying to make a fool of me?'

Eibhlín was feeling weak. She picked up her lightweight helmet for the chariot horse – the one that Mac Cumhaill and Cormac had so offended her by not taking.

'This, you see, is much lighter and yet harder than the

older class of a cap that horses wear into battle. It lessens their load slightly so they can go faster, yet protects them better.'

'What?' He grabbed the helmet from her. 'A nice little cap to protect the poor little horsies. Is that it? *Is that it?*' He flung the thing against a wooden pole. 'In this country, you pale fool, I am more concerned with keeping myself alive than keeping stupid horses alive. That's why I've been king for nineteen years. That's why a horse is not king. Fool.'

Eibhlín's heart sank. She went through several of her inventions. Each was greeted with the same ridicule. Eventually, she took out a cloth-covered object. She tenderly unwrapped it. It was a special hooked spear that her father had designed. Because it was from the man she worshipped, she had sworn to herself that she would never show this to anyone other than the most noble. But she was desperate. And when Glic took this and also flung it in the fire place, she suddenly felt another emotion. Anger. She had nothing to lose, as she could not see herself coming out of this place alive. So she walked slowly over to the fireplace and picked her father's spear out of the ash.

Silence fell on the place, as everyone could see the madness in her eyes. The demented bard had drawn his sword but was standing a safe distance from the spear. The king, of course, had no sword to draw, but pulled out his whip.

She had the stump of the whip caught with the spear hook before he could even swing. She pulled it out of his hand like he was a child. He started snivelling.

'A test,' he suddenly laughed, as the point of the spear touched his belly, still sore from his last encounter with the demon queen.

'A test?' said Eibhlín.

'Yes, of course, my dear, I have only been testing you to see what metal you yourself are made of. That will tell me much more than the metals in your weapons.'

'Really?' said Eibhlín, relaxing a little.

'Yes, of course,' he smiled sweetly. 'Put down that fearsome weapon. We are all friends here.'

She put it down. Glic's assistant cautiously removed it.

'I see now,' said the king, still grinning.

'What do you see?' said Eibhlín.

'It wasn't a pile of fancy metal that was sent to me by the gods, it was the woman to carry the weapons.'

'What do you mean?' said Eibhlín, alarmed.

'You know. Your mission here. You have come to solve my problem. I should have known.'

'Only weapons. That's the only problem I solve.'

'Of course, you can take any of your weapons with you. Whatever you like. Most of my men have no use for anything more fancy than a hatchet and a club. Just as long as you do the job.'

'What job?'

'You really don't know?'

Glic nodded at the other man, who removed the sticks from the doorway and left the hut castle, followed by the two women, and then blocked the door again.

'No. I really don't have any idea what you are talking about.'

Eibhlín looked all around and could see several spots in the rough mud wall where she might be able to get through if she made a dash for it. But there was nowhere to go once she got out. The boat had left as soon as it had deposited her and the other Angledaneland passenger. 'Going to do some trading with less hungry people up the coast,' they had said. If only she'd asked them why they said that.

'Well, my dear,' he said, reaching out to touch her hand. She pulled her arm away as the soft, sweaty palm descended. He bit his anger back and drew a deep breath.

'That's alright, my dear. You can be like that. I don't care. You can be as rude as you want. Just as long as you do the job.'

'What job are you talking about?' asked Eibhlín angrily. 'I'll do work for you if you promise to allow me to get on the next ship out of here, no matter where it's going. What job is it that you want me to do? I could make an iron brace that will hold the roof on this ramshackle castle of yours next time there's a storm. Or I could fix your sword. I assume it's broken, since I see you're not wearing one. Just say what it is you want.'

'You are fiery. Just like her. I see it now. That's why you were sent,' said the king, increasingly pleased with himself.

'Just like who?'

'Don't you know? There's a very nice woman up there in the hills behind us. The only job you have to do for me is to separate her head from her body. It'll be very easy for a temperamental woman like you. You can use any of the weapons you like.'

He kicked the pile of Eibhlín's inventions and scattered them on the floor, then turned away laughing.

'I'm not a soldier. I don't know how to kill. And besides . . . turn and look at me, you little pig man!' she suddenly shouted.

He turned, still laughing. 'You know the strange thing? Those are the exact words she often calls me. You are her perfect match. You can go and do it now, or wait till tomorrow. It's all the same to me.'

'And besides,' Eibhlín continued more quietly, 'I'm just not going to kill some poor, defenceless woman just because you don't like her.'

'Wrong, wrong, wrong. Wrong to think she is defenceless. She is not quite that, shall we say.' He sniggered at his joke. 'Also wrong to say that I don't like her. I actually like her quite a bit more than I like you. I may even have my slaves erect a nice stone circle tomb to put her head in when you bring it to me. I don't want it to be said that I don't treat my women well. And most wrong of all to say that you are not going to kill her. In fact, that is exactly what you are going to do. Unless you want to live here becoming wife and footwasher to your little "pig man" king for the rest of your days.'

He went back and flopped down on his straw. He waved his hand vaguely as if he was telling her where there might be a good patch of blackberries.

'She lives up in the hills somewhere. Wander up there

and you'll find her soon enough. If you bump into the beast, as they call him here, an ugly lump of a boy, don't bother with him. He couldn't harm a fly. But when you are in the vicinity, she'll know. And she will show herself to you when she chooses to. Then, you know what to do.'

'Even if I was going to try to do this, how would I know her?'

'You'll know her. There are not exactly hundreds of beautiful women with twenty-foot tails wandering around the place you know.'

'A tail? What kind of woman is this exactly?'

'Ah, what a woman! My naughty queen. She is going to regret trying to cast me aside,' he said, almost daydreaming.

Eibhlín was filled with revulsion at the sight. She picked up the spear again and prodded him out of his dreaming.

'There's really no point in threatening me with that,' he said, less alarmed than before. 'If you even scratch me, there's no way out for you. The only way out is to do the one simple little job I am asking. Just remove her cap. Then we're both happy and off you go.'

Eibhlín sat down for a minute in the sand again to think about her situation. She was determined not to have anything to do with any of this. She had several reasons. One was that she could not take the word of a rotten creature like Glic. For all she knew, this queen might be entirely good. Another was that she genuinely had never used a weapon against another person. She had no training at all, though she fancied she might be able to wield one of her well-balanced swords as well as most men. The biggest reason of all was that, even assuming that this queen was bad enough to be killed, she really didn't like the sound of the tail or the way Glic chuckled. She had a sneaking feeling this was not any ordinary adversary and that this would not be a match she could win, no matter how good her weapons or skills.

Eibhlín picked out two swords, a snare, and her father's spear. She carefully tied them together with a strip she tore from her clothing. She headed for the doorway.

Glic sat up again and said, 'There you go, my darling girl. I knew you'd see sense. This is a good deal for all of us.'

He shouted for someone to remove the barriers from the doors to let Eibhlín out and told them not to bother her or follow her.

Outside the castle, everywhere was dusty and she was finally seeing the reality. The desperately hungry-looking people she met seemed drained of energy by the warm sun. The castle guards were sitting in the shade of a small tree and sipping something from seashells. She, too, was very hungry and very confused. Nobody seemed bothered by what she did or where she went.

It seemed there was nothing else for her to do except go to the hills to see for herself what this woman was really like and just how impossible it was going to be for her ever to win her way back home. Besides, there was no point in hanging around down here anyway, as she would die of thirst and hunger without anyone even noticing her. The place had been scoured for food by these hungry people.

There wasn't a fruit or nut anywhere, or even a root that might have been edible. No birds that she might net and roast. She had seen one young man eating insects, but even those looked like a hard catch. The people here spent most of the time staring at the ground.

She tied her bundle of weapons around her shoulder and headed towards the hills. It was the first time she'd seen any reaction from the people. When she looked back, everyone had stopped what they were doing. They were all looking up at her, horrified. Nobody went where she was going. Into the domain of their beast. But none of them tried to call her back. Nobody cared to save her. They just stood there with their hands over their mouths. She started thinking, maybe the people of this land deserved nothing better than the likes of Glic as their heroic leader.

The hills weren't very high. She was soon walking in a section where the stone was loose and broken. Given her own trade, she knew well the signs of trades from previous eras. She was walking through what had been a very busy place not that long ago. There was a warren of hollows in the hills where people had knocked out shards of stone to chip into the shapes of tools and weapons. Not having any idea of the danger that lurked in these caverns, she sat into one recess to get some shade and gather her thoughts.

As she sat there, it suddenly dawned on her that this was completely different than the village below. Because the people were afraid to come up here, the place was undisturbed. There were several apple and pear trees, probably seeded here in the times that the stone workers spent their days here. And they were laden down with nearly ripe fruit. There was a clump of briars a short distance further up that looked like it had berries dropping off it. There were animals that had never seen a human and didn't know how dangerous they are. She would be able to snare a rabbit or net a bird with very little effort. For the first time since landing in Angledaneland she started to feel alright. Even better, when she investigated a trickling sound nearby she found a mountain spring with water so sweet she felt bloated by the time she was finished scooping it into her mouth.

She set a snare. She ate three pears. She brushed aside some stone chippings, laid her shawl down, laid herself down, and sank into the best sleep she'd had since she'd left her father's hut in the Fógartaigh rath, what seemed like an age ago.

The next morning, she was awoken by the sunshine warming her legs. She quickly gathered her things, preparing to dutifully carry on journeying up the hill. But she realised she didn't know where she was going or what she was really looking for. She also realised she was more comfortable here than she'd been anywhere for a long time. Plenty to eat. Plenty of heat. No furnace or mouldings to struggle with. And best of all for someone who didn't really like people much, no other people anywhere near. Absolute peace.

She went to check her snares and found a fine, fat rabbit that would nicely supplement her meals for a few days. So she decided to stay right here for a day or two. Or maybe more.

As Eibhlín spent the coming days trying to decide which corners of the caves would be the driest and most sheltered no matter what direction the winds came from, gathering twigs, grasses and mosses to make her nest, other things were happening around. Things were happening far away at home, below in Glic's castle, and nearer still, in the inner caverns of the hill in which she was making her new home.

Back in Éire, the chief of the Fógartaighs had gone to Tara with Eibhlín's father, appealing that someone be sent to rescue her. The Fógartaigh was a kind and gentle friend of Cormac's and this made the king well disposed to the pleadings. He shared the Fógartaigh's sympathy with the woman's father, cold and hard as the man was. As the Fógartaigh pointed out, no one would want to be in that man's position. Even if your child was strong-headed and often got in trouble. Every parent wants to protect their child from harm. Mac Cumhaill was called for.

'Will you go and bring this unfortunate girl back from Angledaneland?' asked Cormac.

Mac Cumhaill took one look at the big, tearful eyes of the Fógartaigh, a chief who always took the welfare of every one of his people to heart, and he knew there was no point at all in arguing.

The only thing he asked was a simple question, but to him a very important one. 'What am I to do if she doesn't want to come back?' said Mac Cumhaill.

'You are surely entitled to ask that,' said Cormac, 'but isn't it a nonsensical question? We both know that that Glic and the ravaged lands of Angledaneland have no welcome for any passing soul.'

'And we both know that Eibhlín is a…' Mac Cumhaill looked over at the worried father. 'Well, can we say that she is very attached to her own point of view?'

Down in the ramshackle castle, Glic was getting curious as to how things had gone. He was preparing to venture up the hill. He was bringing a bundle of plundered gold so that he could pretend it was just a routine visit to bring her a gift, in case he met the demon queen still with her head on her shoulders. But he was hoping against hope that he would meet only Eibhlín. His intention, of course, was not to let her go but to inveigle her back down to the castle and to keep her there until she agreed to become another wife or servant, for his amusement.

But only twenty paces from where Eibhlín had made her bed, twenty paces further in towards the centre of the hill, stood a far greater danger. The demon queen herself knew of every movement in those lands. She knew of Eibhlín from the minute she splashed into the knee-high water as she came ashore from the *currach*. Normally, any rare person crazy enough to climb the hills, anyone other than her puppet king, would have been killed instantly. But here was Eibhlín living like a happy child who had just found the most wonderful hideout, eating the queen's pears and rabbits.

The reason for Eibhlín's continued existence on this

earth was that the queen had been transfixed by curiosity as to what this tall young woman, who seemed to travel alone, wanted in her lands. The reason for her curiosity was that there were very few visitors to this land, other than the chancers and vagabonds who came to try to be the next king. There were no traders, as there was nothing to trade – most of Glic's pillaged wealth was brought straight to the queen. There were no marauders, as there was no one to enslave, with the people so weak and lethargic from just having barely enough food. Mostly, foreigners just left the Angledanes alone to live with their sorry secrets.

There had certainly never before been a visitor of this kind. And what had she brought in the caskets and bags? the queen wondered. She expected that Glic would be up immediately to report on these goings-on, but no. She hadn't seen hide nor hair of him since this woman had arrived.

'Stupid little pig doesn't even realise I know about the visitor, that I see everything,' she grumbled to herself. But mostly, she was just curious.

For a clever woman, Eibhlín was surprisingly oblivious. Most people would know if they were being watched. She had no idea. Yet, everything she did and every time she sat or lay doing nothing at all, there were two pairs of eyes observing curiously. She was watched as the first beams of sunlight stirred her in the mornings. She was watched as she danced a funny dance, washing in the cold mountain pool. She was watched as she set her perfect nets and traps. She was watched as she lovingly drew a small sharpening stone along the elegant blade of her unusual hooked spear.

She was watched right through to the time for lighting a neat, well-sized fire, to cook her food. Then, four ears listened to her humming herself to sleep, seeming to have no sense at all of the danger she was in.

She had forgotten, or dismissed as nonsense, Glic's story about a woman in the hills that she was to kill. She didn't even want to sully the pure good humour she was in with trying to imagine what the sordid little man might have been on about.

This situation continued for weeks. The queen had become quite fond of the young woman, in as far as she ever became fond of anyone.

That was until the much larger boat arrived. It arrived in the early hours of the morning, before orange sunlight cracked the forsaken horizon. The queen saw it anchor in the bay and she saw two smaller boats row ashore from it. Four people got out of the boats. These were not women: they were too ugly. They were not fishermen: they had too much meat on them. They were not Angledanes: they were too sturdy. They were not traders: they were too stealthy, as they headed straight for cover. And she was quite sure they were not potential suitors: they looked like actual warriors rather than renegades or thieves.

The queen's mind immediately assumed that the woman sleeping in her garden, the woman she had thought so innocent was, in fact, part of a devious plot. This was her thought because that was how things had always worked in her domain. Only the most devious, the most cunning, the most wicked, survived.

When Eibhlín opened her eyes that morning, it was to the sight of two beautiful gem-encrusted feet, very close to her face. She looked slowly upwards from the feet. She was dazzled by the splendour of the demon queen. A silken robe of dark purple reached from her slight shoulders to her knees. She was not very tall. When Eibhlín stood up and dusted herself off apologetically, she noticed that she was nearly a head above the queen. A delicate kind of pale beauty surrounded the woman, Eibhlín thought.

'Did you bring visitors?' the queen asked, without any greetings or introductions. As though she was talking to someone she already knew well.

'Blessings on you, kind lady,' said Eibhlín. 'Eibhlín Rua is the name given to me.'

'Did you bring visitors?' the queen asked again, in the same soft voice, with the same eerie look on her face that might have been a smile or might have been something else.

'No; that I did not,' said Eibhlín. 'I am sorry if you were expecting guests. I'm afraid there's only me.'

'Who were those men I saw come ashore this morning, then?'

'I am sorry, but I don't know. I didn't know anyone else had landed. I had been hoping a boat would come some day and that I might be able to get home. But I didn't know one had come today.'

'Why are you wanting to go?'

'Because, well . . . because your king did not seem to me . . . I don't mean to cause offence, but he didn't seem to be quite as great as I had heard tell of.'

Eibhlín was expecting anger or upset from the woman at the insult to her king. But there was still no reaction. Just the same face.

'Why, then, are you not packing your little bag and running down to catch the boat I am telling you landed this morning?'

'Well, to tell you the truth, once I left your king behind and came up here, I found a peace and contentment that I never knew in my life before. And now I'm not in such a hurry to go.'

'No?'

'If it's alright with you, of course, and whoever else belongs to this land.'

Still no reaction from the other woman.

Eventually, she said, 'I am deciding whether to believe you. I can always tell when a human is lying and my heart tells me that you are not.'

'Thank you,' said Eibhlín, suddenly starting to feel afraid. What did the mention of humans mean? What was this woman if not human?

The queen continued as if Eibhlín hadn't spoken, 'But good sense tells me that I would be foolish to believe you.'

Eibhlín felt the coldness of these words like a stream of icy water running down her back. She started moving slightly towards her bedding, making to gather her things.

'There is no point in trying to move away,' said the queen. 'I can cut you down in an instant. The only reason I have been hesitating is that I have come to like you a little bit. You can gain yourself more time on this side of life while you tell me interesting things about yourself. The first thing you tell me that is not interesting, that is the moment when I will run through your heart.'

Just from the tone and look of this woman, small and frail though she appeared, Eibhlín had not the smallest shadow of doubt that what she had said was true and that she would be dying very, very soon. She couldn't see that there was anything at all to do other than to start talking, because she realised that she would prefer to die after her next breath rather than before it.

'I am an inventor,' she said.

'That is interesting,' said the queen. 'Continue.'

'I am very intelligent,' said Eibhlín.

'Yes,' said the queen.

'In some ways,' said Eibhlín, 'but it wasn't very intelligent to come here and walk into my death.'

'No,' said the queen. 'That wasn't very clever, but how could you have known?'

'I make weapons and shields', said Eibhlín.

'Indeed?'

'I have never seen metalwork finer than my own.'

'Good. There is not time in life for false modesty.'

'I have not yet ever met a man other than my father, whom I either respected,' said Eibhlín, 'or loved.' Now she was looking into space.

She didn't know why she said this. She wasn't trying to be interesting anymore. She was just describing the last thoughts that were entering her head before death.

'You are indeed a very surprising human woman and if

you carry on in this way you may find that it will cause me regret to kill you.'

'Well maybe you should kill me now, then,' said Eibhlín, looking the queen straight in the eye. 'I am no longer afraid.'

The queen looked shaken for the first time. Her expression changed momentarily.

'I always stick to my word,' she said. 'Please carry on.'

'I haven't cared for other people very much,' said Eibhlín. 'At all, in fact, now that I think of it.'

'That does not lessen you in my estimation,' said the queen. 'Every human I have ever met has fallen easy victim to flattery, conceit or greed.'

'Instead of making fine bugles or spindles or ornaments, as I once did, I now use my genius to craft new weapons and shields.'

'Do you indeed, my clever girl?' said the queen, smiling.

Pleased with the approval, Eibhlín continued recklessly.

'I have even stopped worshipping Creidhne. She's the one that metalworkers believe they must pay homage to in my land. My secret: I don't believe in her anymore. I think I am better.' She paused. 'I sometimes think the real reason I do this is because I get some kind of satisfaction in thinking of the havoc and mayhem, the torn limbs and the pierced hearts, that will be caused by the fine slender tools that I make.'

'That's enough,' said the queen.

She reached into her robe. Eibhlín could see her shape start to change. Her arms lengthened. Then there was a long spike in her hand, made of some mix of metals Eibhlín hadn't seen before. Eibhlín was completely settled, though she was now certain she was about to die.

She wasn't the only one who was sure she was about to die. As the spike came forward there was a terrible crashing sound and the most horrendous-looking creature Eibhlín had ever seen came blundering through the bramble patch above. This huge creature had the shape of a very tall, but quite pink and bulbous, human body, and a face like a pig's bum, and with only two or three bounds was standing between Eibhlín and the queen.

The queen looked almost as shocked as Eibhlín.

The creature spoke in a young male voice: 'Don't kill her, don't kill her! You'll have to kill me first!'

'What?' said the queen, sneering.

'I love her and you can kill me first as it's the only way you are going to get to her.'

'What? Love me?' said Eibhlín, 'I am flattered, ehh, sir, but a little surprised since I have never had the misfortune of seeing you before.'

The queen's arms extended in an instant, went around and behind the creature, and plucked Eibhlín from in front of him. 'Stupid boy,' she said. 'Meet Siphon,' she said to Eibhlín, still in her grip. 'Unhappily for him, he is the son of your friend, the despicable little pig man.'

The creature got to his knees and said, 'Your Highness, I beg, I plead, have mercy on her.'

'No mercy,' she said. 'Stand up and be a man. I have no time for mercy.'

'Please don't kill her.'

'For your information,' said the queen, looking at Eibhlín, 'I was merely showing our little expert guest the unusual metals in this very fine spike. Nothing to do with mercy. I made a deal. I would kill her on the first boring thing she said. And I can see it would take a long time if I had to wait for her to say something that didn't interest me.'

She pushed the boy aside and spoke to Eibhlín.

'You are free to stay, if you still want to. There are things I can teach you.'

Eibhlín was freed from the grip. And the queen's attention made her blush. The boy started applauding in sheer delight. He probably thought he had found a friend at last.

'I thank you. I would like that very much,' said Eibhlín, oblivious to the cruel kick the queen had directed at her cowering son. Eibhlín was fascinated by the queen. She had no hesitation at all about the offer. Maybe she could learn from this woman. At last, a person who didn't think her strange or awful, who didn't flinch at the idea that a person could dedicate their life to making instruments of war. She thought she might enjoy being like the queen, looking down with disdain on dishonest, pathetic humans, above it all; living up here in peace and solitude. She started gathering her things, looking forward to entering the queen's domain.

'What are you doing?' said the queen. 'I said you could stay, not come. You will live out here in the bushes. And I shall come and talk to you when I feel like it. If I like you more, I may show you my palace. One day. I will leave you now before this curious good feeling wears thin.'

The creature lad started grunting and pointing down the hill. 'Look, look, look!'

'Shut up, idiot,' said the queen, knocking him back onto his bottom with a blow as she disappeared.

She should probably have listened, but she seemed so distracted with thoughts of how a protégée might change her life, that for great good luck she had forgotten about the boat and didn't see what the boy had seen – the approach of Mac Cumhaill, Conán, Diarmuid and Goll, crouching through the tall bracken on the side of the hill. Fionn had taken only his three bravest and most battle-hardened commanders with him – men who understood the benefits of not looking for war where it's not looking for you.

Mac Cumhaill called to Eibhlín in an urgent whisper, 'Quick my child, over here!'

She looked around and then continued tidying her nails on a small sharpening stone. Mac Cumhaill took a risk and stood out from the bracken. Again he whispered, 'Quick, *alanna*, over here, quick.'

'Oh, it's you,' said Eibhlín slowly, casually. 'I'm busy.'

'Come on with me, will you, before your one remembers there are intruders and comes to try to murder the whole lot of us,' said Mac Cumhaill.

'She wouldn't do that,' said Eibhlín.

'Oh, she would,' came a voice from behind Eibhlín. The ugly lad.

'Well, I thought the great Fianna with their great

83

swordsmanship, skill, agility, cunning and strength could not be beaten by anyone,' she said with an overdose of sarcasm.

'We don't want to have to fight her if there is no need for it,' said Mac Cumhaill, 'so come on, quickly.'

'I won't. I'm staying here.'

'Go with them. You're lucky. Go with them,' said the lad with tears in his voice.

'She respects me. I like her. And I like it here.' Eibhlín turned to the boy. 'Why should I go?'

'She will turn against you,' he said. 'She will turn against us all. She thinks I don't know that. She's gone for a sleep now. She does it at this time every day. But it will only last as long as it takes to boil an egg. You should go quickly.'

'No. She might be stern, that doesn't mean she's evil . . . hey . . . hey!'

Mac Cumhaill was lifting the young woman under his arm and gathering the remnants of her weapons in the other hand. She started shouting.

'Shut your gob,' said Conán in a rage. 'You're so smart. You think you know better than everyone. You know that demon for an hour and you think you know her better than her poor unfortunate son who's known her all his life? Shut your gob before you give me a bellyache.'

She actually did go quiet for a minute. There wasn't a person in Éire who didn't flinch when the ferocious-looking Conán opened his mouth in temper. And maybe, too, she was shocked that other people seemed to know things about the queen already – she thought she had just discov-

ered her. Maybe she was shocked at the news that the creature that the queen pushed around was actually her own
son, and the grotesque fruit of a liaison with Glic. The one
she had called 'despicable'. That repulsive thought did not
quite fit in with her image of the austere queen. Or maybe
she was just shocked at Conán's rudeness. Anyway, they
were halfway down the hill before she started yelling again.

As the others were getting into their *currach*s, Mac
Cumhaill stopped to talk to some people on the beach.
Eibhlín was waving and kicking under his arm. Mac
Cumhaill talked to them for a few minutes, pointing up
to the hill and then across to the castle.

When they had rowed a bit offshore and were near the
bigger boat, Goll said to Mac Cumhaill, 'Should we not
have saved those poor people?'

'How do you mean?' said Mac Cumhaill.

'Should we not have got rid of Glic and the demon
queen for them?'

'I told them the truth,' said Mac Cumhaill. 'That gives
them the power to rid themselves of their burden.'

'Still, it would have been easier for them if the two of
them were gone.'

'We came with one job to do, and that is what we are
doing,' said Mac Cumhaill, letting Eibhlín go.

She was quiet now and listening to them.

'Well,' said Goll, 'if you came to do only one job, why
did you take *him* with us?'

He was pointing disapprovingly at the ugly lad huddled
up in the back of the *currach*.

'How else could I have shown those people on the beach that there is no beast and that this chap is harmless?' said Mac Cumhaill.

'Nonsense, you could have just told them, the same as you told them about how the queen is the one who really rules over them through hired vagabonds and how she has a new man every twenty years and has him kill her previous son.'

The boy at the back of the boat covered his ears and started shaking. Eibhlín obviously hadn't known that either, but she just looked at the boy with disdain. Conán was the one who nearly toppled the boat making his way clumsily back to the boy to pat him on the back, saying, 'You're alright now, chief. Don't worry a bit. You're alright now'.

'I could have,' said Mac Cumhaill, 'but I don't think Cormac will mind this one slight deviation from his instructions.'

A freezing northeasterly pushed them rapidly away from Angledaneland and ushered them quickly home.

Of course, the people of Angledaneland did not recover from their oppression. They somehow came to disbelieve what Fionn Mac Cumhaill told them about the demon queen. Some refused to believe she existed. Others didn't believe Mac Cumhaill's assurance that she could never rule them directly, because she had so much disdain for people that she couldn't bear to be close to them for long enough to control a whole country of them. Or that her only method of ruling was through suckling kings like Glic. And that all they had to do was chase him, along with any other chancers who came to take his place. They did not believe that they had the ability to free themselves: that Glic had no powers whatsoever, not even the power to lift a sword. Even though it all made sense to the people on the beach at the time Mac Cumhaill told them, they were somehow not ready to hear it. Even though they saw with their own eyes that the beast of their nightmares was as harmless as a lamb. They started to convince themselves that the foreigners had just put a spell on it to make it temporarily safe. Some people were like that – buried so deep in misery that they were afraid to leave its cold embrace.

The absence of the son for Glic's successor to kill caused a minor problem for the queen. She summoned Glic up to her palace. He knew his time was up. He brought one of the very light swords that Eibhlín had left in his castle, trying to build his courage by telling himself he would finally put this woman in her place and reminding himself how thin her neck was. But of course she was ready for him and killed him slowly. The Angledanes found the mangled body and made up a legend about the heroic battle he had fought.

And soon the queen had a new suitor and a new son in the making. The new man was a small-time thief from Móna, who thought he would like to swap a life of stealing other people's sheep for a stint at absolute power over the unfortunate people of Angledaneland.

From the day they got home, Eibhlín told anyone who would listen how she had been whipped from paradise by Mac Cumhaill. She was too proud to admit any mistake on her own part and always talked about the wonderful, misunderstood queen into whose shoes she might have one day stepped. Of course, she knew the truth. The proof of that was that in all the years she lived afterwards, there was no account ever heard of her trying to board a ship to head back to Angledaneland.

Mac Cumhaill had thought that bringing back the boy might soften Eibhlín's heart. But she never had a minute to pass a kind word or thought to the boy who had offered his own life to save hers.

His affection for her eased in time. He went to live in bogland in the middle of the country and married a nice human woman. The people in that area could not pronounce his name, Grendle Heorot Sionnach. They just called him Grennan. Traces of his features are still to be seen in some of the people from those parts today.

The voice faded with the fire, and Dark was alone in the rath again. He heard a movement in the bushes. A head probed through. Two yellow eyes looked straight at him. Even though it was dark, he knew what he saw. Bigger than a fox and with a longer, grey face. It stared at him, sitting on the pine needles, for maybe five seconds. He didn't move a muscle. It retreated.

3
HELPING HANDS

Before school, when Dark was walking across the yard with milk sloshing in buckets for the calves in the lower sheds, he heard conversation from the milking parlour. He looked out in the back yard. Sure enough there was a red pick-up truck there parked next to Brian's. Dark knew the truck. It belonged to Trevor Saltee, the one neighbour who had never called in while Connie was around. He had a very big farm just across the Brown River. He was gaunt and unsmiling. His shoulders were hunched, and he always had a hard, hungry look. He liked to speak in a pompous, old-fashioned way, with a put-on English accent. These days he called regularly to offer help to Dark's mother 'in the difficult circumstances', but he never came dressed for work and never did any.

Dark listened at the back door of the milking parlour.

'What has you here so early in the morning, anyway?' Brian was saying.

'Ah, nothing of much consequence, my good man. Except that I was passing and said I'd drop in to see how you were getting on.'

Brian didn't reply.

'Any updates on when our good friend Cornelius is getting out?' asked Trevor.

Dark came closer to the door.

'I don't know anything about the man's situation,' said Brian. 'It's not my business.'

'I should rather think, though, that it may be some time yet,' Trevor continued. 'Even with remission.'

'If you know, why did you ask? Isn't that a long time for a minor offence, though?' said Brian.

'I rather think not. Con was his own worst enemy,' said Trevor. 'He lives by his own laws and you can't be going on like that in this day and age.'

'Connie never did anyone a bad turn,' said Brian, with definite anger in his voice. 'I heard he asked that inspector lad not to be nosing around and it was only when the man refused that he lifted him up and put him in his car. He didn't strike or hurt the man in any way. Just lifted him like a kitten and put him back in his nest.'

'A man only doing his job! And then on top of that, he shoved the man's car up the lane with the loading shovel!'

'I'll tell you another thing too,' continued Brian, 'there isn't a farmer in the county who doesn't agree with Connie telling those lads from the department that they're no better than the old land agents. And it was harsh to lock up a man who was never in court before, just for standing up to official blackguardism.'

'Ah ha! It seems you are labouring under a misapprehension. Like many another around here, you have jumped to the conclusion that this man was an agricultural inspector. He was not that. No, sir. In fact that visitor was an inspector from the Department of Heritage. What do you have to say to that, now, sir?'

'Whatever,' said Brian, after a slight pause, obviously a little bit surprised by this information, as was Dark.

'You see, you think you know Cornelius well. But I'm not sure any of us knows him at all. What was a man from that department looking for on these premises? Tell me that if you can!'

Brian shooed out four cows who were finished milking and ignored Trevor's question.

'Well, Con, of course, is his own worst enemy,' Trevor said again, 'coming into court in that state. Wearing a bright yellow suit and the big wild woolly head on him and representing himself. You can't blame the judge for thinking he was making a mockery of the court of law. Even then, the judge gave him a chance and says to him, "Now then Mr . . . er . . . McLean, do you think you can live beyond the reach of civilised society? Maybe in whatever uncouth world you inhabit, the intimidation and assault of a government official is acceptable behaviour?"'

'Were you at the court then?' said Brian. 'What business did you have there?'

'I was there indeed, Mr Brody, as is my constitutional

right, may I inform you. But Con looks straight at the old judge and says, "*A chara*, I mind my business well and I don't want some *gomdaw* in a suit nosing around my yard and rooting through my sheds. That's not part of his job. What was he looking for, anyway?" What did Con mean by that, Brian, do you think? What did he think a man from Heritage might have been looking for on these premises?'

Brian shrugged.

Trevor continued to relay the conversation with the judge. '"Would you at least apologise to the man?" the judge says to Con. "The man has graciously offered to let the matter go if you are ready to apologise and allow him to come and do a full inspection unhindered." But Con says, "To tell you the honest truth, my friends, I'm not a bit sorry. If I said I was, I'd only be talking horse shite." The judge got rather miffed, because the whole courtroom erupted in laughter.'

'Well,' Brian said, looking at Trevor with no pleasure, 'that's the truth. One thing about Connie McLean is that at least *he* is neither a liar nor a sneak.'

The comment had no effect on Trevor. He added with satisfaction, 'Indeed, I suppose you couldn't blame the judge for getting in a rage. He hardly waited a minute before dishing out the big sentence, saying that Connie had complete contempt for authority and that he needed to send a clear message to others who might think they are beyond the law. In case the country would descend into chaos.'

'I have to get on with the milking now anyway, Trevor,' said Brian.

'Oh, quite so. But do give me a call if you get any ideas

about what Con might have been hiding here. We probably should try to find it before the authorities. That way we could make sure that . . . er . . . so . . . so that Helen and the lad don't get in trouble.'

Dark waited for Trevor's truck to turn up the lane before he headed back towards the calves.

That afternoon, he came home from school with a mountain of homework. Sullivan was running an accumulator scheme, as she called it. Every day she caught you for not having some work done, she would double it and add it to the next day's work. And on top of that, there was something in all the other subjects to learn for tomorrow, as well as a maths test. He hadn't the remotest prospect of getting it all done. He sat at the kitchen table. He took out some copybooks with the intention of doing his usual trick – trying to guess what parts Sullivan would check and make some sort of stab at those bits. It sometimes worked. Then he remembered the Old Man's offer, and he stuffed all the books back in the bag. *Feckit, I'll see what that old chancer can do for me.*

When he got to the rath that night the Old Man was not there. And nobody else appeared either. He waited. A quarter of an hour passed. Then thirty minutes. It started raining and the oak leaves started dripping. It was a kind of warm and nice wetness.

When he moved under the biggest yew, he got a fright. He was certain he saw a big branch move. It moved slowly. It moved to better cover him and his bag, which he had brought with him.

After a while longer he started wondering if the Old Man had deserted him too. Got bored with him. He was surprised to feel tears of desolation rising under his eyelids. Then he heard two voices. One, he didn't recognise. It was even older than the Old Man's, and raspy, like a very old goat might sound if it could shape human words.

Then the Old Man appeared. And the fire sprang up in the usual place. He introduced an invisible other.

'I had to drag this old torment along. We call him Dreoilín – the wren man, don't you know.'

Though Dark couldn't see the other at all, still he said, 'Hello Mr Dreoilín.'

'Hello to you, son,' said the voice nicely, and then quickly returned to whining at the Old Man. 'When can I go? I have other things to be doing.'

'You can go when you've helped this boy solve his problem with books.'

'Son, how would you like to make the problem go away?' said Dreoilín

'What do you mean?' said the Old Man. 'Why do you always like to talk in riddles?'

'Well, I can remove your worry by getting the work done for you or I can just remove the worry.'

Dark was confused by this. He found himself a bit scared of the bodiless voice. He didn't want to ask too much.

'I suppose, just get rid of the worry. That will probably do,' he said.

'Grand. Very wise. Then say after me, "And what would

I care about the bookish word when there's a world of great things to be seen and smelt and heard?"'

Dark repeated the words and as soon as they came out of his mouth, sure enough, his cares about what the teachers would say or even what his mother would say were completely gone.

'What way are you now?' asked the Old Man.

'Good,' said Dark, feeling very good indeed.

'Good.'

The Old Man turned to the bushes and said, 'You're of course welcome to stay with us and keep us company here till daybreak.'

A small rusty bird that Dark hadn't noticed flapped off fussily away and for an instant Dark caught a reflection of Dreoilín's leathery old face.

The Old Man said to Dark, 'Don't take offence. He's a sound man in most ways, but there is no druid I ever met who was easy in the company of the little people.'

The familiar smell of burning sticks filled the air. The usual companions were now at the fire. The goblet was more full and the girl who brought it sat not far from Dark. The Old Man cleared his throat and poked the fire vacantly with a pole. He stared into it for a while in silence before starting in a slow and sombre voice.

Old Friends

Some old battles were crowed about gloriously afterwards, by bards – men who did not understand that war was not about glory, only about defeat either suffered or inflicted, cut with rage and fear into the bodies of other men. But there was one particular battle that the bards recorded no songs about. That battle and what followed it shook Mac Cumhaill's faith in himself and in many whom he had considered his friends.

It was late spring one year when messengers reached Fionn and the king with word of an invading army that had appeared with no warning. These gentlemen just peeped over the Sperrin hills in the north one day, marching in a disorderly line. Nobody knew where they had come from. Or how – for there were no reports of ships.

As far as King Cormac was aware, he had no major quarrel with any other ruler or country at that time. And there were no armies, as far as anyone knew, that had been advancing across other lands in this direction. There had been none of the usual signs that tensions might be building up. So the Fianna was caught somewhat off guard with no preparations made for a major war.

Most armies are sent with a purpose and demands. But this one didn't seem to have a country or a cause. War itself seemed to be the only purpose of these malignant men. They just moved forward, cutting down everything in their path. They were without mercy for man, woman, child or animal.

A day's march ahead of them now, the countryside moved before them in terror. The only living things that waited to meet them were birds, wolves, foxes, rats and insects. Even the mice, the rabbits and the badgers sensed that their future was not bright if they were to stay put and they fled with the people and the domestic animals creating a gathering wave, moving south.

As panic spread across the land, the Fianna was so badly caught off balance that it took two days to gather the men and horses. Many had been working with their clans, as was customary if a spring was peaceful. At that time of year the same sturdy horses that could charge through enemy lines with a raging chariot in tow, could just as well calmly plough a furrow. And the men trained in sword and spear would work hard from dawn till dusk, cutting turf and grass and saving both to make sure that warmth and well-fed animals were assured in the winter to follow.

The Fianna assembled and prepared for their first meeting with these hardy gentlemen at the *eiscir* mór. It was decided – Mac Cumhaill decided – that the Fianna should spread out along that fine bank of ground and let them see how well they were able to march up and over it to get to the other half of the country. That was a suitable pattern to meet them in, because of the foolish and artless way they were spread out and marching in a single line. The Fianna had only about 3,120 men active at that time. From the spread of the others it was estimated there were more than 9,000 of them.

The Fianna had overcome far worse odds in the past and Mac Cumhaill allowed that the ridge would level the contest. In fact, if the soldiers were as clumsy and without strategy as they sounded, Mac Cumhaill was starting to hope it might be no contest at all and the invaders might be fleeing within hours.

The wait wasn't long. The Fianna saw them approaching and grunting all the more as they dragged their feet through the bogs below. The early reports from the shocked and fleeing population turned out to have been only slightly exaggerated. They weren't actually wolf-headed monsters, bigger than Mac Cumhaill and breathing poison. But they weren't exactly genial, everyday characters either. They had some of the appearance of ordinary soldiers. Large lumps of men with goatskin tunics, lethally sharpened swords, and iron shields.

Their communication, if it was that, was just a deep, grumbling, gurgling murmur. They were all entirely colourless and dour in appearance. And it turned out they were far from ordinary in other respects as well.

When they reached the foot of the *eiscir*, Mac Cumhaill ordered the men at the top of the hill to stand up, show themselves and have their weapons at the ready. He ordered the buglers to let out the most blood-curdling sounds they could issue. He was giving the advancing men a chance to run away. They didn't, of course. They just kept coming.

When the first of them got to the top of the hill, the Fianna laid into them. The advantage of the hill was enough to ensure that all of these first ones rolled down dead after a short struggle.

The others kept coming, as expected, and Mac Cumhaill thought that within a few hours it would be all done. The bull-headed among them would be sent to their other world and the prudent would get sense and flee. The choice was theirs. Or so he thought. He almost felt sorry for them at that point, with the clumsy, stubborn way they kept coming up the hill only to fall back down it, dead.

However, that was when things took a less agreeable turn.

About half way through the first wave, with many of the enemy dead and only a few of the Fianna dead or badly wounded, Ó Lochlainn of Raghnaill started shouting like a madman, 'Look look, them boys are not ordinary human kind. Them boys are some kind of auld *buan taibhse*, some kind of permanent ghost warriors, or something'.

At first everyone thought Ó Lochlainn was just being himself, getting worked up over nothing. He was pointing down the hill in such horror that he never even saw the heavy foreign sword sweeping towards his head, severing its very thick connections to his body and with it, severing Ó Lochlainn's own connections with this world. He went quiet. At least his head rolled down south rather than up north.

Fiachra ran over and delivered a similar fate to the enemy soldier who had seemed quite unsure what to do now that he was standing on top of the *eiscir* in Ó Lochlainn's place.

'May the bold Ó Lochlainn be blessed with a steadier brain in whatever world he has crossed into than he was in this,' said Conán, not always the most sentimental man.

Everyone else now looked down at where Ó Lochlainn had been pointing. There, an enemy warrior who had fallen back seemingly dead, down into the bog-water below, started getting back up onto his feet as if there was nothing wrong with him.

Soon there were more of them at it. Corpses re-growing missing arms, even missing heads, some who had been lying face down in water for an hour, shaking themselves off and getting ready to come back up the hill at the Fianna. Their wounds seemed to be healed and they clambered back up with as much strength as if they'd only been touched with a feather.

In some kind of doubtful mark of respect to Ó Lochlainn, lying at the bottom of the hill, several feet from his head with its still open mouth, the plague of soldiers that were facing the Fianna were given the name of the *buan* Ó Lochlainns.

It was the mercy of Daghda that protected the Fianna that night. Men's spirits sank very low. They had gone from thinking of a fight where they were only outnumbered by three to one, to a fight with only one finish – exhaustion and then death.

A small glimmer of good fortune arrived with the dawn. The *buan*s retreated a little distance, just out of spear range.

Goll came to Mac Cumhaill saying, 'Whatever kind of yokes these are, they obviously don't like the daylight. We should attack them now, and catch them off guard.'

'Off guard?' intervened Conán angrily, with his crazy eyes looking dangerously at Goll. 'What are you talking about, man? They're not cuddling up to sleep. They are standing there fully armed and watching us. Maybe even hearing us. You want us to go down in the bog among them and let them slaughter us altogether?'

Mac Cumhaill agreed with Conán. It was too risky to

abandon the one advantage they had, along the ridge of the *eiscir*. Besides, the men were too tired and broken up.

'Ten men to take the wounded back down the hill,' he ordered. 'Two men to go to appeal to Conaire, King of Mumhan, and all the clan chiefs of the south for any more people who have had training to come and give us a lift up here. These are not highly skilled soldiers we are facing here. All we need is people who have energy and who can swing an axe or a sword. Five men on rota, watching for these *buan* Ó Lochlainns to make any move during the day. Twenty to go round up oats and any meat that can be got, to feed the soldiers. Everyone else to eat and sleep and store up as much strength as they can for the dark.'

That was it. Before the end of the day, many men and women arrived. The chiefs had not forced anyone to come, but everyone knew that it must have been a desperate situation when Mac Cumhaill was prepared to call for people who were not fully trained. Some had probably guessed that if the enemy got past this defence, there was nothing else to stop them and the entire nation would be driven into the sea in the south, or slaughtered. And for others, the sooner this was won, the sooner the beasts and people from north of the *eiscir* could be sent back home, which would be good for everyone's nerves.

Some who answered the call had retired from the Fianna to farm or to rear children. Some were youngsters who had been doing some training at home in the hope of being selected for the Fianna. One tall boy came up to the hut where Fionn and Conán were sitting. Diarmuid stopped the boy from approaching and asked his name. He wouldn't say. Diarmuid commanded him to go home and get out of harm's way.

Conán and Goll did their best to prepare the volunteers. Those that were strong and fast enough came up to the top of the bank to help the Fianna fighters. Others were organised in a row at the bottom of the hill and were ready to swarm in on any *buan* Ó Lochlainn that made it through, planting him with blows from ash sticks and clubs.

The night went no better than the previous one, with a small number of Fianna killed, many injured and a great deal of energy and spirit drained away from people. Dawn again brought respite.

Goll said, 'We can't go on like this. They only have to kill or wound a handful of us for every hundred of them we cut down, and we will still lose over time.'

Conán said, 'If we follow your plan, that will be a very short time.'

'If I was leading again,' said Goll very slowly and deliberately, 'we'd be down there sorting them out right now. That's all I'll say for now.'

'We're not going down among them Goll,' said Mac Cumhaill.

By the third morning, many of the volunteers were starting to look weak. They were not ready for such adversity. Goll now had a few other men behind him when he again came to Mac Cumhaill. This time he was demanding that a daytime attack be made.

'We can't go down,' said Fionn. 'You and I might survive

it, but many others here wouldn't. Tired legs in soft ground will just make us easy for them to harvest.'

'If we had gone down when I first said it, we wouldn't have had so many tired legs,' said Goll, with his hairless head reddening.

'We wouldn't have had so many legs at all,' said Conán, always ready to spring to Mac Cumhaill's defence.

'We can't go on like this. Working hard and going nowhere. It's stupid,' shouted Goll, pushing his face up close to Conán's. 'There isn't a single one of them dead yet.'

Mac Cumhaill pushed them apart and held Goll by the neck, the old anger momentarily clouding his mind. His hand was on the handle of his dagger. Conán's sword was already drawn. All of Goll's defenders stepped back. But then the gods must have intervened.

'Indeed there are – thirteen of them,' came a voice.

They all looked around. It was the boy.

'I thought I sent you home,' said Diarmuid, glad of someone else to vent the anger and frustration on.

A woman rushed forward, saying, 'You don't speak harshly to my nephew. His load is already more than his share.'

'What did you say, lad?' asked Mac Cumhaill, and turning back to Diarmuid, 'Who is this boy?'

The boy was led up the hill to Mac Cumhaill.

The woman took Mac Cumhaill aside and said to him, 'When he was only four he saw a pirate crew raid his fishing village. Most of his people were murdered. My sister and her husband included, may Daghda treat them kindly.

Others dragged away as slaves. Four days later he was found still hiding in the fox den that had protected him. He has been with me since. He rarely talks but mostly he is well and happy. Except that whenever there is a battle anywhere in the country, big or small, he disappears. At first I thought he was so fearful that he would go into hiding like a dog at the sound of thunder. Only recently he told me that he always goes to the fighting rather than hiding from it. He finds cover behind rocks or bushes. He has a spell upon him that forces him to witness every horror. He believes that if he forces himself to watch and record, he will one day somehow prevent worse things happening and that day his spell will be broken.'

Mac Cumhaill thanked the lady, saying, 'Maybe this is the day.'

Then he went back and looked at the boy. 'What did you mean, son?'

'Thirteen of them are dead. Look over there. And there, and out beyond there.' He started pointing to places in the bog-water, and sure enough, he was right. Amongst the rushes it looked like there were bodies of the *buan* Ó Lochlainns that were still lying there.

'What do we want with the advice of a *garsún?*' fumed Goll, a man who regarded any threat to his point of view as a threat to himself. 'They'll be up soon, and back with the others.'

'The fighting stopped hours ago,' said Mac Cumhaill, 'and those certainly have the look of men who are in no hurry to come back into this world.'

'Well, that's no good to us. So few of them. Maybe they were killed by their own and that's why they're not bothering to get up.'

'Any fewer is progress,' said Conán. 'And I certainly didn't set eyes on them turning on their own.'

'It was dark, you big *stuachán*,' said Goll. 'We couldn't see well what was going on beyond the bottom of the *eiscir*. This is no good to us, because even if it happens that we did kill them, we don't know how.'

Conán was heading for Goll again now and the atmosphere was not good. Many soldiers were looking on, confused.

'Four times,' said the boy.

'Whisht!' shouted Mac Cumhaill at Conán and Goll. 'Listen to this.'

'On the fourth time you kill them, their bodies lie down drained of life, the same as any other poor creature that's been hacked and broken down by sword or axe,' said the boy.

Everyone was silent now. Nobody cross-questioned him. Not even Goll. There was a certainty in his voice that told anyone with an ear to listen that the boy had been paying close attention, absorbing every cruel slash and blow, silently watching every soldier who fell. The horrible reality of it all was in the boy's eyes.

After a silent while, Mac Cumhaill quietly said, 'Good enough. That's the way, then.'

The defenders were gathered and the situation was explained to them.

'Here is the story,' said Mac Cumhaill with a laugh, 'we only have to be about twelve times as good as them.'

One man was sent along the *eiscir* to spread this news to the groups all along its length.

Under normal circumstances, such news would have seemed a fearsome challenge. But that day it was news that lifted spirits. The bickering and dread evaporated. The people became of one purpose again. People slept well and gained new strength and resolve for the night.

A bitter wind took up that night and carried driving sleet. It seemed to get worse with every *buan* that was permanently dispatched to a place beyond resurrection. Even the top of the ridge turned to muck. When day came the cruel weather continued and nobody could keep warm or sleep properly. Fionn ordered that all of the older people be sent home, as there was coughing and sickness starting to spread. The relentless harshness of the skies was becoming as much of a danger to their lives as the invaders' blades. Despite all that, the people fought with great heart. Having looked into annihilation there was no discomfort that could break their spirits.

It went on for twenty more nights. By then several good men of the Fianna had been taken away dead or injured but more than half of the *buan* Ó Lochlainns were lying in the bog, killed four times, never to stir again. They were clearly losing now, but they showed no signs of a change of strategy or a retreat. They never shouted or laughed or cried. They just made the same grunting noise all of the time, traipsing through the cold, wet gory mess below, to come up the hill again and again. Every single fight was ferocious and bitter. If this went on, it wasn't going to end until every one of them was dead.

Early on the twenty-first night, when the fighting had just resumed, Mac Cumhaill took a look at the weary, hunched soldiers along the *eiscir* trying to fight bravely despite the relentless, driving rain and waves of *buan*s still undeterred. He decided to try to bring an end to it. On the rare occasions that the moon glimmered through the clouds, he had noticed one of the *buan*s that never stirred from beneath a *sceach* bush a bit back from the base of the *eiscir*. Mac Cumhaill was inclined to think that he was a leader of some sort. Of course, he might simply have been elderly or injured, as there were no obvious differences from the other grey men.

He himself was tired and didn't want a long discussion. The others would have tried to stop him on the basis that his plan was at least as likely to leave the Fianna without a leader as it was to leave the *buan*s without one.

His plan was not a complicated one. He was going to head down into the bog to bring the fight to this particular *buan* and see how his brethren might appreciate that.

Mac Cumhaill came over the brow of the hill and started to head down towards the *sceach* bush. Several of the warriors came at him, seeing what he was doing. But he slashed out in every direction and mercilessly cut down any of them that came within range. When he got to the bush, he gained more confidence in his theory that the *sceach buan* indeed had every appearance of being an eminent member of this heinous mob. The unnatural beast had a sharp hook in one hand and a sword with a very long dancing blade in the other. Conán and Fiachra now saw and followed, keeping other *buan*s away from Mac Cumhaill as he engaged their leader.

'Give up now,' said Mac Cumhaill, 'and we will let you and your remaining men go home in peace.'

The answer from the ghost leader was a lightning-fast strike from the long blade, which almost seemed to move on its own guidance. In an instant, the sleet stopped and the clouds parted fully for the first time since the battles had started. The full moon that was revealed shone light on every detail. The warriors from both sides stopped their own bloody contests and stood watching. Mac Cumhaill put his head down barely in time to save it. He was not slow to violence in these situations and as the long blade was completing its empty swing, Mac Cumhaill's sword was shearing the ghost chief's sneery head from his torso. Within seconds it was back and Mac Cumhaill had it off again. The creature became angry now and stood back, flailing in every direction. Mac Cumhaill came back at him, avoiding every swing. The leader retreated towards a pile of boulders. As he did, Fionn Mac Cumhaill's sword pierced a third fatal message through his back into his heart. He fell and arose again. He started running away faster. Mac Cumhaill hesitated. It did occur to him that if he let him go now he would lead his *buan*s away, for fear of losing his own last miserable life. That is what should have happened. Instead Mac Cumhaill allowed his anger to overcome him.

He followed behind the rocks out of view of everyone else.

Unfortunately, the ghost leader was not enthusiastic about dying altogether and decided against a fair contest for his fourth life. He had stopped on the other side of one of the boulders and was waiting for Mac Cumhaill to come running. He skillfully tripped Mac Cumhaill with his hook in such a way that he fell onto the upturned long sword.

Fionn Mac Cumhaill let out a terrible groan as the blade went straight through his side. Everyone in the place heard it. But he still had strength and struck the final blow against the ghost leader, who was defenceless as he tried to pull back his long sword from Mac Cumhaill's oozing wound. Quietness fell across the land. All of the ghost soldiers became confused. They started falling slowly back. They must have known their leader was not emerging from behind those stones.

Many on the Fianna side were equally afraid of what they might see behind those boulders. They had all heard Mac Cumhaill's cry. There had been no sound coming from there since then. No sign of Mac Cumhaill rising up to give his famed signal that this saga was finally closed. The weary and bereaved did not see what they so badly wanted: Mac Cumhaill holding his cherished spear above his head and quietly proclaiming a return to civilised ways.

Indeed, for most of the people, the troubles with the *buan*s were past. But for Mac Cumhaill himself and for some of his loyal followers, even harsher trials were still to come.

Behind the rocks there was only one body. That belonged to the leader of the *buan* Ó Lochlainns. There was no sign of Mac Cumhaill, though there was a lot of blood spilled. It was a sorry sight.

At first no one spoke. Conán kicked the body of the ghost leader. Then a soldier by the name of Féilim Ó Broinn wailed loudly, '*Go bhfóire Daghda orainn*, surely the great man is dead.'

'Go easy, man,' said Diarmuid. 'You don't know that.'

'Oh, for certain, for certain,' another person, one of the volunteers, joined in the wailing. 'Oh how boundless is our loss!'

'Where are the bounds of his body then?' said Conán.

'Oh,' says Ó Broinn, a man more dramatic than analytical, crying hysterically now, 'sure he must have been dragged away by some fierce wolves.'

Conán started waving his fist at Ó Broinn.

'Shut your gob, you *amadán*. How many wolves would it take to drag a man that size? And what are you howling about, anyway? Sure you hardly even knew Fionn Mac Cumhaill.'

'Oh, he's a great loss to us all,' continued Ó Broinn. 'The whole nation will be lost in mourning.'

'I'll give you a reason to cry,' said Conán, now in an uncontrollable rage. He started hitting Ó Broinn very hard around the mug and chest and anywhere he could land a punch or a kick. Ó Broinn was on the ground in a minute and it took five men to hold Conán back from knocking the man out altogether.

Diarmuid called for the boy, guessing that he was still

somewhere on the battleground, even though Mac Cumhaill had sent him home again. Sure enough, he came forward from a cluster of rushes when he was called.

'What do you think, son?' asked Diarmuid.

'I didn't see.'

'All the same, what is it that you are thinking?'

'He's alive,' said the boy. 'You must look for him.'

'Thank you,' said Diarmuid.

Few people heard what the boy said. The words of Ó Broinn were the ones that swept around the country like a mountain fire.

As for Mac Cumhaill, while all this was going on he was already far away. One minute he was pressing a potion from his purse into the wound left by the long blade and trying to stand up to call for help; the next, he was lying on a heap of stones in a cold, grey world being kicked and prodded with spears by a circle of *buan*s that surrounded him. In an instant he had somehow been taken, along with the retreating *buan* soldiers, to the bleak world of the *buan* Ó Lochlainns, where an abominable fate awaited him.

He tried to sit up and look around. Everywhere, shades of grey. Thousands of these soldiers stood in every direction. No women or children anywhere in the landscape. This was their horrendous world and they were his new masters.

At first he didn't fight them, because he had no strength and in truth his mind was not in a great state. He put his thumb in his mouth and all he saw was greater confusion. He was reasonably sure he hadn't died. But wherever he was now, it wasn't earth. It didn't seem like there would be any-where for him to run even if he could muster the strength to clobber some of these foul oafs.

That day, nine of them dragged him to a low, grey cas-tle and pulled him down many steps to a dungeon, which was to be his sleeping quarters. He tried to bandage his wound with what was left of his tunic and then tried to rest. But he was hardly there an hour, lying still, bleeding on the wet stone floor, when he heard the door being banged open. He couldn't see a thing because it was as dark out in the passage as in the dungeon. As he soon learned, the *buan*s saw best in black darkness. Their kicks, which he couldn't even see coming, landed very accurately on his head and groin.

At first he thought they were enraged at him for killing their big man and that he was being dragged out to be tor-tured and killed. But he soon learned they bore no partic-ular grudges. The fierce kicking and beating was just an idle pastime with the oafs. From the other underground chambers they were pulling many other people and pecu-liar creatures of all sorts, creatures taken from other worlds, Mac Cumhaill assumed, and kicking and beating them all just as savagely as they did him. Instead of killing him they were dragging him off to work their grey lands. This was going to be his daily routine.

They only fed him a small handful of some kind of black porridge, spilled on the floor of his dungeon every night. On that feed, they demanded forty hours of labour every long day in their world. Because he was bigger than their other captives, they set him to pulling a plough through their hard black soil and when that was all done, he was set to lifting huge boulders so they could extend the walls of the castle. His strength became a curiosity for them and they would gather around as they set him ever harder tasks: digging wells, splitting boulders, pulling loads that their horses weren't able to pull. He completed all tasks rather than appeal to them for any leniency. Without re-acting, he endured whipping on his back till it was bare of skin.

He kept some composure by patiently observing them, counting how many were about the castle at any time, watching for weaknesses in the way they defended, taking note of the regular bad-tempered fights that broke out be-tween them, and estimating which of the other captives he might be able to get to rise up with him. He observed the other peculiar slaves going about, planting, building and washing things for the *buan*s, who seemed incapable of anything other than hitting and grunting. He was trying to make contact with a few of the others, who nodded to him in greeting, and he was waiting for some inspiration on how to escape this woeful place.

Day and night, he would sing as loud as he could, songs of home. During the day, songs of war and songs of tri-umph. At night he had time for sorrow and regrets, and the old songs of grief and lament would not stay off his tongue.

In the beginning, somewhere in the back of his mind, he thought that he would have only a few days of this. He believed his people would not rest till they found out where he was and came to collect him.

But then, after some weeks or months – he had no idea of time there – Mac Cumhaill felt a dark despair start to creep into his soul. He was losing his fight with it. No matter how loudly he sang. Although at that stage he assumed everyone would continue looking for him, he began to lose hope that they might ever be able to find a way to him. Also, his strength to plan insurrection was waning. The *buan*s seemed to be in great supply and his fellow captives were so crushed that few looked like they had the energy to lift a sword let alone strike a *buan* down four times. And besides, there was nowhere to flee to.

These thoughts began to consume him. His spirit began to fail. As he worked on the tiny amounts of food, his weakening mind started to be followed by his body.

Soon, he had only one thought left keeping him alive. When he died, would his spirit then be forever trapped in this barren desolation? Would he lose the one consolation that had always made it easy to risk death in the past – the longing to be reunited with his father, his mother, and with ever-growing numbers of comrades now on the other side? He became very quiet inside.

What was happening back in Éire would have destroyed him altogether had he known it at the time. The story about the spear wound and the wolves continued to do the rounds and to become established as the truth. Few still asked how wolves could have dragged an enormous body away so quickly or how it was that no trace of his weapons or clothing had been found.

And indeed, his presumed death sent a wave of mourning and fear across the country. The people recounted all of his good qualities, as they do when a friend dies, and mentioned nothing of his faults. They talked of his gifts of wisdom, enormous strength, absence of fear and soft heart. And they also worried quietly as to what might happen once enemies heard that the mountainous man they feared was no longer around to ensure that friendly visitors to Éirinn met an enormous welcome and unfriendly ones met a ferocious rebuke.

All of the Fianna were afflicted by sadness and depression. Eventually the king called the leaders to Tara. When they were all settled in the great hall, and food and drinks were being prepared for them in the background, Cormac made a short speech.

He said, not insincerely, 'Fionn Mac Cumhaill was a great man. Part of the reason I've called you together is to celebrate him. I'll miss him more sorely than most. But now the time for mourning and feeling sorry for ourselves has past. As is our tradition, we must try to celebrate the passing of a loved one into a better world. We embrace change and new life. A new era. And I want you to now help me pick a new leader for the Fianna, so that we can rebuild my protection . . . And your own, of course.'

Most of the Fianna took heart in the king's command that it was their patriotic duty to bury their recollections of Mac Cumhaill's deeds in the past, and to set to today's task of rebuilding the army. Many must have had advance notice of the purpose of the meeting, as the discussions about who should take Mac Cumhaill's place didn't take long. Within an hour it was clear that most wanted Diarmuid to lead them.

Diarmuid, who was seated next to the king, raised his voice to address Conán who was standing at the back of the gathering, near the entrance.

'What is your advice to me in this?'

Everyone was surprised that he asked Conán this. Complete silence fell on the gathering. Diarmuid and Conán were not known to be friendly. They were not men who would ever have had much to talk about. Conán was a very large, disagreeable man, fond of bad-mannered jokes and not particular about who he offended. He was happiest in the mountains. Nothing had been seen of him since Fionn's disappearance, until he was summoned to this meeting. It was said that he had been sitting for days in a bed of heather in the middle of the Nine Stones on Sliabh Laigin, a memorial to his own people. Diarmuid was a slender, diplomatic man who liked fine garments and polite conversation and was usually very much concerned to please the king and not to go against the general consensus of the leaders.

Yet Diarmuid must have known that behind the *raiméis* and the great black forest of hair, Conán was as true as a great rock. He knew that Conán was the person Mac Cumhaill trusted most. And Diarmuid was not going to take on the leadership unless he knew this man approved.

Conán did not respond to Diarmuid's question.

Diarmuid stood and looked straight at him and said again, 'Conán, I am asking you, what should I do?'

Conán stood away from the pole he had been leaning against. With the evening sun at his back, he created an enormous shadow falling from the entrance through the parted crowd, reaching the front of the hall.

He shouted at them all, 'Daghda curse you all and Cormac too, for that matter. I don't care whether you're King or slave. No man should ever ask us to bury Fionn Mac Cumhaill's memory. If I had a nugget of gold for every time Fionn put blind faith in me, I'd be the wealthiest man in this world. I'm not about to lose faith in him now. There's nobody in this country who'll persuade me that Mac Cumhaill is dead until they've shown me some proof of it.'

Diarmuid now was silent.

Conán continued, banging his huge stick against the pole with every word, 'On the graves of all my ancestors, I will never rest a day until that man is found'.

Many people turned away from Conán. 'Poor soul. The grief has driven him mad,' they whispered. Diarmuid thought about this for a while. Then he turned to Cormac and said, 'With the greatest of respect I cannot accept your offer.'

'He would not make a suitable leader of the New Fianna anyway, when he's like that,' one of the younger members said.

Cormac was obviously shaken. But eventually he de-clared, 'I regret that you feel that way. But it is the present and the living we have to be most concerned with. I need strength. I need unity. What is needed in the Fianna now is a steady experienced hand on the reins. Goll! Step forward!'

Goll, the bald slayer of Cumhall, feigned humility when asked to resume the role he felt should always have remained his anyway.

He said, 'There is no man here who feels the death of the great Fionn Mac Cumhaill more sorely than I. I should have been more watchful and prevented his rash descent of the *eiscir* into the sword of the fiend. But when a previous king laid heavy tasks at my feet, I never faltered. Unlike others, I will never let sentimental feelings get in the way of duty. From here on there will be proper training in the New Fianna – I will make sure that your army is never caught unprepared, as it was when the unfortunate Fionn Mac Cumhaill led us, disorganised, weak and badly trained, against the *buans*.'

Conán was in a fuming rage. Diarmuid led him from the gathering quickly, before trouble erupted, saying, 'Conserve yourself, we've got greater challenges now.'

They hoped at least a few others might join them. Many good people had stood, apparently torn between respect for them and obedience to the new head man. They quietly waited a while outside, not quite sure what to do next and not knowing what to say to each other. They were both surprised at the only other person who emerged a few minutes later. It was Liath Ní Choinchin.

They might have expected some older, hard-bitten men like themselves; people who had spent too many years next to Mac Cumhaill, shared some dark secrets with him, and travelled with him through all kinds of adventures and troubles. But Liath did not quite answer that description. Sure enough, she was a formidable soldier, full of determination and wiliness. But the shy twenty-year-old was not the most obvious volunteer for the hard road. They both looked at her, waiting to hear what message she brought.

'I am with you,' was all she said.

'You're young and have great things in front of you,' said Diarmuid. 'You shouldn't feel obliged to join us hardened old boars. We're too set in our ways to accept what's going on in there.'

'With respect, I am not doing it for you,' she said curtly.

'I understand,' said Diarmuid, slightly miffed. 'Many women have a fondness for Fionn. But Fionn would want you to go ahead and further yourself. You will move up in the ranks quickly – as long as you don't get involved with us.'

'Do you think that loyalty and devotion are qualities that only come with age?' she said sharply. 'When Conán talked inside there, I first came to understand what the old people always said – people live in each other's shadows. If I give up on Fionn, what is there left of me?'

Conán and Diarmuid glanced at each other. Conán said, 'She knows her mind. Two old boars and a young mule it is then.'

They wandered towards the edge of a nearby woodland to make camp and to get away from the gradually rising spirits that were starting to come from the great hall as the drink was taken in. As they sat around a small fire, looking at each other and realising that none had the vaguest idea of what to do next or where to start looking for Fionn, another person made a welcome appearance. It was Dreoilín, the old druid.

'Whatever help I can be,' he announced, 'I am with you.'

They spent the night there. They talked about what to do and where to start. Liath and Diarmuid believed they were probably looking for well-picked bones. Conán and Dreoilín were convinced, without any reasons they could put in words, that they were still looking for a big lump of a live man. They agreed they'd go the next morning to the site where Fionn fell. Even though Conán had spent two days there after everyone had left and they knew there was nothing to be found, they hoped maybe Dreoilín would get a sense if there was anything otherworldly at work there. And they'd decide from there what to do.

They headed off in the early morning drizzle, four of the least likely companions ever to travel together. The gigantic, wild man; the elegant, sandalled man; the crooked, little ancient; and the slight woman with long, red plaits. The people they met along the way, picking elderflowers, tending sheep and bringing in hay, looked with a mixture of pity and admiration.

'Success or death', were the words that had been exchanged between them over a dancing fire the night before. There were no other ways for this mission to end. None of them would ever give up. And in the cold grey of the morning, success seemed the less likely option.

'How long would you think our mission will take?' Liath asked Dreoilín sincerely.

She had never had dealings with a druid before and was somewhat in awe of this twisted little old man.

Conán overheard and laughed, getting back to his usual form.

'In twenty years, we could still be going around, frightening children – known as the wandering lunatics, who appear occasionally from the forests, turning over stones, still looking for the big fella, and only finding maggots. Sure, look at the tidy little head on Diarmuid, doesn't he already look like a madman?'

'Don't mind him, *a chroí*,' said Dreoilín. 'When you keep a single goal always in the fore of your mind, never letting anyone distract you from it, a door will always open; you will always find a way.'

It took them most of a day to get to the place, near midway along the *eiscir*, where Fionn had fallen. They stayed behind the boulder for a while, looking at the grass as if it was going to tell them something. Then they went to the *sceach* bush under which the *buan* leader had stood. Conán hacked all the limbs from the little tree with his sword. They camped behind the rock. Even at night the ground remained cold and silent. It was as if nothing had ever happened there.

The next day, they started to journey towards the Sperrin hills to visit the area where the *buan*s were first reported. At the end of the first day of that journey, they met a man who said his sister had seen someone that she was sure was Fionn Mac Cumhaill, wandering aimlessly in the woods over further to the west. Their hearts were greatly lifted for a little while. Maybe he was stunned and had lost his memory.

They spent the next two days combing through those woods before moving back to their original pathway. Over the weeks ahead they had many such episodes. People offered them food and often shelter and information they hoped might be helpful. And so they followed rumours of sightings of Mac Cumhaill appearing at dusk, here, there and everywhere. They often parted to hunt separately. Most evenings, they would meet again to decide where to go next, and partly just for each other's company, because by that stage each of them separately was starting to wonder if their own minds were going.

In the north they found nothing either and ventured back down towards Lough Derg, the place that Conán reckoned Mac Cumhaill would surely wander if his limbs were loosened from the control of his brain.

Then one day, after many months of roaming, they chanced into the home of Dailin, an elderly druid and friend of Dreoilín. He chastised Dreoilín for not having looked for the help of his own kind sooner. On Dreoilín's agreement Dailin sent word out for all of the druids of the south to assemble. Some flew. Some swam. And some rode ponies. Nobody dared asked these men about their ways. But somehow all 23 of them were sitting or standing around the big fire at the centre of Dailin's clan encampment by the middle of the next day, because the word of

Dreoilín, their high man, carried more import with them than any instruction from Goll or even Cormac.

They might as well not have travelled for all they knew about the *buans* or Fionn. They were about to disperse again when one man from the far south said to them, 'Would it be beyond the bounds of reason to have a talk with old Brigid?'

A silence descended amongst the Druids.

'Who is Brigid?' asked Liath.

None of the druids answered.

'He is an old *bodach* who is maybe a thousand years old and is said to have been dead and buried more than three times without much effect on him at all,' said Conán. 'These old boys say they don't like him because they accuse him of practising a bit on the dark side.'

Brigid was not much talked of or heard of in this generation. And those who did know him thought it better to steer clear of him. He may have been a failed druid himself, a man who had been excluded from their circle a long time before any of the present men was even born. The indiscretion that had brought dishonour on him was no longer remembered with certainty, though there was a rumour of an accidental death of a man that Brigid wasn't fond of. His state of mind in the past few hundred years was not thought to be the soundest.

The druid who asked the question explained himself apologetically.

'I've heard it said that Brigid once talked of a battle long ago where "air soldiers" had come to the country. Do you not think there's a chance that those boys were some relations of these *buans*?'

Several of the druids complained that Brigid shouldn't be called.

'He is doting,' whined one narrow, soft-skinned priest from Corca Dhuibhne. 'His only power, aside from his abusive gob, is his delusion of being a druid.'

'Have you a better plan, Mangan?' asked Dreoilín sharply.

Mangan pursed his lipless mouth and Conán, always nervous in the presence of too many priests, volunteered to go and fetch Brigid.

Brigid arrived near midnight. He was not a small man and the sight of him sitting on Conán's shoulders was a strange sight indeed. He had insisted on being carried all the way. When he was set down, he made a motion of dusting off the muddy sack tunics that were tied around him with strings of bindweed.

Brigid was cantankerous and full of nonsense. When he had finished dusting himself off, the tall, grey *bodach* looked at his transport and complained in a rusty old voice: 'I'd have been more comfortable if you'd dragged me along the ground.'

Perhaps he had been fed on the milk of otherworld cows, like the real Brigid. Or maybe he had first crossed into this world on Brigid's festival day of *Imbolg*. Nobody could imagine how else this hairy-faced putrid heron of a man had ended up with the name of the beautiful female god of fertility.

He looked around and, rattled, asked 'Which of you

goats dared disturb the sleep of the greatest auld druid in the world?'

'I did,' said Dreoilín, stepping forward. 'And I'd be very grateful if you'd tell us what you know of the "air soldiers" you have been heard to speak of.'

'And who are you, you miserable git, to be asking anything of the great Brigid?'

'I'm Dreoilín, chief druid of all Éirinn,' said Dreoilín, slightly offended, 'and I'll be pleased if you would answer my question as quickly as you like.'

'Sure, I am answering as quickly as I like. That's as quick as nothing at all. And don't I know you're Dreoilín, with your face like wolfhound's vomit and your sad pretence of magic, why would the great Brigid be bothered talking to you?'

'Because the great Brigid will get a slap in the gob if he doesn't,' shouted Conán, picking the *bodach* up by the hair. But his raised hand was frozen in the air by a look from Dreoilín.

'You don't call me to a druid's gathering for over five hundred years, and now that you want something, you remember that I have more magic in my tailbone than the whole lot of you together,' railed the old man, who seemed very pleased with the shocked looks from his audience. 'You are a tragic shower of wasters and I'm heading back to my bed before the sight of you gives me nightmares.'

Dreoilín said, 'I'll certainly respect your druidic powers if you show me you have any. You can start by telling us how to deal with the spirit warriors.'

'I'll have to think for a minute,' said Brigid, putting his finger to his head and looking like he was thinking for no more than one second. 'Well, I've reached my decision. NO. Leave me alone. You have no call on me. I owe you nothing. I have taken comfort from the company of hardly any persons these two centuries past and I owe no person the slightest little thing. So you can carry on with your merriment without me.'

He made a dash for the entrance of the compound, but was caught in the arms of Diarmuid.

Diarmuid let go and the sad, weary look in Diarmuid's eyes seemed to quieten him. Diarmuid spoke softly to him, telling him of the loss of Mac Cumhaill and of the desperate quest.

'Oh!' said Brigid in a slightly changed tone. 'Why didn't they tell me? Sure, I know Mac Cumhaill well. He never passed my part of the country without calling into my cave for a yarn.'

A disapproving murmur went through the druids. Even Diarmuid and Liath looked disbelieving.

Brigid was delighted.

'Your hero! And let me tell you, a man not ashamed to drink a gallon of morning dew in the company of a demon. There were lots of years when he was the only human soul I'd see from one spring to the next. No, Mac Cumhaill was not the worst of you. I'll help as a favour to him, not to any of you.'

Immediately from Brigid's descriptions it was clear that the 'air soldiers' who had visited a thousand years earlier were indeed the same as the *buan* Ó Lochlainns of the recent battles.

'I would say it is a very long time,' said Conán, 'since anyone looked at you and saw a little ray of hope. But if you can tell us any small thing about how to reach the land of these cockroaches I will love you more than your unfortunate mother could ever have.'

The *bodach* became serious.

'First I will need you each to collect a fistful of the pollen of daisies.'

No questions were asked. Right there in the dark, they all spread out and got down on their hands and knees in the dewy grass, looking for daisies and trying to get the pollen out of them. Dreoilín changed into his bird form and flitted, collecting in his beak.

After about an hour, he called them all.

Then he said, 'Now. I want all the useless druids to go home, as what I have to say is not fit for their ears. Dreoilín and Mac Cumhaill's three other cronies will come with me.'

The other druids were not unhappy to comply, but one of them wondered what to do with the pollen they had collected.

'You can keep that if you want,' said Brigid, snuffling in nasty delight into his sacking. Then he looked like he was starting to have little convulsions as spouts of high-pitched laughter broke out of his control, 'as a memento . . . of the day . . . I got a bunch of heroes and priests to go down on their knees before me.'

Liath got in a rage when she heard this. She didn't shout, though. The old *bodach* never saw her coming. In a flash he was on his back on the ground with her foot on his chest and the blade of her sword tickling his neck.

'You. We are very tired. If you had nothing more to offer us only to make fools of us, you should have made haste back to your cave while you had the chance.'

The snuffling laughs only got louder as his old legs curled up.

Conán pulled Liath's sword arm back.

'Just in case those stories about his ability to come back from the grave have been exaggerated, maybe we should keep him in one part for as long as we need him.'

The obnoxious *bodach* stood up and shook the sack-cloths that covered him. A lot of dirt fell off him.

'Well now, my fine companions,' he said, still sobbing with laughter, 'this is the situation. I'll take you there and do the talking for you. You'll have a very short time to get your lad out. When you get back here – if you get back here I mean – ' He snuffled back another bout of laughter and was interrupted by Dreoilín.

'Come on then,' said Dreoilín. 'That'll do.'

'That's not all,' said the *bodach*, 'if you get back here, no-body will ever ask Brigid any questions about how or why or suchlike.'

'But how do you get on so well with them that you think you can keep them entertained?' said Diarmuid, 'And how do you know you can even get us into their place easily? Have you been there before?'

'Now, that's just the thing I mean,' said the *bodach*. 'No questions.'

'But . . . ' said Diarmuid, who was too honourable for making bargains that might have hidden corners.

'It's a deal,' intervened Dreoilín.

'And one other thing,' said the *bodach*, patting Dreoilín on the back as if he was a chap, 'you will invite me to every druid gathering in future and put me back where I belong at the head of the table alongside yourself.'

The others thought this would be too much for Dreoilín to swallow, now that he knew for almost sure that the *bodach* was a creature who was not unfamiliar with dark magic and not unfriendly with enemy forces. But Dreoilín must have been just as desperate in his quest for Mac Cumhaill as his three companions were. He thought for just a minute before he nodded and said, 'Yes.'

The *bodach*'s eyes couldn't hide his delight. He said, 'That'll do me now. Daghda love me. Come with me.'

They followed him a few steps to the open well in the middle of the settlement. He went down on his hunkers. He pulled a bag from amongst his layers of covering. It was a surprisingly large bag. He started laying things out on the ground. They were bones. Five of them. And a skull.

Diarmuid was horrified. But when the *bodach* signaled that he wanted each of them to take hold of a bone, each complied.

'Success or death, old friends', nodded Conán to Diarmuid and the others quietly, as he grabbed what looked like it had been the upper arm of a sturdy man.

Brigid himself held the skull and a rib bone.

Then began a rattling murmuring sound from the *bodach* that would send a chill to the core of the bravest soul. In another instant, they were in the grey land, straight in front of the entrance to the long, low building. They were startled. But they soon gathered their senses as they saw a dozen or more of the all-too-familiar *buan*s trundling towards them. The three soldiers drew their swords and stood in front of Dreoilín. The *bodach* grabbed the bones from each of their hands and stepped in front of them. He kept up his gurgling and Conán then recognised it. It was the very same sound as the *buan*s made. And the advancing grey men stopped to listen. He was holding out a bone. He had their full attention.

Without turning to Dreoilín he growled urgently from the side of his mouth, 'What are you lot gawking at? Do you not have work to do?'

For whatever reason, when the *buan*s were looking at Brigid's bones, they were not able to see Conán and the other three heading off past them into the castle.

They entered the long-walled castle, now unguarded. They went through from one room to the next, all grey and identical square rooms with nothing in them. There seemed to be no central hall, no banquet rooms, no hearths, no king or queen, no evidence of any comforts. It did not seem an excessively joyful place even for its willing inhabitants.

Eventually, Diarmuid noticed a trapdoor in the floor of one of the main corridors. Strange and horrible sounds seemed to be coming from beneath it. Diarmuid lifted the stone cap and flung it aside. They stared into absolute darkness. Conán did a mad thing, jumping in without knowing whether there were steps or even a bottom below them. For luck he hit a floor not far enough down to break his legs. The others followed quickly.

They climbed down a sloping corridor in terrifying darkness. They felt their way along a passage and found many doors. They tapped on each with sword handles. All they heard from inside was groaning. Eventually their knock on one door at the furthest end of the passage, brought a sound that made all of their hearts jump.

'To blazes with you all, can't you even let me sleep for the hour?'

It was, without doubt, Fionn Mac Cumhaill's voice.

Conán had more blind devotion to Mac Cumhaill even than his hound, Bran, did. He was so overcome at the sound of Mac Cumhaill's living voice that he found a huge surge of strength. With one blow from his foot he smashed the massive slate door to smithereens. Mac Cumhaill still couldn't see who it was. He shouted again and lunged at them.

'Get away from me, you heinous curs.'

Then he heard their shouts: 'Come on, come quick, the mountains are calling.'

Mac Cumhaill lowered his voice.

'What? Who is there? Conán? Can it be? My mind is gone.'

'Could it be anyone else?' said Liath.

'Liath?'

'And Diarmuid, and Dreoilín,' said Liath.

131

'Shame on me, shame on me, shame on me; how could I have thought my old friends would have forgotten me. Please forgive me for thinking so little of you.'

'You don't know how near you were to being right,' said Diarmuid. 'You can thank Conán here for knocking shame into the rest of us.'

'There's no time for blather,' said Conán. 'Let's get you quickly away from here.'

When they got out into the grey daylight, they were shocked at the pale and wasted Mac Cumhaill. No one commented until Conán turned to Diarmuid.

'Well I'll concede, those who thought we'd be bringing back a bag of bones weren't far wrong.'

Mac Cumhaill fired a stone that lifted a wandering *buan* off his feet and said, 'There's still a bit of breath left in these old bones.'

When they got back out of the castle yard, Brigid was still engaging his associates. He had now taken many more bones from his bag and he appeared to be swapping them for some grey paste and yellow powder. When he saw the five returning, he surreptitiously stuffed the substances into his layers. He nodded to Mac Cumhaill, who nodded back. Without any chat, he again gave them all bones to hold. Again he touched the skull and recited his cant. Before the *buan*s even realised, the dealing was all done, Brigid and the five were sitting back in Dailin's camp near the banks of the lovely Lough Derg.

It took them a little while to recover their senses. Dailin came out to see what the commotion was about and was stunned and delighted to see Fionn with them where there had been only Brigid and the four wanderers not more than an hour previously.

Diarmuid stood and said, 'Before we go any further, I want to know what potions you got from those monsters and how you know them so well and why you wouldn't leave us go back to free those other unfortunate souls who remain enslaved by the *buan*s.'

Dailin noticed the bones then. He was not a fan of Brigid. His voice also became overtaken by concern.

'I want to know what kind of wickedness has just been practiced in my homestead and whose bones exactly you people are clutching.'

They all dropped the bones. Brigid gathered the bones quickly back into his bag, snuffling and snorting.

'Remember now, no questions.'

With that, he hobbled quickly towards the entrance of the enclosure and disappeared into the night. Nobody tried to follow him.

A chariot was yoked and Fionn was taken to his home where Úna was overcome to see him. Every day that she nursed him to his recovery, his friends would call around and they would sit up late trying to make sense of everything that had happened and discussing what to do about the *bodach*.

Conán wasn't very picky about his company and didn't care for debates about whether Brigid was bad, since he had done them a good turn. Diarmuid wanted Brigid brought before the *brehon*s, who could ask him to prove that he was not involved in evildoings and who could force him to return the bones to rest in peace wherever he had taken them from in case their owners came to haunt them all. Liath favoured getting the despicable *bodach* to bring them back to free the rest of the slaves and destroy the castle.

Dreoilín said, 'The bones, in my opinion, might not be human in the first place. It is likely that Brigid has been trading the bones of the *buan*s who died at the *eiscir* back to their own people. It is best not to test his powers by having him take us back there because he is probably less powerful than he makes out and we might all end up stuck there this time. Furthermore, while I too would like to see him having to account for his bad behaviour, it might be wiser to leave him living in his miserable cave for another thousand years. After all, his ability to travel to the land of the *buan*s might be needed again by our descendents.'

Finally Mac Cumhaill said, 'It's true what the *bodach* told you – that I know him a long time.'

Liath and Diarmuid looked disappointed.

Mac Cumhaill continued, 'And I still can't tell you whether he is good or bad. Probably, like the druid's egg, he is good in spots. But a deal is a deal.'

Conán nudged Dreoilín.

'And you will have the pleasure of having him by your side at every druid meeting from here on. A deal is a deal.'

After a few weeks in the care of Úna, Mac Cumhaill was called back into the leadership of the Fianna. Cormac considered throwing a big party to celebrate Fionn's return but he first discreetly enquired to ensure that the four travellers would attend such an event. He mightn't have always been a wise king but he was wily enough to make up for it.

When Conán let it be known that there might be skin and hair flying if he caught sight of Goll and Cormac with a glass of mead in his veins, Cormac announced that a party would not be appropriate given how ill Fionn still was. Maybe he'd have one in a year or two when everyone was feeling better. Instead, he sent out a message across the land issuing a thousand welcomes home to Fionn.

Of course, he implied that he was the one who had sent Conán looking and that he had never for a moment believed that Mac Cumhaill was a goner.

In fact, everyone Mac Cumhaill met was full sure that they remembered saying, *Conán will bring Fionn back sooner or later.* Goll told Mac Cumhaill that he had made no changes because he knew Fionn would be back shortly. The 'Fianna Nua' story was just someone's imagination running away.

Mac Cumhaill said nothing about any of it. His first act, when he was back in Tara, was to call for the boy who witnessed all battles. The spell was indeed lifted and the boy was growing up with the intention of working the soil and of never seeking out the sight of bloodshed in his life again.

Fionn turned to Liath Ní Choinchin and said, 'Take this boy to Cormac and make sure his aunt and her family are well rewarded for the great help this young man has given us. Then take him home.'

From that day on, Mac Cumhaill was wiser and more

careful with his trust. His friendship became very tightly bound to the four who had risked their lives for him and his mistrust of many others became a silent handicap to him for many a long day afterwards.

Dreoilín never again called another general meeting of druids.

It was very early morning, but a bit later and lighter than usual when the people, big and little, faded from Dark's sight. To his relief, there was no sign of any yellow-eyed, grey-haired hounds.

He thought he heard someone calling his name. And then again, louder. It was back up the fields somewhere, maybe at the house. He left the rath and started running back up the fields. The rising sun cast a redness such as he had never seen in a morning sky.

There in the yard was a huge orange truck parked up against the little 135 tractor that Dark had left out after using it to spread fertiliser in the lower fields the evening before. He couldn't even begin to understand how neither his mother nor the super-alert Georgina had woken up with the noise of the enormous articulated unit coming into the gravelled yard or the racket of his name being yelled so loudly.

In front of the truck stood a man almost the same shape as the front wheel. He was hardly up to Dark's waist in height, but very stocky. Dark certainly wouldn't have liked to tangle with him. He had bright red hair in a huge afro.

He wore a grin that looked permanent and slightly insane. One eye was blue green and looked directly at him. The other was like white china and didn't look anywhere.

'How'ye Art?' said the man, 'Balie is the name they calls me.'

Dark remembered him now. He had seen him once before, a long time back. He had spent a night in the kitchen drinking cans of Guinness, smoking Majors, playing 25s and laughing with Connie and a couple of other lads.

'Alright,' said Dark. 'Connie isn't here, though. He's been away for a long time.'

'Oh, I know that, boss,' laughed the man. 'I was just going down the road there and I said I'd call in to see how the young man of the place is getting on.'

'Alright,' said Dark again, still not sure what the man wanted or how he'd known he'd be down the fields or what he himself was doing driving around the roads in a trailerless truck at five o'clock on a cold Tuesday morning.

'Don't be worried,' laughed the man. 'Connie and me go a long way back. A long, long way. And I can see you're doing grand. I'll let him know that.'

'That's the finest, then,' said Dark, feeling more relaxed, but still not completely at ease until he knew exactly what the man wanted.

The man laughed again and said, 'Well, I can see there's nothing to worry about here. But listen, my brother, here's my mobile number. Connie still has good friends, you know. I'm always on the roads, especially at night, and

137

if you ever need help with anything, you give the Red Lad here a shout. I won't be long coming. Alright?'

'Alright.'

'Good luck, then,' said Balie the Red Lad, crushing his hair on the wing mirror as he climbed back up into the truck.

'Good luck,' said Dark. 'Thanks. And . . . will you tell him I was asking for him if you see him?'

The man closed the door and rolled down the window. Seventies disco music came blaring out. He stuck his elbow out. Still no dogs woke. 'That I will, sir. That I will.'

4
THE WOLF

'McLean, read out your answer to question four,' said Sullivan. She sometimes asked other people too, but she always tried Dark first. Ever since the first day when his mother told her that he was still finding it hard to talk in front of people and could the teachers please maybe not ask him things in class, to give him a while to get better.

Dark, as usual, said nothing. But today was entirely different. For the first time, he didn't feel his entire face and ears getting red hot with embarrassment.

'*Quel surprise*, Mr Dumb. Still waiting for the cat to bring his tongue back?'

'No Miss. I'm talking now.' Dark was as surprised as the rest of the classroom at the words bouncing out of his mouth.

She was startled. But only for a moment. 'So there we are! So the lanky city lad has a tongue after all. I knew I'd be the first teacher here to get you to talk,' she crowed delightedly. 'I knew very well there was nothing at all wrong with you other than being spoilt by your mummy. Alright then. Bring up your work and show it to me if you don't want to call it out.'

'I would, but there's nothing to see,' said Dark calmly.

'What?' Miss Sullivan was really baffled now, 'Why not? I suppose you're going to tell me some feeble excuse like you forgot or . . . or ... or a wolf ate it?'

Now Dark was taken aback. He thought that a very peculiar suggestion for her to make. He had never heard any teacher talk of a wolf before.

'Well, no, Miss,' he said eventually. 'No, the wolf didn't come near it.'

'Are you being smart with me, young man?' She was becoming an even paler white than usual, which was always a sign that she was getting angry.

'No, Miss. He didn't.'

'Stop the nonsense talk. Why . . . have . . . you . . . not . . . done . . . your . . . homework?'

'Honestly, Miss, to tell the God's honest truth, I just didn't want to do it.'

The entire class, silent up to now, nervous about the familiar sarcastic vein that Miss Sullivan was starting into, burst out laughing.

'Shut up, the lot of you!' yelled the teacher. 'Go and stand out in the corridor, you brazen monkey.'

'OK, Miss.'

The rest of the class clapped as Dark walked out. He was amazed. Before now, the school piled new worries on

140

top of his old ones every day and expected him to carry the extra load. Now he saw that there was nothing they could say to him that really mattered. He had enough work dealing with his own troubles and he was not willing to carry extra worries for anyone else anymore. There was nothing she could have said to him. When she opened the door with dramatic politeness waving him out, he heard himself saying in a calm voice, 'Thank you, Miss'.

'And you can stay out there all day, not just for my lessons,' she said.

He spent the day looking out into the goings-on in the blackthorn hedge near the corridor window, seeing things he'd never noticed before. There were two rats cleverly checking that the coast was clear before hurrying out of their home to attend to a discarded chunk of bread. There was a crazy starling coming back every ten minutes to pick a new fight with his reflection in the bottom of a Coke can. There was a black cat that occasionally peered lazily through the nettles but that the other animals somehow knew was off duty. And there was a little rusty brown bird with a cocky tail that fussed into the picture every now and then, surveying the scene. Dark was sure that he recognised the bird and that it was looking in the window at him.

For some reason, Sullivan sent out two of the others with a message to him. The two best in the class. She was always praising them for getting over ninety per cent in every test. What was going on in her mind when she picked the two of them out to talk to him, Dark didn't even care to think about. Neither of them had ever talked to him.

Tadhg was small with blond hair. Ciara was very tall and thin, nearly as tall as Dark himself. She had straight, black hair and greenish eyes.

'She says to tell you, you are to stay out here in the corridor during break too,' she said.

'OK,' said Dark.

They were about to go back in when she turned and said, 'The way she's treating you is not right.'

Dark was surprised. He thought Ciara had never even noticed he existed.

'Thanks,' Dark said. It probably sounded a bit awkward.

'Yeah,' said Tadhg quietly, 'I'm sorry, Art.'

Ciara continued, still looking at Dark, 'I'll tell my dad. He's on the school board. Maybe he can talk to them.'

'Thanks,' said Dark. Then he added, 'But don't worry. It's grand now. I don't mind if she sends me out every day. I've got friends out here looking after me.'

They both looked at each other, puzzled, and then went back in. Dark wished he had said that differently, in case she thought he was a bit crazy or something.

That night, before he gathered with his curious company around the fire, the Old Man asked him how things had gone with his teacher.

'The finest,' said Dark.

'Good enough,' said the Old Man, looking closely at Dark.

'And today,' said the Old Man, 'do you want the work done or do you want to stay not bothered about it?'

'I want to stay not worried about anything,' said Dark.

'Good enough,' said the Old Man again.

The little people seemed in high spirits tonight. Many of them came forth and there was music, not really Dark's style, but it crept into your brain. It was issuing from somewhere in the earth. They danced and frolicked with abandon, the goblet girl amongst them. Dark didn't know what to make of it. The Old Man's ever - present companion Conán saw his confusion and pointed up. There was a full moon overhead.

When things quietened a little, the goblet was brought. Again she sat down near him – maybe only an arm's reach away. And the proceedings began as usual. The Old Man's voice went lower and quieter as he started into his next tale.

'Now,' he said with a wry look, 'did you ever hear of the time Mac Cumhaill could have married into a great kingdom?' The woman with the long, red hair shifted uneasily next to him.

Courting Fionn

The ship that brought Her Highness Tizzie, Queen of Thinlia, to Éirinn was a fussy, fancy, frilly affair. With all its dainty satin streamers and brightly painted masts, it caused quite a stir when it arrived at a bay in Baile Cumain, on the east coast. It looked like a delicate toy next to the rough and ready mongrels that were the ships in which the Fianna addressed the seas. For those who knew Thinlia – a slightly excitable place – the excess of colour and pomp was no surprise.

As the noisy entourage slowly approached Tara, Cormac grumbled. He didn't care much for etiquette and formal niceties. He would rather be out wandering around with his horses or talking nonsense to his fairy woman than be formally entertaining. But the *brehon*s reminded him that as king, he was required to make an effort to at least maintain Éire's relations with Thinlia, which were neither bad nor good.

He organised a middling-sized welcome for them and called a few people together for a bit of a formal banquet to welcome them to Tara.

Tizzie was very slim, pale and, in her own opinion, beautiful. In the opinion of Cormac's human wife, Dearbhla, who did not warm greatly to Tara's visitor, Tizzie was 'under-fed, overdressed and brittle like a clay doll'. Brittle she turned out to be – like cold flint.

When the haughty demands started, Dearbhla stormed off to visit a sister in the north. Tizzie didn't notice or care. She demanded various foods that had to be collected from afar. These included a particular kind of mushroom that sent her into spasms of dance and jerky behaviour when she ate them. She demanded poets all day and musicians and dancers all night, and then turned up her nose at their performances.

The court was surprised at Cormac. His initial grumpiness had been replaced with a definite eagerness to please her. The tiresome celebration went on for two weeks. Eventually Cormac got around to enquiring as to the reason he had been honoured with her ladyship's visit.

'You mean you don't know?' she said sniffily. 'With all respects to your efforts at entertaining and celebrating, had I craved a purgative of coarse shows and plain foods, I could have gone to one of the small, rustic dwellings of a peasant chieftain in my own country.'

Diarmuid, the most polished member of Cormac's court, was the one who had organised the hospitality to the finest detail. His temper slipped momentarily.

'What?! The same mouth that has eaten, drank and tittered to excess now wants to mock the hospitality she so clearly enjoyed!'

Tizzie was too absorbed in her own performance to even hear what Diarmuid said and the king nudged Diarmuid to hold his temper.

'Er, what is it then, that Her Majesty desires?' asked Cormac.

'Why, to see Fionn Mac Cumhaill, of course. I've heard he possesses unnatural qualities and want to see him tested.'

This struck King Cormac as a very peculiar request. He supposed she was a little mentally elevated as a result of the beakers of barley wine she had with her breakfast or that a recent feed of mushrooms had muddled her agenda. Whatever unusual brand of diplomatic canniness was at work in his own head at the time, Cormac decided to go along with it.

Cormac sent an instruction for Mac Cumhaill to come from his home, where he had been resting and tending his and Úna's mountain garden. Mac Cumhaill was very sulky when he arrived in the king's private chambers.

'Cormac, you want me to perform like a monkey for the entertainment of some spoilt royal? This is a humiliation that I respectfully decline.'

'It's not really performing – could you think of it more as showing your mighty skills?' said the king awkwardly.

'It is not my intention to satisfy your requests on this, Chief,' said Mac Cumhaill.

'Well, think of the positive side of it – Tizzie and her crew will go back to Thinlia with the message that there are ferocious and mighty fighting men in Éire and so any thought they might have in the future of bothering us will be quickly put aside.'

'That seems to me a very weak excuse for you not being able to say no to this person,' said Mac Cumhaill sharply.

The king reddened.

'Listen, Fionn,' he said, flustered and slightly angry. 'Listen, old comrade, why don't you take a month off to go hunting after this? You can go down to the Derg and fish away on your own, the way you like. I might even go with you for a couple of days. That'd be the medicine for me. Just the two of us out stalking boar and sitting around a fire.'

Cormac was never insincere when he said things like this. When he was in a pickle, his thoughts would genuinely turn to comradeship and escape. It was just that once he had talked his way through whatever crisis he was currently in, other matters would take priority over plans to head into the country with Fionn. Nevertheless, they understood each other. This kind of plea was as close as Cormac usually got to a direct command to Mac Cumhaill. And besides, Mac Cumhaill rarely valued human company when he was wandering the lough.

And so the shows started. The queen was told that she would have one day in which to ask Fionn to perform feats of strength and another in which she could set him to do tasks requiring great speed.

Tizzie started the first day with her nose pointed to the sky, sending her manservant with messages commanding Mac Cumhaill to lift small rocks. By the end of that day, she was red-faced and excitedly squeaking instructions.

'Now Fionn, can you lift that hill? Right, now lift this cabin with me in it. Ooohhh!'

Mac Cumhaill was rather tired by the time the sun set.

The second day went much the same, with snooty little requests in the morning, sending Mac Cumhaill to the top of the Comeragh mountains and back. Then, by late afternoon she was so worked up that she was asking him to do laps of the country, collecting shells from every beach on the coast as proof that he'd made it.

Mac Cumhaill went home that night, still disgusted with Cormac for having put him through this, but at least consoled that it was over. Or so he thought.

The next day, a messenger from Cormac entered his cabin with a blessing and asked him to come back to Tara – for one last performance. Mac Cumhaill was enraged, but still was bound to Cormac's command.

When Fionn got back to Tara, the king said, 'Just one last thing before she goes?'

'What?' said Mac Cumhaill.

'Well, since you're a warrior she wants to see you in combat.'

Mac Cumhaill laughed, but Cormac didn't.

'I'm sorry, my brother. She wants to set you up against another member of the Fianna, to see how you fare.'

Diarmuid looked at Mac Cumhaill, anticipating that this would not go down well.

Mac Cumhaill looked straight at the king. There was silence for a moment. Then Mac Cumhaill spoke in cold, deliberate tones, 'Given the history of blood between our fathers, you should not carelessly invite the day I break my vow never to use arms against one of my own.'

Diarmuid the diplomat intervened, 'What's taken hold of you, Cormac? Do not let this *straoil* become the cause of further hard words between you and your most loyal friend here.'

As he flustered off to break the news to Tizzie, Cormac mumbled, 'May Daghda look down on me, surely there's no other king who puts up with such insubordination… Alright then, alright, but there's no need to talk about her disrespectfully; that could be bad for relations.'

When the king had left the hall, Diarmuid said to Mac Cumhaill, 'I'm afraid his old weakness is playing up on him again. A few days in the company of any fancy woman and he starts losing his sense and fantasising about having a family with her. He'll deny it high and low, but that's what's making him stupid now.'

'Well, he's going to be a disappointed man by this evening because I'm sorely tempted to put this woman and her crew back onto the sea within an hour if this carries on. With or without their boats,' said Mac Cumhaill.

Mac Cumhaill himself was in for a small surprise. When Cormac told Tizzie the news, she stomped a bit.

But then she said, 'Oh well, I suppose I've seen enough. He'll do.'

'What do you mean, Tizzie, you wonderful, wiry creature from heaven?' said Cormac, who hadn't ever quite mastered the art of flattery.

'Call him here,' she said.

Mac Cumhaill was sent for, and Tizzie duly informed the astonished assembly that she thought her last husband was too weak and that she'd had him smothered in feather pillows. She wanted a stronger man. She had heard about Fionn Mac Cumhaill. And now that she'd tested him, she had decided to take Fionn home for a trial period as her husband.

Silence followed. Nobody knew whether to laugh. The king's colour changed to scarlet.

Mac Cumhaill stepped forward biting his cheek as he said through his teeth, 'To marry a queen of your stature would be an honour, Your Ladyship. However, this is a request I cannot meet.'

'Excuse me!' she shrieked. 'Many's the European prince who would kill or die for the chance I have just offered you, a lowly soldier.' She paused and tried to calm herself. 'Look, you probably don't realise what it would be like to live in a real palace with treasures aplenty and with gates that keep commoners outside. Where they belong,' she said, looking around sniffily.

'With respect, Queen Tizzie,' said Mac Cumhaill still very politely, 'it's a pity that in your time here you didn't observe the benefits of a royalty which serves its people rather than turning them into slaves.'

Cormac was lifted up a little at this sideways compliment.

'Besides,' continued Mac Cumhaill, 'I am happily married to the finest woman I have ever known and could never consider a request like yours.'

'WHAT?!' Tizzie screamed in rage. 'How dare you even address me in the same sentence as you talk about some common mare you tether back at your cabin, the base comfort that ensures you have a big feed of cabbage and pig fat on the rare occasions you decide to call in at home! My people have done their research. Please withdraw your insult this instant!'

Mac Cumhaill calmly offered to call his wife to the castle so that Tizzie could speak to her in person. Cormac and Diarmuid both laughed. They knew that Úna was the kindest soul on earth, but also the deadliest if anyone crossed her or her family. She had a tongue that could tear anyone to shreds and flying fists that would pulverise Queen Tizzie if she got to hear of today's transactions.

'My patience has run out with this,' said Tizzie, turning to Cormac . 'Please instruct him to pack his few things and have him escorted down to my ship within the hour.'

Cormac had recovered his senses.

'I'm afraid, Your Ladyship, there appears little chance that Fionn Mac Cumhaill will change his mind, so it is probably pointless for you to stay with us much longer. I have organised for a good stock of food, drink and, of course, our special mushrooms to be loaded onto your ship in preparation for the journey back.'

Everyone laughed now. The king raised his hand for silence and continued: 'I do hope that the good relations existing between our two countries will be improved by the extended hospitality we have shown you during your stay here.'

She became even more furious at the king's quiet disrespect. She suddenly reached into the folds of her dress and took out a glass bottle. She removed the cork. As a green fume wisped out of it, she blew it towards the king. She announced, with taut laughter, that the vapour caused terrible sickness and sometimes death for anyone who hadn't met it before.

'This little gift from us to your treasured king and his pathetic soldier will serve as a permanent reminder to Éirinn of the day that you made the mistake of insulting Thinlia.'

Even as she spoke, Mac Cumhaill was lifting Cormac away. But several other people, the cook and helpers who had been clearing tables to the side of the great hall, hadn't realised the danger and in seconds sat curled up with cramps and then started sweating and vomiting. The unpleasant Tizzie laughed.

Cormac now became furious. 'Lock her up,' he ordered.

'What?' she screamed. 'Do you dare incur a war with Thinlia?'

Cormac's advisers and *brehon*s whispered to him urgently that maybe he should let her go. The country would be wise to avoid a war over injured pride.

Cormac said, 'I don't care. She's committed a malicious crime against my people. She is no longer a queen in this country. She will pay like any common criminal.'

Tizzie was thrown in a hut, screaming and protesting.

Dreoilín came to see what help and comfort he could bring to the sick. He tried various spells and concoctions and quickly found one that seemed to give the affected people more strength to fight the sickness. They still suffered enormous pain and one person who had already been sick couldn't be saved. But the rest recovered.

At the same time, a debate was going on about what should happen to Tizzie's ship and her gaggle of servants. Cormac's advisers and *brehons* pleaded that he not let them go.

'If they get back with the message that their queen is jailed here, the armies of Thinlia will be obliged to attack,' they warned.

Mac Cumhaill, as on virtually all matters, disagreed with the advice of the *brehons*. He argued that the servants had caused nobody any harm and that the king should let them go or stay as they pleased. Cormac agreed, and it was with great anxiety that people watched Tizzie's ship depart from the shores of Éirinn.

Within three weeks, panic spread in coastal villages as the feared news arrived of ships approaching Baile Cumain bay. With a heavy heart, Mac Cumhaill sent the word around to the already prepared battalions to get ready to fend off the invasion. Thinlia armies were known to be very large and well trained. They specialised in nimble-footed manoeuvres and trick sword movements that would get past the more mullocking moves of some of Éirinn's soldiers of destiny, whose strengths were in heart, might and fearlessness rather than dexterity. Mac Cumhaill hoped that the Fianna would be able to hold out against them, but he knew it would not be without much bloodshed.

He went down to the coast intending to assess the likely landing points of the incoming soldiers. But when he got to a good lookout position, he was most surprised to see only two ships. They were certainly of the Thinlia design. They were already at anchor, far out in the bay, but only one small rowing boat was coming ashore. Mac Cumhaill ran down to the beach to meet the visitors, who clearly were not yet ready for war, and to ensure that none of his men attacked them out of nervousness.

When they landed, a stringy grey man emerged dressed in fancy regalia and ornamented with all kinds of decorations and ribbons and medals. The get-up of one of their senior army leaders, Mac Cumhaill assumed. His ear twitched nervously and he had a scarred face and a tense smile on his crooked lips. He opened his arms to embrace Mac Cumhaill, in the way the Thinliers did with every greeting. Mac Cumhaill disliked that custom, keeping his rare hugs for his family, and for them only on special occasions. But he was so relieved that his people might be spared a war that he gladly hugged the thin general, who started coughing as if he was being choked.

'We've come in peace, Mr Mac Cumhaill,' said the general.

Mac Cumhaill couldn't hide his puzzlement and said, 'What about your queen?'

'We've been told all that happened. And her servants and guards have told of the fairness you showed in letting them go. You have every right to punish her for her crime.'

'Well, that is good news indeed,' said Mac Cumhaill. 'If you'd like to take her home, I'm sure I can convince Cormac to release her on assurance that she'll never come back here.'

'Well, that's the other thing. We were tired of her and while she was away courting you,' the general laughed, 'we took the opportunity to replace her with a kinder, smarter queen.'

All the men on the brow of the hill looked down anxiously, trying to hear what was being said. They relaxed when they heard Mac Cumhaill laughing. 'So. I take it that you are not in a hurry to have Tizzie back then?'

'More than that,' said the general. 'In fact, we've been sent to assure you that the longer you keep her here, the more secure and long-lasting will be your peace pact with the people of Thinlia.'

The general's ships were replenished and his crews rested, though Diarmuid did not volunteer to organise any reception parties. Mac Cumhaill waved the men of Thinlia goodbye as they disappeared out of the harbour and headed back home.

When he laid his head on the cosy feather cushion next

to Úna that night, he sighed, 'I'm relieved that that day is done and wouldn't want one like it again for a while.'

'Well, an awful war averted is indeed something to be mightily relieved about,' said Úna.

'Not just that,' said Mac Cumhaill. 'It's the headache I have from spending a day with a whole crew of jittery, squabbling Thinliers – only eased as the noisy bugles of their boats disappeared across the horizon.'

When Úna gave out to him for being a narrow-minded bog man, unappreciative of other sophisticated cultures, he was tempted to mention Tizzie's observations about her. But on balance he thought it better to let Úna feel she'd got one up on him than to risk having her start a new war.

After some time in captivity, Tizzie calmed down dramatically and was released. At Cormac's insistence, she was trained to help the kitchen staff at Tara and to help the family of the old man who'd died as a result of her vapours. Cormac would call in regularly to see if she had grown more fond of him, which she, for some reason, even in her diminished circumstances, never did.

Of course, she was never allowed to help with the preparation of food.

Dark gathered himself to head home. He would have been happy enough to stay longer. But as usual with the dawn, the birds took their early morning turn as rulers of the country.

He felt lonely as he trudged home.

5

GOOSE FODDER

The principal, Magill, had been waiting at the gate. When Dark's mother stopped to drop Dark off, he almost ran over to the car. He was agitated. He leaned in the passenger door and waved at Dark's mother like he was thumbing a lift.

'Would you come into my office for a minute, young lady?'

Dark could see that his mother was quite dumbfounded at the way she was being spoken to, and she followed Magill almost like another schoolkid would. She even left the door of her car open. Some of the lads from Dark's class went down to pass knowledgeable-sounding comments about the overhead valve train and the CO_2 emissions, and mainly to shut the door for her.

As they walked, Magill tried to maintain some appearance of manners.

'I am very *honoured* at being granted a meeting with

156

you,' he said. 'A pity I have to virtually ambush you to get it.'

'Yes, that is a pity,' said Dark's mother timidly.

'Well, if you had troubled yourself to answer the letters I sent you, you might have saved us both the bother.'

His mother stopped and was about to say, 'What letters?' when she looked at Dark and walked on with the principal.

Just as she was about to disappear into the building after him, her phone rang. Dark knew the sound – it was just an alarm that went off every morning to remind her to call her office with some sales numbers. But today it was like a call transforming her back from a schoolgirl into a working woman. She turned around at the school door, picked the phone out of her bag and put it to her ear. She turned away slightly and started talking into the phone. Then she turned and said, 'Sorry Mr Magill. Something urgent. I really have to dash. But I will drop in very soon.'

When she was back in the yard walking briskly past Dark, she looked into his eyes and said, 'Arthur?'

'Yes, Mam?'

'Will you bring me those letters this evening so I can see what this Mr Magill is concerned about.'

'Sorry, Mam.'

'I need you to help me a little with this situation, love,' she said.

Chronic kindness was her biggest failing. Dark could never remember a minute when she had got really angry with him. Even at the funeral she had swallowed back her own tears, she was so focused on trying to say and do what she thought would be good for him.

Dark intercepted letters only when he knew they'd upset her. What was the point of her reading such letters when they'd have no other result? As far as he remembered, the last letter from the school said something like, Dear Ms McLean, Would you be so good as to attend a meeting with me on such and such a date so that we can find a constructive intervention to deal with your son's learning difficulties…

When Dark reached the safety of the rath that night, the Old Man met him with the usual enquiries. He said, 'Things are good at school?'

'The finest,' said Dark.

'And what are you going to do about those letters you gave the geese to eat?'

Dark was a little bit surprised. 'What can I do?'

'Not much, I'd say,' laughed the Old Man, 'unless you think you'll be able to reconstruct them from the droppings of those fine ladies.'

'Maybe she'll forget about it,' said Dark.

The Old Man just looked at him uncomfortably. Eventually, everyone else seemed to be getting restless at the fire and the fairy girl was impatiently holding his cup when the Old Man said, 'Come and sit with us then, and leave other worries for another day.'

Fathach Island

One day Mac Cumhaill was walking along a white sand

headland on the southwest coast of Corca Dhuibhne. He was thinking how quiet the country had become and even though that was certainly a good thing, he had to admit that he was feeling a bit flat and restless. He was not sure what to do with himself. Úna would have preferred him to be bringing manure out to prepare the field for barley and minding lambs. But the clan were well able to do that without him, and he had already spent the last three months of winter hanging around the home doing very little other than talking with neighbours.

He wanted to be away now. He didn't like hunting at this time of year, when animals and birds were giving birth and minding young. So, two weeks back, he had told Úna he was going out for a short walk, to take a wander around the country and see how the first peep of spring was finding people.

He was spotted by a group of fishermen about to launch three *currach*s. Probably their first time out this year. It was early for them to be going but the weather was unusually calm. Fionn was guessing that the salted fish at home was running out, and hungry eyes looking at them, as well as the same springtime restlessness as was agitating himself, had decided these people to venture out to try their luck.

The big lump of a stranger kicking up bits of seaweed must have been a strange sight to them. They sent a boy over to invite him to join them.

Sea fishing wasn't exactly Mac Cumhaill's greatest passion, but he thought he could do worse that day.

When he stepped over to them, he introduced himself.

'I'm a son of Cumhall and I'd be very honoured to be in your company on this fine day.'

The oldest of the Cinnéide clan, a little man with a grey beard and a weary face, stood creakily from his stumpy stool amongst the lines at the front of one of the *currachs*. The others went silent.

He introduced himself croakily as Nóirín's Caoimhín, and said, 'It's our honour to have you with us Mac Cumhaill, and a very lovely day it is indeed.'

After that, he sat back down and resumed his blank stare out to sea.

The other clan members were very shocked. Ulan Cinnéide, who was in charge of the operation, and was himself quite elderly, explained later to Mac Cumhaill that it was the first time his father had spoken in about five years.

'Did he suffer some great shock or how did he lose the voice?' asked Mac Cumhaill.

'Not that,' said Ulan. 'It is just that the sea has made him so old and tired. It is one thing to be old and remember your parents and their parents and to feel sad at how they have all gone away from you. It is another to have lost many beloved young people, taken by her' – he nodded at the harmless-looking waters – 'before their proper time. It's gone that almost nothing excites him or bothers him enough to throw words at it.'

They started rowing out towards a favourite strip, where shoals of large fish were often hunting smaller ones at this time of year. The day was warm and was becoming even more eerily calm for any time of year, let alone so early in the spring. It was so calm that the water was smooth as jelly.

They weren't striking any fish. But they just kept rowing. Eventually, they realised that they had rowed further out than usual.

Ulan gave a shout to the other boats: 'It's time to head back,' he shouted.

But Mac Cumhaill, for some reason, was gripped by a desire to go further out. Since the sea was so calm, Ulan didn't see any harm in it. He asked the old man, who nodded agreement. He told the others that his boat would follow them in later.

Soon enough, this unusual journey had taken them to beyond the point from which they could still see any land. This was breaking a Cinnéide rule - one that had often left the Cinnéide clan with smaller catches, but with fewer sacrifices to the ocean than other families.

As they went further and further, Mac Cumhaill kept saying, 'Come on now, just a little more.' The four oarsmen started to get fearful. It was too far. They'd be too tired to row back. This went against every thread of wisdom that life had sewn into them.

'It'll be gone dark in a couple of hours, it's still early in the year, Fionn Mac Cumhaill,' said Ulan. 'We can't be abroad after dark, as there are many creatures of the sea that do not look favourably on that.'

'Don't worry about getting back. I'll help with the rowing,' Mac Cumhaill said.

When he took over a set of oars, they picked up great speed and headed ever further. It wasn't a fair thing for him to have done so. He knew they had a fear of being further out than anyone had ever been. He knew they feared reaching a deep hole in the sea, or meeting a giant sea cat intent on taking them down to reside in her damp domain. He was ready for what they might meet, but he knew in his heart it wasn't fair to be dragging these people into mortal danger just because of his own restlessness. He didn't know why he had become so fixed on this idea as he had no plan behind it or no idea of what it was he expected to find if he kept going out in a westerly direction.

In the end, the other men were complaining so much that Mac Cumhaill could not keep them going anymore. Ulan pulled the little flask of water from Brigid's well that they always kept under the front seat of the *currach*, and sprinkled it over everyone present. Just as he was starting to turn the boat, old Caoimhín stood up and pointed with his crooked blackthorn stick.

'Look ahead.'

'I see nothing,' said the boy.

'Me neither,' said his uncle.

But Mac Cumhaill also saw and he knew the strangeness in the old man's voice. There was not supposed to be land out there.

They had to pull the boat for another hour before the others could see what Mac Cumhaill and the old man had been pointing at. Once they did, they all regained their energy. Fuelled by curiosity and excitement, they rowed quickly. As they got closer, they could make out a lovely, green island with extremely tall trees and long grass.

Closer still, they could hear the bare ripple of the blue water on the sandy shore. There would be no danger bringing the boat right in close. They could make out fruit on the trees behind. And fresh streams rolling down gentle hills. This definitely wasn't right. Brigid's day wasn't even passed. No birds should have been nesting yet. Surely no natural tree could be fruiting at this time of the year. But it looked so good that they all, Fionn included, were overcome with the desire to go ashore straight away.

On shore, they walked across the golden sand to a big patch of soft grass, where they settled down for a rest. They refreshed themselves with delicious cold water from a tumbling stream.

After some time, there was a rustling in the trees above them.

'What was that?' said Mac Cumhaill. The others didn't hear.

Next time it was much louder and the rest heard too.

The rustling continued, and after some time they began to ignore it. They got back to eating guavas and other perfect fruit. Then Mac Cumhaill heard a groan. He looked at the fisherman who'd made the sound and said, 'What's the matter with you?'

The fisherman just grunted and pointed behind Mac Cumhaill like a madman.

'It's . . . it's . . . it's a gigantic creature.'

There was a creature walking slowly towards Mac Cumhaill. And it was a very large gentleman, right enough.

It was taller than the tallest trees. Its shadow moved before it, big enough to darken the entire headland that they now stood on. It was covered from its single-toed feet right to the top of its round head, in stripes. Amber and black stripes. It had three arms that it seemed unsure of what to do with.

Mac Cumhaill drew his sword and stood to face the enormous thing. It reached out one of its huge two-fingered hands. The situation was desperate. There was no way Mac Cumhaill could imagine being able to deal with it. Even if this enormous monster could be kept at bay for a while, there were surely more. He didn't have any other armed man with him. They had no hope of reaching the boat with the old man so hobbled, and even if they did, this thing would be able to wade deep into the sea in one or two steps and just pick them up as they tried to row away.

But he tried to keep up heart. He did all he could do. He swung his large metal companion in a desperate attempt to protect them. He assumed the *fathach* would retreat from the swinging sword. But it didn't.

'Its skin is so tough,' said one of the fishermen who had now retreated back down to the waterfront, 'that it knows a sword can do nothing to it.'

However, as the hand came closer, Mac Cumhaill took his chances and made one more almighty swing at it, this time not as a warning. The hand fell right off. The large thing immediately let out a terrible cry and stood bolt upright for an instant. They thought they were all as good as dead at that point. But then it turned and ran off with the other two hands holding the remains of the third.

Mac Cumhaill immediately suspected he had made a terrible mistake. He threw down his sword and walked slowly towards the trees. The fishermen thought he had gone mad and tried to call him back. But they didn't follow him.

For days, Mac Cumhaill listened to the sounds of the *fathach*s talking to each other from hiding places that he could easily see, but did not want to disturb. He began to understand their language. What he learnt astonished him. The enormous creatures were all scared and confused. They had never seen a thing like a sword before. They had no understanding of why anyone would want to carry sharpened metal that could do such terrible damage. They had never known any creature to hurt another.

He started talking to them in their own language.

'I want to apologise a thousand times for what I have done. Myself and my people were afraid. And fear sometimes makes my people lash out without listening or thinking. I don't know how I can make it up to the person whose hand I cut off.'

He expected that it would take days of this kind of talk, if there was ever any chance they would come to trust him. And he expected that at best they would then start negotiating a high reward from him for what he had done. But he was prepared to pay it as he knew he had done wrong and Fionn Mac Cumhaill had seen too many wrongs left undone in his life. He had a determination in those days that he personally would never leave further wrongs behind him.

He was surprised, though. Within minutes of him starting his appeasing talk to them, they started to pop their heads out of the caves and from behind the trees that they thought hid them. Obviously, they had never known a lie either and so to them there was no reason at all to doubt what Mac Cumhaill was saying. Soon they were gathering around him, making chortling noises. Even the one with only two hands.

There were several thousand of them on the island and none anywhere else in the world that they knew of, they said. Though, in fact, none of them had been anywhere else in the world. Nearly half of them had blue stripes instead of orange. There didn't appear to be any chief. They all referred to each other as 'Your Highness'. The young had only two arms and sprouted the third as they stopped running and became wiser.

Mac Cumhaill took the *fathach*s to meet his friends. The fishermen were very nervous at first. But the *fathach*s kept bringing them treats – special fruits from hidden corners of the island. Soon all fear was forgotten and the people started trusting in a way that adult humans had forgotten how to.

Of all of them, the oldest one, Nóirín's Caoimhín, became completely at peace here. Maybe, being the oldest, he had had the heaviest load of mistrust to lose and was the most relieved to be in a place where you didn't always have to be careful what you thought or what you said.

The days and nights slipped by without them even noticing. They explored all day, often carried around by the *fathach*s. At night they sat looking out at the sea. They tried to light a fire on the first night that they spent with the *fathach*s, but realised that the *fathach*s were terrified of it. So they didn't do that again. Anyway, there was no need for fires. It was warm enough. They were eating and drinking plenty, and then sleeping well.

Eventually, Mac Cumhaill said, 'We've all got people and tasks that need us, and it's time for us to bid farewell to this kind place and to go back to our hard world.'

The fishermen sighed, but once they realised how much time had slipped by, the thoughts of how their families would be worried to despair convinced them to get back into the boat without hesitation. All except the old man, Nóirín's Caoimhín. His sons and grandsons argued with him and pleaded with him, but there was no way they were going to persuade him. One of them even tried to wrestle him into the boat, but he soon learned what strength could be in a wiry old body.

After watching this quietly for a while, Mac Cumhaill said to them, 'I can see you love the elder and that he loves you all. But what more could you want for him? Have you seen him as happy and free from aches and sorrows? And he'll never forgive you if you bring him back.'

Eventually, after each receiving a blessing and hearing old stories they'd never heard before, they said their tearful goodbyes to old Caoimhín, and loaded up some fruits and seeds of apple trees that they hoped might grow back in Corca Dhuibhne. Strangely, as they nosed the boat down out through the little estuary, the sea again became as calm as a pond and the journey home seemed shorter.

When they got home, there was great celebration. It had long ago been assumed that the heartless sea had taken more victims. The village had started to blame Mac Cumhaill for persuading the men to go out further than they knew was safe.

Now that they were back, few people believed their story. All the fruits had rotted away within an hour of leaving the island. And Nóirín's Caoimhín was missing.

When the fishermen attempted to take other people out to the peaceful *fathachs'* island, they couldn't find it again. No matter how far out they dared to go, they could not get to the calm waters.

Most people then assumed that the old man had fallen overboard and that Mac Cumhaill had somehow managed to keep them alive at sea for weeks while they searched the dark waters in vain for old Caoimhín's body. It was said in the village that because the Cinnéide boys couldn't bear to think of him dead, they had come up with this story to comfort themselves. And nobody faulted them for that because it was a part of the country in which a good story was always appreciated, regardless of how concentrated or diluted the truth it contained.

But those fishermen and their sons knew the island existed and the rumours are that it still appears from time to time. Some descendents of those Cinnéide men believe that when a fishing boat disappears in stormy weather, the fishermen end up being taken to the beautiful island of the peaceful *fathach*s.

When Dark sat up in the misty blackness, a cock pheasant that had come down from its roost was eyeing him very curiously.

He made his way home.

6
MITCHING BY THE BROWN RIVER

The next day, Dark's mother dropped him at the start of the town leaving him to walk that last bit to school.

'Sorry, Arthur,' she said in a kind of embarrassed tone, 'I'm just in a rush today.'

Dark knew she didn't want to meet the principal again. He scared her. But she didn't think she could say that to Dark. Dark didn't see anything wrong with that. Magill had that effect on most people.

As she pulled off, he looked up the town where little groups of lads and girls were walking vaguely towards the school, with their hands in their pockets, barely talking, looking at the ground, some worried about uniform, some worried about homework and some still half asleep. He looked back in the other direction, past the speed limit sign, and saw the road closing in with cow-parsley and bushes that couldn't be cut back till the autumn because they were full of nesting birds and hedgehogs and maybe further back towards the covert, a den of fox cubs. The choice was easy enough. Once he got in off the road at the first field gate, he was out of sight of the curious. He knew a shortish way back across the fields. It would only take him a few hours.

He got a little lost, and found himself in fields he didn't know. He panicked at first, going through hedges and doubling back, trying to find something familiar. Then he remembered the advice Connie used to give – always go back to the Brown River when you're lost. Then the only thing you have to figure out is which direction to follow it in so that it takes you in under the Rocky Field. And as Connie said, 'if you can't figure that much out you may as well go and shite'.

When he found his way back to the stream, he went to a grassy shelf partway down the bank, out of view. He sat down and took out his lunch. He stayed there a good while watching a large salmon that seemed to have no plan other than to stay flicking his tail barely enough to keep him stationary against the flow. The water was deep and brown. It was beyond time and caring, oblivious to concerns of any kind. The sun was warm. Flies were busy. A water hen kept bobbing in and out of the reeds to see if she should be bothered about his presence. He could see he would be spending a lot of school time here in future. Tomorrow he might bring his telescopic rod and a tin of worms in the rucksack.

In the afternoon, as he wandered home, he texted his mother to say he'd got a lift from a lad who lived further up the road, so she didn't need to pick him up. He had all his farm work done without any pressure. And he still had time to watch some TV. This was definitely a much better way to spend a day.

In the rath that night, the goblet girl looked more perfect than ever before. Dark could hardly keep from glancing at her, even though she caught him every time. The red-haired woman threw something on the fire and it blazed up brighter than ever. Through the flames, as the Old Man cleared his throat, Dark could see a man fishing very contentedly in a small stream that looked very like the one at the edge of the bog.

The Luck of the *Lúdramán*

It's true that Mac Cumhaill had some unnatural gifts that have often been spoken of. Indeed, he sometimes regarded that little bag of inheritances as a curse. He achieved most things in his life fair and square. But whenever he won a contest in battle, begrudgers like Goll would mumble that he must have used the magic spear. When he won a fishing or hunting contest he had heard of people putting it about that he consorted with dark forces. Whenever he won a board game his opponent would claim he had put the thumb of knowledge in his gob. There was one occasion, however, when the thumb story caused difficulties of a different kind.

Gearraí was a man from Fotharta who hadn't landed in this world with an over-abundance of sense. While many children would touch their thumbs off every fish they saw, on the off-chance of getting a taste of Fionn's wisdom, Gearraí still fully believed this was possible at the age of fifty. And he was still fishing, still hoping. Every daylight hour of his life. In fairness, he needed the top-up of wisdom more than most.

One thing he wasn't short on, however, was patience. He had never really figured out how to catch a fish, any fish, after all those years. Even though kindly friends tried to explain to him the sorts of things that might actually tempt a fish to bite into his hook, he still tried his own things.

One unfortunate day, a sea witch, a *bandraoi* of the lowest order, happened to be in the waters of Éire. There were unnatural storms at sea that summer and she'd decided to move up into the rivers and streams for a spell. And in the way that bad luck operates, this lady happened to find her way into the very stream in which Gearraí was always fishing. That day, he was dangling a bit of old leather on the end of his fishing line. The *bandraoi* could take many forms, but generally she moved around as a dogfish, hiding in murky waters, sustaining herself on decaying rats and ducklings.

The *bandraoi* was going along in the dirty drain where Gearraí was fishing. The boys with him should have guessed there was something dangerous in the water, as a family of otters sprang to the bank, panicked by something, and headed into nearby bushes.

The *bandraoi* was bored and irritated. Gearraí's bit of leather strap swung in front of her, and she snapped at it crankily. The first fish the unfortunate man had ever caught in his fifty years. The hook stuck in her. She now became very, very cross indeed and gave a big pull, lodging the hook painfully into her.

Gearraí was so excited that he almost fell into the drain. He started screaming at his friends, 'I've cotch him, I've cotch him, I've cotch the salmon, I've cotch the salmon of knowledge.'

Two of his friends came and showed him how to pull in his fish. They were surprised at how strongly the fish was pulling – they didn't think anything other than frogs and eels lived in that dirty little stream.

When the fish eventually came to shore, one of Gearraí's best friends, a six-year-old boy called Oscar, said, 'Sorry Gearraí, but that's not a salmon.'

Gearraí was very disappointed, and he argued with the boys as they looked at the big ugly fish jumping around on the grass.

'Maybe it's just a different shaped salmon, because it's stuffed out of shape with all the knowledge and all.'

Oscar and the other little boys felt sorry for Gearraí, since he had been waiting his whole life for this. So they told him that maybe if he cooked it up and tasted it, he might just get lucky.

Gearraí brightened up. He set about creating a fire. But all the sticks he used were wet twigs from the stream. And his efforts to light them eventually tired him. In the end, he gave up. He decided he could cook the fish with the heat from his breath. He started blowing on it and saying

'Come on little salmon, cook, cooook.'

The *bandraoi* had planned to lie there till nobody was looking, and then to make her escape unnoticed. But the stink of Gearraí's breath was too much for her. A shrill curse broke out from the fish and the *bandraoi* emerged in full shape. She was a rather pale-faced lady with long yellow hair and thin legs sticking out under a sea-green tunic. She did not have a happy look in her eyes.

Gearraí still thought he had a chance and went up to the *bandraoi*, touched her with his thumb, and sucked his thumb to see if he could get any knowledge. This *bandraoi* did not have a kind nature and she was so angered by Gearraí's slowness that she couldn't bring herself to just fly away and leave the situation alone. So incensed was she that she didn't even think of putting a spell on him immediately. Instead, she started hopping around the place in her rage, slapping him on the head with some kind of beaded rope and saying 'You stupid, stupid, stupid, stupid creature.'

Poor Gearraí wasn't even smart enough to know how to get away. He kept running around in circles and she kept getting madder and slapping him harder.

The boys looked on in terror at this. They had never seen a bad *bandraoi* before, let alone a fish that turned into a woman of any kind. But Oscar had the wisdom to run for help. By the strangest of good fortune, he only ran a few minutes when he bumped into two old ladies walking the pathways of Éire, as they had always done since time began. Although Oscar didn't know it, his appeal for help was ad-

175

dressed to two of the finest healing *bandraois* who had ever stood on hind legs. The ladies didn't like the sound of what Oscar was telling them, and they came with him quickly.

The bad *cailleach* was so consumed by tormenting Gearraí that she didn't notice the time passing or didn't notice the arrival of her colleagues. The old women found her still raging and still slapping Gearraí, now with her fists, a trickle of blood coming from the corner of her mouth where she had pulled out the hook.

Good women though they might have been, there was very little healing in the spell they hit the younger woman with. They uttered a few unintelligible words and the other woman collapsed into the form of a mud minnow. Gearraí looked down at it, still bewildered. One of the ladies hobbled up and flicked the minnow with her stick, landing it expertly in the stream. A small pike happened to be passing and gobbled the *bandraoi* minnow in one mouthful.

Oscar had an idea. He pleaded with the old healing ladies to make a spell to give Gearraí some wits.

'Wouldn't it be a nice thing for him as he heads into his old age?' said the boy.

The taller one laughed. 'Putting wisdom into that head would be beyond our greatest efforts.'

'Besides,' said the other to Oscar, 'you are a bright lad but you, too, have a lot to learn. Sometimes it is best to leave well enough alone. How do you know that wisdom would improve his lot? Gearraí might not have the knowledge of the salmon but he is blessed with the ignorance of the earthworm and that seems to bring him more bliss.'

When the little boys and the old women looked over at Gearraí, none of them could doubt these words. Despite being streaked with bruises, Gearraí was smiling again, putting a piece of grass on his fishing hook and going back to try to catch another salmon of knowledge, completely forgetting the whole episode he'd just been through.

'Furthermore,' said the other woman, 'he is blessed with the luck of the *lúdramán*. There aren't many men alive who can say they stuck a hook in the palette of a beautiful *bandraoi*, tried to cook her alive, and are still in one piece after it all.'

7

No Better Than Each Other

In school Dark was braced for some drama. Miss Sullivan always interrogated people who had been out sick, convinced that overprotective parents kept them away 'at the slightest sniffle'.

He wasn't too troubled. As a token, he had written a note to say he had been sick the previous day. He hadn't spent very long doing it, so it probably didn't look too much like his mother's writing. But what did he care? He would ride on through; whatever.

He was surprised, though. Sullivan never asked him a thing. None of the usual, 'Well, look here, look who has decided to honour us with their company. Let me guess: you were looking a little pale and Mammy thought you might be coming down with Ebola? Or maybe your Daddy couldn't find a plank to block a gateway from his cows so he kept you home instead?' None of that. Not a word.

She was almost nicer to him than usual. She asked everyone else about homework before getting to him. Almost like she was giving him the signal that she wouldn't have an issue if he went missing again. Eventually, of course, she did ask him.

'Well, yourself,' she said in a very controlled tone, 'did you manage any of the homework?'

'No, Miss.'

'Might I ask why not?'

'Because I wasn't here yesterday.'

Dark didn't see any reason to avoid the issue, even if she wanted to.

'Why not?'

'Because I decided to go fishing, Miss.'

Although Dark wasn't trying to amuse anyone, the others started shouting and laughing.

She waited for that to settle down and then said very calmly, 'You do know when you are out you are still supposed to phone someone else to find out what the homework was.'

'Sorry, Miss, but I didn't want to do that.'

'OK, well… well, try to remember next time.'

The message couldn't have been clearer. She didn't even shout or pass a sarcastic comment as she opened the door to the corridor for him.

That was all grand until break time. During break, David Cash came up to him. David was in the same class, but he was two years older than the rest of them. He went in for being hardy. He looked like he'd been shaving for years and he was stockier and stronger than them. And until recently he had been the tallest. He liked to push other lads around. Some lads called him names behind his back. He was half deaf and wasn't sure who was slagging him and who wasn't, so he would randomly come up to people, making out that he thought they had been insulting him; grabbing people and saying, 'Com'ere, what did you say about me?'

Nobody was very fond of him.

Cash was always in trouble with Sullivan too. He had missed a lot of time. People said his family moved around. And he wasn't really able to do any reading or writing. Though he was able to do all sums in his head and he seemed to know everything there was to know about jet engines, World War II and horses.

He came up to Dark and said, 'Here, McLean, how come she always sends you out and she never sends me out?'

'I don't know,' said Dark.

It was peculiar, right enough. Sullivan certainly told them often enough that they were no better than each other.

'Neck and neck for the prize for the thickest plank I've ever had the misfortune to teach.'

Dark was never sure which of them she thought would be insulted.

'I'd feckin' much sooner be out here or outside altogether than packed all day into that glass cage,' said Cash.

For some reason, he was angry with Dark about this. Dark said nothing.

'Here, I have a job for you, Dark,' Cash said.

'What?'

'Since you are out here doing nothing only scratching yourself all day, you might as well take this yoke and follow the two thirty-five for me.'

He pushed an iPhone into Dark's hand.

'What do you mean?'

'Are you feckin' dumb? Didn't I say to you what I want? Take this feckin' thing in your hands and watch the two thirty-five at Newcastle. And if Donder wins you can give me a thumb signal through the door of the class. I have a few bob on him and I might buy you a lollipop if he wins,' he sneered.

Cash doing the big man again. Just wanting to talk loud and let the others know his father was letting him back horses now. Dark took the thing though. Partly because he hadn't played with an iPhone before and it was much nicer than his own phone.

Unfortunately, after messing around with it a bit, he heard some commotion outside and forgot all about it. In the first place, he missed the race. But worse still, he had it in his hand when Magill came up the corridor. The principal got in such a rage at the sight of Dark tuned into horse-racing while he was supposed to be suffering that he hit the thing out of Dark's hands and it fell to the ground. They both looked down. The screen was gone blank.

'That wasn't mine and I'll be in trouble if it's broken,' said Dark.

'Oh, in trouble, eh? Well, that's very touching.' Magill bent down and picked up the thing and put it back in Dark's hand and walked off saying, 'Still, maybe it'll teach you to take better care of other people's things.'

Cash came out at the end of school, already in a rage because he had had no signal through the glass door of the classroom. Then Dark gave him back the iPhone and said, 'It's broken. I'm sorry about that.'

That was all.

He knew where Cash would be waiting for him on the way out. To show off to an audience you had to be predictable. There was a thick elder bush that he always hung around so everyone could see him go for a smoke after school. Dark decided to walk out the road. He didn't want them to see him getting in his mammy's car to get away from Cash. And he didn't want her to arrive at the wrong time and see Cash on his case, and then have her getting on his case about what was going on and trying to take it up with the school and such. He didn't get very far, though.

Cash came running behind him and he just turned in time to catch the first dig on the side of his face. He fended off some of the hits and kicks. At least Cash seemed fairly clumsy and none of the blows were very hard. A crowd surrounded them in seconds. One box landed on his ear and it stung. He got mad for a second and kicked out. He made what felt like a very good contact with Cash's thigh.

Cash grimaced and stepped back a bit and then kept his arms sweeping in Dark's general direction until a car slowed down and a man shouted, 'Hey, you lads, go on home, will ye, and don't be acting the maggot on the road.'

'Let that be a lesson to you, Dark,' said Cash. 'You don't screw around with the Cashman.'

When he had gone away, Dark tried to straighten himself out a bit. He looked at his rucksack with its broken strap on the side of the road and all the books scattered everywhere. He left them there and started walking back to the car park entrance-way where his mother would normally collect him from.

Tadhg gathered his few books and copybooks and came running after Dark with the rucksack.

'Here you go, Art, bud. Cash might be ignorant, but he isn't usually such a pig. Don't know what got into him. Are you hurt?'

'No, I'm grand,' said Dark.

That wasn't quite true, but on the other hand, he wasn't too sore. No worse than when he would take a few knocks in a game of hurling, back when he played.

If his mother noticed, she didn't say anything.

When Dark got to the rath that night, he made no mention of any of this. He was tired of talking or thinking about school things and just wanted to be away.

'How does life find you on this very lovely evening?' asked the Old Man.

'Alright,' said Dark.

'I always found it best to approach a very good day with

183

suspicion,' said the Old Man, 'because such days often have an unpleasant surprise or two in store.'

Other than the girl with the goblet, Dark noticed very few little people present tonight. Only Conán, the Old Man and the red-haired lady sat with him at the fire.

'There were two rotten surprises indeed,' the Old Man started, 'two bad eggs that crossed paths one time. In this case, though, one of them turned out to be definitely a fair bit worse than the other. Since Bal is away with most of the little people tonight at a *Bealtaine* festival in the north of the country, I can tell you this one.'

Bad and worse

Balor was a little red-faced lad. A *fear dearg*. He may have got both the name and his bad temper because he had lost the use of one eye in a row with a crow when he was trying to steal her eggs.

He was considered small even by other *púca*s. And that was saying something, because it was widely known that it was the smallest men amongst the little people who were more likely to turn to the mischievous ways of a *púca*. He was also considered unpleasant even by other *púca*s. Not a trivial observation, considering that being troublesome was a matter of boastful honour amongst *púca*s.

Balor was foul-mouthed. He was contrary. He was a bad-tempered prickly fellow who never tried to tame the tides of anger that overcome everyone from time to time. He liked spreading misery. He was inclined to steal. Whenever he visited a house, the family he visited would always be poorer after he left. He'd have taken eggs. Or a freshly-baked cake. Or whatever nice thing the family had been looking forward to. What was worse, they might find the stolen thing thrown in the ditch the next day, for it was known that Balor stole more for annoyance than out of need.

People hated the sight of Balor, though they didn't often see him in person. He was very fond of the form of a slightly fat badger. And it must be said that he certainly didn't do the reputation of that solid, shy family any good at all. It got to the point that whenever people spotted a gentleman of the badger clan wandering around in broad daylight or sniffing about in places they thought no real badger would ever visit, people would say, 'Shut your doors. The little red fairy man who would steal the sugar out of your tea or the white out of your eye is abroad.'

And mischief was indeed his main satisfaction. When he couldn't annoy people by stealing, he would annoy them by playing unsavoury tricks. When he was hanging around at night he might decide, for no good reason, to scare the daylights out of a herd of cows by making a perfect imitation of a warble fly, so that the farmer might only find them days later, still with their tails in the air, many miles away. Or he might spend a whole night tying knots in sheep's wool so that the farm family might have to spend weeks trying to undo the thousands of odd-looking plaits that his nimble little fingers had created on their animals' backs. And of course, as they worked hard trying to undo the damage, they would often hear the wicked chuckle from the bushes and rabbit burrows nearby.

The trick that won him the greatest dislike was when he tampered with a good well, making the water go brown or giving it a smell of rotten flesh. Many's the person who seriously said, 'May the curses of all the gods and all the powers of the otherworld fall heavily upon that mouldy little cur'. But these prayers never seemed to bring Balor a bit of harm.

Nobody was safe. Balor was as likely to annoy the powerful as he was the poor. One morning at a dwelling near Tara where Cormac was staying, there was a howl of disgust from Cormac's breakfast table. Servants came running to see what was wrong. The first of his three eggs had given off a horrendous pong when cracked. Rotten through. Not good, but explainable. Maybe someone had allowed one of the younger children to collect the eggs and they'd found an old nest, as children are good at doing. But then when he opened the second egg and found it empty and the third and found cabbage in it, everyone knew immediately.

'Curses on Balor, that hairy little red rat-dropping, may his blood turn lumpy!' bellowed Cormac. 'If I get my hands on him I'll kick him to the tops of the trees and let him live with the crows.'

At around the time that Balor was at his worst, a stranger arrived in Dunmore. He was a gaunt, crooked man with a very pale complexion and hungry eyes. He introduced himself as Saile. Though nobody knew it, Saile was a wizard with a lot of history behind him, none of it good. In the country he'd come from, he was considered to be of the lowest character. He had heard somewhere that there was a lot of gold in Éire and that it wasn't very closely guarded – it was a substance that never helped the pot to boil and showing it off was considered by many in Éire as a mark of folly. Only the dead wore it.

Saile had seen lands far to the east where gold in any form could buy him the wives, fine clothes and great mansions that he fancied. He had started collecting gold many decades ago. He had long since acquired more than would buy him every mansion in those faraway lands. He was supposed to have stashes of it buried in many remote corners of marshland in faraway countries. But his interest in the mansions and the estates that it could gain him had long been overtaken by his desire to just go on grabbing more gold. Any method for gaining more gold, hard or easy, was of interest to him. Naturally, easy was preferable to him, since it involved less risk of him getting hurt. He had been lying low for several years, hatching his plan for acquiring easy gold in Éire.

In his first months in Dunmore, he pretended to be a simple traveller. He would move from place to place taking meals that were offered generously by the hospitable people of the countryside. He would chat away with families as they sat eating their meals, talking about the weather and the crops. And he would listen to them and their neighbours who might ramble in to them in the evening for a chat. He was thought peculiar because he never smiled. Nevertheless, hospitality would be extended, as was customary, even to the least pleasant visitors. A bed would be made up for him in the straw. Next morning, he would move on without a word of farewell or thanks. Meanwhile, all he was trying to do was to get to know the country and, what was most important, he was trying to find an accomplice. He needed someone as bad and as greedy as himself to help gather the gold and get it quickly away.

One long summer's evening he was standing under a tree with a group of men in Loígis. The men were taking a small drink after a hot day of haymaking. They gladly shared the cake and cider with the traveller. The talk was free and easy. Saile's ears pricked up when talk turned to stories of Balor.

'Oh, that little vagabond!' said one man. 'He whispered some spell in my donkey's ear and from that day onwards, the donkey will only walk backwards.'

'That's nothing,' said another. 'He knows no limits. He has no fear. He stole all the garments and sacred stones belonging to my cousin, Fenagh the Druid. Just for the *craic*.'

Saile entered the conversation, certain he had found his accomplice.

'Ahem, my good gentlemen,' he said, 'this awful little man sounds like someone I should avoid.'

'He certainly is that,' said two of the other men together.

'Well, could you tell me where I can meet him? Eh, I mean tell me where he stays so I can be sure to avoid that place and never be in danger from him.'

'Well, he travels a lot, because he rarely has fewer than a hundred angry people looking for him with the aim of bringing an end to his miserable trade,' said a stout man.

'That may well be,' said the tallest man there. He spoke as someone who liked to be the authority on all things. 'But a little bird, I won't divulge who, told me for a fact that he has a deep cave where he often sleeps. That would be on the dark side of Sliabh na mBan. That would be a place to be avoided for certain.'

Saile drifted away from the company without a word of thanks, as usual, losing interest now that he had all he could get out of them. As soon as he was out of their sight, he picked up great speed. He was excited and couldn't wait to find his partner. He had already decided what portion of the gold to offer the little rascal. And he was already making plans on how he would dispose of Balor once the job was done.

When Saile got to the dark side of Sliabh na mBan he had no idea where to look. But his luck was in. After a few hours of waiting, he heard a low growl, like a bear, but he knew there were none of them in this land. When he went closer, he could hear that it was the voice of a man. And that the sound was a peculiar mixture of grumbling, swearing and giggling. The grumbling was about everything. The sun was too warm – even here in a trench on the north side of the mountain where it never reached. The days were lasting too long. The trees were bigger than they used to be. The rabbits were stupider and there was hardly any fun in catching them. The swearing was about a wide variety of names of big people, little people, animals and plants against whom Balor had some grudge or other. And the giggling was about various bits of mischief he'd done in recent times.

Saile stepped out into the shadows of Balor's fire. Balor turned on him as fast as a cat and before asking any question, landed a huge slimy spit right between Saile's eyes. Saile almost vomited and threw a spell, but he remembered his mission.

'Good day to you, sir', he stammered, with the stuff dribbling down his cheeks.

'Who in the name of the damned and the dead are you, you long streak of misery, and who gave you permission to enter my private mountain?'

Saile sat down without invitation because he knew he would get no invitation. And he started babbling off his plan. He wanted an accomplice to help steal all the gold in the country.

Initially Balor warmed up.

'So, we'd go around at night taking bracelets and neckties off of all the frauds and wasters who think they are special and robbing the ornaments from the tombs of those who were thought to be a cut above buttermilk?'

'Well, yes.'

'And that will cause great and terrible fuss.'

'I'm sure it may do, but we'll be gone by then.'

'And we could just throw the things in hedges and potato pits where they'll eventually find them, but curse us for the deed.'

'Are you mad?' exclaimed Saile. 'Of course not. We'll take them away. All. Every piece of gold in the country.'

'Hold your horses there, grandmother,' said Balor. 'A lot of the gold ornaments are in Tara and protected by the

Fianna. You won't be taking them too easily.'

'Oh, I will.'

'And how?' asked Balor, 'Since the Fianna are not likely to let us walk away with such stuff without making many spear holes in our backsides.'

Then Saile told Balor of his plot. He had a powder that could cause a great flash of light, blinding all people in the area. When facing the Fianna, he would release it and then take their weapons.

Balor was getting quieter now. 'Take their weapons, eh? And what then?'

'Then of course we'd kill them for the sport of it, so that we could come back any time we wanted.'

'There would be no need to do that,' said Balor, surprising himself.

'What need do we need? We'd just be getting rid of do-gooders.'

'Hmmm,' muttered Balor.

'What? Are you getting scared?'

Balor was quiet. He wasn't scared. He had never been scared of anything in his life. It was another feeling that was bothering him. But he couldn't quite say what it was.

'Oh, not scared then, well I know what your problem is. You are worried about your share.'

Balor wasn't the slightest bit worried about his share. He had no interest in taking stuff to keep. What good would that do him? He was as unhappy as could be with his little cave and the clothes on his back. Having more would only give him more causes than he had time in the day to grumble about. He had never before stolen anything to keep for himself. But he said nothing. He just looked at Saile and still said nothing.

'Don't worry, you'll get half of all the gold.'

Balor's little face was getting redder and his frown was growing deeper. Saile lost his patience.

'Well, look here, if you don't do this then all the stories I've heard about you being a villain are just rubbish.'

Balor was confused. He asked Saile to come back in the morning when he'd had a good sleep. When Saile went, he couldn't sleep in his own cave, so he ventured off into the woods. Soon he found a bed of pine needles made by some good little people. He chased them away, as was one of his favourite tricks, by making wolf sounds. He had a little chuckle at his fleeing relatives. That made him feel better. Back to his old self, he settled into the comfortable bed.

But Balor still couldn't sleep. He kept turning and grumbling. He was sweating and feeling slightly ill in his stomach. About two hours before dawn he jumped up and shouted, 'To blazes with it all.'

He mightn't like it to be widely known, but he had never killed anyone. He didn't like Fionn or the Fianna and he could maybe get used to the idea of them being blinded for a while. But he had to admit to himself that he did not like the idea of them being slaughtered. Who would he have left to torment? And besides it all, he simply didn't like Saile.

And so he headed off for Tara as fast as he could run, hop and fly. At the gate he met a sour captain called Cullen.

Cullen, unfortunately, recognised Balor. When Balor pleaded breathlessly and as politely as he could, 'Let me in you thick clump of bog grass, I've an important message for the *amadán* Mac Cumhaill,' Cullen shouted back, 'Hey, aren't you the rogue who put lizards into a hatch of eggs when I was a boy? Yes, yes,' said the soldier very excitedly, 'it's you, you little blackguard! My mother nearly had a heart attack when the eggs hatched and the lizards crawled out.'

As the point of Cullen's spear barely missed him, Balor decided that there was nothing to be gained by being good. It was just tedious. He went back to his forest bed, feeling better that at least he'd tried to warn the louts.

The only problem was that he still couldn't sleep. He tossed even more and moaned and grumbled until he felt a tapping on his shoulder. He turned viciously.

'Hey, let go, let go,' shouted the shadow looming above him.

Reluctantly Balor opened his ferocious little jaws and released the man's long, bony hand from his teeth. Luckily Balor's teeth were blunt from many years of doing one of his favourite tricks – cutting through the ropes that visitors used to tie their boats in harbours in Éire. Still, the old man who stepped into the moonlight looked cranky and kept shaking his badly bruised hand.

He picked Balor up by the hair and held him at arm's length. Balor was kicking the air and screaming curses. The old man eventually started laughing at him.

When Balor finally calmed down, the man, who had a

grey beard that trailed to the ground, said that he had over-heard Balor's grumbles and wanted to help him.

'I'll tell you what you'll do,' said Balor, getting mad again and punching wildly. 'You can go and jump off the top of a cliff. Balor don't need help from an old wreck of a human.'

'Stop, stop, stop your nonsense now,' said the old man. 'There's no time to lose.'

Balor quietened, temporarily. He heard the authority and the hint of danger from the depths of the old man's voice.

'I'm Hanlon, a humble man,' said the old fellow.

Balor's eyes lit up. Everyone in the worlds beyond humans knew Hanlon. Few had ever met him. He was a roaming spirit of the Dé Danann. He was said to be able to appear in many forms but only rarely appeared at all. The woods were his domain and he was usually visible only to the birds.

Balor saw possibilities here. But that didn't stop him being rude.

'Aye, and I'm Balor, who has no time for modesty. I'm the trickiest little fairy man in the land.'

'Is that so?' asked Hanlon.

'Listen, any chance you'd help me with a few things, you being so great at magic and all that?'

'Maybe,' said Hanlon cautiously. 'As long as you coop-erate with me. What do you want to know?'

'How can I make an egg go rotten while it is still inside the hen?'

'Only by killing the hen before she lays and leaving them both to rot.'

'Thanks *very* much,' snarled Balor. 'Don't try too hard to help me, now, in case you injure yourself.'

'Quiet with the smart talk,' commanded Hanlon. 'You've made your decision and if you were truly bad we both know that you'd be in the company of someone else now and not here prattling to me. So tell me the full story of what our friend Saile has planned, so we can save the people of Tara.'

'There's no point,' said Balor, 'they're not worth saving. The blackguards don't want to believe me so they can get along without Balor's help.'

'We'll go together and they'll listen,' said Hanlon.

'First, tell me how I could make a pike bite a lump out of a man's leg when he's standing in the river trying to spear a salmon. How can I make pimples grow bigger on a youngster's face? How would you make a cow mix her piss with her milk just to give a farmer a nice surprise when he goes to milk her? What is the best concoction to make a pompous druid's fart so foul that he clears all living creatures from fifty paces around him?'

Hanlon didn't answer.

As they flitted through the countryside with Balor's head sticking out through Hanlon's beard, Balor filled Hanlon in on all the details he hadn't already overheard.

When they approached the fortress, Balor started kicking up a fuss. He wanted Hanlon to put some tricky curse on Cullen.

'Just make his toes webbed and stick him to the ground, or . . . or make hair sprout out of his eyes, or . . .'

'Quiet,' said Hanlon, pushing Balor back into the beard, and walking straight past the guards and through the closed doors completely unnoticed.

They went straight to Dreoilín's quarters. Dreoilín awoke and looked around, at first seeing no-one. Then he saw. Balor dropped quietly to the floor and watched. Dreoilín was thrilled by the presence of the ancestral spirit.

Hanlon introduced Balor and told Dreoilín that, despite what everyone thought of him, he was a good little rogue. Balor expected Dreoilín to set Hanlon straight. After all, there were many times when Balor had tormented the life out of Dreoilín, stealing his potions and tying his long hair to his bed head.

But Dreoilín just looked down and said, 'I suppose we all know that. That's why I didn't turn you into a bar of soap the last time you put itchy dandelion powder into my sandals.'

Balor was somewhat upset at his loss of bad reputation. But right now, he wanted to get the business of Saile off his mind. Hanlon, who would not meet any humans, asked Dreoilín to take Balor to Mac Cumhaill with the story.

Dreoilín left Balor with Mac Cumhaill, telling him everything he knew about Saile's movements and what his intentions were. In the meantime, Dreoilín went back to his rooms to work with Hanlon on something that would protect people from Saile's blinding flashes.

By morning, Mac Cumhaill had a group of men ready

and Dreoilín had a protective ointment prepared. Hanlon had disappeared back to the woods, his work done. Mac Cumhaill wanted to march straight into Saile's hideout and to take him back to Tara for the king to decide his fate.

But the rogue in Balor was still alive and well, and he wanted it done differently. Since he'd done such good work, Mac Cumhaill decided to let him have some entertainment.

Mac Cumhaill and Balor went to Saile's house.

Balor shouted, 'Saile, my old friend, come out and see what I've brought you.'

Saile was cautious – that was how he had got to be such an old wizard. There was no answer.

Balor shouted again, 'Saile, I've brought you a gift.'

Still no answer, but Mac Cumhaill spotted a shadowy movement behind a hole in the wall of the hovel.

Then came Saile's sickly voice, 'Balor, little . . . em . . . friend, I thought you were lost. What exactly have you brought me and who is your giant, oafish friend?'

'Oh, he's just a fellow I thought you might like to try your special charms on.'

'Aha!' said Saile, throwing the ash plank back from the doorway. 'Excellent thinking, my little dwarfish brother, excellent.'

Saile walked to within two paces of Mac Cumhaill and then pulled his hand from his pocket, and released something into the air. A flash of white light seemed to fill the whole space around them, just as Balor had said.

'Oh, no,' whimpered Mac Cumhaill, with his arms outstretched. 'What has happened?'

Saile cackled. 'Now,' he said, walking right up to Mac Cumhaill, 'let me see what this big galoot can do without his sight.'

He started poking his stick at Mac Cumhaill. Fionn danced this way and that, trying to get away from his tormentor and tripping over stones and bushes as he did. Balor joined in, of course, unable to let such a good opportunity to annoy Mac Cumhaill pass him by. He kicked Mac Cumhaill very hard in the shins. He threw stones at him. He scrawbed him with a briar and rubbed nettles on him, laughing like a lunatic all the time.

Eventually, the cautious and cowardly Saile was convinced that the big man was helpless, and he came right up. He grabbed hold of Mac Cumhaill's spear saying, 'I'll have that if you please'.

'Let me advise you friend,' Mac Cumhaill said, the play-acting gone from his voice, 'it will be a matter of great regret if that spear parts company with me.'

'Oh, you'll have it back in a minute,' laughed Saile, as he gave a big tug which he assumed would remove the weapon from the blind man, 'but it will be in your heart and not in your hand.'

'That spear was my father's and it is loyal,' said Mac Cumhaill more quietly.

'Let go, let go, you fool,' said Saile. 'Here Balor, throw more rocks at him or something to make him let go. He's starting to stare at me as if he can see, and it's starting to scare me.'

Balor was an expert rock thrower. He picked a nice-sized one, took aim and hit Saile very hard in his flabby belly. Saile bent over crying out, 'FOOL! Fool! I might as well kill you now rather than later, as you're no use to me.'

Saile made one last grab for Mac Cumhaill's spear, this time intent on impaling the bad *púca* on it. But as he did so, he finally realised that Mac Cumhaill was indeed staring straight at him. What was worse, he had the same big grin on his face as the *púca* had. By the time Saile had realised he had been outsmarted by the *púca*, Mac Cumhaill had already introduced himself.

Saile was put in a large cabbage bag and transported to Tara. The fact that he had shown his intention to kill both Mac Cumhaill and Balor in front of the several witnesses who sat in the bushes absorbing the entertainment did not go well for him. The *brehon*s presiding had no doubt at all that he was a truly bad fellow, and he was condemned to working for life as a slave to a friendly dragon who lived in a remote cave in Alban.

Balor's heart gave a little twinge of jealousy when he heard the king pronounce that Saile was the worst blackguard of a man he'd come across in a long time. But he also enjoyed the party that Mac Cumhaill and the king threw for him at Tara. He became very friendly with Conán, and spent the entire evening sitting on an arm of the king's throne, with Conán on the other side, encouraging him and breaking up with mad laughter as the *fear dearg* passed rude comments about the king and all of his guests. Whenever the king got tired of mischief and practical jokes in the castle, he would send Balor away on holidays to visit the castles of royals whom Cormac considered boring. Balor would usually arrive back refreshed, with a message sincerely and regretfully breaking the news to Cormac that the little gentleman musician whom Cormac had lent them had not quite behaved himself in an exemplary fashion while he was abroad. The king could recount nearly all of these messages, word for word, as they amused him greatly.

As he left the rath, lonely again, Dark was thinking he should have made some effort to defend himself against Cash. He should have felt angrier. He was starting to feel angry now – for all the good that was – with himself, mostly. Just because someone else was having a bad day, why did he always just suck it up?

He remained cross as he fed the calves, not even talking to any of them as they pucked the buckets and looked up at him, expecting more.

8
MINDING NIAMH

As usual, Dark was in the schoolyard before most of the others, as his mother had to get to work early. So was David Cash, as usual, even though he walked to school.

For a while, Cash stayed at the other side of the yard, kicking a Coke can against the wall to keep his feet warm. But then he wandered over when he thought no one else was looking and sort of slapped Dark on the back and said, 'Sorry, Art. Sorry about that yesterday. Are you alright?'

'The finest,' said Dark.

'I'll make it up to you,' said Cash earnestly.

'No need,' said Dark.

'I will. If you ever want a pup, just tell me. It's just I was scared about the phone. It wasn't really my phone. It's the uncle's. I don't have a phone at all.'

'By the way, it was Magill broke it,' said Dark.

'Oh, Jaysus, so that only makes it all the worse what I done to you. Oh, man. Maybe Magill is right about me.

Maybe I am just as thick as horse shite and I probably am going to end up in jail.'

'Don't listen to anything Magill says to you. He knows nothing about anything.' Dark was surprised at himself saying so much.

'Do you reckon?' said Cash, staring intensely at him, trying to figure out whether Dark was making fun of him.

'What kind of pups have you got, anyway?' said Dark, trying to take the uncomfortable seriousness out of the conversation. He didn't like serious conversations.

Cash brightened up, 'All sorts. Brindles and blacks and little terriers. All classes. The loveliest pups you ever seen. And all out of great rabbiters. Come back with me some day after school and I'll show you.'

'I will,' said Dark.

Cash started to wander off again, and as he got a distance away, he turned and shouted in his usual voice, 'By the way Dark, you nearly broke me leg with that kick, ya crafty hure.'

In maths class, things were back to normal. Miss Sullivan got in a rage with Dark over nothing much and sent him out to his usual place. Out in the corridor, Dark gave a lot of thought to how well a little greyhound might settle in at home with Georgina and Psycho, the two old collies.

As the break approached, the thought struck him that he would be better off talking to the dogs themselves. And he'd better talk to Niamh too.

He slipped into the classroom once Sullivan had

headed for the staffroom. He picked up his bag and went out. He went to the back of the school, as the staffroom window looked out on the front gates. As he headed quickly to the hedge at the back, Ciara spotted him and said, 'Hey Arthur'.

He stopped and feebly said, 'Hi'.

Then he kept going. As he pushed his way to make a gap in the bushes, which he was fairly expert at by now, he heard some of the sixth-year lads who were smoking at the back of the oil tank shouting, 'Hey look at McLean go!' and 'Good man, Dark!'

Cheering struck up, sure to draw the attention of old Úna who was on yard duty. It didn't matter. He was out of there very fast and made his way quickly across the fields, over two further ditches and a six-foot-high stone wall. Within three minutes he was in the clear, back out on the road to the Brown River, a half a mile outside the town.

He had the telescopic rod with him this time, but he didn't get a nibble. It was too sunny. He headed on home.

When he got there, he went straight into the house to see the collies and get some crisps to add to his sandwich. When he had eaten, he put on his wellies to go out and bring some meal to Niamh in the back garden.

Niamh had been Connie's favourite cow. She had a lot of grey in her coat – apparently she had some of an old shorthorn strain in her – and the kindest, gentlest eyes Dark had ever seen in any creature, human or otherwise. But she hadn't gone in calf this year. Brian said that in tight times like these no farmer could carry a dry cow for a year.

But Dark had eventually persuaded his mam that it would-n't cost anything if she let him keep Niamh. He had fenced off the back orchard which had been overgrown for years. He didn't intend to let anyone remove Niamh from there until Connie came back to see to her.

As he was about to go out, he heard a noise in the yard. Like someone banging closed the steel door of the tractor shed or hitting an oil drum. The collies started barking and wanting to get out. Dark moved the net curtains on the kitchen window and looked out across the yard. He could see nobody. Maybe he'd imagined it.

Then, just as he opened the house door, he heard a car door shutting. Whoever was there must have seen him.

A pick-up truck pulled out of the yard. He only saw the departing tail at the far end of the yard and he couldn't see the number but was pretty sure of the colour and make.

He went out into the yard to see what had been taken. The old stone quern and trough were still out at the barn door. He went to the milking parlour and everything seemed in order. He went to the tractor shed. The door was not closed properly. Things had been tossed about in-side there. But strangely, the welder, the angle grinder, the spanners and everything else seemed to be in there still. Dark was very puzzled.

There was only one person who had that kind of truck around here. But why would Trevor Saltee have been in the yard? Looking for what? And why would he sneak off when he saw Dark come in?

Within an hour, his suspicions were confirmed. He got a text from his mother. 'Art? Where are you?'

Dark didn't reply. His phone was not supposed to be switched on at school, so she'd understand.

But she sent another a few minutes later, 'Arthur, you can reply to me. I know you're not at school.'

Dark replied. 'Felt v sick so came home. Ddnt want to trble u.'

'OK, love. Wrap up warm and I'll see you later. Who would have sent me an anonymous text about you, by the way?'

'Dunno,' replied Dark.

That was it.

He could not begin to figure out what Saltee was searching for. He went out to the tractor shed and looked again amongst the oil cans. The crate for scrap steel was half empty, and the rest of the contents were scattered on the floor.

When Brian came to do the milking, Dark had the cows in for him as usual. He asked Brian, 'Is there anything you can think of that Trevor Saltee might want around here?'

Brian was quiet for a minute. 'You should have no dealings with that man, Arthur,' he said, 'I don't like to put in a bad word. But you should know. When that fella came to the area twenty years ago and bought Brown Hill farm, no one knew where he came from or where he got his money from.'

'What would he want, though?'

'Everything that he thinks he can get; the land and

everything else, I'd say. I notice he's gone very friendly with your mother. I'm sorry to say this to you Arthur, but she's too nice a person to be up to dealing with the likes of him. She sees only good in everyone and there's none that I know of in Saltee.'

Dark already knew that Brian wasn't fond of Saltee, to put it mildly. It wasn't the first dire warning he had issued about Saltee wanting to take the land while Connie was away. Dark didn't see how that could happen, so he didn't get too alarmed by Brian's forebodings.

He stuck to his point: 'But if he was after the land, why would he be rooting around in the tractor shed?'

'Why, indeed,' said Brian, almost to himself. 'You might very well ask. And why would a man want your hundred acres when he's already got three hundred of his own and a serious aversion to work? But the answer is, Arthur, that some people always want more of what-ever is going. That's the beginning and end of Trevor Saltee. There's nothing more to him. If you could remove the craving to have more than his share, Saltee would no longer exist.'

Later, Dark thought maybe he should write to Connie and tell him that Saltee was nosing around, since his mother didn't want him visiting jail. But Dark wasn't much for writing and Connie probably wouldn't want to be bothered with letters when he might have bigger worries. Dark had really only seen jail on TV. He wondered if Connie was in a prison gang. He didn't think he'd be obedient enough for that. Or if the warders were every day trying to hammer manners into him with truncheons. That wouldn't work well either.

That night, Dark had to get his mother to call the vet. One of the first-time calvers got into trouble. He and his mother were out holding torches and fetching buckets of warm water until near midnight as grumpy old Ned Kelly cut her open, took out the big bull calf, and stitched her up again. It wasn't the first time, but his mother hated it more every time. She was squeamish. The reason she was a vegetarian was that she couldn't even think about blood and here she was having to deal with this. Dark kept telling her to leave it to him. But she didn't want to do that either, as that made her feel guilty that he was carrying too much.

After he got washed, Dark was pleased to be going to the rath.

The Old Man didn't get up from the fire to ask him about his day. He just said to him, '*A mhic,* maybe you should take that pup.'

It looked like they'd been waiting a while, as the little red-mopped lad was hopping mad and cursing at Conán for sitting in the least draughty spot.

The cup was brought for Dark and for the first time Etain spoke, 'Your health, Arthur'.

Her voice surprised him. It wasn't small. It was warm and familiar. He nodded his thanks and drank.

The Old Man poked the fire with a very beautiful sword that Dark had never seen him with before. Then he started talking.

Prize Daughters

Bressal, the king of Laigin, was a weak and useless man. But he did not know that. He believed himself appointed by gods and privately thought it was a great injustice that he wasn't king of all Ireland, of all the world in fact. He survived only because Cormac, the high king of Éirinn, was in Tara, which was near enough to Bressal's place in Dún Ailinne. And Cormac was a great believer in avoiding hassle. So, to prevent an outright uprising in Leigheann, he quietly managed most of the affairs of that province without Bressal knowing anything about it.

Bressal had once been on a boat trip to visit many lands to the southeast, and from the day he came back he was never done tormenting everyone in Laigin. He had his fort done up in colours so bright that even the crows were terrified to come near. He would tell those subjects who had to toil hard every day just for survival that they were a very uncouth people; that if they were better farmers they'd be able to grow grapes and dates for his household – like the Gauls did. He also demanded that all chiefs in his area keep wine in their homes and change to wheaten bread. Some chiefs complained that Éirinn's weather didn't ripen wheat well and that traders looked for too much good wool and leather in return for small flasks of wine. Most didn't even bother to argue. They just kept small quantities of wine and wheaten flour available for the rare event that Bressal actually visited them.

Bressal's worst excesses were with his own daughters. He had heard somewhere of a king in Cornobha setting up sporting events with his daughter's 'hand in marriage' as one of the prizes. Bressal thought that if this was what kings abroad were doing, then surely kings in Éire should get with the times. He had three daughters, whom he didn't love greatly, because he was so fond of himself that he had very little love left over.

On the evening that this idea struck him (Bressal never arose from bed before mid-afternoon), he sent his lackey, Fergal, to call the girls to the great hall.

They arrived in the hall and waited several hours for their father to get there. Bressal always made people wait for him, even if it meant sitting outside the door, as he believed that nobody of any importance ever arrived on time. His daughters were cross, but also curious, as the only times their father had ever spoken directly to them had been to shout at them.

When he burst through the doors, he waited for his daughters to bow before he spoke. He looked them over for a while and then turned to Fergal, saying, 'Do you think they'll do?'

'Oh', said Fergal, grinning and rubbing his little twisted hands together, 'I'd say they'll do very nicely.'

'Do for what?' snapped Deirdre, the youngest and hottest-tempered of the three. Her face reddened.

'Don't you speak to the king in that tone, young one,' whined Fergal, shaking his finger at Deirdre.

'Don't point at her,' said the quiet and very serious middle sister, Anúna. Fergal was scared of Anúna. He knew her reputation. She may have been quiet, but when she was angered she was fearless and ferocious. Fergal had no intention of inviting a shower of her infamous kicks and he stepped back to the other side of the king.

'What do you mean, Father?' said Niamh, the oldest daughter and the only one who was always respectful to her father, no matter how badly he behaved.

He didn't even bother to respond. He continued talking to his weasel servant as though the women were not in the room.

'So, do you think we'll get princes and gentry coming to the competition?'

'Oh, yes,' grinned Fergal again, looking Deirdre up and down. 'Sure, I might even take part myself.'

Without saying anything further, the king and Fergal swept out of the hall, leaving the daughters very confused and worried.

They didn't have long to wait before finding out exactly what was going on.

The king was so excited by his idea that he talked about it to a visiting chief that very evening. He had declared that he'd have three competitions – sword-fighting, spear-throwing and wrestling. King Bressal was drunk and boastful.

'It will be an event to show everyone in Éire that I am a king of international standing.'

'Grand news, indeed,' said the chief.

'We'll have a high class of foreign princes and great noblemen in the competition, as happens in more civilised countries.'

'That should be very exciting for us all, I'm sure,' responded the chief politely.

'And glory be to the name of Bressal, the winner of each competition shall walk off with a daughter to marry and produce his children!' shouted the king.

The chief was so shocked that he didn't know what to say. He certainly couldn't have told Bressal what he really thought for fear of losing his lands and having his family left with nothing. But he told two of the servants and asked them to warn the women and to tell them that they should flee, as it sounded as if Bressal was quite serious.

When the girls heard, they were very upset. But they didn't doubt the Chief's account. Deirdre and Anúna were certain that the only way to avoid a terrible fate was to leave the castle the very next morning. They were adventurous people and had made lots of friends in houses great and small around Laigin. They had learned over time that all their father's stories about his glory and popularity were false. As people came to trust them it became clear to them that few people thought better of their father than the girls did themselves. Many could see what a vain and stupid man he was. So the younger women knew they had many houses where they could hide safely without fear of anyone telling their father where they were. The eldest daughter, Niamh, was a different matter.

She was such a simple and kind-hearted person that she was unable to see anything other than good intentions in any person, even her father. Even though she was now thirty-three years old, she had never ventured beyond the castle walls to mix with other people. Not because she hadn't wanted to, but because she didn't think it would be right to break her father's strict rules. She couldn't bear to hear him shouting angrily at her and threatening to hit her. She decided, despite her sisters' pleadings, that she would not run away. She really believed that her father would calm down and realise how such rash plans would hurt them.

The next morning, the younger women again tried their best to persuade Niamh to come with them to safety, but to no avail. The parting was the saddest moment in all of their lives since the death of their beloved mother when they were young girls.

When he found out what had happened, the king took his anger out on Niamh and locked her in a hole in the ground. He decided to go ahead with the competitions but for just one prize. He couldn't be rid of her soon enough, he said.

And sure enough, within days, word was put out that Niamh, first daughter of Bressal, King of Laigin, was to be the grand prize in a sporting and fighting competition to be held in Athy. Niamh was ill with fear and desolation. Word traveled abroad and soon chancers and scoundrels of every sort were arriving. They had all heard of fairy tales and were claiming to be Prince This and Sir That. Most of them were wearing ridiculously-coloured regalia and armour that was too heavy for them: most unsuited for the muddy roadways and forest paths of Éirinn.

The actual competitions were not even worth reporting. Fergal was the main organiser and he understood nothing about sports or contests. But he knew that Bressal wouldn't care as long as there was a big platform for him to sit on, lots of banners bearing the coat of arms he had made up for himself and a pompous ceremony for him to preside over.

The sword, spear and wrestling competitions were performed in a muddy field away from the main platform. For those interested in such events, they were a great disappointment. None of Éirinn's best warriors took part. They knew that Mac Cumhaill would not have approved. Mac Cumhaill himself was across the seas to the north at the time, helping a friend to deal with a troublesome serpent.

The competitions were squalid and chaotic, with all three contests eventually rolling into one big brawl. The various princes and noblemen ended up wrestling around in the muck, like the low-minded curs they really were, kicking and biting each other in their greed to abduct a woman whose name they couldn't even pronounce.

After about an hour, there was only one man standing up; though he was so short it was hard to tell that he was on his feet. Nobody knew much about this man. He had only appeared in town the day before the contest. Though some of the princes and noblemen had taken to mocking him, he had not risen to the provocation and had spoken to nobody. He had no sword, no spear and no armour other than the thick black hair that surrounded his arms and chest. He had been a very aggressive fighter. When the brawl had descended, he had worked his way through every part of it, delivering sturdy blows of a thick black stick to any of the participants who didn't run away from him.

'Any man here who believes that he is the winner, stand up now and talk to me,' came a deep, slow voice from the hairy runt. Large, wild eyes looked out from his head. There was absolute silence for a while, as most of the great 'noblemen' on the ground decided that playing dead was their best option.

Eventually, one man fumbled to his feet. This tall, blond fellow had been prancing around Athy in the weeks before the contest, proclaiming himself the prince of Lithuania and the certain winner of the princess's hand in marriage.

'Ahem, my good little chap,' said the 'prince', trying to drum up his most haughty voice, 'I believe that I should point out that this is a competition for men of honour and high station. Not for midget farm hands or stable boys or whatever it is you do. I'll give you a couple of gold coins here if you'll be so good as to take yourself off to tend to my horses.'

The short barrel-man barely moved a muscle. He raised his stick, maybe just a fraction, and perhaps there was a slight movement that looked as if he was considering taking a step in the arrogant man's direction. But the wildness in the little man's eyes was probably enough. The Lithuanian prince's courage deserted him and he dropped his elegant sword and ran like the wind in an easterly direction away from Athy.

Nobody else had anything to say.

Neither Fergal nor Bressal was at all happy about the

214

outcome. They had hoped they'd be shipping Niamh off to one of the grand houses of Europe, providing the king with an excuse to go there on regular trips on the pretence of visiting his dear daughter. However, none of their guards were up to a contest with the barrel-man. And both of them were quite scared by the very look of him. In the end, Bressal decided that the best thing to do was to get the whole thing over as quickly as possible so they could get the dangerous little man away from there.

When the little man was brought around to the victory stadium, a sigh of horror went around the crowd. Niamh herself was quiet. She had done her crying. To her, it didn't matter what the winner looked like. Anyone who was prepared to take her away without knowing her or caring what she thought about him was just as horrible whether he was a prince in fine clothes or a beggar in rags.

Bressal called the little man up onto the platform. He asked him what his name was.

'Barli,' grunted the man, without bowing or doing any of the usual things that he had been told Bressal expected of visitors. He clearly didn't like the king any more than he seemed to like anyone else around the place.

The king laughed politely, trying to gloss over the little man's roughness.

He asked, 'Ahem, and what kingdom will my daughter be marrying into, Mr Barli?'

'Kingdom my backside,' growled Barli. 'Can we finish this? I need to head off before nightfall.'

A murmur of laughter went around the crowd.

The king fumbled angrily. He pulled Niamh by the hand, and said, 'Here! At least it's one less mouth to feed. Begone with both of you and if I don't ever see either of you again it won't trouble me a bit.'

There were many tears from the servants and castle guards as their beloved Niamh was put on the back of the great black horse, behind Barli.

Barli turned to make sure that Niamh was safely on board. He made her put her hands around him so she wouldn't fall off. He was seen to pat her hand and some noticed that he didn't do so roughly. And then the horse took them off faster than any steed the people there had ever seen so that in minutes they were gone from view and onlookers differed as to which direction they had taken.

A great pall of shame fell over the castle. In the following days, many of the servants and guards started leaving. Of all the horrible ways that Bressal had behaved in the past, for most people this was the worst thing that had ever happened in the Athy castle. Neither Bressal nor Fergal saw anything wrong with the whole thing. But Fergal was smarter than Bressal and he soon realised that they had underestimated the anger of people.

When he heard that the two younger sisters had ridden with friends to Tara to demand action from the high king, Fergal realised that the whole episode mightn't turn out well for Bressal. He too packed his bags and sneaked out of the castle one afternoon while Bressal was still sleeping, leaving only Bressal and a couple of his toady nephews in Athy.

When Cormac, the high king, heard the full story from Deirdre and Anúna he was incensed. He felt guilty for not having found out more about the big event that Bressal had been organising. He felt very bad for not having put a stop to Bressal's bad behaviour long ago. He sent for Mac Cumhaill, who returned from serpent-hunting a day later to hear the whole sorry tale.

In the meantime, Fergal arrived at Tara, claiming to be enraged about what had happened to poor Niamh and asking to be made a humble servant of Cormac. Fortunately, the sisters had already told Cormac all about Fergal's part in the competitions and in Bressal's other mischief. And unfortunately for Fergal, Cormac was not as easily flattered by the slippery Fergal as Bressal had been.

'Oh, I've made my mistakes in working for such a weak king as Bressal, Your Highness,' he said insinuatingly, 'but believe me, all I've wanted all my life is to serve you.'

'Is that right?' said Cormac.

'Oh, yes, all my life, I say. I've waited for a chance to serve the greatest king on earth. The greatest king in the universe, O Cormac.'

He bowed low.

'If I was the greatest king, I would never have allowed Bressal to inflict such cruelty on his daughters.'

'Oh, but how could you have known, O Great One? You have such weighty matters on your mind.'

'Get up, you git,' said Cormac, bored now. 'Your first task is to tell Fionn all you know about Barli.'

'Oh, willingly, willingly, Sire,' said Fergal, red with embarrassment as everyone laughed at him getting up from his knees.

'And then,' said Cormac, 'since you say that all your life you've wished to serve me, I'll grant your wish. For all the rest of your life you will serve. Get to the outer enclosure and serve my daughter's donkey and make it your concern every time he fancies some food, has a sniffle or feels an uneasy temper, just as you did for so long with Bressal.'

The information that Mac Cumhaill got from Fergal was of little use. In fact, he got little useful information from anyone. All he seemed to have was a description, a name and excited tales of a very fleet horse.

At the back of his mind, the name and description troubled Mac Cumhaill. He felt that somehow he should know who this Barli was.

Mac Cumhaill asked Dreoilín for help.

'Sorry Fionn,' the old man said. 'If you needed me to put a spell on a known person or to give you special powers against him, I might be able to help. But if we don't know what part of the country or the world he comes from or went to, it is very difficult for me to do anything useful.'

Mac Cumhaill tried to use his thumb of knowledge for some inspiration as to where to start looking, but not a single idea came into his head. This made his men very worried because often when the thumb was most lacking in inspiration, there were other magical forces at work.

Mac Cumhaill had his men moving out from Athy, stopping at every village in every direction, asking people whether the huge, black steed had passed through. Mac

Cumhaill reckoned he would have had to stop somewhere to tend his horse, and even if people hadn't seen him stopping, then surely somebody somewhere must have seen him passing through.

But even though everyone wanted to help, there was not a single person with anything to tell. The days were passing since Niamh had disappeared with the barrel-man and people were starting to despair for her ever returning safely.

Mac Cumhaill himself had taken a path in a north-westerly direction, and within the day he had gone as far as he could go, reaching the wild ocean at the northwest coast of Baile Lugda. He was feeling tired and confused. He decided to spend the night with his acquaintance, Luan, the high king of the little people, whose castle was under a big rath in Baile Lugda.

That evening, he told Luan of his desperate quest. Luan was very sympathetic.

'What kind of king or man could give away his daughter like that?' he said, shaking his bald little head.

'The funny thing,' confided Mac Cumhaill, 'is that ever since I first heard the description and name of the man I'm looking for, I've had a funny feeling that I should know him.'

'What was his name and appearance?' asked Luan.

When Mac Cumhaill again repeated the little bit of information about Barli that he had already told in surely a thousand places already, Luan raised his right eyebrow. Mac Cumhaill was about to get angry as he was almost sure he saw the corner of a grin fleet across Luan's lips.

'What do you know?' he demanded, standing up too suddenly and banging his head on the ceiling.

'Well, I have a feeling that you might be right – that you should know this Barli fellow very well.'

Mac Cumhaill sat back down.

'Do you remember the time of that terrible war between your big people and ourselves?'

'Yes.'

'Do you remember the most ferocious warrior from our side? The one you spent more time fighting than any other?'

'Marla Barla!' exclaimed Mac Cumhaill, thinking back on the terrible days when good men on both sides had battled each other over hills and marshland in the most futile war ever fought. 'But …'

Before he talked further, he remembered the little people's great warrior. He had been very slender – not at all built like the descriptions of the sturdy Barli. Of course many years had passed. And the accounts of Barli's black eyes certainly rang true. And the great, black steed that had disappeared so cleanly into the landscape certainly had the sound of little people's transport about it. But the deciding factor for Mac Cumhaill was when he remembered the tactics used by the burly man in Athy. Fighting some of the most dislikeable characters on earth, this little warrior had shown great mercy. Mac Cumhaill realised that the reason the mystery fighter had used only a thorn stick was that he had seen the competitors were no match for him with the sword and he hadn't wanted to kill any of them – only to scare them away. Such an act had all the marks of the valiant Marla Barla.

Mac Cumhaill felt some relief as he allowed the thought to creep into his heart that no harm would have come to Niamh. He asked Luan if he would be so good as to take him to Marla Barla's residence that very night.

When they got to the small rath near Lough Neigh where Marla now lived with a small group of his friends and family, there was a welcoming glow under the black-thorn hedge to the front of the fort. The guards ushered Luan and Mac Cumhaill straight through. Inside, a great party was going on. Mac Cumhaill's heart sank. He assumed he was too late and that young Niamh had been forced into marriage.

But soon a very familiar figure ambled over to them. Next to the king and the other little people, Marla looked very large. He was indeed built like a barrel of muscle. He bowed to his king and then came over to Mac Cumhaill. A great, beaming smile covered his face.

'It's been a long time, brother,' he said to Mac Cumhaill, 'but I guessed I'd be seeing you pretty soon.'

'Hello Marla,' said Mac Cumhaill. 'I'm afraid I'm here on serious business.'

'You're looking for a missing princess?'

'Yes.'

'Don't look so worried – you won't have to fight me over this,' laughed Marla. 'She's over there.'

Marla was pointing to a high-ceilinged corner of the fort where there was much dancing and merry-making.

There, sure enough, was a woman much too tall for the company. But other than that, she was laughing and chatting like everyone else. She had seen Mac Cumhaill now and started moving towards him, but in no hurry.

Marla Barla explained what had happened. He had been in the area of mid-Laigin, looking for a good otter to use as a guard on his fort. He heard the story about the big people's king in that area, holding a competition with his own daughter as the prize. He was such a big fairy that he had the advantage of being able to pass as a very short human, so without saying who he was he had moved amongst the people of Athy, making more enquiries. When he had asked why Fionn Mac Cumhaill was allowing such a thing to happen, he had learned that Mac Cumhaill was out of the country. So he had decided to do Mac Cumhaill a favour. He had entered the competition himself and when he had won it, he had taken Niamh away to safety.

'You could have done me a bigger favour by letting me know that you'd taken her,' said Mac Cumhaill, pretending to be angry.

'Ah, well, I couldn't make it too easy for you,' laughed Marla Barla. 'But you figured it out – eventually!'

After they had established that Niamh was in no rush to get home, Luan sent a messenger to Tara to tell her sisters that she was safe, and then Mac Cumhaill and Luan settled down to enjoy the festivities and the hospitality of Marla Barla's fort. There were many tall tales, riddles, jokes and tricks that were shared in Barla's fort that evening.

The next day, when Mac Cumhaill was leaving, Niamh came to him very apologetically saying, 'Fionn, I hope people won't be too offended…I mean, do you think people would mind if I stayed here a while longer? I'm sorry you've had a wasted journey.'

'Don't you worry, *alanna mo chroí*,' said Fionn. 'I always found that anyone who has time to set themselves up in judgement of other people's private business is not a person whose opinion I would care about in the first place. The good people of Laigin, not least your sisters, will be happy with the report I bring them. Besides, I would stay here myself if I could.'

Within a month, a message was sent to her sisters. By that time they were ruling Laigin from the castle in Athy. Their father had disappeared and nothing was ever heard of him afterwards. The message was a wedding invitation.

Marla Barla and Niamh married in what was the most interesting and unusual wedding ceremony in the history of Éirinn, with little people and big people celebrating together and arguing about where the couple would live and what gifts their children would have. They were the happiest couple in the whole of history and they lived very long lives with each other. When their many children grew up, some of them chose the fairy way and others went to live with big people.

When the story, the fire and all the company evaporated, cold rain was dripping through the oak tree under which

Dark was sitting. It looked like it had been falling for a while. His parka and pants were already wet through.

When he got outside the rath, it was spilling and he was starting to cough and splutter by the time he climbed into his bedroom.

9
SAVING THE WREN

He was still coughing at school time. It was only a tickle, but his mother said, 'Art, I'm just sorry that you had to be out with the vet last night. You're working too hard. This can't go on.'

Dark said, 'Don't worry, Mam. It's nothing. Nothing to do with being out with the heifer.'

When it came to homework-checking time that morning, Sullivan didn't even ask him. She just opened the door and he went out.

He wasn't long in the corridor when he saw the familiar wren land in a bush opposite him. The wren was so busy looking in the window and trying not to be noticed that it didn't spot a magpie approaching it, hopping down from branch to branch in the ash tree above it, turning its head from side to side so as to look at the wren with one eye and then the other. Dark spotted the magpie's plan when it was almost too late. No time to go to the door to shout the magpie away. And the windows were double-glazed so the wren couldn't hear him clapping.

The only thing to hand was the fire extinguisher, lying in the corner. He jabbed the window with it, base first to be sure the glass would give. He hadn't known that double-glazing broke with such a bang. It was certainly enough to alarm the wren and frighten the magpie away. It was also enough to bring the teachers out of every classroom off the corridor.

'What in heaven's name is going on, young Arthur McLean?' said old Mrs Moriarty, the Gaeilge teacher. Everyone called her Auntie Úna and said she was a little bit cracked. She had been there as long as anyone could re-member and had taught all the parents and Jim the care-taker and she was old even then. 'Are you hurt, love? Is someone after firing a shot at you through the window? A plague on their souls!'

'Not at all,' said Dark.

'Oh, dear. Well, whatever happened, it must have put the heart sideways in you. Don't you worry about it now,' said Mrs Moriarty, looking up at him kindly.

'What, then?' said Sullivan, shoving in front of Auntie Úna. 'What on earth are you after doing *now?*'

'The young man just slipped and had an accident, can't you see that?' said Mrs Moriarty sharply to Sullivan. 'Great God almighty, anyone with an eye in their head can see that. If you didn't have him shut out in the corridor every bloody day, it mightn't have happened.'

'Excuse me, Úna,' interrupted Magill, just now arriving

on the scene, 'I think you are wanted back in your own classroom. Miss Sullivan and I will deal with this.'

'So, what are we after going and doing now? Hmmm?' said Magill, turning to Dark.

'I just did it for the wren,' Dark said.

Magill paused for a minute and then he said, 'Ah, I get it. That's supposed to be funny. He's making a little joke of us, Miss Sullivan; he is telling us he did it for the lark. Right?'

The whole class had come out for a look. Even Ciara.

'No, sir,' said Dark, flustered, 'I didn't mean to joke. I mean…I didn't mean that.'

'See, I knew there was a little skanger hiding in there,' said Sullivan, 'pretending like butter wouldn't melt in his mouth, and the minute your eye is off him he is vandalising the place.'

The strange thing was, as the principal and Sullivan were ranting away, and as Dark stopped listening to them, the magpie came back. Dark was sure that it too was now looking at the carry-on inside and for a second he thought he saw the magpie's head take the shape of a scrunched-up man's head. And that face was laughing at his difficulties. There was no doubt about that.

The principal complained loudly: 'I can never get through to that mother of yours on the phone. She will have to learn that it is not wise to ignore me. You phone her and tell her what you've done now and that if she could be bothered to come down to see me, I'll be in my office waiting for her.'

227

Dark took out his phone.

'Either way,' Magill said, 'I am calling the police.'

Even Miss Sullivan seemed surprised at this, but she sauntered back to her classroom.

Dark knew his mother would get in a panic straight away if he called her – for a long while now all unexpected calls had that effect on her. But since the principal was going to call the police either way, Dark didn't see the point of bringing his mother into it. So he pretended to phone her.

The moment of chaos seemed to have passed. Everyone except Dark went back to their classrooms. It was quite cold standing in the corridor then.

Dark went out to bring the fire extinguisher back inside. Only as he opened the door did the magpie lose interest and leave his perch on the ash, cackling as he flapped away to do some other mischief.

Just after lunch, there was a big 'whooo' sound from people staring out of windows across the school. Magill had been as good as his word. A squad car had arrived and a *garda* strolled into the schoolyard. Even though he was hatless and not too serious-looking, Dark, watching now from the window of Mrs Moriarty's class, was suddenly frightened. He had never thought he could get arrested or anything like that.

Magill came into class and called Dark out to meet the guard, who was standing in the corridor where the window incident had occurred.

'I can't interview him without a parent present,' Dark heard the guard saying to Magill.

Dark couldn't hear what the principal said back to the guard, but there was definitely something about 'a most uncooperative single girl… irresponsible parent… out of control…'

And then old Auntie Úna came out of class again and went up to the guard, saying something.

The guard didn't hush his voice when talking to other adults, like a teacher. He turned back to Magill and asked, 'Is this right, what Mammy Moriarty is saying? Out in the corridor for hours every day?'

The principal was shaking his head vigorously and waving Úna back to her classroom.

The guard came back over to Dark and asked him out into the yard for a private chat. He said in a cross voice, 'Any time you like now, sonny, you can tell me what happened here, because vandalising school property can get you in a lot of trouble and I don't have time to waste with lies or bullshit.'

Dark said, 'I broke the window.'

'Are you being smart? I can see that. Why?'

'I didn't mean to.'

'Would you just tell me what happened, like a good man.'

'I can pay for it.'

'Oh, right, I'm sure. And how would you propose to do that, now?' said the guard, still impatiently.

'I've got two calves of my own. I'll sell one of them.'

The guard looked up from his notepad and the biro that was irritating him because it was only writing patchily.

He took another long look at Dark. He put away the notebook and faulty pen. His tone changed completely.

'You're the son of Seán McLean, the Lord have mercy on him? Staying up there at Connie's place?'

'Yes. I don't know how much glass costs. Do you know would one good six-month-old calf cover it or would I have to sell the two of them?' asked Dark.

'You don't have to sell anything,' the guard said, very quietly. 'Pat Curtain is my name. I'm a friend of Connie's.'

'I would rather my mother didn't have to pay for it.'

'Or find out about it?'

'Yeah.'

'Listen, don't worry about that,' said the guard, still quietly. 'They have insurance. You're a good lad to offer. I don't know what you thought you were playing at, but I'm just going to tell Magill that you had a dizzy spell from standing out there, and knocked the fire yoke against the window as you fell.'

'He won't believe you,' said Dark.

'I don't give a fiddler's what he believes. You just don't make a liar of me. Alright?'

'Alright,' said Dark.

'And try to keep out of the old goat's way in future so that he's not calling me up here every day. Alright?'

'Alright.'

Dark listened as the guard went back in and chatted and laughed and patted Magill on the back. The principal wasn't smiling.

As he left, the guard shouted back at Magill, 'By the

way, that ould extinguisher is out of date. That could turn into a much more costly mistake than a little bit of broken glass.'

Dark was ushered back into the classroom by Magill, who never said a word to him. That was his last time in the corridor.

As he walked down the fields to meet the Old Man that night, he marvelled at how well Dreoilín's spell was working. A year ago, if he had been shouted at by the principal and then questioned by the *gardaí*, he might have said he didn't care, but in truth, he'd have curled up in terror. Now, he really didn't care much at all. Or didn't care that he hadn't done any school work or homework in a long time. He didn't give a hoot about any of them.

He started coughing again as he made his way inside the rath. The red-mopped little rogue, Bal, grabbed him less roughly by the arm and brought him straight over to the fire. Bal pulled the cup roughly from Etain, adding something to it from a rolled-up leaf he took from his cape. It tasted so bitter that Dark spat part of it out. Conán laughed.

'Drink up, you cur, and show some appreciation when a man is trying to cure your bad chest,' said Bal.

Dark drank up and he did feel better, for the moment.

The Old Man asked him how he was doing.

'Has any one of you ever seen such a thing as a magpie with a man's face?' Dark asked.

The Old Man laughed. 'Ask Bal. A man can see queer things if he looks closely enough at any situation.'

231

That was all. Then he started talking and everyone stared into the flames and fell silent.

The Greatest Battle That Never Was

Mac Cumhaill had just left Tara with Conán, burdened by the king's instructions to hunt down and kill a young man called Skellig, who had had the temerity to attack the king. Before they had got far, Fionn was summoned back by Cormac for another conversation that would drive him to the very edge of fury and despair.

When they re-entered the chamber, the king invited them to sit with a sombre assembly, mainly of *brehons*, men to whom Cormac now delegated too much of his thinking. In recent times Cormac gave a lot of his own thoughts over to his hobbies – activities the *brehons* persuaded him he had great hidden talents for, like designing watermills and painting pictures of dogs. His talents in those fields remained well hidden but Mac Cumhaill felt that his real talents in the field of pragmatic cunning were also starting to become blunted by engaging with these ineffectual men. Goll was also already there. Judging from the silence when he walked back in, Fionn himself had recently been the subject of discussion.

'Fionn,' started Cormac in the gravest tone he could issue from a face that had been badly bruised by the attentions of Skellig, 'my apologies for calling you back, but these wise gentlemen have just brought me dreadful information. A massive attack on our nation is imminent.'

'Oh?' said Mac Cumhaill, imagining for a moment that

the plump, tight-mouthed owl-men had actually divined some original information.

'Yes, information they have gathered from sea traders has it that the Crúca Róma forces may be about to attack our land. And they tell me their opinion is that our forces are, eh, somewhat unprepared.'

Mac Cumhaill was not too impressed. Though this was the news he had most dreaded hearing, news that meant a likely end to all that had worth, his first feeling was rage. He had been warning Cormac for years about the Crúca sweeping across the countries to the east. Many of the smaller chieftaincies in the lands nearest Éirinn now answered to the Crúca. And there had been several attempts by the Crúca to take Halban. Cormac well knew that Mac Cumhaill had led many men to fight alongside the Halbanach, as much to expose his own soldiers to the methods and weaknesses of the Crúca as to help the Halban kinsmen protect their possessions. He had warned Cormac many times that the next head of the Crúca would want to add new ground, so as to turn himself into a god in his people's eyes, and that Éire's remaining beyond their grasp would one day become an unbearable provocation to them.

Cormac's advisers, these very men now assembled, had for years dismissed all this, assuring Cormac, 'Why would they consider invading here when their trading boats can do business? Fionn thinks like a soldier and only sees the makings of a war, where level-headed people see the makings of good beneficial dealings.'

The truth of the matter was that some of the *brehon*s and

many of the lowland people were fond of the shiny cloths and smelly soaps that the traders brought in return for meat, wool and metal. A trade that went on even in years like the present one when there were people in Éire going hungry and cold. They hadn't wanted Mac Cumhaill doing anything that might upset the cosy relationship.

Now, of course, from their daily dealings, they were the first to hear that there was an army and a fleet of giant ships gathering just across the water. And when they had added the suggestion that Mac Cumhaill was to blame for the Fianna not being ready for this, it seemed that no voice had protested. Not Cormac. And not even Goll.

As Fionn stood to leave, he looked from Cormac to Goll in a rage that he could not even put words to. Conán had no such inhibition. He shouted at Cormac: 'You are a great man in several ways. But it would really round you off if your memory was less selective. You forget that you were the one who said Mac Cumhaill was wasting the lives of young men, taking armies over to Halban to train. And you forget how many times he asked you to put aside builders and resources to build fortresses and ambush sites at all of the coves where the Crúca might try to land. And you forget how many times he asked you to stop the traders who come here with wine and go back with information. Information on landing points. Information on the state of our defences. Information on which chiefs like nice things and might be open to offers of high office under Crúca rule. Information on which chiefs might be open to bribery during a harsh winter such as this one, when aching bellies are making the people restless.'

'Sit down now, honoured gentlemen. Cool heads. There's no point in raking over old arguments now,' said Cormac urgently to Mac Cumhaill and Conán, all pompous recrimination replaced by fear. 'I was not meaning to blame anyone. Not in the slightest. We all need to stick together now. What can we do?'

'And, by the way,' said Conán unnecessarily, turning back as he left with Mac Cumhaill, 'did you remember when Skellig was boxing the head off you earlier this morning, that it was you who boasted you were a great man to spot talent and you that insisted that Skellig be made a senior man in the Fianna even after Mac Cumhaill told you that doing so would be like giving a barrel of golden whiskey to a man already drunk on his own importance in the world?'

After they'd left, Conán asked Mac Cumhaill, 'What are you going to do?'

Mac Cumhaill just shook his head. 'I have nothing left inside me. I will leave them to it now.'

Conán parted from him. Because he couldn't think of anything else to do, he resumed the journey south to attend to the now minor problem of tracking down Skellig, the man who had turned on Cormac. Cormac had laughed at Skellig for demanding that he be made head of the Fianna, and Skellig had rushed Cormac in a tantrum. He punched the royal head several times and fled before the guards realised what was happening.

Conán was going to stick to the plan Mac Cumhaill had

set earlier that day: to disobey the king. Since it was partly the king's own fault for feeding the wrong-headed boy's notions about himself, they would capture Skellig, but spare his life and send him somewhere he could do no harm.

Fionn himself headed southwest to try to forget the major problem of the Crúca.

It was only a few years since the Crúca had moved into the neighbouring land. They took the ground of Togodum and Caract. Every season, they controlled more of the middle and south of that land. These Crúca armies made servants of entire nations. They turned all of a people's crafts, all of their farming and all of their metalwork to the service of a foreign Crúca headman. Up to then, most peoples had laws and regulations as suited their own temperaments and their own ways of looking at the world. But the Crúcas enforced the same set of laws on every different kind of people, no matter what the beliefs of those people were. Instead of liberty, the once proud followers of the great Cunobelin now had bathtubs, wine and servitude. Mac Cumhaill knew better than anyone in Éire how overwhelming the danger was. He knew the Crúca too would have learned something from Halban. They would not launch unless they had several armies ready, each massively outnumbering the Fianna and they would attack with overwhelming ferocity at several points simultaneously. Their timing was perfect. They knew that at the end of a winter after two bad summers when the grain had sprouted before it could be harvested, the apples had rotted, the turf had been too wet, and there wasn't even fish oil to light a candle and shorten the cold hungry late winter evenings, the population's fighting spirits would be in a delicate state.

He knew that people would now be expecting that Fionn Mac Cumhaill would somehow lead them through this. The people had little idea what they were in for or that stopping the Crúca now would be almost impossible. He knew all that. But the only way he could see to avoid massive bloodshed and likely eventual defeat was total capitulation. He was not capable of making the sensible choice. It could not happen while he led the Fianna. So it was best if he left them alone now. Under Goll and Cormac the resistance would be feeble and the misery soon over. And that was what was making him feel like he had a heavy boulder in his stomach.

As he set out walking, he was traipsing from one mountain to the next looking for a man called Lorcán, a man he regarded as wise and true. He wanted to talk to him in the hope it would clear his own thoughts.

Lorcán wandered alone in the most desolate hills. He had been the most popular poet in the land at one time. But he had no time for any of the newer styles and soft tastes that had consumed some of the people in the lowlands. Not when ordinary people still had to employ all their wits just to keep death at bay. He became unpopular when he didn't humour certain chiefs who asked him to go easy with his words. He had taken to solitary living and didn't seem to feel any loss.

When Mac Cumhaill eventually spotted Lorcán, it was late evening. He was leaning on a long ash plant, looking out into the distance from a mountain ledge high on Sliabh Laigin. He was a tall, lean man, younger than Mac Cumhaill. He had red hair and a wary look about him all the time. He welcomed Mac Cumhaill as always and Mac Cumhaill gave him a flask of whiskey he had been given by a man he knew, as he passed the foothills.

'I trust, my large friend, that your life is progressing in a manner that is to your liking,' he said to Mac Cumhaill.

Mac Cumhaill didn't answer.

They sat by a small fire, burning the backs of their throats with cups of the harsh drink. What settled Mac Cumhaill in Lorcán's company was that he wasn't offended by silence and that he didn't feel the need to speak unless there was something to be said. After a while of staring into the fire, as on many occasions before, Mac Cumhaill just started talking to Lorcán.

'To tell you the truth, I am not the right man for this time. We are caught on the wrong foot. Nothing Cormac or I can do or say now will change that.'

'Why would they want this trouble? Haven't they had a bitter enough taste of your methods and your madness in Halban? Maybe their leader is the only one who wants it. Would that not give you some hope that it mightn't be so impossible to shake their determination?'

'I think it's just too far out of my reach this time,' said Fionn.

'What is it that they already know?'

Mac Cumhaill lay back and looked at the stars, with his hands behind his head, thinking about Lorcán's question.

They would know from Halban that the Fianna will run towards them rather than away from them. That their rock- and spear-throwing contraptions instill no fear but only make easy targets of the men fiddling and trying to set them up. And they would know that the orderly lines of men marching behind a wall of shields held no terror. Their lines weren't long scattering when four or five chariots raced into them, each carrying only one or two men with deathly red paint on their faces, lime in their hair, and naked as the day they were born, screaming in fury and slashing in every direction. They would understand how many soft young men with a fear of the sight of their own blood were needed to overpower one Fianna soldier who sees a glorious death as a transition he is ready to make any minute of any day.

Mac Cumhaill said, 'Our ambushes, better hill fitness and wild surprise attacks always made the Crúcas fall into disorder.'

'Yet, they come. Is there much that they do not yet know?' asked Lorcán.

'They may know some things but their methods are so uniform and their previous successes so great that they seem unable or too proud to adapt. They still don't under- stand that the orderliness and regalia which might have frightened other nations is seen here as weakness. To peo- ple here, they look like dancers rather than soldiers. And then when they are knocked into disarray and descend into random cruelty against ordinary people, they don't under- stand that in these parts that does not make people want to submit. The Crúcas haven't realised that here, cruelty only makes peaceful domination an everlasting impossibility. That each injustice is stored and passed on until the time comes to correct it, even if the opportunity takes generations to arise.'

'But I don't believe that kind of thinking brings Fionn Mac Cumhaill satisfaction – seeking consolation in the knowledge that after defeating your people they will not have a comfortable reign here. So what are you going to do?'

'I don't know for sure. But if I was to go back, the first thing I would do is to stop the merchants and cut off the Crúca's supply of information.'

'It sounds like they have already got as much nourishment as they need from that well. Would it not be possible to poison the well instead of closing it off?'

This was all that was said during the night in relation to the country's problems. However, much else was talked about, as was always the case when Mac Cumhaill met Lorcán.

Mac Cumhaill spent the night on a heather cushion in Lorcán's cave. The next morning was as clear a day as Mac Cumhaill had seen in a very long time. From the mountain top he could see the peaceful green carpet spread as far as the sea, clumps of trees starting to peep out at the spring light and soft crooked boundaries between the big infields of various clans, looking random to someone who didn't know how many generations it had taken to work out every finger length of them, and small patches of brown where turf had been cut last year. There was smoke here and there coming from homes where mothers were up and preparing porridge or whatever bits of food they had magically found to nurture the ones they loved. He could hear whistles and dogs barking from some early starters, boys who were out rounding up the few black cows to tease the last drops of the year's milk out of them. On the lower slopes he could see a man with the patient calmness of an expert, coaxing a fine white horse in to stand alongside a red bull, already harnessed to a wooden plough. Up closer, a mountain ewe with two bony lambs had stopped to inspect him, deciding whether to risk carrying on about her business despite this big intruder standing on her track, or to retreat until he had gone back to wherever he came from. Mac Cumhaill fell in love with his country again.

As he wandered back towards Tara, he was spotted by Conán. 'There you are! I knew you'd be back. Goll owes me a flask of whiskey.'

'How did you know, as a matter of interest?' said Mac Cumhaill.

'You are always complaining about wanting to go off on your own and live the quiet life,' said Conán truthfully, 'but at the back of it you know you wouldn't survive a minute wandering the bogs if you knew there was excitement and trouble going on without you.'

Mac Cumhaill didn't have time to put up a denial of his friend's observations, as Goll spotted them and came out demanding to know what Mac Cumhaill's plans for the Crúca were. And where Skellig's head was.

'Don't worry about Skellig,' Conán intervened, 'some of

my men have him cornered and he is not going anywhere.'

'That won't do,' said Goll, 'Cormac wants his head, and if you are not up to that task, I am.'

'I don't doubt that,' said Conán. 'Do you not think though, that Cormac should be engaging his formidable brain with more important matters now?'

'You should be glad he is not yet looking for your own head, with the lip you gave him yesterday,' shouted Goll.

Conán laughed at Goll, only making him redder and meaner.

Fionn intervened. 'I will deal with Skellig myself. Conán and Fiachra and I will go to see to that now. In the meantime, I would be obliged if you would take charge of the Fianna and start taking in and training all the new people that Cormac wants.'

The contortions were wiped off Goll's face and he wandered off, no longer bothered about Skellig, Conán or anything that Mac Cumhaill might have up his sleeve.

Conán was puzzled at Mac Cumhaill's interest in Skellig. But he didn't say anything. He called for Fiachra and the three of them set out for Fotharta in the southeast corner of the country where Skellig was hiding in a copse of trees.

This young man, Skellig, had come to Cormac's attention in the battle with the *buan*s. As a new recruit tearing into the *buan*s with a fervour and fearlessness that had made many take note, Cormac had insisted that Skellig be made a group leader. Mac Cumhaill cautioned that the fearlessness seemed born more of a belief in his own immortality than in any sense of gallantry. Cormac didn't understand Mac Cumhaill's opposition and listened to the whispers that Mac Cumhaill feared that the might, speed and cunning of the young man undermined his own status.

Initially, Skellig had given the impression of being a very strong leader. His men either loved him or were terrified of him or both. Anyone he thought was undermining him or questioning his authority in any way was beaten and kicked by Skellig in front of everyone else. None of them would even tell this to Mac Cumhaill at the time, because they were so afraid of Skellig's threats. They could see from his eyes that no threat he made was idle. When he said, 'If you go crying to the bosses, I will attack your wife and tear your children apart like dolls,' his calm stare left them in no doubt.

By now, Skellig was making his even grander plans. At first, the large young man had persuaded himself only that he was the rightful leader of the Fianna. However, yesterday even as he had made his strategic retreat from Conán, his admiration of himself had grown further. Now that he'd seen Cormac bruised like a mortal, he started to believe it was time for him to overthrow Cormac too. The entire army he was going to do this with consisted of seven weak-minded men who must have been mesmerised by Skellig's grandiose delusions.

Within a few hours, Mac Cumhaill was at the small grove of hazel trees accompanied by Conán and the much-trusted Fiachra.

They left their shields and weapons down and sat relaxing on a mound a few paces beyond the trees. They

243

had seen one of Skellig's companions scurry inside, giving up his observation post, so they knew Skellig wasn't far away. At the back of the clump was the sea shore and there was nowhere for Skellig to go.

'Now is your chance to assert yourself,' shouted Mac Cumhaill. 'Come out here to me now, because time is precious and I don't want to waste another minute of mine on you.'

'Your day is past, Fionn Mac Cumhaill,' came the voice of Skellig. Conán and Fiachra instinctively went out to flank the spot the sound was coming from.

'Come out, you *gombán*,' said Mac Cumhaill, 'while there is still good humour on me.'

'Old man, I'd rather you would just retire and enjoy the stories of your glory days,' came Skellig's heavy voice, 'than make me cut you down here in this lonely place.'

There was a terrible yelp from the trees and one of Skellig's companions came running out. Conán had spotted where they were sitting in the trees and lobbed a spear in. The youngster came running towards Mac Cumhaill, throwing down his weapons. He had only a slight gash on his hip, as Conán had not thrown with any serious intent. However, a bellow came from Skellig, 'Traiterous coward,' followed by a spear thrown with ferocious intent. It went straight into the man's back and the poor fellow dropped like a log.

Mac Cumhaill could hear Skellig growling at the others with him: 'If any of the rest of you wants to run to the losing side, go now and the same will happen to you.'

Mac Cumhaill picked up a fairly large boulder and rolled it like a marble in the direction of the voices. It flattened bushes and small trees as it went and stopped at Skellig's feet, exposing him entirely.

'Come out, I said,' said Mac Cumhaill, still calm. 'You'd better hope that gormless Déise chap lying there is still drawing breath, because there are fairly serious consequences for murder.'

'A man killed in combat is not murdered,' said Skellig. 'I'm an army commander. That's what I'm trained to do.'

'To kill your own? I must have missed that part of the training,' said Fiachra, his face boiling with anger.

'Shut your gob, you,' said Skellig. 'This is between the old man and me now.'

The other six men with Skellig took this as their cue, dropped their weapons and ran back away from Skellig, to circle out on the beach and re-emerge behind Conán.

'We made a terrible mistake. He only told us this morning that he had hit the king,' said one of them.

'Whisht now, the lot of you,' said Conán. 'Go and lie on the sand and don't stir until we come to talk to you.'

'You had your chance, son of Cumhaill. Now it's your time to go,' said Skellig, stepping forward, his entire face contorted.

He drew back his arm with another spear in it. To give him credit, the man had enormous power. The spear came fast and true, not lobbed, but straight, speeding its way through the air destined for Mac Cumhaill's chest. But it was fired with rage rather than stealth and Mac Cumhaill

245

only had to angle his battered bronze shield to its approach. The spear glanced off and broke its head on the rock.

Skellig then raced forward with his sword drawn. It was a very long blade with fancy scrolling on it. Mac Cumhaill hadn't seen it before and guessed the man had had it made for himself at the time he started getting notions about being the greatest warrior in the land. Mac Cumhaill was still contemplating this as the weapon was swinging with enormous force towards his neck. He ducked at the last moment and felt hairs being cut from his head. His timing was so good. He really was feeling good this day. He grabbed the retreating hand that held the sword and followed it, dragging Skellig with his own momentum to the ground. Skellig had a big hand, but Mac Cumhaill's completely locked it and, as Skellig fell, there was an unpleasant sound of bones crushing. The fancy sword fell harmlessly to the ground.

'Is he two-handed or just a *ciotóg*?' Mac Cumhaill shouted down to the men, lying on their faces on the beach.

'Only the left is all he can use,' said one.

'Well, you're lucky then,' said Mac Cumhaill, looking back down to Skellig, 'because it means I can leave you an unbroken hand for picking your nose.'

'No, it's you who got lucky and caught me off balance,' said Skellig, grunting with the pain. 'You tricked me.'

Mac Cumhaill said, 'Are you starting to understand yet that you will never be a soldier?'

'What is to be my fate? Are you going to slay the best prospect of a successor who could do better than you? Are you going to rob your own children of a worthy defender?'

'Conán, can you check the state of that lad lying over there with the hazel sticking out of him?'

Conán looked at the wound, listened to the man's breathing, and immediately pronounced, 'I think he'll be alright; our great new leader can't even succeed at spearing a man in the back.'

Mac Cumhaill looked back down at Skellig.

'Maybe your luck is turning. I'm not going to squash you just yet.'

'What's going to happen to me, then?'

'I have just the job for a majestic fellow like you,' said Mac Cumhaill.

Skellig was then tied up and brought to a cave.

The men lying in the sand were called over and questioned. In the end, Mac Cumhaill chose to believe their story, that they had been told by Skellig that he had been appointed the new head of the Fianna, and so they obeyed when he commanded them to travel with him. They were all young, and Mac Cumhaill allowed that Skellig might have seemed a very impressive character to them, with his strength and his boasts. He said he would give them a chance to prove themselves, and, if they came through it, there would never be another word spoken of this mistake.

The first of them was set to guard Skellig, keeping him fed and watered in the cave and keeping him quiet whatever way he saw fit.

The second was sent to the local people to find a handy

woman who might be able to attend to the wounds of the injured man.

The other four had a more curious job. Mac Cumhaill explained to them, 'You are to leave all your weapons here. Go down to the village there and find anyone who is prepared to swap your fine tunics for the old shawls and goatskin wraps of herd boys. Do you understand?'

'Yes.'

'Are you sure?' said Mac Cumhaill, testily.

'Yes.'

'Well, then, when you have that done, you are to spread out, up along the coast from here. I am giving each of you something you can trade with and each of you a message to pass on. Here.'

They held out their hands dutifully. Mac Cumhaill reached into his pouch. To the first lad he gave a cluster of river pearls, brownish but pretty. To the second, he gave five nuggets of gold. The third got ten white, blotchy eggs, the work of golden eagles. The fourth got a miniature harp that could play a fine melody at the slightest touch of the most tuneless hand.

Mac Cumhaill's information was that there had been greater merchant activity in this corner of the country over the past months than any other part of the eastern coastline. Strange indeed for a part of the country with little to offer a trader other than rotten cheese and hairy wool. Since some of this new wave of merchants were apparently interested in enquiring about more than the weather, he intended to arrange for them to be told about more than the weather.

The first man, who was to wait in a cove three hours up the coast, was to look for someone who would trade his mother's precious pearls for a new bronze adze. Nothing else would do. And it didn't really matter whether he ever got one. But he was to approach every man with a boat that came in there looking to make this trade.

'And what do I say when they ask what I need the adze for?' said the first man.

'You want to carve yourself a canoe so you can take part in a great war at sea.'

'What war?'

'You don't know, but tell them that anyone who can carve a canoe from the trunk of a black cherry, the magical type that can become invisible in the murky waters and move silently and undetected at night, has the choice of training for that instead of for the war on land. You have been told that the seas will be crawling with men ready to give their lives, silently working from the dark water underneath, opening the bottoms of ships and seeing how elegantly they stand when the sea is inside them. And then when the war to defend Éire is won, that will be only the beginning. There will be a hundred thousand men in small canoes like yours silently crossing to make land in every little cove and beach, and moving swiftly so as to finish the war in the enemy's own territory.'

The second man was going to a bay just a short walk north, to wait in the sand dunes for traders. His story was to be that the last of his chief's gold was to be traded for shackles as he wanted to be able to get a few teams of the prisoners that would be working his land after they were trapped here in the war.

'What war, will I say?'

'You will say that all you know is that it is the Fianna's war. The Fianna are luring a foreign army in here. Out of respect to those massacred in Halban, there can be no foreign soldiers left alive, but those slaves that survive the sinking of the boats will need to work one year here to earn their freedom and to make up for the fact that every able hand in this country is holding a sword in a neighbouring land instead of steering a plough in his own this year.'

The third man was stationed to the southwest. He was to trade the ten eagle eggs for whatever charms the Crúcas use to appease their water lord.

'Why will I say I want that?'

'You will report that it is because that unsavoury gentleman has followed the Crúca war boats into our sea. We don't want him here at all. They can keep him. He is a scourge to our fishermen, farting and spluttering and throwing up storms without notice. Fionn Mac Cumhaill says that if we bribe him to leave the waters quiet for a few days, we'll get rid of every single one of the ships that brought him here.'

The fourth man was to stay here at this bay, waiting, and then approaching any strangers who came. He was to ask them what they could offer him to persuade him to part with the beautiful little harp.

'But you are not actually to give it to anyone,' said Mac Cumhaill.

'Why?' said the soldier. 'Is there some magic secret to it?'

'The only secret to it is that I happen to like it and want it back, if that's alright with you,' said Mac Cumhaill.

'And what story should I tell them?'

'You are a half-witted bard who has lost his verse, but are full of lament. You are a musician who has lost his tune, but are full of wailing. You want to find something that will bring light back into your life.'

'Why should I say that to them?'

'You have a long, dreary explanation to give them. You tell them you are so despondent that the music has left the country. There is only the silent sound of people waiting, metal sharpening, the sound of looming slaughter now, in the hills that once rang of a thousand welcomes. Sure enough, you'll say, the coast looks normal. But it's only a deception. Once you go inland from the coast, the entire country is converted into a warren of traps. That there is no man in the country who has not received years of training in how to ambush and attack Crúca platoons from the flank or the rear and how to scatter them and run them into traps. Everyone has been schooled in the methods and weapons of the Crúca. There have never been so many blades and spears stashed away in secret places. There have never been so many hide-outs and hill retreats prepared. The druids too have spoken and lent their unholy blessing to the mayhem that is to follow and nobody is afraid to die.

In fact, they would welcome a glorious death. There is no man over twelve in the country and very few women who have not trained and sworn to avenge their friends across the water and sworn not to let their fate be ours. The only music now is fighting songs. They infest the place. The invader is not even to be allowed to return to his boats. His boats won't exist,' said Mac Cumhaill. 'Are you with me? And you can moan on about the fact that this is not a country for poets anymore, and such. This country is now no more than an open grave waiting for fifty thousand men to fall into it. And after that there will be no wall to stop the *Éireannach*s going across to take back the defenceless lands from Móna onwards and to meet the Halbanachs coming downward. And then ask the trader can he not show you something that might lift your spirits in such a dark time. Keep on and on like that at them until you have sowed your droning despair in their unfortunate hearts.'

Mac Cumhaill and Conán departed, leaving Fiachra to supervise these men in their work. They would all have to meet Fiachra every evening to report on whether they'd met any trading boats that day and how well they'd swallowed the stories.

Mac Cumhaill headed west. He got to Corca Dhuibhne where he knew the finest *currach* oarsmen lived. There he recruited twelve young men, willing to go on a dangerous adventure. He also got the loan of two horses and made sleds that two fine *currach*s were dragged across the country on. When they got back to Fotharta he tested the oarsmen again. He told them more about this mission and

252

how dangerous it was and that some of them might not come back.

'There's nothing on this quiet little sea to scare us,' said one of them. 'Don't we know from when we were small that any day we come back from the sea alive is a day to be merciful for.'

They stopped a couple of days in the port, resting up and gathering things for the next journey. Mac Cumhaill wanted to allow some time for the information carried by the traders to filter through the enemy ranks to soften the hearts of the paid soldiers and to throw sand in the eyes of the already reluctant commanders. The leaders would be unsure of whether the information was good. Even if they suspected bluster they would know that the surprise was gone and that the *Éireannach*s were warning them that their mission would not meet with hospitality. The Crúca were the ones having to do the guessing now. And that would make them nervous. He knew only too well how these things went.

In the meantime, he set the young fishermen in the water again to see which was able to use the sticks most quietly and with the greatest agility. There was little between them but he picked six. The others were to wait there in Fotharta in case he needed to come back for a second team. That instruction made those selected less exuberant.

Then at midday on the appointed day, he went down to the water's edge to prepare for the job that he truly thought might be his last. Conán was to have arranged a bigger boat to carry the whole lot of them to their place of work. Fionn couldn't see any boat there, at first. He shouted for Conán, with a strong note of anger in his voice. It wasn't like Conán to let him down.

'Calm yourself,' said Conán, appearing from behind a sand dune where he had been sheltering. He was with another man, a very weather-beaten fellow with a white beard and a bald head.

'Where's the boat and who is this you have with you?' said Fionn.

'The boat is around on the other side of the headland, ready and waiting for you these past twelve hours. And the man I have with me would be the owner of the same boat and a man you should recognise.'

Fionn took another look, and said with no small surprise in his voice, 'Crothán? Is it you?'

'None other,' said the old man, laughing.

'The last time I saw you, I had you up with Cormac on rather serious matters. I didn't think I'd be seeing your barnacled mug for a while again,' said Fionn.

'No more than I hoped I'd ever see your own stinking mountain of self-righteousness again,' said the old man, still laughing. 'Bad luck to you for bringing an end to my good fortunes.'

'Good fortunes got by raiding the boats of harmless traders leaving these shores, as I remember,' said Fionn. 'And who do you think would have had to face the consequences if the countries that these trading boats came from were to come looking for revenge?'

Fionn turned to Conán.

'I thought I asked you to bring me a reliable seaman and his boat.'

'With respect, Fionn, you asked me to bring the best man that ever put foot in a boat. This is he. This old sea dog might be a little bit of a rogue, but there is no better man to follow a boat through the roughest of seas. He is famed and feared for this very reason. And, you may as well know, despite his slight weakness for theft, he is a close and old friend of my own, and as reliable when he gives his word as any man or woman who ever stood on hind legs.'

Fionn didn't know much about Crothán, but if Conán was ready to vouch for him in this way, that was a fair start.

'Good enough,' he said, spitting in his hand and extending it for Crothán to shake.

Crothán responded with firmness.

Crothán's boat wasn't pretty. She had more scars on her leather pelt than an old tom-cat. The main mast was a roughly-cut ash bough and the second one was slightly askew. The lattice of ash boards inside her were blackened from weather. But she was a fine, sturdy lady and looked like she had already ably survived a good deal of wrestling with wild seas. Fionn immediately felt a pang of old Crothán's love for her.

The *currach*s were then tied onto her, to trail like two big children. Other peculiar cargo was also ordered by Mac Cumhaill. There was a three-pronged iron fork that he had asked Eibhlín Rua make up for him. Typical of Eibhlín, it was more ornate and sharply barbed than was ordered, but it would do the job. She had also supplied four large augers made in shiny hardened iron. Then there was a very large sack of rotting bladderwrack seaweed that had a smell you could trot a donkey on. Possibly smelling even worse was the next item that was loaded. It took four men to load it. It was wrapped in cloth, tied in ropes, and seemed to be moving on the deck.

They set off at dusk. But before they were long out, one of the young fishermen started to panic.

'Where's the water from Brigid's well? We can't go!'

'There's none on this boat,' said the old man, 'and I've survived a lot of adventures without it.'

'I suppose you wouldn't necessarily want to be drawing the attention of the superiors onto the kind of work this boat is usually involved in,' said Conán.

'We have to turn back,' said the young man. 'Without the good will of Brigid, our work is doomed!'

Fionn had no intention whatsoever of turning back.

Conán pulled the lad over to him and said to him very sternly, 'In this life, boy, there are times when you can wait for some god to help you. But most times in life you have the responsibility for your fate in no hands other than your own and you can let the gods take the credit afterwards.'

'I'm not afraid of you. Threats don't work,' said the young man, getting very agitated.

Conán looked at him with a wicked smile and said 'The funny thing is, people often say that about threats. But luckily, in most cases, they do work when they are justified and sincerely intended. For example, in this situation you are in, if you don't settle yourself down, you'll be on your own too, out in the watery waves without the comfort of any boat under you.'

Then one of the other fishermen intervened.

'Isn't there plenty of charmed water in the *currach*s alongside us?' he said. Surely that would protect us well enough.'

That was the end of that.

The old man was very experienced in this sea. It was where he had done most of his pirating – which, of course, he swore was all in the distant past. Even though the seas weren't high yet, it was tough going because the help wasn't of a high standard. There was no room for the old man's usual crewman. The boat was just too small. Conán had claimed he'd be able to do all that needed doing as he'd been out with the old man many times before. However, it turned out all he had was strength and curses, but no idea at all of how to follow the old man's shouted instructions in regard to the sails or the tiller. The *currach* boys tried their best to help but they had never been on a boat like this before and just kept tripping over each other. In the first part of the journey it looked on several occasions as if they might all get tipped into the sea without a single wave, a sea monster or any other enemy to blame.

If he brought them back from this trip, Mac Cumhaill told Crothán, he could rob all the traders he wanted and he certainly would never be the one dragging him off to Cormac.

The place Mac Cumhaill wanted him to aim for was

south of Móna. They wouldn't need a harbour, only a quiet sheltered bay within easy *currach* reach of that island.

It was a simple crossing and the wind was with them. The boat moved, creaked and flexed her boards as she worked effortlessly with the deep sea. They made it well before dawn. They set anchor in a small bay surrounded by sheer rocks from which no human was likely to spy them.

'What do we do now?' said one of the *currach* men.

'We wait,' said Mac Cumhaill.

'Wait for what?'

'For weather,' said Mac Cumhaill, turning to the boatman. 'You think we are in for a storm, Crothán?'

Crothán was a hard man to age. He'd looked old and awkward on land, but since they'd set sail he looked very comfortable in his leather skin.

'I promised you a storm Mac Cumhaill, and that's what you're going to get.'

'I think you're wrong about that,' said the most forward of the young *currach* lads. 'The sea is calm. I'd always know when there was a storm coming.'

The older man just looked at him as if he had expressed nothing more interesting than a fart. He looked back at Fionn.

'By the gulls, by the calm, by the streamers of light coming through, I'll tell you now it will be blowing something fearsome before the sun goes back down tonight. And raining down in cart loads. I'm not a glad man to be out in the sea waiting for what I know is coming, rather than warm and comfortable in a shoreside cabin waiting for it to pass.'

258

'Well, maybe,' said the lad, realising he was out of his depth, 'maybe the signs are a bit different on the seas this side.'

All still ignored him.

'That's good then,' said Mac Cumhaill. 'And visibility?'

'You won't be able to see in front of your nose,' said the seaman. 'It will be a bad night for any kind of work.'

'It will be a perfect night for the work we have in mind,' laughed Conán, 'and you'll all be very glad indeed of the fog and the rain when there are Crúca arrows trying to locate your flesh.'

One of the *currach* men went white.

Conán wasn't one to miss out on entertainment.

'Years of travelling the most wicked and violent of seas without a worry and you're getting nervy about a few harmless men, who have no personal grudge against you, trying to kill you?'

Mac Cumhaill patted the lad's head, which, instead of comforting him as intended, just brought forth the contents of his belly. The lad was alright again after that, but Conán wasn't all that happy about having to lean overboard with his hairy backside in the air, trying to wash the stuff off his tunic while everyone on the boat sniggered at him.

Everyone, that is, except the cloth-wrapped parcel, which, of course, contained Skellig. Mac Cumhaill now took his dagger and slashed open most of the bindings. The unfortunate Skellig stood up, and, with his great height, he lost his balance, almost falling out into the deep water below. He was large now in every respect. He had obviously been well fed by his minder, as he had some belly and a spreading rear. And he had a thin beard growing out from his yellowish face. When the gag was taken off him, he immediately started talking as though he was continuing a conversation of only a minute previously.

'I may have made some misjudgement, however; I will admit that.'

Maybe there was hope for the man, Mac Cumhaill thought.

'Well?'

'If you'll get me my sword I'll fight you again and this time I'll show you that you are old and past it. I may forgive you then for what you have done to me.'

That was the second laugh of the morning for everyone else on the boat. One of the young *currach* men gave him a tap of an oar and knocked him down.

'Now, let's be polite to our guest,' said Mac Cumhaill. 'He has important work to do today.'

'What work?' said Skellig. 'I need to approve of any plan before I'll participate in it.'

The young fisherman gave him another tap of the oar, since the previous one had earned him such approval.

It was a peculiar day. Just around the coast, as far as they knew, lay one of the most formidable armies the living world had ever seen. Here they were in a rickety old pirate boat, waiting for a storm that might itself sink them, and getting ready to go around that next headland and face into likely death. Yet there was a spirit of merriment that had sprung up on the boat. It started with one of the young lads asking the old seaman what was for breakfast.

'There's a good few dead cods like yourselves down there in a box if you want to cook them,' he said.

The young fellow went down to examine the box and shouted up, 'How many should I cook up for now?'

'Cook the whole bloody lot up,' said the captain, 'because from the little that Mac Cumhaill has bothered to tell us, we mightn't be needing too much food tomorrow.'

The boy looked at Mac Cumhaill.

'Indeed, you might as well,' said Mac Cumhaill. 'Pessimism is part of the trade of seamen, and we may surprise this old dog and survive. But if we do, I'll be happy enough if the worst pain I am carrying home with me is an empty stomach.'

From that point, the *craic* and gallery rose up. There was nothing else to do and it was a glorious day, praise be to Daghda. They all started telling yarns. Even the young lads had a sense of the rare time they were trapped in and were telling funny ones they'd never told before. The old seaman told a world of tall tales about near misses, wild seamen and enormous sea monsters.

By the afternoon, one of the Corca Dhuibhne men revealed that he was a good hand at gob music and the dancing started. It was mostly the young lads, but at one point Mac Cumhaill and the sea hound stood up and, arm in arm, they danced some kind of a reel that had the boat rocking dangerously and the seabirds heading inland.

Skellig sat quietly, sulking throughout.

By mid-afternoon, a breeze carried a few drops of rain their direction, reminding them of their situation. They all looked up at the gathering clouds and the old man didn't seek any acknowledgment of the accuracy of his prediction because they'd all rather he was wrong and that Mac Cumhaill was wrong and that all they had to do was to lift the anchor and head for sweet home. Quietness fell on them. Mac Cumhaill started giving instructions and making sure everyone understood. Any misunderstandings in the storm would mean certain death.

Time moved quickly now. The dusk wasn't long coming and the seas were rising quickly. Soon the boat was rolling and rising like a cork. Even inside this bay, the waves were getting enormous. Crothán and Conán were pulling ropes and timber every way to try to keep her facing into the waves. They were all counting the waves intently. The old man had informed them that in these seas it was every sixth wave was the monster.

Mac Cumhaill turned to Skellig. 'You were asking what you have to do?'

'You need to tell me the plan and then I'll see. You don't order me around like I was one of these green chaps.'

He got another tap of the oar, this time a bit harder.

'Listen here,' said Mac Cumhaill, coming up close to him. 'These green chaps are the ones whose skill will determine whether you and I live or die today. So I'd talk a bit nicer to them if I were you.'

Skellig said nothing.

'Another thing – ' said Mac Cumhaill, 'you have one job

to do here. I'll tell you what it is. You might not like it, but you will count yourself lucky to be allowed to do it, because if you weren't needed for this, you wouldn't be needed at all. Do you understand?'

No response.

'Do you understand?'

'Yes.'

Skellig finally seemed to be coming to understand what he'd been told all along – that Mac Cumhaill had saved him from certain execution and now he was seeing in Mac Cumhaill's eyes that Mac Cumhaill was not above unmaking that decision. He suddenly became agreeable. The plan was set in motion. The enormous sack of bladderwrack was opened. Skellig stood like a tree as two men set to work tying the seaweed to his body. They ran strings around and around his now portly belly, giving him an enormous skirt of seaweed. They also tied much of it to his hair and beard, just for appearance. A long rope was tied around his belly and the end of it fixed securely to one of the *currachs*. A large torch made of a cloth soaked in fish oil and wrapped around a *sceach* stump was lit and put in his left hand. The three-pronged weapon that Eibhlín had made was put into his right hand.

Then Mac Cumhaill said to him, 'Now, listen again and listen well. This is your test. You have to make sure that this torch stays alight and that the fork stays out of the water. That's all you have to do. If you fail, that is the end of you. If you succeed, you may live.'

'That's easy,' said Skellig, holding the torch and the fork

high in the air. 'I can do more than that. Give me a sword and I'll wipe twenty of them out.'

'Easy? Oh, I forgot to mention, jump in there.'

'What?!' shouted Skellig. 'Don't be mad! I don't swim.'

'That's fine. The weeds do. Throw him in,' said Mac Cumhaill.

Skellig had made the mistake of standing to voice his protest and when he made a lunge at the lads, it only took the slightest effort for them to topple him over the side. He went out of sight at first but Mac Cumhaill gave a tug of the rope and sure enough he came back to the surface, bobbing up and down with the support of the thousands of little seaweed bladders.

'Remember the fork and the torch,' shouted Mac Cumhaill.

They had to pull him closer to relight the torch. Then the first *currach* was put in the water and three men set to rowing it with Skellig in tow. Sure enough, the night was so black and wild that when they were only a short bit from the boat, you couldn't see the *currach* at all. You could only make out the comical sight of the enormously angry and seaweed-strewn Skellig making good and sure to keep the torch that lit him high in the air and the fork equally visible in the other hand.

Everyone was too tense now to laugh at Skellig anymore.

The old man shouted, 'He might be the best of the lot of you. When you all get swallowed by Her Majesty here, he at least has a chance of getting washed to shore.'

The second *currach* was then pushed over the side of the

boat. The seas were so big now that a wave almost lobbed it straight back on board. The seaman and Conán held it tight while Mac Cumhaill and three oarsmen got into it. Conán wanted to come with them, but Mac Cumhaill pushed him back. He was needed to hold the *currach*s steady and help the others quickly in and out of them. Anyway, he would have sunk the *currach* for sure. As it was, Mac Cumhaill's enormous weight put the *currach* lower in the water than it would normally be. In the lashing rain and wild winds, Mac Cumhaill asked them one more time whether they thought they were able for it. They all agreed they were. It was just like bringing home a big load of fish.

'And if it gets too much,' shouted one of the lads, in his element now, 'we always throw the catch overboard.'

This was going to be the lead *currach* and the boys in the other *currach*, towing the buffoon, knew their only job was to follow and circle at a distance, keeping sight of each other with uncanny skill, the way Corca Dhuibhne *currach* men have always done in a bad storm.

The lads knew more or less where they had to go. They had to stick to the coast and head north until they got to what they didn't want to see. Mac Cumhaill just hung on to the sides of the little *currach*, it taking all his efforts just to stay inside it, while the boys sat there effortlessly as if their bodies were part of the structure.

They cut the *currach* straight up on mountains of water. They dipped into valleys where they couldn't even hear the wind, with the enormous walls of water surrounding them. How much worse it must have been for the other boat with the weight on the rope pulling them and going slack, as their cargo navigated waves behind them. But on they went. Mac Cumhaill couldn't make out whether the other boat was even following anymore, but the lads seemed to know it was.

After some time, they turned the first headland and were relieved. As they came to the top of each wave, they were all peering through the sheets of rain trying to see lights, fires, the signs of a camp and most of all, to see great ships sitting in the water. But Mac Cumhaill's heart sank. There was nothing. They saw only another headland far in the distance, with the seas only seeming to get worse. He cupped his hand and shouted into the ear of one of the oarsmen, 'It may be around the next one, but it's too far for you to row in this. We'll head back and move the big boat closer tomorrow.'

The oarsman just shook his head and shouted back, 'We could sink as easy going back as going forward.'

It took hours to get near to the next finger of land sticking out into the water. Again, their spirits sank further as they inched around. Nothing to be seen. Mac Cumhaill decided it was better to put into land to risk being found by some Crúca patrols while waiting for the storm to pass than to risk heading back with the men so tired.

As they pulled in further around the headland to try to find a more sheltered spot to land, they saw it. This was a large water channel rather than a bay. And tucked away, some distance in, there were thousands of little fires flickering, spread over the entire hillside. And down below them, rocking in the turbulent waters, they could clearly see the dark outlines of very large ships. Many of them. Even in this foul weather on this miserable mission, there couldn't have been a man of them who was not struck by the deadly beauty of this sight. The awe that had defeated so many peoples nearly took them too. But they didn't stare long. A giant wave came crashing over them, punishing them for their pause. They went under, but came back up, all still in position. Mac Cumhaill's large hands came in handy for bucketing the water out and as they gradually became stable again, they resumed their focus.

New strength was found. The *currach* cut through the water towards the ships, faster than they'd moved the whole night. The boys obviously understood that stealth and speed were their best chance of having a new story to tell. Within minutes, they were at the first great boat and pulling in under it. It would have taken the most alert watchman to have seen their approach. They were as dark as the water and they were far below the normal level of attack for such boats. Their featherless oars made no familiar warning. The danger to them, as it turned out, was not through being observed. It was more from the ship herself. Sometimes high, exposing a lot of belly, more times trying to roll back on them and submerge them under her, she must have had a sense that they meant her no good.

When they had the right position, the creaking and moaning she was doing hid all sound of Mac Cumhaill's activity. He had felt his way along the crusted timber looking for the end of a board and then feeling for the dowels. He took from the floor of the boat one of the augers that Eibhlín had given him. Once he had a start with the auger he was able to hold himself and the *currach* steady. He kept turning. It took a little while, but soon he felt a give. The dowel was gone. Then another one below it. Then two from a board above them.

He signalled the lads to move. They headed to the next ship, where they did the same again.

He was deciding whether to try a third, when he heard terrible creaking from the first big lady. He had only created the most basic injury to her, but this wild sea, given any opening, was doing the rest. A rip was appearing in her side. He signalled the boys to get away out of sight fast, to beat back for the headland.

As they worked their way back out to sea, they saw the sight that would surely catch the attention of the now alert watchmen. A light on the sea. A very large, ugly, angry creature bearded in seaweed and waving a three-pointed fork and roaring incomprehensibly. The watchmen wouldn't have had the advantage of knowing that there was a *currach* twenty paces in front of this apparition, pulling it up and down through the waves, and that in fact it was the occupants of the *currach* that this lunatic deity was yelling at, rather than them.

As Mac Cumhaill's *currach* was closing around the headland, he could see the two ships listing, one of them already with its lovely curved nose heading towards the sky. The other *currach* stayed a little while longer cutting back and forth across the bay, dragging its foul load. A terrible commotion was already striking up on the shore.

Soon they followed too. Almost as though on time, when they got back around the corner into the long stretch, the sea eased enough for them to start to feel for the first time how wet and cold they were, even the men pulling the oars. They struck on in silence almost afraid to undo their good luck by talking about it. After a while, one of them noticed that they couldn't see Skellig. Mac Cumhaill's *currach* pulled alongside the other as they drew in the rope. It was slack. At the end, it was gnawed. The unfortunate man had got into such a rage at his humiliation that he must have chawed through the rope.

'We'll go back and look for him,' said one of the lads, starting to turn the *currach*.

'We all will,' said the lads in Mac Cumhaill's boat.

'There's no need,' said Mac Cumhaill, pointing to the shore. There, true enough, was the torch, still waving. The weed had floated him in.

'Will we fetch him?'

'No,' said Mac Cumhaill. 'The *amadán* could have saved his teeth – I was going to set him down over there anyway. He's better off not coming home.'

Despite Mac Cumhaill's promise of letting Skellig live, it wasn't something he'd discussed with Cormac yet. And while Cormac, in the right mood, might well show him mercy for having deliberately speared a member of the Fianna, he would be much harder to persuade of the value of a man who had inflicted such a sour bruising on his own royal person.

'If he has learnt anything he might be able to pretend to be humble and start a new life for himself over there.'

'But won't he tell the story, tell them that their god doesn't actually care one way or the other whether they take their ships out of our sea?'

'He won't. He's not stupid. He knows they'd not be able to look at him as a reminder of how they'd been fooled. That they'd torture him for any other information and then let him fight to death with some wild animal for their sport.'

'It's a big chance to take.'

'We've taken bigger chances tonight,' said Mac Cumhaill.

And that was the end of that.

He'd promised Skellig his life if he did the job asked of him. Skellig had done that. So he would live. He mightn't like landing up where he was, but he didn't have friends to miss and at least he had his health and his voice.

They made it back to the sailboat before dawn. Old Crothán was leaning over the side talking mournfully to Conán, seated on ropes behind him. He was more than surprised to see them.

'What was that about? I thought you told us we'd have the whole night of a storm,' said Mac Cumhaill.

'She shocked me. I haven't seen her throw up storm and then take it away as quickly as that in my life before. I've just been standing here debating with myself what it meant. If it happened while you were still inside the bay at your work, it would mean she was offering you up to them. If it happened after your work was done, it would mean that they are the ones who have displeased her and that the storm was her way of offering something in defence of the people of Éirinn.'

'You're nearly worse than they are, old man,' said Mac Cumhaill. 'The sea doesn't care for any of us, one way or the other.'

'Don't say that too loud, now', warned Crothán in an alarmed voice.

The lads were all nodding earnestly in agreement. Mac Cumhaill was reminded that men of the saltwater really belonged to another domain. The kings and chiefs of the land could come and go as they pleased, as far as these boys were concerned. These lads all served only one mistress. From the young and bold to the old and wizened, they all addressed her with tender respect.

'You don't want to make my job of getting you home any harder,' said the sea hound.

He was very keen to put more water between him and the enemy shore before the cover of darkness started to lift. Nobody had any argument with that.

As they got further, the full realisation of what they had just done and appreciation that they were still alive started to hit the young lads. One of them started shaking. The others became giddy with the relief and laughed like lunatics, as the old seaman's yarns resumed, only taller. And Mac Cumhaill was right: the pain of hunger on the way back to their homes was one they were very glad to be alive to experience.

Within weeks, stories were coming through from friendly traders. The new headman of the Crúca Róma had received communication from his gods. An invasion of Éirinn would be a catastrophe. All the omens were telling him that there might be cruel traps set by these bloodthirsty madmen. He would be remembered and deified as the great and wise leader who pulled civilization back from a quagmire. The irrefutable signal from the gods had been voiced clearly to him when Neptune had conjured up a freak storm and made two perfect ships fall like stones through the water, and the water had turned calm again in an instant. The likes of it had never been seen before.

From then on, the excuses starting to filter down to the Crúca's subjects became more colourful and varied. The Crúca had left Éire alone because they could get all they needed there through trade. They didn't bother because it was too small. They stayed away because the place was peopled by ungovernable braggarts who wore nothing but paint on their moist, white flesh and the lime they wore in their matted hair got into their brains and made them insane and fearless.

That was more or less the end of that episode. There was a spate of raids on traders' boats over the next years, where they would be relieved of their satins and fine goods and sent on their way. They were especially likely to be put upon if it was known they were carrying drink. Cormac would get upset when his supply of wine started running low and Mac Cumhaill and Conán were always sent to investigate. But strangely, they had very little luck in catching the old sea hooligan responsible for all this misfortune. Traders became reluctant to visit these shores for many years afterwards. There is no account of how old Crothán ended up, whether the sea finally lost patience with him or whether he continues to amuse her in his raggedy little boat to this day.

The brave *currach* men were rewarded with silver bracelets and Mac Cumhaill held a feast for them at his own clan homestead. He didn't bother warning them not to tell anyone about their adventure as he knew this would be too hard a task for them. But he also knew that once they went back to entrusting their lives to the great waters of the west, their stories would become enmeshed in the tapestry of other colourful tales from those parts and would never get back to the traders.

So this was one of the greatest battles that never was. A great victory never celebrated because nobody died. And because very few souls on this earth ever fully knew what really happened that time. Not even Cormac. Mac Cumhaill didn't have faith in the king's ability to hold his tongue when in foreign company.

Years later, Mac Cumhaill met Cormac out trying to perfect the mill he was still attempting to build on the Slaney. The king said, 'I don't like to boast about being right. But as I think you'll remember I predicted, the Crúca never did bother with us. You were too busy worrying about nothing.'

Mac Cumhaill just said, 'Yes, chief. The poets don't exaggerate when they verse about your greatness. Indeed, you'd be a horse of a man if you could shite trotting.'

Bal's cure was short-lived and costly. When Dark found himself alone in the morning not only was his cough back, but he also now felt groggy and had a terrible headache. When he got back to the house he crept into his bed, groaning.

Two hours later, when he woke up, he was still suffering and barely able to do the feeding, as each of the calves looked like they had two heads on them.

10
LOSING CONTROL

In class that morning, Dark still couldn't see straight. It took his best efforts just to sit calmly without letting his thoughts run out of control. When he shut his eyes he was getting a stream of weird dreams dancing in front of him. Like a pile of the worst nightmares all jumbled up together with bright lights and pounding noises thrown in. When he opened them again, Miss Sullivan still had two heads.

He was extremely relieved when it started to go away. He was just quietly vowing that he would never trust Bal again when he realised that a single-headed Sullivan was looking at him and cracking her fingers. That was not good. She obviously hadn't decided yet what new course of action to take with him now that she couldn't put him out. She was apparently in the middle of some kind of quiz and she repeated the question she had just asked him.

'Well, yourself there, are you deaf? What is the tallest mountain in Africa?'

'Kilimanjaro,' Dark said.

She seemed surprised for a moment. Then she said, 'Is

that what you've written down? In case you hadn't noticed, everyone else has been writing down answers for the past forty minutes. What have you written there?'

'Nothing.'

'Exactly. Well…' Everyone was expecting the usual command to depart. Instead she said, 'Write it down now.'

There was a giggle around the class.

'Where, Miss?' said Dark.

'On your hand, on your bag, where do you bloody well think? On your bloody geography copybook.'

Dark didn't do anything. He wasn't trying to be smart. He didn't have any particular desire to make her mad. He just didn't happen to have brought any books with him that day. In fact, all that was in his rucksack was his sandwich, his DS, the telescopic rod and a plastic bag with a scoop of calf nuts he wanted to feed to two weanlings that were in the road paddock, on his way down the lane later.

'Are you refusing?' she said, her voice rising dangerously.

'No, Miss. Not really.'

'Then up. Up you go and stand in the corner.'

Dark went to the corner. Instead of looking out at the goings-on in the hedge, he was put facing the class. It wasn't too great.

But Sullivan had bigger problems. Again there was a murmur of insurrection. Sullivan was one teacher who had never shown cracks in her iron grip before. But now, the giggling from the others turned into whispers and then there was a long, elaborate belch from the back benches.

When she looked around for the culprit, laughter and twenty random conversations that had been pressed beneath the surface since first bell broke out into the open as if there was no teacher in the room.

'Hey, Quirke, who won the minor match last night?'

'Yer one is uuuuseless, she'll never win Idol.'

'Canavan should have been on the team.'

'Brendan is deadly cute.'

'What did the cop say to you, Dark?'

'Did he give you a few skelps?'

Then there was a loud bang. Everyone jumped. A wood-backed duster that somebody had nicked from her desk earlier had just hit the metal blackboard with such force that only Cash was going to be the suspect. The laughter rose up. Julia Fortune fell off her chair she was laughing so much.

For one moment, Sullivan seemed not to know what to do. Dark almost started to feel sorry for her. Then she walked slowly, dramatically, to the top of the class. Silence resumed as people wondered what she'd do next.

She picked up the duster from the floor and she turned very slowly, completely composed again. She had a smile on her face.

Very sweetly she asked, 'Who wanted to know what the guard said to Mr McLean here?'

Nobody answered. Absolute quiet had returned.

'Was it…let me see now. Was it, maybe, you, Mr Cash? Did you want to know what the guard said to Mr McLean? Would you like me to arrange for you to find out? I'm sure they'd be interested in talking to a thug who tried to assault a female teacher with a dangerous projectile.'

Cash went as white as a sheet of paper. Somehow, Sullivan had known what nerve to touch. Cash had a mortal fear of the guards.

She carried on, very pleased with herself.

'Ah. So you're not prepared to respect me or any of your classmates. But you still have a little bit of respect for the…long arm, shall we say, of the law?'

'I didn't mean to hit you, Miss', he stammered. 'Honest to God.'

Anyone could see that that was true. The duster went nowhere near hitting anyone. He had just wanted to make a bit of noise the same as everyone else.

'Ah, so you admit you threw it! Leave God out of it. We bend over backwards for you people and this is the thanks we get. Go and tell the principal what you did. I'm sick of looking at your ugly mug.'

David Cash left the classroom. He left the building. And they all watched through the window, including Miss Sullivan, as he left the school yard through the front gate. Sullivan carried on as if nothing had happened.

That night the Old Man asked why Dark had such a sour look on him. Dark told them some kind of outline of what had happened.

'Most peculiar carry-on,' said the Old Man. 'Maybe you should stay away from that school business altogether yourself for a day or two. Go down tomorrow morning to see what kind of form that young fellow is in and to see what kind of a pup he has for you.'

That sounded like an excellent plan to Dark, and he felt lighter now for being back into the Old Man's world.

'How did you know about the far away mountain?' asked the Old Man.

Though he thought about it a bit, Dark couldn't answer that question. TV probably.

When Etain brought his cup, he spoke to her. 'You didn't let him put any of his cures in it tonight?' nodding at Bal.

She just laughed.

The Old Man started. In the magic flames Dark was suddenly staring into something like a small fox hole and looking back out at him was the most twisted little man's face he could ever have imagined.

The Festering *Bronloider*

*Bronloider*s were grumpy and fussy little creatures. Nobody knows where they came from or who they were related to. They were much smaller even than the average *fear dearg* or *púca*. And unlike our familiar little people, they were not elegant in any way. Their arms were too short to reach to their little feet when they bent over. They claimed they were unable to do anything for themselves, and unless big people in neighbouring houses brought them food, they yelled and moaned, saying that they were dying of starvation. They were always whining and complaining and were odd in a whole clatter of ways.

Despite all their oddness, back in Fionn Mac Cumhaill's time, any village having a *bronloider* choosing to live nearby was always considered very lucky indeed. And that wasn't just because they were extremely rare. It was because of a very strange thing that happened to you when you were near one of these awkward little creatures. Your head would suddenly fill with warm and lovely dreams. Whatever it was that you liked most in the world would come right into your head in thoughts so clear you felt sure they were real. People who worried about where tomorrow's food would come from would have their heads filled with the smells and images of feasting – there would be bountiful mountains of mutton, salmon, buttermilk and cake. Someone who liked flowers would imagine they were in an endless landscape of wonderful blooms, smelling as real as if they were walking amongst them. Someone fond of company would spend endless days by roaring fires surrounded by tellers of the most amazing stories, singers of the most wonderful songs, and everyone happy and never getting old. Fionn himself, when he was once near a *bronloider*, was overwhelmed with the feeling of sitting in a boat on a vast lake. There was a dry, cloudy sky above him. A small deer appeared at the distant edge and looked out at him from amongst the large trees warmly cladding the banks. And his mind was as clear of complications as the trout that were feeding undisturbed from the glassy surface.

There was only one time ever when there was a problem with a *bronloider*. That was in a village above in the northwest, in the area of Baile Lugda. This one *bronloider* called Thum came to the settlement. People were very pleased, expecting the good hallucinations that others had spoken of. They had heard about all the beneficial effects they can have on people's moods. And Daghda be blessed, but there were some people up there in those parts who would have needed a good lift just to get them to the normal level of mild satisfaction with life, not to speak of happiness.

They were extra pleased when they discovered that their *bronloider* did not have the usual habit of grumbling about his dietary needs. This one seemed to demand no cake or meat at all from the locals. So, to people from that part of the world, it surely seemed that the *Lughnasa* celebrations had come early – they were going to get their good times at no cost at all to themselves.

They didn't have long to wait for the dreams nor for the unpleasant surprise that came with them. This particular little gent started having exactly the opposite effect of a normal *bronloider*. Anyone who came within two hundred paces of him would start having the most awful dreams. The dreams were different for everyone. Each person's nightmare would be about their own worst fears. So people who were afraid of wolves would imagine themselves surrounded by a pack of the most ferocious, growling grey lads with the largest teeth and the most merciless eyes you could imagine. And people who were scared of heights would be jabbering wrecks, persecuted all day by the terrible certainty that they were standing on a cliff ledge, narrower than half the length of their feet, looking far down onto a raging sea smashing into the rocks in Moher.

People most certainly hated having him around, especially because the children were not getting sleep at night. They were so upset by the horrible images that the *bronloider* had created in their minds. They were seeing all kinds of horrors from huge waves washing across the countryside, great cracks opening in the ground taking them into a bottomless cavern, to doorways that turned into monsters' mouths and swallowed everyone who walked through them. Many became terrified to close their eyes even for a blink.

The people gathered and demanded that their chief ask the *bronloider* to move away. The chief agreed. He went to the tiny cabin made of a wad of mottled green and brown dock leaves, caked together with spit and bird droppings, where the darling little man now resided. As the chief approached, he could hear *caoining*. It sounded like the awful little horror was wailing at his unfortunate hedgehog companion for having taken some breadcrumbs off the ground. The chief had a strong feeling that this wasn't going to go well. Then as he got closer, matters became worse. A nasty dream hit him like a stone in the middle of his forehead. He had always had a mortal fear of spiders, and now as he got closer to the *bronloider*'s house, he thought he saw the most enormous pair of red eyes staring at him from behind a bush. He knew it was just a dream. He knew that this was impossible. But he also knew what those eyes belonged to. Though he was a brave person, his heart almost stopped with fear as the gigantic spider stepped out from behind the bush and sneered at him. The poor man stood his ground for a few seconds more and then he turned and ran away from the imaginary creature faster than he had ever run in his life before.

Two days later, he was still shaking, and it was said he was never fully right in the head after that. He was certainly now in full agreement with the other villagers that they needed help. A messenger boy was sent for Fionn. Mac Cumhaill had never heard of such a problem and was very curious. He came at once. The people described their predicament in more detail than he would have preferred. Mac Cumhaill didn't need much convincing about the bad currents that were in the dream air around those parts. He had had a poor feeling descend upon him from several miles back.

But he had a plan. He had a strong mind and he thought that if he could keep his mind focused on his favourite thoughts, there would be no room for bad dreams to get in. So, when he walked towards the dirty green mound, he kept saying to himself, 'Pancakes. Mmmm. Deeeelicious pancakes. Mmmm,' because Mac Cumhaill had a terrible appetite on him and a mountain of pancakes was just about the nicest thing he could think of right then.

It worked, but not for long. As he got closer, he started to see over the pile of fried batter and on the other side of it was a low, narrow cave and suddenly he was inside it and deep underground. The kind of caves that you couldn't turn around in. Now he could see himself and feel himself going down into a tiny, twisting tunnel, black with dark. He could feel the terror of getting stuck and not being able to wriggle back.

'Pancakes, pancakes,' he shouted as he started running towards the *bronloider*'s front door. But it suddenly got much worse. Water. First he heard it. Then he felt it. He could see the cave filling with water, rising towards him. He was trying to reverse out, but he wasn't able to budge. He felt complete terror. More terror than if facing the most vicious band of swordsmen, unarmed. But somewhere in the shadows of the nightmare he could still see the outline of the dock leaf roof and pushed his hand through. In the *bronloider*'s living room sat the malignant little creature, dressed in a black suit like he was in mourning. He was sitting on a tree root, smoking a pipe.

The *bronloider* was shocked and indignant to see the enormous stranger staring hazily down into his ruptured house.

'Who and what are you? Get OUT of my house, you great big bog monster,' he shouted.

Fionn Mac Cumhaill was in a panic, like someone holding their breath for too long. He knew that if he let the cave dream go on for a few seconds longer, he'd have to turn and run away. So he grabbed the *bronloider* in his great hands and shook him a bit harder than he meant to, saying, 'Stop it! Stop it! Stop it! You desperate little sack of misery!'

The dream stopped instantly, as the little man's pipe dropped out of his mouth and broke on the floor.

Now Mac Cumhaill was able to act more calmly, but he

was still sweating and he talked quickly for fear the dream would return.

'You're asked to leave this village immediately and take your woeful dreams with you.'

'What? Why?' said the *bronloider*, lifting his black hat and scratching his yellow head.

'Do not stop at any other village in this country,' Mac Cumhaill continued. 'If I hear of you tormenting people again, I'll toss you out onto an island in Lough Corrib, where you can bother nobody but the birds.'

'What disease have you got, you big *amadán*? Every one of your louse-eaten brethren likes the dreams of my people,' said the *bronloider*, in genuine indignation.

Mac Cumhaill was finally starting to realise that the creature did not know the effect he had been having. He set him down on the tree stump, picked up the slightly broken pipe and put it into his mouth, and started explaining all the terrible thoughts that he had been inflicting on people.

The *bronloider* was most upset and could think of no explanation for it. Then he started his unmerciful *caoining* and whining, lamenting that he must be some kind of abnormality and a disgrace to his family, all of whom had been loved by the big people.

'Well, is there anything different about you?' asked Mac Cumhaill. 'Anything that might be festering the dream air that's coming off you?'

'No,' said the *bronloider*. 'No. Except... maybe. Maybe. I wonder. I've got this awful sore foot that's been troubling

285

me for a hundred years or more. Maybe you'd take a look at it for me.'

Mac Cumhaill looked down and instantly saw a wound so old that it had grown grass and tiny bushes around it. He was about to ask why on earth the *bronloider* hadn't cleaned and healed the wound. But then he looked at the short arms. He realised that it would be unkind to laugh.

Instead, he took the needle-sharp tip of his spear head and poked out the big splinter that had caused the original wound. Then he pulled out a bottle of potion used for quick healing of battle wounds. A little of this and the *bronloider* was feeling better in less than no time.

He jumped up and kissed Mac Cumhaill. That was not a memory that Fionn Mac Cumhaill would cherish. But even if he hadn't done that, Mac Cumhaill would have known the *bronloider* was happy again, because as he was preparing to leave a new dream swept over him like a warm breeze.

'Mmmm. Pancakes. The best pancakes you'd smell in a year of walking the world.'

He left the house feeling like he was floating.

After some time, the villagers started picking up the courage to go closer to the *bronloider*'s house – all except the chief, who was so scared that he never went to that part of his lands again.

And every year when Mac Cumhaill was passing any-where near that part of the country, he would rest for a while in the woods at the back of the little *bronloider*'s house. He would lie on the ground and look up at the sky

through the branches of the big ash trees that grew there
and he would allow his mind to wander for an hour or two
into a world of wonderful, happy dreams.

The morning was dry and cold. Dark's parka was still
damp from the previous night's rain. He was coughing
away coming up the fields. He was so used to it now that
he wasn't cautious anymore. As he approached the window the light went on in his room.

Through the slightly open sash he heard his mother
saying to his empty bed, 'You're coughing a lot dear.'

Then she called out in an alarmed voice, 'Arthur!'

He couldn't slide the window up or she'd get an even
worse fright. There was a window in the back bathroom
that he knew how to open from the outside. He ran
around to that as quietly as he could. He was in there in
a minute even though he knocked bottles of shampoo and
medicine off the window shelf.

He shouted, 'Coming Mam,' as he met her in the
doorway. 'I was just at the loo.'

'Oh my God. You gave me a terrible fright.'

'Sorry, Mam.'

Then she thought some more about it. 'In the dark? In
your jacket?'

'I was just cold.'

'Your jacket is wet, Arthur. What is going on? Come
on now. Tell me.'

'OK. I thought I heard one of the heifers moaning

and I just slipped out to check that she hadn't started calving.'

'Oh, dear. Why didn't you call me, son?

'I didn't want to trouble you, Mam.'

'You can't take all this on, Arthur. It's too much.'

'It'll be fine, Mam,' Dark said and went to bed, but he didn't sleep. He didn't like to see his mam upset and worried. Not at all.

11
AN ILL WIND

Unluckily, that very morning there actually was a bit of a problem with the cows. Though he knew it wasn't going to improve his mother's outlook in relation to the farm, Dark had to ask her to stop the car on the laneway. There was no choice. There was a cow off on her own in the Road Field. She had broken away from the herd as though she might be about to calve. He needed to head her down to the yard so Brian could take care of her.

When he got back to the car, his school shoes were covered in mud. He cleaned them off pretty well, he thought, with newspaper.

His mother was going to be late for work now.

'Blast Connie and his precious cows,' she said, staring at the windscreen with tears of frustration in her eyes. She almost never swore. 'That's all I can say. A pox on him.'

His mother had wanted to put the cows up for auction the day Connie was taken away. She said that Connie agreed that that was only fair. Dark had been against it.

He had already known back then, he had heard from Brian, that anyone who got out of cows was prevented by Europe from getting back into them. Connie wouldn't be allowed to have his cows again. That would be the end. There would be nothing else for Connie to do around here. He would have to move away. That was why Dark had insisted that he'd be able to help Brian keep them going. It was just stubbornness, really.

He had learnt a lot, though, and most of the time, he managed. But some days, like this one, he also cursed Connie a little bit for leaving him in the lurch like this. And his mother too. And every-bloody-body else. All inside his head.

When the car stopped, he considered heading off to the river or to see Cash. If he was to tell the truth, he was only going in to school now in the hope he'd get the chance and the courage to talk to Ciara. But he probably should have followed his first impulse and headed someplace where it was easier to be.

It was maths first class. It was always bloody maths. Or bloody geography. Bloody Sullivan anyway. Why would any geography teacher want to teach maths? Or the other way round? She did it on purpose, he wouldn't be surprised, just to be always in his face.

She asked him about the intersection of a Venn diagram. He might have known the answer, actually, but he was just too tired to think. Before he could try, she said, 'The answer you have written down, I mean, of course'.

He just looked at her.

She said, 'Right, up you go. You know where to go.'

Dark did.

As he walked up, some remaining clay, which had been drying in the warm classroom, fell off his shoes. She stopped mid-sentence when she spotted it.

'Sorry, I'll get the broom, Miss, and clean it up,' said Dark, making his way to the cupboard.

'You will do exactly as I say,' she said. 'Stand right where you are. We can't have you trailing muck halfway across the room.'

Dark stood still right in front of her desk.

'So...' she said, in a pleased voice. 'Mr McLean here decided to bring half a cake of dung into our classroom. Everyone, take a look here at the overgrown city boy who can't even clean his shoes.'

'It's only clay, Miss,' said Dark quietly.

'Oh, well excuse *me*. Only clay. Not to worry, though. You're not the first clever lad in this school to think there's more future in traipsing around in bog holes than in learning. Don't worry, your boots will soon be permanently stuck in cow-dung. And you'll have plenty of time for regrets later when you are still out clodding around chasing bullocks as your classmates drive past you in flashy cars.'

Dark said nothing.

'Take off those filthy things and you can hold them for the rest of the class. Double period, what a pity.'

Dark did. Unfortunately, his socks had got wet in the field too and they were not looking great. She just pointed at them, holding her nose away.

'Those too,' she said, 'those too. Put them in your pockets.'

He did that and then just looked down because now he was embarrassed about his feet. The wetness had marked his toes. And because she had him now and he didn't want her or someone in the class, anyone in the class, to see his eyes. She seemed pleased.

Then she turned and looked around the class.

'Now. Who will volunteer to clean up the little show-and-tell contribution that McLean decided to bring us? Let. Me. See.'

She was expecting to do her usual picking of 'volunteers'.

Dark heard one chair push back, as someone stood up. He didn't look up. Then another. As they pushed past him with the broom and dust pan, he saw it was Tadhg and Ciara. Others stood up too, offering to help. Mostly to break the boredom.

She wasn't happy with that either, though. She stared at Ciara, who looked intently down at her task as her long thin fingers held the broom more tightly.

Sullivan spoke directly to her: 'What's this? Are you two trying to be smart?'

She sat up on the teacher's table, a thing she never did. She put down her chalk beside her and started dangling her legs like a kid. They were all waiting for her again.

Eventually she said, 'If there's only one thing I teach you for life, it is not to throw yourselves in front of a falling wall, thinking you can prop it up. Let's be honest now. Arthur here has made his own decisions.'

She paused for effect. It was the first time he could remember her saying his first name.

'There's no reason for any of you to ruin your own lives just because you feel sorry for him.'

She paused again.

'How would that make your parents feel? Ciara? Tadhg? How would your hard-working parents feel if they heard you were giving up on your education for a young fellow who doesn't care at all about his? Because that's the truth. Arthur simply doesn't care. Anyone can see that.'

She turned slowly to Dark and paused before asking, 'Isn't that true, Arthur?'

He knew it was what she wanted but Dark had to say, 'Yes, Miss,' because it was the truth and he was too tired to think of anything more complicated to say.

She turned back to the others.

'So. You see. Why don't you settle down now and I'll forget all about this – I'll keep it as our secret.'

Everyone sat down. Tadhg looked very glum. Ciara just kept her eyes down.

That was it. It was as if she had decided to rub Dark out that day. She had not succeeded in tormenting him into leaving school, so now she would just pretend he had done so.

From that minute on, she addressed very few words to Dark. He didn't care.

When Dark turned into the Bog Field that night, he stopped dead. It was a still night with a good moon. There was not a leaf rustling on the trees in the ditch next to him, but at the other side of the bog, the trees of the rath were swaying like they were in a violent storm. Then it stopped completely, in an instant, and the rath trees also became as calm as the ditches around the field. He felt real fear. He suddenly realised that he was very alone and he didn't really understand anything about this place. A gateway between worlds – but how did he know that all the forces which stepped through that gateway were kindly ones?

He stood for a while.

He considered the alternative: going home and forgetting he had ever ventured onto the forbidden ground. But that was hardly better. He decided to go on, whatever might be waiting for him. He focused on the courage of the Old Man and the laughing face of Conán and the looks from Etain and hoped they were going to be the people he found there this night.

He approached slowly. He felt fear like a weakening tingle in every muscle of his body. But he got there and felt his way through, more cautiously than ever, as though whatever was in there tonight might not notice him.

Inside, it was black dark. Much darker than he had ever seen it before, even on moonless nights. He became so afraid that he felt limp and he had to sit down.

And then, all of a sudden, it was fine again. The Old Man arrived and it was as if nothing had ever been wrong in the world.

It was strange, though, Dark thought. The Old Man usually saw into every slight mood and thought he had. Yet, if he had noticed Dark's shaken terror this night, which surely must have been written in bold on his white face, the Old Man didn't make any mention of it at all. It was as if he was distracted by the story he was about to enter.

As the others gathered, they all looked cold. Even Etain was pale. He touched her slender fingers as he took the cup. They were as cold as the metal. Even the fire burnt reluctantly.

As the Old Man cleared his throat, the scene Dark soon saw before him in the flames wasn't a warm or comforting one.

The Winter of the Black Wind

Cóbh was never a place renowned for good fortune. When the message came one day for Fionn to go there, he was immediately overcome by a sickly feeling of foreboding. It was a peculiar call from a peculiar place. A boy was stuck up in a tree and Fionn was wanted there, to see what could be done.

'What kind of thing is that to be asking the leader of the Fianna to attend to?' growled Goll at the young man who brought the message. 'Can't ye get the whelp down from the tree for yourselves? Next you'll be calling Fionn Mac Cumhaill every time your cow is sick or your hen stops laying.'

'I dunno,' said the lad, looking at the ground. 'I was only sent with the message.'

'No luck will be had from answering that call,' predicted Conán, quite correctly.

Nevertheless, the image of the boy became peculiarly vivid in Mac Cumhaill's mind: a small fellow high up on the weak upper branches of one of the few tall larch trees that grew in Cóbh. In his mind, he could clearly see the tree leaning out and overhanging a part of the bay that had no bottom. He worried about why this image was coming through to him. What dark forces wanted to draw him to that place? But he could see the lad perfectly and he knew the little boy was innocent and afraid. He could almost hear the boy or the tree calling his name. He had no choice. He had to go.

When they got there, the scene was exactly as he had envisaged. The violent waters were already reaching waist height, submerging the bank where the tree was rooted. The tree was leaning outwards like a bent old man over water that was much, much deeper and very angry. It looked as if that water's plans did not include good deeds or kindness as far as anyone present was concerned. The little red-headed child of no more than ten years was on the branch that reached furthest out. He was too frightened to move a limb, let alone climb back in. There was freezing rain blowing, and the lad, suspended in the wind with only a light tunic on him, was surely nearly paralysed with the cold.

It didn't look as if there was an easy solution. There were no ladders long enough to get up to where the boy was. The branches he was clinging on to were mere twigs and would certainly have broken before any grown man could climb near him.

They had to do something quickly though, as the boy was wailing and sobbing softly. A kind of sound from someone getting ready to give themselves over to death. He would not hold on much longer. His family were all gathered near the tree, along with neighbours and friends, and they were trying to keep back their own tears and looking pleadingly at Mac Cumhaill to do something to save the beloved little boy.

Mac Cumhaill's heart was sore when he decided on a plan, because not far inside him he knew it was a trap. He knew it was going to go wrong and that the bad luck of Cóbh was about to become his own personal bad luck. But he had to try something. So he told Diarmuid and Conán to wade in under the tree and make ready to catch the boy. He himself got ready to lower the tree. He climbed as high as he could without the tree shaking, and tied a rope around the trunk. Then he got back down and started pulling the rope back in towards dry land, trying to pull the enormous tree towards him.

'*Wisha,* Daghda love him,' said an old woman, 'Fionn Mac Cumhaill is gone soft in the head. We may as well pray for the boy now. That tree was three hundred years old when I was a child and stronger than a thousand men.'

But Mac Cumhaill put his whole strength into it. A couple of other men tried to help, but their efforts made no difference in the contest between Mac Cumhaill and the great larch. Finally, a sigh of amazement went through the crowd as the roots started snapping and the tree started to creak and groan. Slowly at first, with Mac Cumhaill pulling harder than ever, it began to straighten. Then, as he pulled harder, gradually it bowed inwards and came closer to the ground. Soon Conán and Diarmuid were easily able to grab the little boy to safety.

Then, just as Mac Cumhaill was going to let go, a massive, unnatural, black gust of wind came from nowhere. A main root snapped, the rope went slack, Mac Cumhaill fell on his back, and almost instantly the great tree pounced. It came crashing onto Mac Cumhaill. The crushing noise it made was so ferocious that few there had any doubt that instant but that Mac Cumhaill's stay in this world had been brought to an end.

The crowd had fallen silent, as everyone stared at the horrible scene.

Conán started shouting at them: 'Wake up you *amadáns!* Go and get axes. Go and get saws. Go to the neighbouring clans and get more men. We are going to cut this evil tree to smithereens and set Fionn free!'

He was shouting like such a madman that the people thought it was better to do what he said than just to stand there gawking.

Soon there were thirty or forty people chopping and hacking at the body of that dead tree. Even if they didn't believe that Mac Cumhaill would come out alive, they were all infected by Conán's frenzy of anger towards the tree and whatever evil had taken hold of it. There were young and old at it. Even the mother of the rescued boy, who was wrapped in blankets in the arms of an older woman, had taken an axe and was chopping more fiercely than any man. It was as if the whole village had suddenly erupted in rage at the merciless bad luck that had stalked their people for centuries. They were hacking and chopping at fortune.

Eventually, the trunk was eaten away enough and started to give. The heavy roots tried to stand back up, bending the partially severed stump upwards like a broken arm. The body underneath was covered in stale blood. To the surprise of many, it groaned. Mac Cumhaill's bronze shield with its dark ruby centrepiece was bent out of shape, but it had somehow protected his chest. He was still alive, but only barely. He was carefully edged onto a canvas-and-pole stretcher, and the family whose boy he had saved asked for him to be brought into their home. The little boy sat by his bedside, trying to get him to swallow a spoonful of warm porridge every time he came close to waking up.

Dreoilín and a handywoman were sent for and they came with the best of herbs, splints and bandages. After a few weeks, Mac Cumhaill was starting to feel less pain and was trying to sit up in bed to play card games with the little boy. But he had two broken legs that were set in splints and they were going to take the whole winter to heal.

When he finally left the house supporting his weight on hazel walking sticks, he thanked the family deeply for their warmth. The little boy still thought it was all his fault.

'You don't worry about anything in the world except enjoying your youth and looking after your parents,' said Mac Cumhaill. 'It's a miracle you're alive, and you should make the most of every day you get from now on.'

But as Mac Cumhaill set off on his crutches, he was a very worried man. He knew that there were other forces at work. The black gust that came and disappeared so suddenly, knocking the tree onto him, was no ordinary wind.

Sure enough, it wasn't long before his foreboding bore bitter fruit. Stories started coming from all over the country of terrible accidents and chaos being caused by mysterious gales coming from nowhere. Bridges were blown down when people were crossing them. Fishing boats were overturned by massive winds from the shore, even though the water had been completely calm minutes before and the thatch was being whipped clean off cabins without warning and dropped, point downwards, back in on top of them.

Most of the bad events seemed to be happening to members of the Fianna. Lookout posts were demolished when Fianna soldiers were sleeping inside them. Horsemen were blown clear over a cliff in Scariff. Soldiers out guarding one of the king's dwellings had a wall hurled on them by a gust. In all cases, people said the wind had a mysterious blackish tint to it.

Mac Cumhaill went to Dreoilín and asked what he thought. Dreoilín went to Lough Garr to talk to his ancestors. He returned after three days with an account that had come to him – from more than three hundred years before – of a renegade god called Cass. He was a brother of Daghda but Daghda had told him never to darken the family door again. In ancient times, people knew Cass as the Black Wind. He had done enormous damage back then and eventually had been captured by a very powerful druid, and held inside the spirit of a young larch tree.

'And where was that larch tree?' asked Mac Cumhaill, already knowing the answer.

'In the town where all bad luck seems to begin and end,' sighed Dreoilín.

'Hmmm,' said Mac Cumhaill. 'And I set it free.'

'Cass must have drawn that little boy to the tree and then scared him up, hoping that someone would come and break down the tree to free him – and it,' said Dreoilín.

'Most importantly,' asked Fionn, 'what is our challenge now? What must be done to destroy him?'

'Fionn, dear son,' said Dreoilín with tiredness in his voice, 'I truly don't know. But he did call you specifically to that tree. And he does seem to be attacking the Fianna more than anyone else, as if he was trying to gain ground before you are fully recovered. So it's possible you have something that he's scared of.'

Mac Cumhaill thought about it all that night and the next day. He was sure Dreoilín was wrong. This ferocious force, the Black Wind, had left him as good as dead and he was supposed to think that it feared *him*?

Úna, who was always practical in her way of thinking about things, asked, 'Well, what is it that he really likes?'

'Spreading his own misery to all of humanity. That, it seems, is all it takes to put him in a pleasant mood,' said Mac Cumhaill.

'And you – are you not in his way?' said Úna. 'Do you think he doesn't know you have some kind of blessing of the other gods?'

'It didn't feel like that when the tree was crushing my bones,' said Mac Cumhaill.

'Daghda between us and all harm!' said Úna. 'Aren't you still alive when no one thought it possible? There are a thousand times you would have been dead by now, if their knowledge and the protective hand was not upon you.'

'That is true.'

'Well, then. Your very existence scalds him in two ways. The first is obviously that you represent a danger to him in his activities of torment. The second is that you have something he always wanted and can never have again – the approval of his brother. The fact that you survived the tree, which no other human would have been spared from, will only confirm that for him. He will do everything to get you. And now that you're injured, he's thinking it's his best chance.'

'Good enough,' said Mac Cumhaill, 'so he's hitting lots of the Fianna to draw me into battle.'

'Well, you just can't go, you know,' said Úna. 'Not in that state.'

'Yes,' said Mac Cumhaill, not really listening.

'Can't you see that's just what he wants?' said Úna.

'Yes, but I can't let him carry on.'

That night, there was another attack on a Fianna camp and an old man who cooked for the soldiers was strangled by the wind tightening like a bindweed around his neck. That decided Mac Cumhaill.

He went back to Dreoilín and asked for some help with

spells or potions. Dreoilín gave Mac Cumhaill an oyster shell, doubtfully.

'It worked to contain a sea breeze once,' said Dreoilín.

Granted it was a west coast oyster shell, as big as Dreoilín's two hands. But Mac Cumhaill looked at it with disbelief.

'Is that all you can do? How am I expected to get a screeching hurricane into that?'

'If you can get the head of the gale in, the rest will die, but I can't tell you how you might lure it in.'

Mac Cumhaill knew there was only one bait. That day, despite appeals from Diarmuid and Úna not to do it, Mac Cumhaill sent out word to all parts of the country that he would be waiting at Cashel to fight the weakling outcast, Cass.

As the word went from mouth to mouth, other winds picked it up and carried it in whispers, far and wide, so that it was no time at all until the Black Wind knew it. Even though rattled at the insult it suspected a trick; that Mac Cumhaill would never be foolish enough to come out on his own to fight it when he wasn't even able to stand without crutches. But it went to Cashel to look and sure enough saw Mac Cumhaill sitting with his back to the great rock, and a semicircle of people a good distance out from him, watching in fear.

Fionn Mac Cumhaill was pale with pain and with cold. The wind wasted no time and went straight in for an attack. In a horrible dark *whoooosh* it swept through the crowd, knocking people in every direction, and whirled around

Mac Cumhaill's enormous chest. Mac Cumhaill groaned with agony as the wind tightened its grip. It was trying to squeeze so tight that Mac Cumhaill would not be able to breathe. At first it looked as though it had succeeded, as Mac Cumhaill's face became red and then blue. But he sucked in with all his strength, and his chest filled with air, and he blew out in an enormous shout. The wind was furious and moved away with a phwaaaa sound. Mac Cumhaill knew there would be more.

The second time it tried the same. This time Mac Cumhaill knew his chest was stronger than the wind, and he immediately breathed in and the wind retreated again, sweeping some of the spectators up into the sky and dropping them miles away in its anger.

The third time it came at him, Mac Cumhaill guessed it would do now what he feared most: attack his neck and try to strangle him. If it got around his neck he feared there was nothing he could do to save himself. But for luck, in its rage, the wind rushed at him and picked leaves on its way. This allowed Mac Cumhaill to see it coming a split second before it arrived. He put up his arm and in its blind anger the wind missed Mac Cumhaill's neck and wrapped itself around his arm instead. Not seeing its mistake until it was too late, the wind wound itself in such a tight bind that Fionn's arm pained; his neck would surely have been broken had the wind found its target.

But the wind's mistake was Mac Cumhaill's opportunity. With one sweep of his other hand, he clamped the shell onto the head of the tight wind. He slammed the shell shut before the thing knew what was happening. The rest of the wind fell off his arm. At first he wasn't sure that he had Cass inside the shell. He waited for another attack. The whole crowd waited in silence. But after a few minutes Mac Cumhaill lifted the shell above his head and everyone knew it was over. A great cheer went up and the people came to carry Mac Cumhaill on their shoulders all the way back to Tara.

Though Mac Cumhaill now had one arm in a splint as well as his two legs, the spring that followed was a beautiful and happy one for the people of the country.

The shell was taken out into the bottomless parts of the ocean off the coast of Cóbh, where the dark water drags hard on the best boats. It was weighted down with stones so that it should sink forever and never be seen again. However, many people still believe that even from within its shell, deep under the water, its horrible anger sometimes stirs those seas into unexpected swells, tormenting and sometimes marking large and small boats passing these parts with a curse that draws them downwards.

Everyone disappeared suddenly when the story finished, rather than fading out gradually as usual. The black darkness was restored in the centre of the rath. Dark got out of there as quick as he could, and although he was sure he heard a great storm brewing behind him again, he didn't look back once as he headed back up the fields.

12
A NEW HOUND

Dark's mother dropped him at the speed limit sign. She hadn't ventured closer to the school since Magill had talked to her the last time. Dark waited for her to be gone around the turn on the road before he headed back the same way. The turn for the Drishna *boreen* was only half a mile out the main road. Connie used to call it the Famine Road, 'built on crushed skeletons'. There was very little likelihood here of meeting anyone who would be curious at a lad with a school uniform walking away from the town.

Cash lived about two miles out. Dark had gotten directions from Brian that morning.

Dogs barked and five, of various shapes, wandered up to smell and inspect Dark as he approached the front door. A blonde woman opened the door almost immediately. There were two very small children looking out around her legs.

'What do you want, sonny?'

306

'Is David in?'

'Are you a friend of his? Will you do me a favour and take him to school with you? He says he's not bothered.'

'I wasn't thinking of going myself,' said Dark.

'Oh, right. Water always finds its own level I suppose. DAVEY! Come out here will you and see this man.'

Cash was in a tracksuit and looked surprised and confused, as if he had just got out of bed. He was scratching the back of his head.

'McLean? What has you here?'

'I came to see about that pup,' said Dark.

Cash brightened up immediately. 'Oh! I thought they might have sent you to call me down to school or something.'

'Hardly,' said Dark. 'They'd hardly send me.'

Cash thought about that and then laughed. 'No. Hardly. Come on out here with me, then.'

They went around to the back of the house. Dark had never in his life seen so many huts and cages and sheds in one garden. Cash must have seen Dark's reaction.

'Do you like animals and birds then? Here, I'll give you the tour.'

There were budgies, rabbits, coloured pheasants, ferrets, feather-footed bantams, ducks, a small horse, a black donkey and many, many dogs. By the time they were all fed and talked about, two hours had passed. The mother looked out the back door and said, 'Davey, you and your father need to get rid of half of them animals, you have me broke feeding them.'

There were two litters of pups to choose from. Dark knew his dog the minute he set eyes on her. She was about average size for her litter and not too shy and not too bold. She was white with brindle markings. And she was fat for a whippet. She came right up to him and licked his hand and eyed him.

Cash said, 'Looks like she's picked you, buddy.'

'OK,' said Dark.

'She should be a right lady after the rabbits seeing as her mother is one of the best.'

Dark wasn't concerned about that. Hunting rabbits with dogs had never interested him. But when he held her in his hands and felt her snuggling warmly into his stomach, he knew he was going to spend a lot of time with her.

Cash brought him over to the two caravans at the side of the house. One was modern and looked ready for the road. The other looked like it hadn't moved in a long while. It was on blocks and a climbing rose draped the roof.

'This is where I stay, when we're not away off,' Cash said, 'so as I can mind my gran. She never comes with us anymore because she says the way the country is gone these days pains her heart.'

A small woman pushed the door open. Her face was brown as hillside bracken with deep gulleys running through it.

'Who's this, Davey?' asked the woman in an ancient voice.

'This is my friend, Arthur McLean, Nan,' said Cash.

The granny looked Dark up and down. 'McLean? From the Killane Road out there?'

'Yes,' said Dark.

A toothless smile lightened her face. She gave him a pat on the shoulder.

'God bless you, *a mhic.* I knew your grandmother and your grandfather well. The Lord rest their souls, two decenter people never walked on the face of this earth. In the summer time when we'd be stopped out that road, I used to call around there and they'd always buy whatever little things I'd be selling and there'd always be tea and great welcome. I knew their lads growing up too. Seán and Cornelius. Two fine boys. They often came up to the caravan to bring up a billy can of milk or some clothes or other things that their mother thought would be useful for me with all my childer. And they wouldn't be afraid to sit around the fire with us and sing a song or listen to yarns. Where are they now?'

Dark wasn't ready for that.

She saw and changed the subject.

'That's a fine, fair name they put on you. It fits you just right. Arthur,' she said, emphasising his name in a distant tone.

He couldn't say why, but it was as if she knew him before. It was the first time in a long while that he really liked the sound of that word again.

Then she laughed and said, 'You are growing into a great big man too, God love you. Look at the height of you already. Come in, come in.'

Arthur and Davey came inside and sat on the chairs she pulled out at the table.

Then she laughed and said, 'So, you think school is only a cod too, Arthur McLean?'

'Sort of,' said Arthur.

The old lady laughed harder. She brought out two bottles of orange and a packet of fig rolls for them. She left them to talk about the dog while she went back to watching *Telly Bingo*. When the biscuits were all gone, Arthur decided he would head on home. He said thanks to Cash's grandmother.

As he was leaving, she said a peculiar thing. She blessed him and laughed saying, '*A mhic*, you'll have to watch out for the little folk that they don't steal your heart away. The old people always said there was a great kingdom of the little enchanters somewhere out Killane way.'

As he was heading out the gate, he held up the little box that Mrs Cash had settled the pup in for the journey, 'Thanks very much Davey.'

'No bother, McLean.'

'See you tomorrow?' asked Arthur.

'No.'

'Monday then?'

'Not going back there, Arthur.' There was finality in his voice. 'I'm no one to them. I have better things to be doing.'

'Fair enough,' said Arthur.

'Call up another day, though. Any time you want.'

'I will,' said Arthur.

When Arthur got home, he spent a couple of hours settling the pup by the Aga. She ate the bread and milk and
corned beef and tuna he gave her. And she got out of her
bed to pee on the floor five times in an hour. That was no
bother, as the old flagstones on the kitchen floor soaked up
what he couldn't mop. The two old collies took to her immediately and even started growling at each other to work
out which of them would get to mind her and lie next to
her and show her the ropes. Georgina won in the end.
Arthur was glad, as she had the greater need.

That night, the Old Man and Conán asked for a detailed description of the newcomer. There were some
questions about the shape of her ears and her eye colour
that Arthur would have to check on later.

'I can develop a terrible fondness towards a dog,
Arthur,' said the Old Man. 'You must treat her with great
respect. A dog will always pay back kindness, in loyalty and
love. She will never have to think twice.'

Arthur noticed that the little people didn't seem too enthusiastic about this subject. Bal was positively sulky.

'You wouldn't have so much fondness for the friggers if
they were five times the size of you and came digging the
earth to look for you,' he said.

'Most of them can't even get the scent of *sí*,' Conán
laughed. 'They mightn't bother you either if you weren't
so averse to water.'

That only made Bal's face more contorted with anger.

Etain brought the goblet and sat in next to Arthur on a
log. A terrible fondness would hardly describe what Arthur

felt then, as the lovely liquid made his mind melt and the words of the Old Man transported him through the flame.

Fiachra Loses His Fight

Fiachra Mac Duibhne had joined the Fianna very young and trained with a terrible determination, no matter what the weather or no matter what festivities were going on.

He had become one of the greatest members the Fianna had ever known. He was a very short young man, and he wasn't bulky. He never boasted of his achievements. But he was fast, fearsome and unflinching. His friends were wary of him, because of his strictness and dedication. He stuck absolutely to the rules and had no sympathy or understanding for anyone who strayed. He was ever vigilant and some said he never slept. Enemies quickly learned to fear him for he had a stamina and ferociousness in battle that was unmatched. The leaders came to know about him and from early on, he would be selected for missions that needed only the most trusted and committed.

Mac Cumhaill didn't like to discourage such dedication, but he sometimes thought that nobody could keep going indefinitely with such fervour.

'Have you no life outside of this, son?' he often asked Fiachra, laughing.

Fiachra would respond, not laughing at all, 'No, chief, I don't.'

One evening, sitting at a slow fire and waiting for a pot to boil, Mac Cumhaill asked him what he meant by that.

Fiachra said, 'Many years ago I left my father when he needed me.'

There was silence. Tears welled, strangers to the hard man's eyes.

'Sorry, chief,' he said, blowing snot into the fire and trying to dry himself up.

'Get the dirty water off your chest, boy,' said Mac Cumhaill. 'There's no shame in tears.'

'I can never forgive myself for it,' said Fiachra.

Then he told how his mother had died when he was very young.

'After that, it was just Daddy and myself in the house. I liked him. No. That's not it. I adored him. I went everywhere with him. He was a *currach* maker. The best. He was very good indoors too, doing the cooking, taking care of me and telling me stories. But then, when I was about ten, my father changed. He started being visited by a ghost. He stopped all his woodworking. He stopped even leaving the cabin. He took to his bed, without any talk of plans to get up. I had to take on all the inside work as well as learning to snare rabbits and collect debts from people my father had built boats for, so we wouldn't starve. That was in the middle of the winter so at first I hoped that when the weather cleared up a bit maybe he would shift out of the bed and sit next to the hearth and heat his strength back. I kept the fire blazing.

'But nothing changed. He would just sit on his straw mattress looking terrified and talking to the ghost. I wasn't able to see the ghost and often didn't believe it was real. I was tired of having to work so hard. I was angry because I'd lost my mammy and now even Daddy seemed to have stopped caring for me. I shouted at my father to wake up and start helping. After maybe two years of this, I took a notion one day and just packed my few clothes, I cursed him and left. I walked many miles until I found an old warrior who promised to train me for the Fianna. I worked and trained very hard until I was accepted by yourself as the youngest ever member of the Fianna. But ever since I have never felt good. Not for one day. Not for one minute. I left my sick father alone and didn't even tell him where I was going.'

'So,' Mac Cumhaill said, 'is that why you've never taken a partner and had a family of your own?'

'Yes. Since I let my father down, I don't deserve to be loved by any other person. How could they trust me not to desert them too?'

'You were young,' said Mac Cumhaill. 'We all make mistakes when we are young. You have to close the door on them some time or they spawn other mistakes.'

'I can't,' said Fiachra. 'I think about him every day; I try to put him out of my head by fighting harder than anyone else, by hunting better than the others, by working harder in the castle. So I'm that exhausted that I might get an hour's sleep.'

'Well, what about going to find your father then?' said Mac Cumhaill.

'I tried that. I went back there a few years ago. The people in the clan all said they were proud of how well I'd done. But they all got quiet when I asked about my father. I went down the path to our little old shack. A woman welcomed me. She said, "I'm sorry son, he hasn't been heard of in a long time".'

'Well, since it's going to be a long night and since this pot is never going to boil,' said Mac Cumhaill as casually as if he was suggesting a walk over the hill, 'why don't you take a turn with me to the land of the unsettled. We'll see what they have to tell us about the whole episode.'

Mac Cumhaill didn't make such proposals often. He liked to keep quiet about the few special abilities allowed to him by higher powers, to avoid fuelling rumours about him. He looked closely at the reaction. Fiachra paled. But he didn't laugh or run away like most men would do at such a proposition. The depth of Fiachra's misery was such that he agreed without hesitation.

No sooner had he agreed than they had travelled far without any sense of moving and were now sitting in the same position, still facing a very poor fire, in the middle of a stone hall. The hall extended into other halls as far as the eye could stretch. The roof was so high you could barely make out the details. All around in every direction were moping images of human forms floating aimlessly, draped on furniture and lying forlorn on the floor. The last time Mac Cumhaill had been here was to have a conversation with a very frightened old soldier, killed in battle but suspended in these halls, too paralysed by fear to make the next step into the other world.

Right there, not a hundred paces from them, was the

only clear image. His form was vivid and real. He was hunched in his old brown tunic, sitting on the floor, rocking slightly.

He looked up when they walked over to him. He looked the same as the day Fiachra had left him. He still had the face of someone trying bravely to swallow back great pain. He didn't recognise either of his visitors, but he smiled faintly at seeing humans.

Fiachra bent down over him and whispered in his ear. 'It's me. Fiachra. I'm very sorry.'

The father tried to stand. For a second or two he didn't believe it, staring through the years, and then he hugged Fiachra.

'A fine man! My little child!'

'I am very sorry, Father,' Fiachra kept saying.

'Sorry? For what?'

'For giving up on you.'

'I can't lie to you. I was heartbroken from the day you left. But I knew I was the one who left you first. So I always prayed you'd found something better to do than to spend your life nursing a skeleton.'

They went on talking, each vying to take more than his share of the blame for their separation and hardship.

Eventually, Mac Cumhaill said, 'We have to be moving soon, Fiachra. That pot will be boiling over and our bit of meat will be ruined.'

Only then did Fiachra remember to introduce Fionn Mac Cumhaill to his father. Warm greetings were exchanged and much gratitude was expressed by Fiachra's father for all Fionn had done for his boy, not least in bringing him here to this place, where humans dreaded to tread.

'Will the three of us go back then and we can talk about it all over a few mouthfuls of rabbit stew?' said Mac Cumhaill.

'You go,' said the father. 'I can't.'

It was as if someone had punched Fiachra very hard in the chest. His face filled with pain again. He had assumed they were reunited for good. Of course then he realised that if his father had been free to come back, he would have done so long ago.

He started pleading like a child: 'Come back with me and I will make things right. I will never leave you alone again.'

'I can't,' the father said, pointing over his shoulder, where there hovered a ghost as ugly and foul as the darkest deed. 'This thing will definitely never leave me alone.'

Fiachra could finally see it – the thing that had enslaved his father all these years. The thing, if the truth be told, he had doubted. It was real.

'It will never leave me alone,' said the father again.

'I know an old lad who might be able to help,' said Mac Cumhaill.

The ghost, who had remained impassive, seemed to shift position slightly at this.

The father was eventually persuaded to come back to their fireside, if only to spend a few hours on earth with Fiachra. The spirit came with him, he said, but could no longer be seen by Mac Cumhaill or Fiachra.

Mac Cumhaill sent a boy to Lisheen, where he knew Dreoilín was often to be found wandering in the bogs in the company of frogs, inspecting his forest of rushes and mumbling to his ancestors. Dreoilín flew to their fireside and then changed into his human shape.

He needed no explanations. He could see the ghost immediately and recited a long verse appealing for the restoration of Daghda's protection over the poor man. Almost before the words were finished, the ghost had fled back to its own land, without a murmur of bad or good wishes to the man he had plagued for twenty years.

The father was overwhelmed. It took him a little while, looking timidly this way and that, to start to believe.

Then he said, 'It's the first time in so long I feel like a living person. Nothing squeezing the good out of every thought, before I even get a chance to translate it into an action. It feels like somebody just rolled away a huge boulder that has been flattening my body.'

From that day on, Fiachra visited his father every day and they would often go hunting and fishing together. Fiachra became interested in many things. It was as if his own life had been suspended just as his father's had, and he was trying to catch up on all that he had missed.

Over time, he became hale and hearty, where he once had been keen and lean. That made him better company, but a much worse soldier. He found excuses to miss any events that involved travelling far from home.

One day, Mac Cumhaill said to him, 'Fiachra, I am sorry

to tell you this, but you are no longer suitable for the Fianna.'

Fiachra actually looked relieved and said, 'But I have been trying really hard to stay good at soldiering.'

'Yes,' said Mac Cumhaill, 'but your heart is not in it.'

'You saved my father and this is how I repay you? What can I do to get back as good as I was?' asked Fiachra.

'Nothing. I have been thinking about that this last while. The basic problem is, you are too happy to be a good soldier. All of the best here are being eaten up inside by various things. That's what makes us mean when we have to be.'

They parted as friends and Fiachra took up bee-keeping, supplying honey for the tables of kings, as well as making mead. His temperament infected the bees and he rarely got stung. He went on to have the biggest collection of hives in this country or in any other that Fionn Mac Cumhaill had ever visited.

The mornings were getting lighter and even though the fire vanished earlier than usual, there was already a glint of light over the hill fields and the birds were already well into their proclamations.

Arthur wandered home and had a sound sleep before the alarm clock called him. He was giving himself an extra half hour these days, as the worst of the calving was well over. He thought his mam would be relieved about that.

13
WISHING TO BE AWAY

No trouble from Sullivan at roll call about the previous day's absence. And she skipped over David Cash's name altogether. No homework questioning either. Her policy of ignoring was in full force. He still didn't care. He took out the DS and played it under the desk. By first break he was very bored.

Cash and the Old Man were right. Why should he be wishing the long minutes away in here? He wasn't needed here. At home, there were many animals that needed and appreciated his attention. There were good things he could be doing.

And as for the sí's fort, there was not one thing in that world as dull and miserable as one minute in Sullivan's classroom, with its yellowing posters of badly-drawn smiling people, and brightly-coloured walls that someone thought would trick young people into thinking this was a happy place.

He would only have to figure out how to get out altogether without getting his mother in trouble. He left at break time through the front gates.

That afternoon when he sent his usual text telling his mother he had got a lift home, she phoned him to say she was coming home anyway. She sounded serious and a bit scared.

'Arthur, there are some people coming to the house to see us this afternoon. Just be honest with them.'

Arthur washed and put his uniform back on. When she arrived, she tried to wipe crumbs from his mouth with her handkerchief. Even though he was a head taller than her, she patted his hair as if he was still little. It was only because she was nervous.

Shortly after that, Georgina ran out barking madly, as a car crunched its way up the gravel. The pup, Pumpkin, ran out after her. Arthur ran after Pumpkin. Georgina couldn't be expected to understand that other dogs didn't have the same natural instincts for car-chasing as collies.

It was a large, metallic blue Passat. It made his mother's car and everything else around the yard look old and somehow lacking in colour. Arthur went back in with the pup.

Two men came to the door and his mother invited them inside. Arthur was sent out, and from the door he heard them talking to her in serious tones. He couldn't make much of it out. Then she called him back in.

'Arthur, I think you know Mr Jenkins from school?'

Arthur looked at the first man. He seemed vaguely familiar.

'And this is Mr Malley. He is with…er…the HSE, you know – the, um, health board, sort of.'

Jenkins stepped forward, in front of Arthur's mother, with a hand extended to Arthur.

'Arthur, I'm the home-school liaison officer.'

Arthur said nothing. He'd seen the man in Magill's office, now he came to think of it.

'Your mother is a difficult woman to pin down,' he said with an attempt at a laugh. 'I've been trying to get hold of you both for weeks now, and in the end, I had to bring my friend here, Mr Malley, with me to get the favour of an interview at all. Mr Malley is a social worker. Have you ever heard of such a species before?' He was trying to be funny, but Arthur just went on looking at him.

'Do you know what our jobs are?'

'No.'

Malley intervened. 'Arthur, we've just come up here to take a look in on you and see how things are going.'

'They're going grand,' said Arthur.

'Arthur,' said Malley, 'the reason we are asking you these questions is only for your own good. We are on your side. So you can answer freely.'

'OK', said Arthur.

'Well, to be honest, we're not so sure that things are going so grand,' said Jenkins. 'My information is that you are not doing very well in school – on the rare occasions you decide to attend. And from outside the school we've had reports of you wandering the fields during school hours. You do know that when we get reports like that we cannot ignore them. What would be your own view on that?'

'On what?'

'How well are you getting on at school?'

'The finest,' said Arthur.

'Well, when last did you do any homework?'

'A while back.'

He turned to Arthur's mother. 'When did you last check that he was doing his homework, Mrs McLean?'

She was flustered. 'I'm sorry. I've been so busy. He's been so busy. We will make sure he does better.'

'And when did you last bring any books to school, Arthur?'

'I dunno,' said Arthur.

His mother looked at him questioningly.

'And are those reports that we've been receiving from concerned neighbours about seeing you lurking at the river, are those incorrect? How many days a week do you actually stay in school?'

'Two or three,' said Arthur.

His mother now looked shocked. Arthur was sorry. But he was also puzzled over who could have been reporting him.

Jenkins turned to Arthur's mother again, and said, 'If you were in our position, Mrs McLean, how do you think this would look? A mother who claims to be unaware that her son is going to school with an empty bag and mitching every other day?'

Arthur's mother said nothing.

Jenkins turned to Arthur. 'What do you think will be the final result for someone who doesn't bring any books or make any effort?'

'I don't know.'

'Do you think learning is just going to *happen* to you?' Jenkins was sounding a bit less patient now.

'Maybe.'

'Well, I have bad news for you, Arthur. It won't. And you will very soon find yourself with no future other than being trapped here, not able to read or write or succeed. Is that what you want?'

'I don't mind,' said Arthur.

'He can read and write perfectly well,' said his mother, reddening.

'You are going to need to make a lot more effort,' said Jenkins. 'Now, there are some other issues Mr Malley wants to ask you a few questions about.'

Malley now stepped forward. 'Would you like to take a walk with me?' he said, very sweetly.

Arthur looked at his mother. She nodded.

Malley wanted to go to Arthur's room.

He said, laughing 'Do you mind if I make notes, Arthur? It's just that I have a very bad memory.'

Arthur wondered if Malley thought he was five years old.

'You can call me Joey,' said Malley.

Then he went from general questions to fairly detailed ones. He asked Arthur what he usually had for supper. How often they had take-away. What time his mother came home at. Whether he sometimes went hungry. He asked him who is at home when he gets home from school. He asked him whether he was having to do a lot of farm work.

More information from concerned neighbours it seemed. Then he started asking about his mother. How often did she talk to him? Did she ever leave him alone at night?

Next he said, 'Arthur, I noticed some beers and wine in the fridge when Mum was getting out milk for our coffee. Would there often be a lot of drink? I mean, for example, would you often see Mum getting drunk with friends? It's OK to tell me.'

Arthur didn't like that. His fear of these men turned into something like anger. Sneaks in cashmere jerseys trying to get him to spy on his mam.

'You leave my mother out of this!' he heard himself saying.

The social worker's lips tightened. 'I see,' he said. He started writing furiously.

And then he brought Arthur back to the kitchen.

'Arthur, we are just trying to help.'

'If you want to help, there's a scoury calf-shed to be cleaned,' Arthur said loudly, almost in someone else's voice.

Arthur's mother looked as surprised as the two officials.

They didn't stay long. His mother was very upset for a long time after they left. But she didn't give out to him for all the trouble he had landed her in. His mother always blamed herself for everything. He made her tea and said he was sorry.

Down at the rath that night, he told the Old Man a bit about it. He didn't understand what the titles of the men could mean.

'Why would it be, Arthur,' he asked, 'that when a boy

is having trouble in the *school* that these *brehon*s of yours come to the conclusion that the problem is in the *home*, where everything is fine and there is no problem at all? Or none that is any of their business, anyway.'

'I don't know,' said Arthur.

'Do you think you should spend the night with your mother instead of listening to an old man *raiméising*?'

'No,' said Arthur. 'She'll be asleep.'

'Good enough', said the Old Man.

Then Arthur felt the Old Man put his arm around his shoulders as they walked over to the fire. It felt very nice.

Etain gave him his cup with a smile and sat next to him again. Soon the Old Man's words flowed and transported him.

The Hardy Sangster

There once was a land occupied only by woeful sangsters. A sangster was a creature much bigger than a human. They were noted for the ugliness and abundance of their heads. Though a sangster would display only one ugly mug at a time, it had many. Only one of the many was the working head, where any business went on. And only close family members knew which one that was. Since the only way to kill or hurt a sangster was to hit its real head, anyone needing to quieten one of these fellows was faced with a very good chance of himself getting sliced and eaten without inflicting the slightest damage on the sangster.

Sangsters were chronically unhappy entities. One of the results of this was that they liked to fight a lot. The only good thing about them was that they didn't like to leave their island. Even though they were extremely unhappy with every aspect of it, they were convinced there was no better country on earth, and no other decent creature liked to visit there. So they continued breeding and fighting with each other as they had done since the first brother and sister sangster had landed on that island many centuries earlier. Most outside didn't know about them. And of those who did, most didn't care about them.

However, at one time, there was a particularly nasty young sangster youth who caused so much damage and attacked so many others that he became too much even for the sangster bosses. The story told at the time was that the elder sangsters made the mother tell them which was his real head and told her that if he caused another minute of trouble they'd send him to dig in the mines. There were no mines on Sangster Island. Anyone who got sent to the mines never came back.

His mother was not pleased. As far as she was concerned, they were punishing her for doing too good a job. Every young sangster was supposed to be raised as an unmannerly, uncontrollable, sulky hooligan. And she knew she had done such a good job on this cur that he would not listen to her even for a minute. He could as soon attack her with a long knife, if she tried to advise him to calm down. But she had no doubt that the senior sangsters would be true to their word and disappear him the next time he attacked someone. It would be a matter of great shame for such men to be suspected of showing any mercy.

So she got her brothers to help tie up her little darling. They caught him in a net and as they ran chains and ropes around him he lashed out and killed one of his uncles who had mistakenly let his good head show for a minute. They put the young sangster in a big barrel, and pushed him out to sea to a point where the barrel got caught in an ocean current and was swept away.

That very ocean current that cooled Sangster Island happened to be one that warmed the west coast of Éirinn. By the time the barrel had been a couple of days at sea, the angry young sangster was able to free himself from the chains and rope. No splashing and flailing could work the barrel back against the flow. There was no way back home for him. He just had to allow the barrel to carry him wherever it was going. When it landed, he was awfully hungry and he proceeded straight towards a small village called Umall, on the western tip of Éirinn. He announced that this was his new country and that all the creatures he found living there were invaders. This, apparently, was his argument for eating them.

The local hard men tried to attack him with stones and hurley sticks. They thought they were having great success in their surprise attack, for they knocked his putrid head to a pulp. But no sooner had they turned to walk away, slapping each other on their backs, than a replacement head popped out and ate three of them in one mouthful.

The remaining people fled the area (except for one widow woman who found the sangster very attractive and stayed behind with him).

And of course, as always when a stew started getting too thick, someone suggested that Fionn Mac Cumhaill be sent for. It is not that Mac Cumhaill enjoyed being the first port of call no matter what extraordinary mess was going in any part of the country, and it was not that he always had a very strong preference for the people he was supposed to rescue over the creatures he was supposed to rescue them from. But what choice did he have other than to come? There was to be no rest for him.

He came with Dreoilín, Conán and a couple of young soldiers. On the road to Connemara they discussed the problem. Dreoilín said that from the descriptions people had given, the troublesome stranger sounded like a kind of creature he had heard tell of from a faraway island.

'If it is indeed a sangster,' said Dreoilín, 'then we're probably wasting our time going there. There's no way to kill him without knowing which head to kill. And there's no way to know which head to kill unless someone from his family tells you. And sangster families aren't renowned for helpfulness and don't live anywhere near here even if they were.'

Mac Cumhaill decided he was going to try to fight anyway and see what happened. They didn't have much further to go, as the sangster, who had started moving inland from Umall, met them on the road. He headed for them roaring, with his big mouth open and his huge arms flailing. Mac Cumhaill went straight for him and lambasted him with a blow of a club. The head was knocked clean off him like a loose stone off the top of the wobbly walls the people marked their ragged boundaries with over in those parts.

But no one celebrated. Just as they feared, another head popped up to greet them with even greater toxic rage. And this one was harder to connect with using the club. This went on for a while, until Mac Cumhaill finally realised that Dreoilín was right.

There was nothing for it but to take one of the bigger risks of his life and head off for Sangster Island. He left the two young soldiers taking turns, hitting heads and resting, with strict instructions to keep the sangster occupied till they got back. He headed down to the sea, happy enough for the chance of some solitude. He felt like a swim anyway, as he hadn't been in saltwater for a year.

It wasn't so great a distance into the Westerly Ocean to reach the current, and, swimming against it, it took him nearly a week before he spotted the bleak Sangster Island, a bit off to his right.

He was surrounded immediately when he went ashore, but fortunately not eaten. These sangsters had never seen a visitor before and were not sure whether they were allowed to eat them. They decided to take him to their king instead.

The king happened to be in a good mood that day. When Fionn described the problem, he immediately slapped his brow and said, 'That sounds very like the hardy pup that was supposed to be taken to the mines. Bring his mother here'.

The massive old *cailleach* kept changing heads uncomfortably when the king asked her why she had made a sailor of her son, when they were waiting for a chance to send him mining. For a minute, Mac Cumhaill felt sorry for her. What else would a poor old woman do but protect her child? he thought. But his sympathy didn't last long. The old sangster mother took a run at the king and nearly scratched his eyes out.

'If you find the cur, I'll kill him myself. The runt promised to send me dead bodies from wherever he landed and he hasn't sent me a thing.'

'Well now, if you would tell this big lump of a visitor how he can coax the real head out of your delinquent son, he can do your work for you. And be advised that if you try to scratch the eyes out of any of my heads again, I'll boil you up for soup!'

The sangster mother had no hesitation.

'Call out, "Torment, Torment, Torment," and the big ugly mug will come popping out,' she shouted in her deep, gravelly voice, 'and you'll know it because it has a tiny red mark over the left eye.'

'Thank you, indeed, and blessings on your business,' said Mac Cumhaill, backing out.

Nobody heard him because the hall had erupted into a major squabble over some food the servants had just brought in. Even the king was kicking and knifing everyone around him.

Mac Cumhaill ran back to the sea before they realised that a nice-sized meal was leaving the island.

It only took two days to swim back to Umall. And not a minute too soon, because the two young men whom he'd left fighting the sangster were so exhausted they could barely raise a sword.

Mac Cumhaill rushed up.

'Torment, Torment, Torment,' he shouted.

At first nothing happened. He fired every foul curse he could think of back in the direction of Sangster Island. Then he tried again, but with an attempt at imitation of the deep gravel voice of the sangster mother.

This time there was a crackling sound, and out popped the ugliest of all the heads in the universe. The 'little' red birthmark his mother had referred to would have been hard to miss. It was in fact a blazing conflagration the size of a frying pan over his left eye.

What nobody present had known was that a sangster with its real head out becomes a thousand times more ferocious. Within a second of the head appearing, three heads had disappeared off middle-aged Umall men who were standing around observing the unusual events that were unfolding in their usually quiet settlement. Everyone else scurried out of the way of the sangster, its red blotch throbbing with rage. It was looking everywhere, probably trying to locate the source of the motherly voice.

Mac Cumhaill stood firm. Retreat now would only allow the monster to calm down and hide away its good head. He had to keep it riled. It came for him faster than a cat strikes, which is faster than any other animal can blink. Fast, but mercifully predictable. If Mac Cumhaill had not observed closely the slight swelling of the eyes that had occurred immediately prior to the strikes on the other men, he too would have certainly had important parts of his body partitioned from each other. His head would undoubtedly already be keeping company with the heads of the harmless Umall men, swimming in the digestive juices of the whelp's belly. Instead, Mac Cumhaill had crouched down just a moment before he thought he was in the sangster's striking range. Only his sturdy spear stood upright with its base firmly jammed on a rock, to greet the palette of the sangster's great cave of a gob, as it attempted to enclose Fionn Mac Cumhaill's head inside it.

The spear had no retreat through the rock and had no option but to extend itself through the roof of the mouth and the brain, what little there was, of the sangster's one true head. This did not have a good effect on the sangster, who fell down dead without a word out of him. Mac Cumhaill struggled to retrieve his prickly accomplice from the hoary cartilage of the sangster's skull. That same article had saved his skin on many another occasion and he certainly had no intention of deserting it now.

Mac Cumhaill then left the people of Umall to their confused mixture of lamenting for the lost and relief at the end of the torment. He had other business to see to back home. He heard afterwards that the local people were too scared that another head might pop out, and left the sangster on the roadway for nearly a month before they finally dragged it down to Clare and flung it off the cliffs of Dooneen.

The widow who had stayed behind with the sangster had twins the next year. Although they had only one head each, they both had the distinctive red blotches all over their faces leaving little doubt that yet another drop of malignant blood had thereby been added to the already dangerous concoction flooding the veins of people from those parts.

As they were heading out for school the next morning, his mother stopped the car in the lane.

'Please promise me you will stay in school and I will promise you I will make things better.'

Arthur didn't like the sound of either part of this. But he could see she was still upset from the visitors yesterday.

'Sorry, Mam,' he said again.

He fully intended not to duck out of school again until he had a better plan for not getting caught. He would stay put at least until he had figured out how to do it without Trevor Saltee spotting him. He had realised by now that nobody else could have been reporting. No other neighbours would spoil a mitching day. And Miss Sullivan wasn't rushing to report him for leaving school, that was for sure.

14
DOORWAYS BROKEN OPEN

That morning in school, a thing happened that did not make Arthur feel too good.

It was at break time and all the lads from his class were hitting a *sliotar* up against the boiler-room door. They often did that before school. It was a steel door and there was a great bounce out of it. Tadhg shouted for Arthur to come over. Arthur hadn't tried hurling since he was in primary school, back in Cork city.

Someone gave him a hurl. The idea was to stand back at the hedge and hit the *sliotar* as hard as you could at the door. At first he couldn't get the hang of it. Then his hands started to remember how to flick the ball up onto the stick and clip it towards the target.

There were five of them at it each stepping up in turn and throwing shapes like Seán Óg in an All-Ireland final, placing the ball carefully on the ground, eyeing the target, legs apart, spit into the hands…

Gerry Kennedy was giving the commentary: 'And Miley Coakley carefully addresses the *sliotar*. He says, "How'ye, *sliotar*." And then Coakley deftly lifts the ball in the air. And yes, yes, yes – it's on target, what a cracker of a shot! This will be the decider, the goal that brought the cup home to the Rebel County. No, wait, the feckin' eejit is after missing it.'

The lads were laughing so much that half the shots weren't even hitting the door, but hopping off the bricks and going everywhere. By the time it came to Arthur's third turn, he found it helped him to concentrate if he pictured someone in the door. He hit harder every time. Soon he had it aced. He was picturing a sangster, with a different head each time, each uglier than the last.

Kennedy was saying, 'They call him the terminator back in the wilds of Killane. He kills insects. There's no man alive prepared to stand in goal in front of the man they call The Dark. One man did, may the Lord have mercy on his perforated soul ... '

Arthur was getting angrier and fiercer for some reason that he couldn't explain and striking the door harder each shot. Then he stepped to take a shot and the sangster's face blurred and started to turn into a more familiar one. He couldn't quite make it out.

Kennedy said, 'A hush has fallen over the crowd. They have never seen this before. An angry Dark.'

'Are you alright, Arthur?' said Tadhg.

Kirwan and Doran started singing, 'Ooh-ah, it's Art Mac Lee-ah.'

Arthur didn't stop. He had never felt rage spilling out of him like this. He got the ball on the stick. He looked again at the door. The outline of the face was still forming when he struck. It was his most powerful connection, giving an unmerciful crack of the stick. In that split second when the *sliotar* was powering in a perfect horizontal line towards the target, Arthur gave out a cry. He realised it was his mother's face. He wanted to call the *sliotar* back. Why was he raging at her? That's not the face he should have been hitting. It wasn't she who had made Seán McLean ride a motorbike like there was nobody who needed him to be careful.

Then there was a very loud bang and the door lock complained severely.

'Jaysus lads,' said Kennedy, dropping his ruler microphone, 'run for it!'

Arthur just stood there.

Kennedy looked back and said, 'Come on Art, don't worry mate, we'll all tell them we saw some knackers trying to break in.'

Only Tadhg stuck around. He went up to the door to examine the damage. There was a massive dent in it and the lock had given way.

'It's only a smallish dent,' said Tadhg, consolingly. 'No need to be upset.'

Arthur blew his nose onto the ground, to hide the tears. Tadhg awkwardly patted him on the back.

'I'm grand, thanks,' said Arthur. 'Just pulled a muscle there. Not worried about the door at all. They've got insurance, you know.'

Later, when the message went out over the PA asking whoever broke the door to please come to the principal's office, it was a break for Arthur from playing the DS. He stood up immediately.

'Well, well,' said Magill, when Arthur walked in. 'What a surprise!'

'You asked who broke the door, Sir,' said Arthur. 'It was me, Sir.'

'I'd never have guessed,' said Magill, lying back in his leather chair. 'The only problem is, I'm not a fool and I know you couldn't have done it on your own.'

'I did, sir. It was an accident. I hit a ball too hard against it.'

'You really test my patience, McLean. I think you enjoy it.'

'It's true, sir.'

'That's a steel door. I'll tell you one thing for a scientific fact. You did not do that damage with a *sliotar*. Christie Ring himself wouldn't do that. You had accomplices. Were they from your class? Were they outsiders? Who were they?'

'Maybe it wasn't as well made as it looked,' said Arthur.

Magill stood and walked behind Arthur to close the door. He stood behind Arthur for a long minute and then walked back to his seat. He said, 'Don't talk rubbish to me boy. I'm too long at this game. I'll do a deal with you. You give me names, and this time I won't call the guards.'

'I can't do that Sir,' said Arthur.

'You fool, you gormless fool!' shouted the principal. 'Do

you think that kind of honour amongst thieves will get you anywhere in life? Do you think they'd do that for you? Look where false honour got your uncle!'

Arthur felt rage again. He felt like jumping across the desk and boxing the top of Magill's baldy head. But he didn't do anything.

Strangely enough, there was no more mention of calling the guards. Arthur started thinking Magill musn't have liked whatever the guard had said to him in the school yard on the last occasion.

After an awkward silence, Magill said, 'Right, you don't want to say anything more? That's fine. I'll tell you one thing boy, I'm as near as this,' – he was holding up his right hand showing a tiny gap between his finger and thumb – 'I'm as near as this to just going over there to you now and giving you the hammering that your precious mother obviously needs help with giving to you.'

Arthur just stood there. He was sure of one thing. He was not going to be able to stop himself hitting back.

Maybe Magill saw this. He looked away for a moment.

'OK then. OK then. OK. Detention indefinitely. How do you like the sound of that? Until you come to me with names, you will stay inside at your desk every break time and for one hour after school. Every day. Each and every day.'

'I will like shite,' said Arthur. He was surprised. He hadn't meant to say that.

The principal's jaw dropped.

Arthur had never been rude to a teacher before. But

that was just how it was. He would stay on the grounds, at his desk if that was what they wanted, for the full day every day for his mother's sake. But there was nobody on earth going to keep him from his life for a minute longer than the school day.

He walked out and went back to class.

After school, Magill was at the gate. When Arthur approached, he said, 'Back inside, you.'

Arthur just looked at him and walked past. Magill did nothing about it.

When his mother picked him up, she asked, 'Is something wrong, Arthur?'

'Nothing,' said Arthur.

The rath had never been quite the same to Arthur since the night of the Black Wind. He was always a little cautious now. He knew for sure now that there was much more here than simply good. It had never occurred to him before then that danger could flow out into the fields and could reach out over the boundary into his ordinary world. He now understood why people feared these places and left them be. He thought much more of the *sí* and what they might be thinking of his intrusions. And of other forces that might cross through this doorway while he was sitting there. He was more hesitant approaching the place.

But once he was in there, in the safe company of the Old Man, his friends and Etain, he felt like travelling with them forever. It seemed he was OK in one world or the other but not in between.

The Old Man asked him what had happened at school. 'Nothing,' said Arthur. 'Nothing.'

Etain brought the cup and stared at him. He thought of what Cash's granny had said about enchantments, but he drank without hesitation.

The Old Man raised an eyebrow. They settled at the fire and he started describing a cat.

Beatha's Sacrifice

Fionn Mac Cumhaill and his good woman Úna were both very fond of cats. The best one they ever had they got from a neighbour as a tiny white kitten, only half the size of any other of its litter. Úna named it Beatha (meaning life), because she thought that for a thing that small to have survived, it must have had a great hunger for life.

Beatha spent most of his young life next to the roaring fire that always burned in the hearth of *Teach Mhic Cumhaill* which was situated in the lovely hills of Baile Dunchada, a stone's throw from the eastern sea and two stones' throws from Tara.

Beatha had taken a fancy to Mac Cumhaill's great chair and would curl up on the feather cushion there all day long. Úna would laugh at Mac Cumhaill. Nobody else, not even the king when he visited, was allowed to sit in Mac Cumhaill's chair. But when little Beatha was there, Mac Cumhaill would just give him a few strokes and pull up another seat, whispering to the little, purring ball of fur, 'You terrible, lazy, little monster, you surely know how to live well.'

Beatha wasn't ever going to be big but he turned out to be a mighty little cat. He went hunting every night, but only after the fireside company had gone to bed. People would ramble in at dusk every evening for a few hours of news and stories. This kept Úna company when Mac Cumhaill was away, and of course, when Mac Cumhaill was at home, the numbers grew, as people would be wanting to hear what new yarns he had brought from his travels in the big wide world beyond them. Beatha would go around making friends with all the visitors and would only start his own rambling when the last of them had bidden him good night. Even before he was six months he was a great mouser and was even tackling the occasional rabbit.

At the same time as the little cat was growing up carefree in Mac Cumhaill's house, trouble was brewing in the desolate little seaside village of Bré. A group of seven *bandraoi*s had gotten together with the idea of starting to do a bit of work outside the law.

For some reason, when a group of people came together to reject the good and to praise and seek out the bad and the unkind, it was mostly *bandraoi*s. When druids or *púca*s went to the bad side, they usually acted alone. Úna's theory was that even when they were bad, women were able to cooperate with each other but the men gone bad were so cantankerous that they could generally only work alone.

And who knows why these ones turned away? Maybe they had seen no reward or appreciation after many years of good work – which is never well rewarded, because a calamity averted is never fully appreciated. Or maybe some of them had their own misfortunes or sadnesses. Maybe they were just lonely and bad company was more to their taste than none at all.

For whatever reason, there now was this group of *bandraois*. And it was discovered later that they had made certain vows to each other. The cant they had all had to recite was:

> *I now understand that goodness and kindness are mere illusions of the soft-minded.*
> *I believe that the ways of the world are overwhelmingly bad and unkind.*
> *I have abandoned the follies of good* bandraois *and druids, giving lifetimes to futility, attempting to hold back the tide of the wickedness of nature.*
> *I am now at one with the callous world.*
> *I will serve the bad spirits that are to be found in all foul and heartless doings.*

At night, they stood in circles holding hands and calling the spirits of dreaded long-dead *cailleachs* and wizards.

'Come back, come back to us O inspired ones,' they would repeat in low, croaky tones like frogs, 'Come back and walk again among the living ... Revive, O ancient wickedness.'

After their chanting was done, they sat and drank their favourite drink. It was a mix of *sladdie,* the sea grass beverage that gives a lot of coastal people great strength and fortitude, mixed with the most powerful whiskey, nine times distilled. And they rubbed powerful, secret herbs on their bodies. And they would fall asleep around the dying embers of their fire as they concocted plans to bring the age of *cailleach* rule to Éirinn and then to all of the world.

In the daytime, they were holding sessions for people who wanted curses put on their neighbours. This was always good business for bad *bandraois*. And in truth, if badness did not already lurk in people's hearts, the dark *bandraois* would have had very little to do. There were always people with scores to settle, people so embittered they felt justified in consorting with bad forces and soliciting evil enchantments.

This trade served two purposes for the *bandraois*. It helped them to start to fill a chest of treasure that they would need for their greater plans. Every piece of silver and every gift was stashed away, as their living needs were few. They ate eggs, hens and vegetables from their own garden. They kept their house perfectly tidy and nothing went to waste.

The larger purpose it served, of course, was to increase the overall air of bitterness and malfeasance in the country. Each bad or mean deed reverberated and caused further grudges and bitterness and a desire for more vengeance that could spread and last for generations. That was a good start for the kind of power they aimed to build when they eventually displaced Cormac. This group had no shortage of bad intention. Especially late at night when the *craic* was high and the drink and herbs were lubricating their thoughts.

The *bandraois* were placing curses of all sorts. One

widow complained that her neighbour was running more sheep than he was allowed on the common grazing ground. The *bandraois* cast a spell that made all of the man's sheep fall over and die, leaving him and his young family with nothing to keep them from starvation that winter but the kindness of other neighbours. One man went to them to complain that his sister had tricked their parents into giving her the family home. He didn't mention that his parents had asked him to leave because he had been thieving from them and from his sister. Not that that extra knowledge would have stopped the *bandraois*. The *bandraois*, of course, didn't care who was right or wrong. If you paid, you got your spell. They gave him a potion that would weaken bones and the horrible cur gave it to his sister's young son, causing both of his legs to break.

In return, the *bandraois* were demanding pieces of gold, sacks of corn, assistance with building a stone temple, and various other things that were quickly making them very well set up.

The *bandraois*' intention was to keep their business secret from the powers in the country until they had gained more strength. They had wanted to be better prepared before tackling Mac Cumhaill and his sort. So, part of the bargain with every person who came to them for a curse was that they must take a vow of secrecy or risk their lives. No admission was ever to be made. No glee was ever to be shown. In fact, the purchaser of the spell was to go to the home of the victim and commiserate over the terrible bad luck that had befallen them.

The *bandraois* didn't leave their customers with any uncertainty about this. Each was made to say out loud, 'In requesting this evil today, I bond myself silently to evil. If ever I break my bond of silence, strike me down with the force of lightning.'

It probably would have remained that way – a secret whispered amongst the bitter but unreported to the powers of the land – had it not been for a project that went wrong.

There was a widow called Nan who was very upset with her son-in-law. Her husband had fallen from a tree and died when the eldest of their seven children was only ten. She had worked night and day to rear the children. She had prayed every day for her eldest daughter to fall in love with a good man who might help her a little with the other children. Maybe a man with land and cows or at least with some heart for work. Instead her daughter married Seánie, a man with no land, no cows, no interest in work and nothing only a mouth on him to talk and eat all around him. She couldn't get rid of the ugly feelings she had towards Seánie. He offered her no comfort or help with her other children, only promised to add more children for her to provide for.

So when she heard about the *bandraois* from one of her small-hearted friends, she couldn't help herself. She went to the *bandraois* and asked for the man, Seánie, to die so that the daughter would be free to find a better match. By the time she was leaving the *bandraois*' house, she was already regretting it.

She ran back inside shouting, 'No, wait, please forget all that. Cancel it.'

But the *bandraoi* at the door shooed her out, saying, 'Go on away with yourself. When you have saved up another two dozen duck eggs, you can come back with the next request.'

Nan got down on her knees and pleaded. 'You can keep the eggs I brought you today for free. No need to do anything to earn them. And then tomorrow, I'll bring you some silver which I had stored away for her dowry.'

But this only made them angry.

'Have respect for yourself, woman,' said a tall one who emerged from the dwelling to push her to the ground with a rush broom. 'You have done what was in your heart, now stand over it.'

Nan stood up and went home in dread. As she got further from Bré, her spirits started to lift and she thought that she was just being stupid. These *bandraois* didn't have so much power. Nothing would have happened. She prayed to Daghda that all would be just as it was before. After all, she said to herself, why would those women bother with the effort of a spell when they knew that their action wasn't wanted anymore?

What she didn't know about was the curious code of honour that bound this group. One of their rules was that once a job had been taken on, it would be done.

She was feeling a bit better as she got close to home, and had promised Daghda that for the rest of her life she would do nothing but good for the people around her. Especially her daughter and Seánie. However, as she crossed the little wall near the front of her clan's camp, she heard the sobbing of her wonderful daughter. Her pride and joy. It was a sound that pierced her own heart. She had known how much her daughter loved Seánie. She now knew that she would never be able to live another day with herself, in the knowledge that she had let wickedness take hold of her heart and that she had caused such devastation to her own beloved child.

She fell down on the ground. As she lay there, she told the neighbours who gathered around her everything that had happened and exactly where the *bandraois* were living.

And then she died.

Whether she died of guilt and shame or whether it was the curse of the *bandraois* against anyone who gave them away, it was never known. But even if her life had added misery to the world, in her death she had done some good.

Word went straight to the king and from there to Mac Cumhaill.

It was mid-winter at the time. And a very cold and wet winter it was. Mac Cumhaill was getting older and he now liked to spend most of the long evenings by the fireside with family and friends, rather than in the camps around Tara or away on hunting trips. The news of the business with the *cailleach*s upset him because it disturbed what had so far been a very peaceful winter. But it didn't terrify him as it did some of the Fianna. His upbringing in the company of a druid woman had given him some knowledge and strengths. And he had met some very fearsome *bandraois* in the past. For his own comfort, he decided to plan his campaign against them from home.

Maybe the bad news made everything around him appear in a greyer light. There was a down draught and the fire seemed to be poor. His food tasted less appetising. The conversation around the fire was dull. Even his lovely little cat seemed to be a source of irritation.

'What are you looking at me for?' he grumbled, pushing Beatha off his chair. 'I have enough people looking at me expecting me to work miracles. Don't you have mice to catch?'

'Leave Beatha alone,' said Úna. 'The little creature is not to blame for this. He's only looking at you for a scrap of food or a bit of a stroking, like he always does.'

Mac Cumhaill felt bad. He wasn't in the habit of taking his temper out on the defenceless. He made a purring sound to call the cat back.

'It's just that you're upset about this other business,' said Úna, reaching out to stroke Beatha.

Beatha chose Úna and curled himself around her leg.

Mac Cumhaill called Conán and Diarmuid to his home. They each came with five of their commanders, all of them soaked from the incessant rain. None of them had the inclination, on such a miserable evening, to devise a complicated plan when a simple one might do just as well. They would go the next night and surround the nice, stone house that the seven troublemakers had built. They would tell them that their game was known. Guessing that they were not yet prepared for a war, Mac Cumhaill expected that the *bandraoi*s would give up sensibly and accept a deal that exiled them to some remote island. At least it was worth hoping for that.

The next morning, a group of 13 soldiers moved across the mountains to the miserable village of Bré. The *cailleach*s were mostly nocturnal and the only souls moving at the hour they got there were a mangy dog and a mean east wind blowing in from the cold, dark sea. They went to the new stone house on the hill above the village. They approached carefully. But they needn't have bothered. There was no life. No sounds. On the door they could see a jackdaw flapping, one leg tied to the door bolt.

Mac Cumhaill went to free it and it repeated the message it had been given.

'The deal you've come to propose, we regret we have to refuse. But why don't you offer it to your mothers? Send them off on a boat to some freezing island. You see, we know everything you think, even before you think it, you bunch of *lúdramán*s. Our advice to you is to get away from this place as fast as your thick legs will carry you. If you are still here when we come back, the raven of death will peck your eyes and we will have your livers for supper this very evening.'

Mac Cumhaill let the bird go.

Mac Cumhaill was angry. Most of the men, including Diarmuid, were not. They were nervous. They looked around them all the time, thinking they were being watched and that the *bandraoi*s were about to reappear at any minute. The threats were one thing. All *bandraoi*s, good, bad or in-between, were renowned for the eloquence of their threats.

But Diarmuid asked the question that was really worrying them all.

'How did they know we were coming today?'

'Don't be getting all shaky now,' shouted Conán, irritated with the pale quietness that had descended. 'It was probably just a good guess on their part.'

'Maybe,' said Diarmuid. 'But what about the bit about the island?'

'It's hardly the first time that has been done with witches. And that foul wizard was sent off to Achill only ten years back,' said Conán.

'Maybe they can read our minds,' said one of the younger men.

'Maybe, maybe,' said Mac Cumhaill. 'But not unless they have surpassed the powers of any *bandraoi* I've known.'

When he got home, Mac Cumhaill decided not to think about the possibility that one of his commanders might have informed the *bandraois*. He knew all of them on each team. He didn't even want to imagine any of them being in league with dark *bandraois*.

But Úna re-awoke the worry when she said to him the next morning, in her usual, matter-of-fact way, 'Of course you realise it must have been one of those people of yours.'

'No person of the Fianna would ever betray us like that.'

'What about that Liath one? She's much too sweet to be true.'

This was an old tune. Úna never thought good of Liath Ní Choinchin, though she was easily the most promising young commander in the Fianna, fearless, smart and true. Úna thought Mac Cumhaill had a special liking for her because she reminded him of Liath Luachra, the warrior woman who had helped bring him up and taught him much of what he knew.

'I don't believe there is a fair reason for you to suggest her over any of the others,' said Mac Cumhaill.

'Except that she's a wily little vixen, you mean? I have never trusted a woman with red hair and she has boatloads of it.'

'Now, Úna,' said Mac Cumhaill.

'Well, even if she hasn't turned on you yet, there is someone who has. A spy there must be.'

Mac Cumhaill reluctantly agreed that he had to start suspecting a spy. Maybe the *bandraoi*s were holding information or a threat over one of his people.

Later that day, Mac Cumhaill called Conán and his commanders back to his house, but did not call Diarmuid's people. He explained that nobody from the group should talk to any other soul about the plan he was about to lay before them. They all swore to that. The plan involved trapping one of the witches who was known to collect two buckets of dirty green water from the Bré pond just before dusk every evening.

Mac Cumhaill, Conán and his five commanders laid in wait, with nets. They also had a flask of *praiseach* pollen – most *bandraoi*s were so addicted to this stuff that a good whiff of it blown at them would send them into a blind reverie, making it much easier to approach them without having a lump of flesh or an eye ripped off. But the *bandraoi* never showed up. Eventually, after dark had fallen, a whisk of wind flew across their heads and they were sure they heard hoarse laughter as the flying *bandraoi* disappeared beyond a thicket of woods.

Apparently, again, the *bandraoi*s had known in advance.

Next day he planned with only Diarmuid and his men present. This time the plan was to create a haze of *bandraoi* bait by heating a mixture of foxglove petals and honey. When the *bandraoi*s from all over the region descended on the place, Mac Cumhaill would call out to them all that there were seven bad ones amongst them. He hoped that the others would know which were the Bré women and would give them up because they were giving all of the rest of them a bad name. And he intended to threaten all *bandraoi*s with expulsion unless they helped him catch the seven bad ones. It wasn't an idle threat. If there weren't ways of selecting *bandraoi*s for expulsion, there were always ways of expelling every *bandraoi*. Nobody would want that because the good ones did a lot of healing and helping in their clans. But if the good ones let the bad ones hide behind their cloaks, he would have no choice.

He started the fire. He started cooking the concoction. The sickly smell wafted all over. Soon strange women of every size and shape started appearing. When no more seemed to be arriving, Mac Cumhaill said his say to the hundreds assembled there.

But he got no help. They all just giggled and sniggered. One old woman came forward and told him that every one of them knew who the bad ones were, but that they were all absent tonight.

She continued, 'They said to me, "When Mac Cumhaill sets his clever little trap tonight, send him our regards and tell him if he keeps going the way he's going, his remaining days in this world will be few and unpleasant."'

Mac Cumhaill went home, furious and confused. It seemed almost impossible that the *bandraois* could have a spy in Conán's group as well as someone in Diarmuid's group.

Liath came to him. She informed him quietly that some of the men in both groups felt quite offended that they had been suspected.

The next day, Mac Cumhaill could think of no new plan. He just sat by the fire in his big chair. The day after, he didn't leave his home either. He sat stroking the cat, which must have sensed his distress as it stayed close and provided a consoling distraction to him.

Mac Cumhaill felt at a loss. More days passed. People were getting anxious. Every death now, whether natural or not, was attributed to the *bandraois*. And when you attribute a death or misfortune to a *bandraoi*, it is not the *bandraoi* who gets the primary blame. People immediately start to wonder which of their neighbours or family paid the *bandraoi* for the curse. And when they think they've figured it out, they start considering going to a *bandraoi* themselves to do harm to the person who may never have done them any harm at all. And so, the contagion of evil started to take hold of people.

After a while an unpleasant murmur arose from some corners of the land. One of Diarmuid's men was the first to say it out loud: 'Mac Cumhaill, of course, was the only one present at both planning sessions.'

And then, 'Mac Cumhaill, of course, has always had a soft spot for women with powers.'

And, 'Mac Cumhaill, you know, was brought up by herb women – even if we are told that they were good, how do we know for sure?'

The rumours were getting even bolder: 'And anyway, don't you know that Mac Cumhaill has a few special tricks of his own. Of course, we all know that he sold his soul to a black *bandraoi* in return for them.'

It is part of the way of rumours that if they are repeated often enough they become facts.

'Oh, there's no smoke without fire,' people would say.

To his discredit, the king himself had heard these rumours and when the tests with Diarmuid and Conán failed the king also started to wonder about Mac Cumhaill.

'Well,' he reasoned, 'if there aren't any truths there, why is Mac Cumhaill just sitting by his fire while things get worse?'

Conán heard this and said to the king, 'Cormac, if you really believe that, then on my heart I will leave down my sword and spear this day and I will never fight in defence of this kingdom again.'

Cormac had wine taken, and he continued: 'Of course I don't believe that he is in cahoots with them. But you do have to wonder if he is not just turning a blind eye. There are things you don't know about Mac Cumhaill, Conán; things that none of us really know. On those long, dark forest and mountain days of his outcast childhood there was a lot of time for bitterness to build up. It would only be natural that he might have a well of anger against normal people, buried deep inside him. And when he goes off wandering in the hills, he spends time with some people who we wouldn't really have much in common with and who he would be better keeping at sword's length away from.'

Angered though he was, Conán did not tell Mac Cumhaill of this conversation then, as he suspected he would never fully forgive Cormac.

After several more days sitting listlessly by the fire, Fionn heard Úna crying from the garden one morning, 'Come and see Beatha!'

What was she wailing about? Beatha was right here, sprawled under the table – his new favourite spot since Mac Cumhaill had taken back permanent occupancy of the chair. He recalled the way that Beatha would run to take his chair the minute he stood from it.

'You don't do that anymore,' he said to the cat.

And then other thoughts were coming into his head. He remembered being puzzled that the old woman who died while revealing the secret of the *bandraois* had talked about seven women, but everyone he'd talked to since spoke of only six.

And he said to himself, for the thousandth time, shaking his head, 'there was no one else in the room when I talked to my commanders.'

As he said this, he looked down again at the cat who, as usual, was now looking straight up at him. The cat realised too slowly that Mac Cumhaill had finally understood what was happening. He had it by the tail as it tried to scurry out the door. It was screeching and scrawbing like the world was falling down.

In the meantime, Úna had made it back into the house, holding a little body. Despite the mud on its skinny pelt, it was clear immediately that this was the real Beatha. The cat in Mac Cumhaill's hand squealed even more ferociously and curled itself up to put deep scratches in Mac Cumhaill's arm but Mac Cumhaill didn't pay any attention.

Their poor little Beatha looked dead to Mac Cumhaill. But Úna claimed she could still feel a faint heartbeat. She took him to the fire to warm him and to try to get little drops of sugar water into him to give him some energy. She cuddled him and sang him a lullaby that sounded beautiful even above the complaining of the other cat.

Mac Cumhaill took the other cat outside and held it over the deep well in their back yard.

'*Bandraoi,* you can choose. Die as a cat in this well, or help me catch your friends.'

The cat looked at him and spoke: 'Anything you ask, I'll do,' she rasped, probably thinking she could change her mind once he let her go and she got out of his spear range.

'That's good,' said Mac Cumhaill, taking out a knife and slicing off the end of her tail. 'Because you'll be stuck as a cat forever if you let me down.'

Mac Cumhaill knew that when a piece is missing from the form that a *bandraoi* has changed into, she is trapped.

The cat squealed and stomped, more in anger than in pain.

Mac Cumhaill told her to tell her friends that he and Úna would be away tonight and that this would be a good time to enter *Teach Mhic Cumhaill* and lie in wait for him.

The cat disappeared sulkily but quickly. Clearly, all the great vows of loyalty to her friends meant quite a bit less to this lady cat than her own well-being did.

Mac Cumhaill called for Conán and Diarmuid. When he told them the *bandraois* would be calling to his house this evening, the tone of his voice told them not to question him. They helped him to prepare a huge net smeared with lard that was laden with *praiseach* pollen.

They lay in wait. Sure enough, by dusk the bandraois started arriving. They were so sure of their information now that they had become completely brazen. They did not take the slightest bit of caution. They walked right up to the house and started trying to open the door. When all six of them clustered at this task, the net fell on them. They squealed and squawked as they were winched up in a great bundle with legs and arms sticking out in every direction.

That very night, they were taken on a boat and deposited on one of the coldest and most desolate islands in the northerly sea.

As for the seventh, when she came back to look for her tail, Mac Cumhaill had decided that she was safer in the form she was in. He kept his word and told her where the tail was. It was in the lake. The *bandraoi* now swore at the cat's body which she occupied, because she knew that every sinew of it would resist any adventure in water. There was no way she was going to get into that lake. So she spent the rest of her days as a half-tailed cat. And what's more, she had to learn to catch mice. And to eat them. For there were no people willing to give scraps or show kindness to a treacherous creature like her.

Soon enough, the real Beatha was drinking milk and sitting up. It was only a few days before he had his strength back and was back to his old ways – sleeping all day in Mac Cumhaill's chair and catching mice and rats with great enthusiasm at night.

Mac Cumhaill had always hated to see the way Beatha would play with the little creatures before he killed them; even though he had seen it a thousand times with other cats and knew it was just nature's harsh way. He would give out to Beatha, saying, 'Kill the little fellow, Beatha, can't you see the terror in its little eyes? There's enough misery in the world. Kill the poor thing or let it go about its business.'

The strange part was that he soon started to think that Beatha understood him. Beatha became a curiosity to visitors. Mac Cumhaill would make them wait up to see Beatha hunt. It was a thing that none of them had ever seen before in a cat. Beatha would prowl like a normal cat;

pounce like a normal cat; but he would take hold of his prey by the back of the neck, as he'd seen Bran doing with hares. He would give one or two hard shakes. And that would be the end of it. Of course, nobody now dared to repeat what many of them again started thinking – that Mac Cumhaill had taken more than his meals from the good women who had brought him up. For it was widely known that cats took instructions from nobody other than those with the powers of a *bandraoi*.

15
EVERYTHING SLIPPING AWAY

Up to that time, it was true what the Old Man had said, that the only hassle was at school and that things were grand at home. But that day, home started to close in on Arthur too.

He woke up that morning and remembered there would be more hassle at school today. Magill didn't take kindly to being disobeyed.

Arthur wasn't really scared about it all, but thought he just didn't want to bother with it. And he couldn't go mitching anymore. So he just told his mother, 'Mam, I think I won't go to school today.'

'What? Arthur, love, I'm sorry, but you can't do that.'

'I could stay home and work on the farm and do something useful instead of sitting around in school all day.'

'You need your education, Arthur. And besides, it's the

law, and we'd both get in trouble. You heard what those men said.'

'The school wouldn't report me, though, I'm fairly sure. It's only Saltee. You can talk to him, tell him to mind his own business.'

'I'm sure you are wrong there Arty. The school has got to report you.'

'David Cash is allowed to stay home. They're not following him up.'

'Well, they should be. And they most definitely would follow us up. Besides, you're alone too much already. It worries me. You need to be with people your age.'

'I can go up then and spend part of the day with Cash,' said Arthur, 'once I've helped Brian with the farm work.'

'Well, now that you've raised it, that's another issue I've wanted us to talk about.'

Arthur did not like the sound of this.

She looked out the window and started talking in a shaky rehearsed way, not like herself.

'I think I've been a little unfair on you, allowing you to do so much farm work. If we went on like this your teen years could entirely pass you by.'

'Don't worry about that, Mam. I wanted to do it. I still want to do it. I'm not missing a thing.'

'I know. You insisted. But I shouldn't have listened to you. It's too much.'

'So what are you saying?' said Arthur. 'We can't leave the farm idle. It has to be kept going so it's running fine when Connie comes back.'

'No, it won't go idle. But I've been getting a bit of advice on it.'

'From who?' Arthur was starting to panic as the penny dropped.

'And the advice seems to make sense. We couldn't sell the ground. But we can lease it out to someone else who could farm it productively.'

'From who, Mam?' asked Arthur again. 'Who has been giving you advice? It's Trevor Saltee, isn't it?'

'That would free you and me up to go back living normal lives.'

'I don't want to live a normal life, whatever that is,' said Arthur. 'It's him, isn't it? I don't want him around the place. He's a sneak. Did you know he's been snooping through Connie's stuff?'

'Trevor?' She did sound a little surprised.

'Yes. He was here the other day. Nosing around the tractor shed.'

She paused for a minute. Then she switched to the autopilot voice she used whenever she didn't want to think about something anymore.

'I'm sure he meant no harm. He's been very helpful to me. He probably…he maybe just wanted to see what new machinery he would need to put in, when he takes over the running of the place.'

Take over. So that was it, that's what Saltee had been after all along.

'What does it mean, a lease? Does it mean he'll have the yard and the milk quota and all?'

'Yes. Well, he'd need it to be able to run the farm, wouldn't he?'

'And we'd only have the house here then?'

'More or less, with a bit of garden, I suppose. But he's a reasonable man. I'm sure he wouldn't mind us using one or two sheds for storage or to keep your two calves in.'

'What about the garden at the back where I keep Niamh?'

'That's a field, I'm afraid, Arthur, and so it goes with the farm.'

Arthur felt like he was going to go mad. 'What does Connie say? Have you even asked him? If you had to rent it out he would rather it be to anyone else in the county.'

'It's not really his call, Arty, since he's not here to help,' said his mother. 'Trev says he'll drain and level the lower bog, and make the whole place more productive, which he says Connie was advised to do years ago but never got around to.'

'Where the rath is?' Arthur asked. 'You can't *do* that. You can't level a rath, Mam. It would . . . it would cause . . . great misfortune.' He sounded, even to himself, like a helpless child.

'Oh, those are only old *pisreógs*, Trevor says. I just need to get more on top of our situation. I have little enough time at home and I'm fed up of it being consumed with mountains of regulations, records, surveys, official paperwork and inspections from the department.'

Arthur could see she had her jaw set and she was fixed on her course. She found decisions hard to reach and, when

364

she had made them, hard to break.

This was the worst thing yet; the worst possible thing. He just looked away from her. His anger was gone.

She put her head on his shoulder the way he used to put his on hers when he was shorter.

She said, 'It's the best thing, dear. You'll see in time.'

Arthur went over and lay down in front of the Aga, next to the dogs. He started rubbing Pumpkin.

'Look, I can see you are not wanting to go to school today. How about I just give you a sick note for this one day. I'll phone the secretary to say you've still got that cough. I can drop you over at your friend Cash's place and you can hang out there for a while. That might do you good.'

Arthur didn't move. He just felt like he was going under water and a numb quietness was coming back over him. The same as before.

'Well, look, love, we'll talk about it more later then. I'll just leave you to walk over to David Cash's place when you've given the dogs a good mind. Maybe you could take them out for a walk first. You'll still need to do all kinds of chores like that, you know.'

When she left, he rolled over on the floor and stared at the smoky ceiling. He lay there for a long time. Then he headed out and went around the fields for a few hours. He stared for a long time into the Brown River. It looked cold and muddy after yesterday's rain.

His mother was home before five, long before he expected her. She had brought a stack of chocolate cookies, doughnuts and coke. The last time they had eaten this kind of grub together was the day she had had to tell him about moving from Cork. They ate in silence.

He asked her later if he could borrow her laptop to play *Fallout*. When he brought it back, she was still sitting where he had left her, at the table with her head in her hands.

She said, 'I'm sorry, Arthur. It's the only way.'

Arthur said goodnight and leant over her chair to give her a kiss on the forehead.

That was the first time since the Black Wind that he had no fear. In fact, he would even have welcomed any dark force he met there. Because the truth is, he started wishing, or maybe deciding, that when he entered the rath today, he would never come back out of it.

The only force he met was a kindly one. He didn't need to say anything. The Old Man put his great arm around Arthur's shoulder again and Arthur felt that he was being lifted back into the clear air where he could breathe without feeling sick in his stomach.

The Old Man said, 'You don't feel like talking today, but that's alright.'

Then he did a strange thing. He laid Arthur down on the thick layer of leaves that floored the rath. Etain arrived with a much larger chalice than usual and held it to his lips.

Soon he was in another place, in an even more comfortable bed. He sat up and looked around him, confused. He was on a thick cushion of moss and heather. There were rocks all around him, giving shelter from a harsh wind. In every direction the ground fell away, covered in sheets of purple-flowering heather. He was just under the top of a mountain. Nothing in any direction seemed as tall. He knew it. Sliabh na mBan. He had been here once with Connie.

Standing a distance away, at the very top of the mountain was the Old Man. His long robe and sheepskin shawl were pasted against him by the fierce wind. As well as the beautiful sword, he had the battered bronze shield with a ruby heart. He was surveying the terrain in every direction. When he came over to Arthur he sat next to him on the heather and started talking about a young soldier.

On this day, his visits into the world of the Old Man and all his histories started to run together and the rest – school, home – disappeared altogether.

The Bear Who Would Be King

There once was another Art who left an impression on the Fianna. Regrettably, it wasn't an exceptionally good one. He was a young fellow who came here to train with the Fianna for a while. Art meant 'bear' in his language and he was given that name because, from early on, he looked remarkably like a bear from the forests of Gaul. He was short, hairy and built like a boulder.

The place that he came from was a small, isolated mountain domain within the land of Móna, not far across the water. That pocket of Móna was controlled by the great queen Angharad. Angharad had a gift for leading people. Her kindness and warm-heartedness had a way of opening people to her. She ruled by the consent of the majority of her own people. And she naturally forged friendships and trust with leaders in neighbouring territories, ensuring that Móna never had immediate enemies. In the peaceful situation she had created, she hadn't seen a need for taking resources from her people to feed and equip an army.

As with most people, her weakness was related to her strength. Her ability to find whatever bit of goodness lay in people's hearts, and to nourish that, worked well generally. Most people, when they found someone who thought well of them, didn't want to disappoint that person. And in that way Angharad would inspire people to rise above themselves. That's all lovely and good. However, wasps can make their way into that particular churn of buttermilk. What Angharad was not able to understand was that there are some people who either possess no nugget of good nature at all or have it so well buried that it is unreachable. By not understanding that, Angharad was always exposed to treachery.

Angharad, who was a cousin of Cormac's mother, had sent a message to Cormac requesting that this young man, Art, be allowed to train with the Fianna. She made the request as a favour to the boy's father, who was a dear friend. The boy had his heart set on soldiering and had complained that he couldn't learn much from Angharad's small group of unarmed guards – men and women who had never seen combat.

High-minded Angharad never even wondered whether there might be any reasons, other than youthful whim, that

Art was so bent on training with men who were not so fortunate as Angharad's defenders –the men of the Fianna had been led into many arguments that had been settled with blood and metal rather than talk and compromise, had partaken in wars with all manner of opponents.

Art had some good in him. He was clever. He was a surprisingly good athlete for his short stature, mostly excelling at lifting and throwing heavy rocks. He had natural aggression and took easily to weapons both in training and in competitions.

Very soon he was one of the best young men in the Fianna. What he lacked in deft defence with a shield he compensated for by being such a ferocious, roaring attacker, ensuring that his opponent was the one needing the shield. What he lacked in speed with a sword he made up for with the deadly force of his blow whenever he did make contact. He was fond of a hatchet, which was a terrible instrument in the hands of such a burly man. And with a spear he excelled in both accuracy and propulsion. In games of strategy, where the teams of young men were sent into the forest to try to outwit the others, he did very well too, coming up with some very cunning schemes to get to his goal first. Even if that meant crossing a river in flood, or spending several nights alone in a forest that was patrolled by a dangerous injured boar or a bad-tempered *fear dearg,* he would find a way to see it through.

For all that time, he never showed any bad character. He was competitive, right enough. But so were many of his young colleagues in training. He was always friendly and cheerful with the other men, giving as much slagging as he got. With his trainers and the leadership of the Fianna, he was courteous and didn't look for any favours on the basis of being Cormac's guest.

He only revealed other aspects to his character after the episode with Aoife.

Cormac, though not a picturesque man, was in the habit of breeding exceptionally beautiful daughters. Aoife was one such person. She was a half-sister of Gráinne, who was better known. But Aoife and her full brothers and sisters were brought up in a place away from castles and fuss, in a fine dwelling that had been built for their mother on top of a fairy fort. This allowed the mother to easily spend time with her own people down below, when her children did not need her.

Aoife was the eldest of that family and she was only barely out of childhood when Art first saw her, playing with the younger children on common grazing ground near her enclosure. He came that way regularly from then on. He found every kind of excuse to detour his errands and his training missions so they would run past the house next to the fairy fort. After some time he got the courage to talk to her. He called her over to the chariot track he was standing in. He had let his imaginings run so far ahead of him that in his own mind he was already virtually betrothed to her. He made the mistake of thinking that she had reached a similar stage in her thinking about him.

In fact, of course, she had never seen or noticed Art before and she was very cautious when this rather hairy young man called her roughly over onto the track.

She was timid.

He was forward.

He grabbed her hands and pulled her to him and said, 'Aoife, my loved one, let us run away together, for I can't bear one more day of looking at, but not touching, your beauty.'

Aoife was more than mildly alarmed. She screamed and pulled away from him. She ran back to the field, gathered the younger ones, and headed straight into her house.

For a clever man, Art was slow to appreciate what had happened. He confided in Mac Cumhaill that evening.

'I don't understand what was wrong with her. I offered her my love and she ran away without a word.'

Mac Cumhaill spoke kindly, assuming it was just that the young man was inexperienced and therefore awkward in matters of the heart.

'If you like her, you have to approach her kindly and let her get to know you. And then you have to hope that what she gets to know of you, she likes too. At that stage, you could be onto something grand. Just take it easy for now. Do you understand?'

'I do,' said Art, but in a slightly sullen tone that Mac Cumhaill wasn't all that fond of.

The very next day, Art went back and did the same again. This time he went to the back of the fairy fort and called. Aoife was not a cowardly person and she had been thinking that maybe she had judged this man harshly the previous time. She was worried that he might have thought the reason she ran from him was because of his brutal ugliness, whereas in fact she would talk to anyone as long as they were right and honest. She had decided she would hear what he had to say if he came again. So when she heard his call, she went to him again. Again, he grabbed her hand. But this time even harder so she wouldn't be so easily able to run off when he said what he wanted to say. She was immediately frightened again, even before he opened his mouth.

'You see Aoife, I love you. So that is what I needed to tell you. You are the one I have chosen for myself.' He was smiling broadly, expecting her to be very pleased about this information.

'Who are you, and what are you talking about?' said Aoife.

'I'm Art. I am going to be a very powerful man – a king, in fact, in my own country.'

'Please let go of my hand. You are hurting me.'

'First tell me you are not going to be a naughty little donkey and run away again while a man is only trying to talk to you.'

'Let me go, please.' Aoife was crying now.

His heart didn't soften at all for the one he claimed to love.

'I just can't do that until I get you to stop your womanly chattering and understand the importance of what I am saying to you.'

This was a mistake. Aoife's tears had sent the little ones fleeing to report to their mother. Before Aoife could say another thing to him, Art had been lifted off his feet almost as if the pull of the earth had reversed itself. He then floated a short distance and dropped heavily into a viciously thorny dog rose bush on the other side of the fairy fort.

He was back talking to Mac Cumhaill that evening. Mac Cumhaill was less patient with him this time.

'Did you not hear a thing I said to you yesterday?'

'I did, but that's not how I do things. I want her to hear what I have to say.'

'I would think she has gathered by now what it is you want to say. You have to accept that she does not want to hear it again.'

'It's just because I'm a bit on the short side. Once she learns what a mighty warrior I am, she will see past that. Send a messenger down to tell her and sort it out.'

'I don't think your, ahem, minor height problem is the main thing to worry about here. It is said that Aoife's eye has been caught by a gentleman from her mother's world. And who could fault her indeed, as they are a far more beautiful people than us, and live longer, happier lives, and with much finer music. I am quite sure that next to that tiny buck you would not look so stunted at all.'

Art reddened in anger. Maybe he had expected more tact from Mac Cumhaill about his height. Or maybe he was angered about the notion that he had of being jilted, made worse by the fact that his replacement was a fairy man.

His anger only worsened when Mac Cumhaill continued.

'Laughter aside, I am obliged to punish you for

disregarding my advice and for causing upset to this young lady who has done no harm to you or yours. The punishment is that you are barred from the *Lughnasa* hoolies this year.'

Mac Cumhaill knew that, to any young man, not being allowed to participate in the great harvest festivities was a sore thing. He didn't intend it to be the special punishment it was for Art, who prayed to Lugh every day. To Art, *Lughnasa* was the only festival worth going to and he believed that every year he partied with Lugh, he got a little bit more of Lugh's beauty.

'That's not just, Fionn', said Art. 'I did nothing that others haven't done. Holding a girl's hand.'

Mac Cumhaill ignored this.

'Maybe then, my son, this will help you to bear my advice in mind for the next young woman you fall for, because you are not going to get anywhere with your approach.'

'I'm not interested in "the next young woman", said Art angrily. 'Don't you hear what I'm saying?'

Mac Cumhaill laughed. 'Art, I know what I am talking about. Jealousy can poison a man's heart faster and more completely than the extract of any plant. You need to walk away from this situation. You will need to start looking for another young woman, because, from what you tell me, any chance you had with this one is scattered, shall we say, to the *sceach* bushes!'

'I won't accept it,' said Art, too blinded by anger to even notice Mac Cumhaill's joke. 'She will see me and if it is her family that tries to stand in her way, they will pay.'

'I'm not sure that's a family you want to get mixed up with,' said Mac Cumhaill, still laughing. 'Are you so stupefied by your anger and wounded pride that you have not realised what happened to you today? Do you not realise who Aoife is? Is the fact that she is a daughter of our king not enough for you to be persuaded that you should mind your mouth and your head? And the fact that she is the daughter of a woman of the little people, the very one who spared your life and kindly did no more than blow you into a thorny *sceach* bush today, is that also not enough to persuade you to swallow your false pride?'

'How can this be?' said Art, temporarily subdued. 'Why is she not then in a castle with Cormac? How can she also be the daughter of a fairy? That is not natural. It must be what they give him in the goblet. But what kind of king is this Cormac? How can you respect a man who willingly imbibes some vile potion that causes him to become enchanted by a weasel woman? I refuse to believe it.'

Mac Cumhaill now was silent for a few minutes. There was no more laughter.

Art cowered a little as he realised he had gone too far. He witnessed the big man biting back a rage.

Eventually Mac Cumhaill spoke slowly and dangerously: 'Listen to me now and look at me when I am telling it to you. If you ever speak ill again of our king, our little brethren, or indeed of our Aoife, you will not have to worry about any of them. I will consider then that you have proven something I do not want to think of you and

375

I will end your time in this world without any further warning to you.'

Art did listen well. He was a good learner. He immediately apologised and snapped back into the role of the good, obedient soldier, learning his trade. After some months, Mac Cumhaill went back to assuming that it had all just been the folly of a young man with his brain bent out of shape by his first love. He even wondered if he hadn't taken it too seriously and spoken too harshly to Art.

Mac Cumhaill was in this frame of mind when Art came to him and asked that he be allowed to stay on in the Fianna rather than going home, as he was fitting in so well. Mac Cumhaill did not regard this with much suspicion. To show the young lad that he appreciated how he had reformed, he went to Cormac on Art's behalf with this request.

What Mac Cumhaill didn't know was that Art had not moved the smallest fraction from the views he had expressed in his meetings with Mac Cumhaill. The only wisdom that had penetrated his bear-like stubbornness was that it would be better for his own health not to seek Mac Cumhaill's assistance again. Every night after training he would head off on his own, telling the other lads that he just wanted to do more running to keep his fitness levels high.

In fact, he always ran to one spot:. a clump of yew trees that overlooked Aoife's dwelling place. There he would hide himself and stay awake as much of the night as he was able, watching the comings and goings.

Since the dwelling was next to the fairy fort, the night

time was when things really came to life. At first he was shocked to have what Mac Cumhaill had told him confirmed. He saw various fairy people leaving their fort at all hours and going in and out of the human dwelling. And many were the evenings he also saw Aoife's mother slip from human form back to fairy form and wander down into the hollows of the earth.

And much less often, he saw a chariot arrive late at night with one man in it. The unmistakable man would be greeted at the entrance to the fort and presented with a tiny, golden goblet. He would then go into Aoife's mother's dwelling. He would only emerge in the late hours of the morning when the sun was well up, shamelessly unconcerned about who might report him back to his human wife, chatting away to the fairy wife and giving instructions to the children as he was leaving. Though there were no fancy robes or formal tunics, neither was there the slightest attempt at disguise. Obviously, Cormac assumed that none of his people would see anything wrong with this. Art's anger with Aoife turned into a frenzy of disgust at all these happy, normal goings on. He convinced himself that this was a breach of the laws of the world and an offence to Lugh and Daghda and all the gods.

It seems that Art started to believe then that he was a holy agent of the gods and that anything he would do against such wrongdoing would be blessed. That allowed him to absolve himself of any feeling of guilt for what he was about to do next and indeed for many of the less than admirable things he was to do in his later life.

Incidentally, the person that Art decided to target to channel his divine vengeance upon was the young fairy man whom he saw as his competition. Art had seen the slight fellow come shyly knocking on the door of Aoife's house every evening. The tiny but beautiful young man would walk out with her to a spot just in front of the yew trees and sit there talking, laughing, weaving fantastic images in the air and holding her hand for hours every evening. When they touched, the faint background magic music from the earth beneath the fort seemed to somehow get louder and sweeter. It was driving Art into spasms of rage. But he would go back there the next night for more. And he would sit, quietly paralysed, watching and eavesdropping on every bit of idle talk.

His first attempt to do something about this was clumsy. One evening, he heard the fairy man saying he would not be able to visit the next night, as there was a grand wake at another fort. The *sí* were no different than the big people in regard to wakes. Everyone was deeply interested in the shadow of death and all the young people had to leave the fort to participate in the festivities in their cousins' domain.

Art decided to disguise himself as a *púca*. He huddled himself in smelly goatskins and cut himself a blackthorn walking stick. It was not a bad disguise. His face was naturally hairy and malevolent. When he hunched, he was almost small enough to pass as a large, over-fed fairy man. He went to knock on the door of Aoife's house at the same time that her fairy buck would usually do so. She opened.

'Yes, sir, what were you looking for?'

'Come outside to talk to me,' he said in the squeakiest voice he could muster.

'No, but you can come in if you're hungry or tired. Our house and table are always open to weary travellers.'

'It's me; it's me, Séafra,' said Art.

She laughed first and then she looked again.

'What foolery is this?'

'No foolery, starlight,' said Art, who had all of the lovers' terms of affection burned into his brain, 'I am your own sunbeam. I've been turned into a *leaprachán* by a *bandraoi*.'

She looked doubtful. But she had to admit that through the ugly beard and long hair, there was something familiar about his face. She didn't fully believe, but she started thinking how awful it would be to reject her own love, if it really were true. She decided to go and sit with him in their usual place and to listen to what he had to say. She would test him to see if he knew any of the secrets that only two people in the whole world could know.

'So, aren't our stars looking good tonight?' he said, pointing up.

'Yes, but why are you pointing at the bear, my dear? Ours are over to the west.'

'Of course. I just started thinking recently that the bear is a particularly fine arrangement.'

She edged a little away from him.

'Anyway,' he continued, 'let's talk some more about what we'll name our beautiful children.'

'Yes, what had we decided on again for the first-born? All the confusion tonight must be making me forgetful,' she said.

'Oh, now, let me see,' said Art, enjoying this bit. 'The trauma of the body change has also made me forgetful. Was it Bréagán?'

'Aha,' she said.

'Or Fionnán?'

'I don't think you are … '

'Or, let me see now, was it Senan?'

She looked very disappointed. It was of course what they had agreed and she couldn't now doubt that this sneering lump was what remained of her lovely Séafra.'

Now, sensing victory, he tried to hold her hand.

'I'm sorry, ehh, Séafra; for some reason I don't feel like that tonight.'

'But what has changed?' said Art in mock indignation.

'Nothing really, it's just that…'

'You said to me once that it didn't matter what I looked like; you'd still love me because our souls are intertwined.'

Aoife was shocked. This was another of the things that nobody else could have known.

'I'm sorry,' she stammered. 'You are right.' And she slid her hand awkwardly into his.

He gripped it very tightly and she looked at him again, starting to realise there was a reason he looked so familiar. She tried to pull her hand away.

'What is it, my dear?' smiled Art.

'If you are Séafra, you have changed in many ways.'

'In what ways would those be?' said Art, still smiling.

'Well, you are hurting my hand. And…I don't know; even though I can see you are bigger than him, you somehow seem much shorter.'

Art stopped sneering. A sudden rage welled up and overwhelmed him and he cast off the stinking goatskins, threw back his shoulders, and said, 'Arthur, the most heroic, at your service. You have misunderstood me before and now I will tell you the truth of what a fine man I am and of how lucky you are that I will still take you, forgiving you for having engaged with a weasel, a dancing deceiver. I will never forget though, that you have crossed into forbidden worlds and I will always ensure that as my wife you never do this again.'

Aoife was shocked. At first, she was stuck to the spot by fear.

Casting off the disguise didn't matter to him now, as his plan hadn't included staying in disguise very long anyway. He had only intended to stay in disguise long enough for other fairy people passing from the fort to the house and back, to see him with her and carry the news.

'No need to stare at me like that,' said Art. 'You will come to like me. But now you can go inside and gather your things and we will leave.'

'What are you thinking? What are you talking about?' Aoife suddenly found her voice and started shouting.

'You have no future here now, as you have been seen with a *púca,* the one night that your lover is away. They've seen you.'

'You boar,' she screamed. 'I will explain to them and to Séafra.'

Art laughed. 'They don't trust humans anyway. Not even half humans or whatever it is you are, I would say. So they will never believe whatever fanciful stories you tell them about being tricked. Now, I'm your best hope. You ought to be very grateful that I have stuck by you despite your un-reliability and your doubtful ancestry. So go and get your things before those wicked little ferrets come to get their vengeance on you.'

Of course, Art's arrogance had been growing much faster than his knowledge or wisdom and now overshad-owed all his other mental powers. He in fact had no idea of how the little people would react to what they had seen, yet he thought he could speak with authority. When Aoife went inside, supposedly to get her things, needless to say, she did not come back out again.

After the first hour, he thought she might just have a lot of womanly things to gather. After another two hours, as the early summer dawn was arriving, he finally started to admit that this plan was not going right. They were not kicking her out.

But maybe, he thought, when Séafra returned, he would reject her and then she would come out to him. He would go there the next night to be ready to forgive and rescue her. The next night, he got his answer and it wasn't the one he had been expecting. He went to his usual spot in the yew trees, not figuring out that they would have realised this was where he had been sitting when he had eavesdropped on all their intimate secrets. He had just settled into his nest of yew needles when a small whirlwind struck up, filling the air with these needles, hitting against him like tiny darts. He knew they were deadly poisonous and that if he got some of them in his mouth or nose he could be in serious trouble. He held his nose and ran out with the whirlwind following him for several hundred paces before it stopped, dropping the needles to the ground.

Art lay low for a few days, somewhat frightened by this experience. Even he, at first, accepted that they had probably not done their worst to him. But then the dark nature that was hardening into his personality started to get the better of him again. He started telling himself that as a divine agent he could not give up; that it was probably his divinity that had protected him; that they would truly not be able to do anything worse to him; that he must go back and take more drastic steps. He told himself that he had made a fair attempt to do things nicely. Now, he decided, it was time to stop tinkering and to make these people – Aoife included – respect and fear a warrior of his stature.

That evening, after training, he raised some eyebrows with his colleagues when he collected his hatchet and spear before heading off on his 'further training routine'.

'What do you want them with you for?' asked Conán, who had been working with the young men that day.

'Oh, just in case I see a weasel or some other vile creature on the path,' said Art, grinning.

'What do you mean, boy?' said Conán. 'Who in their right mind would go chasing a weasel with a hatchet?'

'Only joking,' said Art. 'I think there's a boar that crosses one of the paths I run at night and I was thinking I might be able to bring you all back a nice surprise for our feed tomorrow morning.'

'Right then,' said Conán, still not fully persuaded. There was a glazed look in Art's eyes that Conán did not care for.

When he was telling Mac Cumhaill later, Conán said, 'It was like the look of a preachy druid that thinks he's the only one that can know the wishes of the gods.'

'Don't worry about him', said Mac Cumhaill. 'I had a good talk with him a while back and he has settled well since then.'

'All the same,' said Conán, 'I asked Donn and Uileog to follow him at a distance.'

'Good enough,' said Mac Cumhaill.

But indeed it wasn't good enough. Not by a long shot. Art moved very quickly. He headed straight for some bushes directly in front of the well-beaten path between the fairy fort and Aoife's mother's dwelling. By the time the other Fianna men got there, only a hundred paces after him, they couldn't see him. They could see tracks where he had left the path but lost them after he entered a stream. But they guessed he was around this settlement somewhere, as the land beyond was open country. So they went to hide in the yew trees to see if he got up to anything.

Everything happened very fast then. It turned out that the little people were expecting Art. Aoife had persuaded them that he would not give up. She knew he would be

384

back. They had set a net in the yew trees. The trap snapped shut; two hazel trees swung back into an upright position, closing the net on their prey and lifting it completely off the ground.

Several little soldier men who had been standing invisibly waiting for their quarry, now appeared. They cheered at their success. At the back of them appeared Séafra. He was a timid young man and not much for this kind of thing. He was happier with a fiddle than a sword. He felt a bit sorry for Art in the net because he knew how crazy the love of Aoife could make a person. On the other hand, he was angry with Art for scaring Aoife and for spying on them and he wanted him given a serious talking to.

As he turned to walk back inside to Aoife, someone shouted, 'There are two of them!'

And then a human voice: 'We mean you no harm.'

And another fairy voice: 'It's not him at all, they're both too big.'

In an instant Séafra heard another human voice right above him. He looked up just in time to see the raging head of Art as he swung the axe with all his might, bringing it down at the speed of light, aiming to split Séafra in two. Séafra didn't get out of the way in time and left one foot behind. He filled with pain and his blood gushed out. His chances of escaping one-legged from the second murderous blow were very slim. As the axe was no more than the thickness of a hair from his neck, it stopped dead. It was caught in a web. Séafra looked back along the web to see Aoife's mother on the other end. He had never in his life seen her perform fairy magic before; always, he thought, acting more like a human wife for Cormac than a fairy wife. But he was very glad she had chosen today to reveal her skills.

Everyone closed in on Séafra and watched Aoife's mother tend to his wound. There was nothing she could do to re-attach the little severed foot, as it was too badly broken by the blunt axe blow. All she was able to do was to stop the blood flowing, ease the pain and make it heal immediately.

In the commotion, Art broke from the web and fled. Despite his pig-headedness, he had a good sense of preserving his health. Nobody bothered chasing him. That would come.

For now, they cut down the two Fianna men and found out from them why they had been sent. Stories were exchanged between them and the little people, piecing together all of the evening's events.

When things quietened down, the anger started to well up in the fairy fort. Cormac was warned that he would be better to stay away from his fairy wife that evening. Mac Cumhaill came down to talk to the local fairy chief, a man who went by the name of Ceann. At first he would not even receive Mac Cumhaill. When, eventually, he relented, he made no secret of the fact that he was a very angry little man.

Mac Cumhaill could see where he got the name from. He had a head on him as big as a fine turnip, even though his little body was no bigger than a mediocre carrot. Mac Cumhaill thought it would be wise to keep his amusement at this sight to himself.

'You have every right to be angry,' said Mac Cumhaill. 'I can only apologise a thousand times for this.'

'But you knew and didn't stop him,' said the chief.

'I didn't know he was capable of any real wrongdoing,' said Mac Cumhaill.

'Why, then, did you send your two men to follow him?'

'We were just curious really to see what he was hunting, but we had no suspicion he had anything more on his mind.'

'But you knew all along about him tormenting Aoife and did nothing. She's like one of ours and you did nothing to protect the child from this foul man.'

'She is like one of ours too,' Mac Cumhaill said, feebly, 'and I did punish him and forbid him to go near her again.'

'Forbid! He obviously took a lot of heed. Coming here every night without you knowing it. And you never even thought to warn me!'

'I thought he was honourable,' said Mac Cumhaill, 'but I see now that I made a mistake with him. I can't undo that.'

'There are no words of regret that can undo what has been done wrong here. A payment will be sought. My guards are already preparing to fly. Art will be killed and anyone who attempts to protect him will be killed too.'

'Art has invited whatever misfortune befalls him,' said Mac Cumhaill, 'but let us deal with him and do not allow your soldiers to kill other humans or we may be into a terrible war that no amount of talking between myself and King Luan can prevent.'

'Luan does not come into this. Every local chief of my people has full authority to deal with situations like this as he sees fit.'

Mac Cumhaill knew only too well that this was true. With the *sí,* a local grievance could be settled locally. It made it very hard to prevent outbreaks of war, as some local chiefs of the good people could take a broad view of what constituted fair revenge. There was no guaranteeing that this band of angry little people would not cause a lot of misery this night, ensuring that the big people would be out with Mac Cumhaill the next day demanding further retaliation. And so it could go on into a bitter war.

'I put myself at your mercy, chief,' said Mac Cumhaill. 'Tell me what is to be done to avoid this getting out of hand and causing much damage to innocents on both sides.'

'A good young man has lost a limb. The fact that he is not split in two is not down to lack of intention. We will avenge this and the consequences may fall upon us all as they choose.'

Mac Cumhaill did not know what to say next. A feeling of dread overcame him. The very worst kind of war was one between the peoples who share a country, because they already know each others' every move.

In the silence, another voice spoke: 'It is our request that the retribution is left to Fionn.' There stood Aoife, her face still marked from tears, talking now with the mature tones of a woman twice her age.

'You both claim to need to act on my honour and on the injury to my loved one. But we have decided that we do not want any death to overshadow our wedding. We want Mac Cumhaill to take care of this. And we demand that Mac Cumhaill not kill the bear. He must be banished so that he can never torment us again, and the people in the land he is banished to must be warned of his fault so he can be watched at all times. That is all. Any further action on either side will be a further injury to Séafra.'

There was nothing more to be said. Both Mac Cumhaill and the fairy chief were in awe of this young woman and her lover. They both knew right then that more would be heard of them in the future.

Mac Cumhaill left quietly, sending Donn and Uileog to raise all members of the Fianna at the camp with the instruction that they were to bring out the hounds and scour the countryside looking for Art.

Mac Cumhaill had again misread Art. He thought he would at least have had the good sense to realise how grave the situation was for him now, and to lie low or flee. But not at all. A few hours later, Art arrived back into the training camp. Only Mac Cumhaill and Conán were there. They could hardly believe their eyes when he wandered over and said, quite casually, 'Reporting for training. Where are the rest of the boys?'

A black rage spread over Conán's face. Art never saw the first blow coming into his face. Conán's fist landed so hard that Art, tough and all as he was, crumpled. He barely felt any of the other punches landing all over his head and ribs as he tumbled onto the ground. Mac Cumhaill didn't attempt to hold Conán back.

When Art woke up, he was on a chariot with his hands tied. From there he was taken and put into a wooden cage on a boat with cattle.

'I want to talk to Fionn,' he started shouting. 'This is an indignity. I demand to talk to Mac Cumhaill.'

Uileog and Donn, who were given the privilege of seeing him off, looked at him and said nothing.

He shouted at them, 'I am a far more important warrior than either of you. One day I will be a king. Do as I tell you now and go to call Fionn so that I may be released from this humiliation.'

'Do you find it humiliating to be alive?' asked Uileog quietly. 'That can be cured.'

'You touch me and you'll regret the day.'

'There's no need for you to see Fionn, as he sent a special message,' said Donn. 'He says to let you know that the only reason you are alive today is that Aoife asked for you to be spared. However, once you are put on this boat, that promise to Aoife is over. After that, if he ever meets you again, whether in this world or some other, he will crush your head.'

'Will he indeed!'

'And he's the least of your worries, I'd say,' said Uileog. 'Aoife's grant of mercy to you is also ended this minute for the little people. If they see you after this day, they will give you plenty of time to wish you had met Fionn first for a quicker and less painful transfer to whatever world you will go to after this one. The *sí* are sweet people when they meet sweet people. When they meet a sour person, they can turn very very sour.'

Art's protests were quieter from then on, and he made no more demands to be put back onshore. The boatmen took him along with their other cargo, to his own country. Mac Cumhaill sent a message to Angharad asking that Art be watched closely at all times and not be trusted with weapons. He asked Cormac to give the same message to Angharad, in case she thought that Mac Cumhaill was being hard on Art.

Regrettably, that was not the end of Art. Angharad's ways did not prepare her for the kind of sly treachery that now lurked near her. Art took it on himself to go and work for no reward in Angharad's service. He impressed her so much with his hard work and deference, dedication and politeness that she soon got into the habit of exchanging greetings with him. Increasingly she found it hard to believe that this was the same man of whom she had had such dire warnings from Cormac and Mac Cumhaill. She started to think that maybe they were just being overprotective of her and that they had blown some minor mistake out of all proportion.

One day, she decided to call him into her rooms to discuss the situation.

'You are indeed the best and most loyal worker a queen could ever wish to have,' she said.

'It is my greatest honour to serve you,' said Art. 'I only wish you would let me serve you better in the skills that I am really trained in.'

'And what are those?' she asked.

'In the skill of defending a precious leader from attack,' said Art carefully.

'Well, I have had no need of such defence as I rather avoid making enemies,' said the queen.

'That is one of the things that makes you so great. But, and I don't mean to worry you, but…'

'But what? Art? You can be honest with me.'

'Well, when I was in foreign lands I heard talk that there may be forces seeing your land as an easy target for attack and pillage.'

'I have avoided it this long through reaching agreement with people in a civilised way. I intend to keep doing that.'

'Alas, not all people in the world are as committed to honour or good intentions,' said Art, slowly. 'I have heard rumours that there may be a force gathering that would overrun this country without any discussions with you, enslaving and slaughtering our people and taking all before them.'

'Oh, I doubt that is true; my neighbouring leaders would always warn me if such a problem was building up.'

'They may not know yet either.'

'Well, what can I do about it anyway, even if it is a remote possibility?'

'You could have some defences. I could do that for you at no effort or cost to you.'

'Well, maybe, if it would cost the people no extra in taxes, it can't hurt…You say you have gained sufficient experience in these types of things?'

'Yes. I am the best there is. Oh, but then of course, according to our friends across the water, you can't trust me with a weapon or leave me untended.'

She looked at him long and hard. She said, 'Tell me your side of that then. What was that all about?'

'It was a major misunderstanding. I caught a fairy man trying to molest a young woman. When I tried to save her, he flew at me with a dagger. As I was attempting to take it from him, he fell over it and cut his own foot off. Mayhem broke lose. As you maybe know, when a big person has a clash with one of them, the big person is automatically wrong in their view. The scheming fairies put a spell on the woman and made her vow that she loved the fairy man and that I, in fact, had been trying to kill him for other reasons.'

'Oh, the treachery! What other reasons could you possibly have had?'

'Exactly. What could have been in it for me? Rescuing a damsel in distress. They tried to say it was jealousy and Fionn Mac Cumhaill just wouldn't hear my side of the story.'

'Well, he can be a bit full of his own opinions at times,' said the queen helpfully, 'and I suppose Cormac just believed what Mac Cumhaill told him.'

'Exactly. But I can tell you, after being shipped off in disgrace like a criminal, I will think long and hard before I ever consider doing anything to help them again.'

'Oh, well don't let one bad incident mar your entire life,' said Angharad, reaching over to touch the calculating brow of the bear-man.

393

He was finding it hard to contain his joy beneath a conjured frown.

'But what can I do? Loyal soldiering is all I know.'

'Well, that's what you will be employed to do for me, then. Though I have to remind you, I don't need very much protecting because I prefer to get on well with everyone and not to keep many possessions. But I do always keep a few guards, mainly to fend off drunkards or madmen who pester me. Not a grave job, but you can join them if you wish. Go and get yourself weapons and protect me.'

'But what about the instruction from Fionn?'

'Ah, I will talk to him the next time I see him and we will laugh about the entire episode, I am sure.'

The very next day, Art was travelling the countryside looking for the half-skilled and the willing. There were small bands of bullies to be found in most of the chieftaincies around Móna at that time. They survived by extorting silver and grain from villages in return for not burning them down. Art offered these men a deal they couldn't turn down. There was going to be only one force taking protection taxes from the villages from now on. They could either be with Art's force or be killed. If they joined him, they would get training and respect. They would even get a grand new title conferred by Art. Sir This or Sir That. And they would be forgiven for all previous robberies and murders.

Art knew how to get his point through quickly. He recruited the first band of hoodlums he met, and together they killed the next two bands. After that, all joined or fled.

With the villages too, he burnt the first two where elders asked any questions about why they should pay him any taxes. From there on, he quickly became the glorious protector of all villages in Móna.

In a matter of months he had a sizeable force and he controlled all of Angharad's countryside. She became completely isolated. The love they had held for her was completely outweighed by the fear provoked by Art.

Then one day he told Angharad he had to remove her from the castle to protect her from an invading force.

She said, 'This has gone too far, Art. This is not what I had intended. The people are scared of my army. I want this to end.'

Art barked at her. 'Quiet, foolish woman. You had your chance.'

She was escorted at sword-point, thrown into a cabin on a remote hillside and a guard left with her to keep her fed and stop her wandering. Art hadn't lost his shrewdness and he reckoned it might come in useful to be able to show her to the people at some point in the future. And she would look better at that point if she was alive.

Art issued a proclamation saying that Angharad had been taken ill, and that she had pleaded with him to take on the role of king. He had loyally taken on the heavy burdens of State. That was that. King Art began his reign.

Art soon recruited balladeers. They complied with his requests to make a glorious history for him. Soon the songs people were expected to sing at firesides in Móna claimed that their glorious warrior, Art, had slain a huge, winged lizard that breathed fire. They also claimed he had accomplished many great deeds while in Éire. Most common of all, though, were heroic songs about how he had raided and harried fairy people wherever he encountered them. Any fool would have known these tales were untrue, as there is no human ever who has set out deliberately to harass and torment the *sí* and lived to tell the tale.

He never freed himself from the wound that Aoife and the *sí* had inflicted on his pride. One of the increasingly bizarre proclamations from him puzzled even his most obsequious advisers:

> *Relations between humans and fairies are against the laws of the gods and are unnatural. Henceforth, anyone engaged in such relations will be considered to have offended the gods and will be struck down. Furthermore, any children of such relations must not see the light of day, as they create an unbearable torment, reminding us forever of the sins of their parents.'*

In spite of his increasingly entrenched obsession with the *sí* and his mistrust of women – none was allowed to join his realm or to enter his castle – the people of Móna soon became immersed in his way. The initial fear of saying anything negative about him gave way to habit and then belief. The people there started saying things like, 'Under King Art's glorious rule, crime is a distant memory.' That was true. The Sirs ruled absolute and anyone even suspected of a theft or assault would be accused of damaging the king's property and would be killed without further ceremony.

Many of the neighbouring kingdoms were amused and flowed with tales of the increasingly isolated and eccentric King Art, meeting endlessly with his Sirs, touching them with his sword as he conferred new titles on them every month, and spending hours deciding on the contours of their armour and the colours of the feathers and emblems of each. In Éire, though, there was little royal amusement. Cormac wanted Art's reign ended and his cousin Angharad reinstated.

Mac Cumhaill refused. 'We are not honour-bound to reinstate her as she dismissed our warnings. Besides, it doesn't do us any harm to have an army of raving lunatics that has to be gone through by anyone approaching us from the east.'

'You are a calculating man at times. But you won't enjoy it so much if Arthur decides to bring his lunatics over here.'

Mac Cumhaill knew that wouldn't happen. Arthur would be terrified in case any of his men got to hear the truth of his disgrace or discovered the truth of his previous tangles with the fairies.

'And you?' said Cormac craftily. 'You were not at any time deceived by Art's flattery?'

Mac Cumhaill went across the sea that night with Conán and Bran and took Angharad from her mountain hut while the guard was sleeping. When word got to Arthur, he calculated that his old enemies had drugged the guard. He announced to his people that the wonderful, gentle Angharad had been whisked off by the evilest of fairies and he entered a period of mourning for her.

Angharad was in fact brought back to Éirinn where she lived to old age as a guest of Cormac. Soft-hearted to the end, she bore no bitterness. She wouldn't even say a bad word about Art. She would just go quiet when his name was mentioned. Other than that, she charmed everyone she met with kindness and concern. They included Aoife and Séafra who came to visit her often, and who named their first-born child Angharad.

As for Art, he died young. Reputedly his heart burst open with rage after his castle collapsed into its moat and he discovered that the foundations had been removed stone by stone by some unseen forces. All the removed stones could be seen in a pile a mile away, erected in a gigantic likeness of Luan, the king of the *sí*. He couldn't bear it. However, his era made such a mark on the minds of his people that folklore about the great King Art made it sound like it lasted a hundred glorious years rather than the actual five miserable years.

16
MINDING THE SECRETS

When the Old Man faded, Arthur was lying on the soft bed of leaves and looking up at the old yew tree again. He sat up, alarmed, beginning to realise it was daytime. He'd be late for the feeding and all.

He could hear other voices calling from a distance, maybe beyond the far ditch of the Rocky Field.

He climbed to his feet. He had a terrible pain in his stomach and his mouth was as dry as if he'd been chewing sloes. He pushed out through the bushes and whistled because he felt too weak to shout loud enough for anyone to hear from that distance.

A huge figure burst through the far ditch of the bog. Arthur was very confused. Even with his blurred vision, the figure could only have been Connie.

Connie came running in great steps, water splashing as he missed the rushes. Another man ran more carefully behind him. Brian.

As they reached him, they stared at him for a moment, not seeming to know what to say.

Then Connie said, 'It's, eh, good to see you, bud.'

'Oh, thanks be to Jaysus, thanks be to Christ,' Brian kept saying.

Arthur's eyes were slow in adjusting to the daylight. 'What are *you* doing here?'

'The bold *gardaí* couldn't find you so they let me out to look for you!'

'But I'm only an hour or two late,' he said, trying to assess how high the sun was. 'And it's Saturday. So I'm not even missing school.' The mention of the guards in all this was beyond him.

Brian looked at Connie.

'Actually it's Friday, Art. You've been missing for a week.'

Arthur didn't know how that could be. But he couldn't think about it. He was just so thirsty. Getting water was about all he could think of. Before they could stop him, he was on his knees scooping up from a pocket of black bog-water. When he stood up again his legs buckled.

Connie lifted him up. Arthur didn't have the strength to object.

'Let's get you back,' said Connie. 'There's someone above in the house going to have the happiest day of her life. Jesus Christ, you're gone massive! Skinny and all as you are, it'd be easier to carry Brian.'

When they got into the kitchen, his mother stared blankly, her face grey. Then she collapsed and Brian caught her before she hit the floor.

When she recovered she couldn't stop kissing Arthur and giving Connie the occasional kiss too and saying, 'Oh, God. Oh, thank you.'

She was hardly coherent for a while, touching him as if she didn't believe he was real.

Then she said, 'I'm sorry Art. That night you went missing – I stayed up late and thought more about the idea of leasing the farm and your reaction to it, and I realised what a mistake it was. I went in to wake you to tell you it was OK. But you were gone. It felt like after all the time you and I had been treading our way carefully along a difficult cliff path together, I forgot for just a second and let go of your hand, let you slip away, and the world had finally come to an end.'

Connie called an ambulance.

Arthur said, 'I'm fine. I'm not sick.'

'Just in case,' said Connie.

'Should I call the guards?' said Brian.

Arthur had had some water and Lucozade. Connie wasn't letting him drink as much as he wanted. Just a little at a time. And then some chocolate. And cookies. He got a little bit sick but then ate more.

By the time the ambulance men came, Arthur was standing again and feeling OK. They took his temperature and his pulse and said he was grand.

His mother kept holding his hand. He found it all quite hard to take on board, because as far as he was aware, he had seen her only a few hours before.

Not long after, the *Garda* inspector from Macroom came

into the kitchen where he and Connie and Brian and his mother were sitting around the Aga with other neighbours who had gathered in to share in the good news. She was accompanied by the guard that Arthur remembered from the fire-extinguisher incident – the one who said he was Connie's friend.

By now, his mother was feeding Arthur stew and tea and ice-cream and chocolate – anything he asked for. And Pumpkin, who seemed to have grown much sleeker, was licking his legs.

'God save all here,' said the inspector.

Arthur was bracing himself for a bollocking.

'Will yis have a mug of tea?' asked Connie.

'Seeing as it was Her Ladyship here who took you off the last time, Connie, and me who had to interview Arthur at school, I'd be afraid of what the two of you might put in it,' laughed the guard.

'We McLeans don't hold grudges,' said Connie, adding a drop of Powers whiskey into each cup before he applied the tea.

'And so, now, tell me, where were you all this time, young man?' asked the inspector, getting serious and turning to Arthur.

'I was down in the rath. I fell asleep or something.'

'You can't have been – my lads looked in there twice and they were sure there was no one there.'

'It's the truth, though,' said Arthur.

'We even had sniffer dogs,' she continued. 'They came on nothing more down there other than a peculiar den, maybe a very small fox den, but with no smell or sign of a fox anywhere around.' She laughed. 'Come to think of it, one of the dogs came out yelping after sticking his nose in the den, whatever was in it. Maybe a mink or something. But you're not going to tell me you were hiding down there, now, are you?'

That was an odd question, Arthur thought.

'No, Guard.'

'It wouldn't fit a lad a quarter your size. You must have been away with someone. Who took you away?' she insisted. 'You don't have anything to fear from them. We will deal with them.'

Arthur didn't answer.

'Hmmm? You're probably still in shock. Maybe I'll ask Guard Curtain here to call out to you another day and you can tell him a bit more. Would that be OK, Helen?' said the inspector to Arthur's mother, finishing her tea and whiskey.

'The main thing,' intervened the younger guard, 'is that although you put the heart sideways in all of us, you are alive. And that has given every man and woman out there a great lift today.'

'Well, that's true enough,' said the inspector. 'And I suppose, what harm? You're back and you're not going to give us all any more frights like that, now, are you?' She was looking very sternly at Arthur.

'No, Guard.'

'And you should be very thankful to Guard Curtain here, by the way,' she said as she was leaving. 'He was the one that persuaded me to look for Connie's release so he could help find you.'

Guard Curtain winked at Arthur as he left.

'You're some cur,' said Connie with a note of praise, when things calmed down and the *gardaí* had all left. 'I'll give you that. You do know that the good inspector thinks it was all a ruse to get me out on early parole?'

The next day, when he was alone with her, Arthur vowed to his mother as he had already done to himself never to do anything that might cause her such grief again. When he had seen her ashen face, it was like getting a glimpse from the grave of how his death would have destroyed her. He loved her and didn't want even to think about it again.

With Connie back, things got better on the farm. Connie was the same as before, as if nothing had happened. Arthur, too, was nearly the same as before, as if nothing had happened.

Connie was teaching Arthur the drums, and had bought him an electric guitar. The two of them made a lot of noise in the milk-tank shed after the evening milking.

School was a mixed bag. Arthur still didn't see why he couldn't be at home minding the three extra calves Connie had given him as a reward for springing him from jail. And he was still being ignored by Sullivan and falling completely off the scales on most other subjects too. He didn't hate going to school so much, though. Other teachers were OK. He was doing well in Irish with Mrs Moriarty. Mr

Kirwan had heard about the door incident and wanted him to try out alongside final-year lads for the first hurling team. And on his first day back, after the others were done asking him where he'd been and if he was alright, Ciara came over to him and touched his hand, kind of accidentally, for a few minutes as she sat next to him on the wall. That had felt very nice. She and he talked nearly every day now.

But then the social worker came back. Connie opened the door. He didn't know that Arthur was sitting on the sofa under the stairs and could hear everything

'I want to talk to Arthur McLean. You must be the uncle. May I come in? The name is Malley.'

He didn't sound nearly as officious as when he'd been talking to Arthur's shy, nervous mam. Arthur disliked him even more this time.

'Afraid not, friend; we don't need what you're selling.'

Arthur was very relieved to hear those words. He wasn't ready for more questions about his home and his mother. But he was hoping Connie was not going to get in trouble with Malley for stopping him coming in.

'Look,' said Malley, still in an apologetic tone, 'I'm sure you mean no harm, but you should understand that you are not going to help the boy's case by obstructing me in my work.'

'Arthur is fine. He is happy as a pig in shite when he's at home. If you want some real work, why don't you go and investigate old Magill. He's been tormenting the children of this area for two generations.'

405

Malley was sounding shaky now. 'You may as well know, we get regular reports from his principal and from concerned neighbours. And we know that he ran away from home for a week. We are not in the business of ignoring a cry for help. The boy's chances of being left in this setting are already highly unfavourable.'

Arthur curled up on the sofa. He had never even thought of that.

Connie just laughed and then started talking in a fast, quiet tone that Arthur hadn't heard before.

'First, your reports from neighbours are from one neighbour only. Am I right? Do yourself a favour and go ask any other neighbour. Second, Arthur didn't run away. You have no basis for saying that. Third, I need you to go back to your office and write a report that says Arthur McLean has the best, most loving, most hard-working mother who ever stood on hind legs. Because that is the simple truth. And then you close the file on Arthur and move on to someone who does need your help. Fourth, and it's really most important you understand this, nobody is going to take Arthur McLean away from his family.'

'I hardly think it suitable that a man in your position should be telling me how to do my job. And I don't like what sounds like veiled threats. What if I were to have a word with your parole officer?' Malley's voice was squeaky now.

Connie laughed again.

'So you don't like to hear threats, only to make them. Well, don't view this as a threat. It is merely a sincere and

406

entirely factual description of the situation you have walked into. I failed my beloved brother's son once. Every day I was away pained me as much as the day Seán died. It won't happen ever again. Have you ever seen the Nine Stones on Mount Leinster, Joe Malley? No? Well there is a circle of old friends surrounding Arthur now, each as hard as those granite rocks. If you open your eyes you might see them looking back at you. You need to watch the hedge when you are out walking or look in the eyes of the guard who stops you on the road home or maybe take better note of who works at the cubicle near you in your office. Or listen more carefully to the little foreign doctor who is working in the A & E the next time your wife goes in with bruises.'

'That's not only insane, but scurrilous.' But Joe Malley now sounded like a scared kid.

Connie continued as if Malley hadn't spoken.

'I'm only trying to tell you something that you need to know. You have no business here. Anyone who tries to come between Arthur McLean and his family will rue the day. This is not a threat. It is a plain statement of fact, the kind that it is better to know in advance than to find out afterwards.'

'I'm going now.'

Connie changed tone as if he were talking to a neighbour.

'How do you find the new Passat on the juice, Joe?'

'Jesus!' said Joe Malley as he shut the car door.

Arthur heard the car turning on the pebbles and

starting to head off. Then the car stopped and Malley was back. Connie hadn't moved from the doorway.

'What's that in the laneway?'

'I see nothing,' said Connie.

'There's a huge, orange truck roaring up the lane towards me with a crazed midget looking out the window, swearing at me and giving me the finger.'

'I can't see any orange truck.'

'It was there a minute ago,' said Malley, sounding desperate. 'Where is it gone? Jesus Christ. It was straight in front of me. What's going on?'

'Don't you worry about that at all,' said Connie calmly. 'When you go home, have a nice cup of tea. Then remember to write that report and close that file. And just forget about us. And do take better care of things in your own home from now on, won't you, Joe?'

Malley went. His car never left first gear as he crept down the lane.

Connie came back inside, humming away to himself as if nothing had happened. He still didn't seem to notice Arthur on the couch. He had a quick chat with the dogs, then picked up his jacket and headed off out for the evening.

The next day, Arthur's mother said to them, 'Look, will ye both be on your best behaviour because there is going to be a fellow, that social worker guy, calling in on us. In fact I thought he was supposed to come yesterday.'

Arthur kept looking at his breakfast cereal. Connie kept studying the *Racing Post*.

'Do you hear what I'm saying?' she continued. 'I just need you both to make a little effort so we can get this guy off our backs. OK?'

'OK, Mam,' said Arthur.

'Yes,' said Connie. 'We'll try our best. Won't we, Art?'

He winked across at Arthur.

There were no follow-up visits from Malley.

Magill hadn't gone away, though. Arthur's mam was still avoiding returning his texts. And Arthur didn't even need to intercept his letters, as she was dumping them herself. Arthur couldn't work out why she was avoiding him, because he knew she was worried about how he was doing in school.

One morning it got a little crazy. Magill was waiting at the postbox which was conveniently near the speed limit sign where his mam normally dropped Arthur. Posting a letter at ten to eight in the morning!

As Arthur got out, Magill came straight over and sat into the front seat.

'I know you are a very busy young woman,' he said, 'but we do need to talk.'

What could Arthur's mother say at that point? Arthur got into the back so she wasn't left alone with Magill. She pulled the car in off the road.

'You know, we don't have to carry on like this. I'm sure a…nice…young woman like you has better things to do than sitting getting an earful from me every other day.'

Arthur could see his mother turning pale under the gaze of Magill.

Suddenly he realised why his mother had been so freaked out by all the text messages. And why she had been trying so hard to avoid a meeting with his principal. He couldn't absorb it. This leathery goat who was leering at his mother had a grandson in sixth year!

'Not to say that I don't *enjoy* meeting you,' he laughed smarmily. 'Quite the contrary. But I am certain there are…more pleasant things we could be talking about.'

'OK,' said Arthur's mother, in a resigned tone.

Magill continued: 'What I mean is, you and I could work together to sort this problem out and make young Arthur here less of a worry for us.'

'What did you have in mind?'

'There are treatment programmes available these days.'

Arthur felt a chill sweep over him.

'What do you mean?' said his mother.

'Well, there are other young lads taking medication and doing very well. You wouldn't believe me, would you, if I told you that two of the quietest boys out there on the school grounds used to be hooligans too.'

'Give Arthur drugs, you mean?' said Arthur's mother. 'No, thank you. We're against…I'm against that.'

'Typical,' muttered Magill, dropping his head in his hands and abandoning the smarm.

'Excuse me?'

'Of course, it's always the ones most in need of a strong hand that think they know better than the professionals,' fumed Magill, his manner returning to normal. 'Well, young lady, let me tell you some home truths then. This smart alec here is making poor Miss Sullivan's life impossible. She is only trying to do a day's work – which I trust you can relate to. Do you work at all yourself, or are you depending on State handouts like so many of the single mothers we see coming in here these days?'

His mother squirmed. She was no good at defending herself.

Arthur could hear a familiar voice behind him speaking angrily: 'Listen here, you fat little badger fart, that's no way to talk to a widow woman, who works harder every single day than you'll ever work in your life.'

But nobody else heard it.

The principal continued: 'The other children are now giving her backchat too and one or two of them are swearing at her. Ciara O'Connor, one of the quietest girls from one of the slightly better families in this godforsaken backwater, ups and says to Myra Sullivan yesterday, "Miss, I think you are basically a mean person and I don't care a damn what you say to me from here on." Did you ever know the likes of that? The poor woman is only trying to give these children a better way of living than their parents.'

'Has Arthur been rude to this teacher, Mr Magill?' his mother asked meekly.

'Well, not directly, but some of these other children have.'

'So. I'm sorry to hear that, but I really don't see how I can help.'

'Miss Sullivan says that Arthur is putting them up to it

and staying in the background himself, looking out the window. They all watch your boy now and take their lead from him.'

'Specifically, what are you saying?' his mother said.

The principal became angry.

'Specifically? *Specifically*, is it now? Aren't we getting very grand? Do you not understand what I am saying, woman? I hope you are not taking his side. That is what has half the children ruined. Parents. "Oh, my little Johnny would never do anything wrong…" '

His face curled up like a nasty little *bronloider*'s, for all the world, when he said this.

'I was just asking what you meant.'

The principal shouted, 'I'm saying that he is the ring-leader, the root cause, the wily fox … He is behind all the ructions. Now do you understand *that?*'

'I really don't like your shouting. I don't think it's right to be talking like that about any person, young or old,' his mother said.

'But what would I expect? As if he wasn't a gurrier al-ready, coming from the inner city, and then to bring him into that house to be further tutored in blackguardism by a notorious jailbird the likes of Con McLean. Do you want him to end up like his uncle? Is that what you want? Con was just like this when he was here. Always quietly day-dreaming, in a world of his own, you'd think, never want-ing to spend a minute at his books, and up to a power of mischief at the back of it. You couldn't beat sense into him and believe me, I gave it a good try.'

Arthur spoke: 'I'd rather end up like him than like you anyway. I don't want to end up buried alive.'

Mr Magill reddened with rage. 'What more need I say? Your son and brats like him are the reason they never should have taken the stick out of the classroom.'

'No more,' said Arthur's mother.

Arthur saw that she bit her lip to hold back the tears.

Finally satisfied that he'd struck home, humiliating her as was his daily amusement, Magill switched back to being Mr Smarm.

'Well, my dear, as I'm trying to tell you, if you cooperate with me instead of trying to pull away from me, all sorts of good things could happen.'

He opened the door and stepped out.

'There we go. See you again. See you, Arthur, and do try to remember what we've discussed.'

That night he heard his mam talking to Connie. She wasn't telling him anything much about Magill, but she was saying, 'I just don't know what to do, Con. He's so far behind. And that lousy cow Sullivan just gives him zeros. He's not that bad.'

She was sobbing a bit, Arthur thought, and he didn't want to be hearing that sound ever again.

'They say he'll probably only get into the woodwork and technology stream next year.'

'And what's wrong with tech? It didn't do me any harm.'

His mam said nothing.

Then Connie said quietly, 'Listen, isn't he happy

enough, Helen? That's the main thing. Don't worry about anything else. Everything else will fall into place.'

'Do you think so, though?' she said.

The next morning, she said she couldn't drive Arthur to school, as she had an early meeting. Arthur understood. He could have cycled the seven miles, but it was very wet and the bike had no reflectors. She asked him would he wake Connie to ask him for a lift.

Left to his own devices, Connie considered it an unnatural act to get out of bed before midday. His cows were never milked before one o'clock and the evening milking usually started when Connie came back from wherever he went gallivanting at about midnight. So it wasn't an easy job to raise him. There was no point in calling, because he wouldn't even hear the loudest shout above his own snoring.

But he didn't get cross about the cold water trickling through his hair and beard. As the first drop reached his open mouth he said, 'Mmm, that's a grand drop, Missus.'

The rest of the contents of the jug had to wash over his face to make him sit up. He didn't swear much. It almost seemed he was pleased to be asked.

When they sat into Connie's old Land Cruiser – he called it the *Queen Mary* – before he started the engine, he said to Arthur, 'Any idea why your ma doesn't want to drop you off today?'

Arthur hesitated. Connie was looking straight at him. 'I think it's Magill. I think he might be freaking her out a bit.'

Nothing more was said about that. Connie slowed and

hooted as he drove past Trevor Saltee's gates.

'If I have to be up at unholy hours,' explained Connie, 'I don't see why he should have a lie-in.'

He didn't stop at the speed limit sign. Or at the gates. He drove the thirty-year old Land Cruiser, with the exhaust hanging off it and doors held tight with baler twine, right into the school grounds, where only teachers' cars were allowed. Right up to the front door.

Magill picked up his courage and came out to tell Connie, 'You there; you there, get out of the grounds; you can't come in here with that contraption.'

'"You there"? That's not very polite,' said Connie, opening the door and stepping out. 'Pretending you don't remember my name after beating the shite out of me every day for four years.'

'Keep your distance, you great oaf,' said Magill.

'Come here to me,' said Connie, laughing. 'I don't want to hurt you at all. My brother's wife tells me she believes you are an amorous man.'

Magill was retreating towards the door, but not fast enough. Connie got him. By the ears. He lifted his two feet off the ground, and held him right up at eye level. There he dangled for what seemed like ages, kicking and saying, 'Don't, don't hurt an old man, Cornelius, let's all be sensible, let the past stay in the past, please.' He was almost squealing.

Several of the other early people gathered around.

'I'm not going to hurt you at all,' Connie repeated. Then he pulled the principal closer to his bushy beard and

415

it looked as if there was going to be a head butt. But instead Connie gave Magill a big kiss and then dropped him.

'Oh, my Lord Jesus Christ preserve me,' said Magill in utter confusion and disgust. 'Oh, sweet mother of the divine Jesus, what are you after doing?'

He put his hand to his mouth and literally ran inside, pursued by the lunatic laughter of Connie and all the lads in the yard.

Connie shouted in, 'Come on back out here Magill, you good thing you. You taste as sweet as mouldy rosebuds.'

Every day after that, Magill hid inside whenever he heard the Land Cruiser approaching. Connie would give a few revs of Mary's fine old diesel engine, before driving off with all the bystanders shouting, 'How'ye, Connie,' and 'Good man, Connie.'

One afternoon, Arthur took the familiar trip back down to the rath – even though he had been strictly forbidden to ever go near the place again. When the Old Man appeared, he said, 'It's good to see you again, *a mhic.*'

It was daytime and the Old Man was on his own. No Conán. Or Etain. Or Bal.

Arthur said, 'There's a favour I wanted.'

The Old Man started talking as though he hadn't heard Arthur. He was looking away.

'In case we don't see you again for a while – do you remember I was telling you before about how Mac Cumhaill was always guided by the spirt of Cumhall, never forgetting, never letting go? Well, that wasn't entirely true. There were occasions, only two, when the guiding voice was lost to him and those were days of dark regret. Days when Mac Cumhaill made grave mistakes. One of those times involved a terrible mistake with Diarmuid, a man who was almost as close as a son to him. It's why you never saw the spirit of Diarmuid wander with his old friends. That's a story I won't ever tell you. The other of those days was when Fionn Mac Cumhaill let his guard slip and had his own son taken when the boy was only eight. Taken to another world. The darkness that descended that day was blacker than the moonless night. His heart nearly burst with the wish to be able to tell the boy he was still ever looking for him and thinking about him; that he would see him now and then in a lone young deer that sometimes edged down to the waterside on winter evenings when Fionn Mac Cumhaill sat alone on the banks of Lough Derg, staring out across its choppy grey green expanse; that their spirits were still united and that he was certain they would meet again.'

Arthur stared quietly back. He had never seen an old man weeping openly, making no attempt to stop the tears that were flowing in streams from him, and sobbing like a child. Arthur didn't know what to say. He preferred things and people to be as he knew them. Not to change. He looked at his feet and waited a while. Then the Old Man, back in his old voice said, 'Now. What was it you wanted to ask, *a mhic*?'

Arthur asked if he could call the wren again.

Dreoilín appeared and said, 'Arthur, is the lack of worry starting to wear off? I'll polish it up for you.'

417

Arthur surprised himself and spoke up, just as Dreoilín was about to again cure him of caring a damn about the school work or anything.

'I was wondering, would it be possible this time for you to do it for me, the school work, if that wouldn't be too much trouble?'

'Well, it's not exactly much more trouble,' said the bird, 'but what difference would it make to you? Having no worries is the same feeling whether it comes as a result of having done tasks that seek to enslave you or as a result of having stopped caring about them.'

'I understand. And thank you for that.'

'So, what's the problem?'

'It's my mother. She…well, she is kind of a bit worried about me, I suppose,' Arthur said, slightly embarrassed. 'So I brought some of my books down in the rucksack today.'

Arthur was sure he saw a smile drift across the Old Man's face.

'But, doesn't she know,' said the bird, 'that you're doing more important things?'

The Old Man intervened.

'Dreoilín, you're wasting time arguing with this man. Why don't you just do as he has requested?'

'Sure, what would I know about algebra and ox-bow lakes?' said Dreoilín.

'I thought you were supposed to be the greatest magician,' said the Old Man. 'If you can't do it, why did you offer to do the work for him?'

'I'm not that good. I can't put what's in those books into that head,' he said nodding towards Arthur, 'or maybe I can do it this once. But when you get back from whatever yarns this old chancer takes you on today, there will be someone in your own house who will be able to help you with all of your work every day.'

Arthur took out his English copybook. To his amazement, the synopsis of *Hamlet* was all written in his own scrawl. And in the maths book, the algebra was all done. And what's more, he didn't need to revise for the upcoming Irish test because it all suddenly looked as easy as if he had been speaking the language all his life.

He was still staring down in confusion when the Old Man stood and said, 'A daytime welcome can quickly wear thin in the home of the *sí*. But you will always be welcome here any night that you decide to come back to us.'

Then he and Dreoilín were gone.

When Arthur went home, there was no one there except Connie who had come into the kitchen to make himself a thick sandwich with cheese, crisps and ketchup. He made a second one for Arthur.

'I don't suppose…' started Arthur. 'There wasn't anyone else in the house when you came in?'

'What are you on about, bud?' said Connie.

'Nothing.'

Later, when his mother came home, Arthur said, 'Maybe if I wanted help to do a bit of the school work now and then, you'd be the one that they said could help me?'

His mother let her handbag slip onto the floor. She

419

started talking really fast. 'Arthur, love, yes. That's the…those are the most wonderful words…Yes, I'll try, of course. Who said? No, but I've always been hopeless at explaining anything… It's not me who should help you… But hold the thought… I think it might be Connie.'

'Connie?' Arthur was surprised. 'But I thought you said Connie only got as far as the woodwork and metalwork in school?'

'Connie?' she laughed. She picked up a letter from the table. It was addressed to Dr Cornelius McLean. 'Why do you think they call him that?'

'I dunno,' said Arthur. 'I thought it might be some of his friends having a laugh. You know the strange names they call each other.'

'Connie did the tech alright. And then got into UCC. And then on a scholarship to Berkeley. Some big degree in ancient archaeology. They made him a professor. The youngest ever. And he was writing for newspapers and playing in a band and things were really starting to go great for him. And then one day shortly after…well, immediately after Dad's funeral, he threw it all in. He said the only work he was interested in was here. And he came back to run the farm full-time and fell back in with his old, strange friends and got himself into all kinds of shenanigans that you don't need to know about. And, well, you know the rest.'

'Ancient *archaeology?*'

'Old buildings…Old bones…The ways people used to live…Don't ask me.'

Arthur never asked Connie about any of that. He preferred him the way he was. But the next day he asked Connie if he wouldn't mind helping him try to figure out some maths. He was so far behind that he didn't understand any of it. He was expecting Connie to laugh at him or tell him a joke. But Connie seemed delighted. He opened Arthur's maths book as eagerly as he would the *Vintage Tractor Trader.* His voice even changed when he was at the books.

He said, 'Hmmm. Now let me see. Let me see. Let me see. Oh, Christ. How do they always manage to turn simple, clear and beautiful ideas into a hotchpotch of unutterable horse shite?'

He scanned through Arthur's books in less than an hour.

Then he closed them and said in what was going to be a very familiar tone, 'Now, you see, bud, there's very little to this. Don't mind the book. All you need to understand about algebra is this…'

After that, in the afternoons, before doing any school work, Arthur rambled around the farm with Connie. He learned how to milk the cows. He found out how to poach the river on Tuesdays when Trevor was away down at the mart making notes on what everyone was getting for their cattle. He learned how to tickle the trout and remove them from the river without ever a hook being stuck in them for sport. He shot pigeons and trapped magpies. He was often sent on dusk raids to rearrange and relocate objects on Trevor Saltee's very tidy farm. These missions included knocking down perfect stacks of hay bales and moving cows from one end of the farm to another. They were carried out not out of any vengeance – Connie didn't have that in him. It was purely that Connie delighted in how Trevor would hop from one foot to the other when he came into the yard in a rage, yelling, 'You wouldn't happen to know anything about my flipping cows at all, I suppose, Con McLean?'

'I am hard set to mind my own, Trev, let alone keep an eye on yours,' Connie would roar across the yard, laughing like a madman. 'Will you come in for a drop of tea, like a civil man, and not be standing there looking out of your mouth at us?'

Trevor would leave, muttering in rage, but afraid to say any more to Connie.

And Connie wasn't going away as much as he used to. Lots of nights he stayed home now. Often the friends would visit and talk till the early hours. Arthur's mother seemed not to mind them as much and would sometimes stay up playing cards with them and listening to their bullshit. Other times it was just the three of them in the house and Arthur would hear Connie teasing his mother about whatever TV programme she was watching or her telling him about some of her work stuff. Arthur didn't know if something was getting going between his mother and Connie, but if it was, he wouldn't really mind now.

One very cold December day Connie said to Arthur, 'I see you're not going down to the rath anymore.'

'I do still, now and again,' said Arthur.

'You've had enough of the *sí* and all those people?'

'I thought you didn't believe in them.'

Connie looked at him questioningly and then said, '*A mhic,* I think you already know that they walk among us. It took me longer to accept. I ran off to search the world for scientific explanations. But I always knew that I am part of it and it is a part of me. I had to come back where I belonged – at the gateway of the worlds.'

He had never addressed Arthur in that way before. Arthur went quiet.

'Com'ere, I have a couple of things you might like to see.'

'What kind of things?'

'You have to first let me know that you'll be OK.'

'What would that involve?'

Arthur knew Connie well enough now not to assume any task was going to be too easy.

'It would involve hiding your knowledge well and not ever ever telling anyone, under any circumstances, ever.'

'OK.'

That would be no bother for Arthur, as there were a lot of things he'd been hiding well and not telling anyone about for a long time now.

'Seriously now,' said Connie, looking very intently at Arthur, 'if they know, they will come to try to take these things away and lock them up in a vault to be studied by people who won't understand anything.'

Connie looked all around to make sure there were no cars coming down the lane, no sign of Arthur's mam at the windows, no sign of Trevor at his lookout post on the Brown Hill Field where he sometimes stood with binoculars, trying to catch Connie doing something illegal. Then he nodded to Arthur to follow him out to the back of the hayshed into his tractor workshop.

He started removing stacks of dead batteries, buckets of burnt engine oil, and armfuls of blue baler twine, all from the bin where he kept stuff he was reluctant to dump in case he found a use for it some day. Then he lifted the massive steel bin from its spot. There was a dirty carpet offcut covering the floor under it.

'Pull that back, Art,' he said.

Arthur did. The floor underneath was completely clean. There was a steel door in the middle of it.

'What's that?' asked Arthur.

'What does it look like?' said Connie.

'It looks like the same kind of safe you keep the shotgun in'.

'There you go. Here are the keys.'

Arthur was just as anxious to cut to the heart of this matter, as he was entirely curious now. He put a key into each of the locks and opened the cabinet as he had watched Connie doing with the gun safe. It looked empty at first.

'Put your hand in,' said Connie.

That instruction worried Arthur. Knowing Connie and his tricks, his hand could touch anything from warm cow-dung to a nest of pet rats. And all there would be after that would be roars of laughter from Connie. On the other hand, this door definitely hadn't been opened in a long time. If it was a trick, it was a very elaborate one.

He looked into Connie's face. There was no trick here. He was absolutely quiet and his mouth was serious for once. He actually seemed to be shaking.

'Go on,' he said, almost whispering.

Arthur did. He felt something cold like metal. There were two objects. He could feel what they were. He ran his fingers over the fine curves and ridges. Heavy enough for the size of them. He held his breath and lifted them out. Under the bright lights of the tractor workshop, there was no doubting it. The long scabbard had all of the intricate engravings. The sword handle was still perfect. The large ruby remained in the heart of the magnificent shield, proud of the dent where it had protected its owner from a falling tree. The bronze that connected ancestors still duskily reflected the lights of the shed. Arthur felt a cold shiver move across his shoulders.

'We'll have to find a new place for these,' said Connie, 'and there's more. You are now a part of it. They live among us and they also live through us. That's a weight on your shoulders, but I think you are able for it.'

Arthur didn't feel any weight. This brought everything together. Even before Connie spoke, Arthur knew what he was going to say.

'This is not the end, *a mhic.* It's only the beginning.'

GLOSSARY

Note: *When pronouncing Irish words, the letters CH should be pronounced like the end of the Scottish word 'loch', to make a harder sound than the CH at the end of 'much'.*

A chara: (formal) term of address (from *cara,* friend), pronounce: a-CHAR-a

A chroí: term of endearment (from *croí,* heart), pronounce: a-CHREE

Alanna: term of endearment, usually only used for a girl (form of *leanbh,* child)

Amadán: fool, pronounce: OM-a-dawn

A mhic: term of endearment towards a man or boy (form of mac, son), pronounce: a-VICK

Bandraoi: druidess, pronounce: bon-DREE

Banshee: a female spirit whose wailing predicts death

Bealtaine: the first day of the summer quarter of the year; the first of May, pronounce: BAL-thinna

Bodach: lout, pronounce: BUD-uch

Boreen: narrow, unsurfaced road or lane

Brehon: learned interpreter of the law; judge

Bronloider: from the Irish *brionglóid,* dream, pronounce: brun-LOYD-er

Buan: permanent, recurring, pronounce: BOO-an

Cailleach: witch, hag, pronounce: CAL-yoch

Caoineadh: (caoining) – keening, pronounce: KEEN-ah

Chaw: chew

Ciotóg: left-handed person, pronounce: kith-OGUE

Craic: fun (can also be used to mean 'things in general', as in 'How's the craic?' meaning 'How are things going?'), pronounce: crack

Currach: a coracle or skin boat, pronounce: KUR-roch

Eejit: idiot

Éireannach: Irishman, pronounce: AIR-a-noch

Eiscir: long-ridged embankment of earth naturally occurring in the landscape, pronounce: ESH-ker

Famine Road: road, usually going from nowhere to nowhere, built as part of a work-creation scheme during the Irish Famine (in the mid-19th century) by starving peasants; the idea was to create work in order to justify giving money to the poor, but in fact the people were so ill and hungry that they often died while working.

Fathach: giant, pronounce: FAH-hach

Fear dearg: literally 'red man', like a *púca*, a lone traveller from the realm of the little people, given to practical jokes; those who crossed him could expect bad fortune, pronounce: FAR JAR'g

Gaeilge: Irish language, sometimes anglicised as 'Gaelic'

Gallery: Great craic or fun, high jinks

Garda: (correctly Garda Síochána) Irish police force; also, a police officer, pronounce: GAR-da

Gardaí: plural of *garda*, often used collectively to mean the police (or 'the guards') in general, pronounce: gar-DEE

Garsún: boy, pronounce: gar-SOON

Gob: mouth

Go bhfóire Daghda orainn: may Daghda help us, pronounce: guh VORE-ah DAG-da URR-ing

Gombán: fool, pronounce: gom-BAWN

Gomdaw: fool

Guard: a police officer (also known as a *garda*)

Gurrier: a rough, disreputable person

Hooly: party

Hurling: fast ball game, played with sticks (hurleys), with similarities to field hockey and lacrosse

Imbolg: the first day of the spring quarter, the first of February, the feast of Brigid

Leaprachán: leprechaun

Lúdramán: idiot, fool, pronounce: LOO-dra-MAWN

Lughnasa: first day of the autumn quarter of the year, the first of August, associated with the harvest and sacred to the god Lugh

Mitch: play truant from school

Mór: big, great, pronounce: more

Mullocking: acting clumsily or in an ungainly, rough manner

Oíche Shamhna: the last night before *Samhain,* 3 October (Hallowe'en), pronounce: EE-ha HOW-na

Olagón: wailing, pronounce: ULL-ag-OWN

Pisreóg: superstitious belief, pronounce: pish-ROGUE

Praiseach: charlock, a yellow-flowered weed, pronounce: PRASH-ock

Púca: mischievous sprite, pronounce: POOK-ah

Puck: To poke or butt something, to give someone a dig

Raiméis: nonsensical talk, pronounce: rah-maysh

Rath: overgrown mound isolated in the Irish landscape, believed to be sacred to the *sí,* usually avoided by farming people

Samhain: the first day of the winter quarter of the year, 1 November, pronounce: SOW-an

Sceach: whitethorn (hawthorn) bush, sacred to the little people, pronounce: sk-yach

Scrawb: scratch or scrape

Seanachaí: storyteller, pronounce: shan-a-CHEE

Sí: fairy; fairy people, pronounce: shee

Slag: to tease

Sleeveen: miserable, ingratiating creature

Sliotar: small hard ball used in the game of hurling, pronounce: SLI-ther

Straoil: a slattern, an insulting word for a woman, pronounce: streel

Stuachán: idiot, pronounce: sthu-kawn

Teach: (Mhic Cumhall) house (of Mac Cumhaill), pronounce: choc (vick cool)

Taibhse: ghost, pronounce: THIVE-shah

Wisha: Word sometimes used at the beginning of a sentence, similar to 'ah, well'

PLACE NAMES AND PERSONAL NAMES

Note: *Names that are pronounced the same way in English are not included.*

Aoife: pronounce: EE-fa

Baile: settlement, territory, pronounce: BAL-ya

Baile Cumain: on the east coast, the territory of the Cumain clan

Baile Dunchada: just south of Tara, the territory of the Dunchada clan

Baile Lugda: in the northwest, the territory of the Lugda clan

Beatha: Irish word for life, pronounce: ba-ha

Bré: town on the east coast, pronounce: bray

Bréagán: pronounce: bray-gawn

Caoimhín: Kevin, pronounce: keeveen

Ceann: head, pronounce: ky-ANN

Cinnéide: Kennedy, pronounce: kin-AY-da

Cóbh: harbour on the south coast, pronounce: cove

Conaire: pronounce: KUN-a-ra

Conán: pronounce: cunn-AWN

Corca Dhuibhne: on the southwest coast, pronounce: CUR-ka GWEE-na

Creidhne: a god worshipped by metalworkers, said to be the artificer of the Dé Danann, pronounce: kred-neh

Crothán: pronounce: cruh-HAWN

Cumhall: pronounce: cool

Daghda: the good god, the senior deity, pronounce: DAG-da

Dearbhla: Dervla

Dé Danann/tuatha Dé Danann: the people of the goddess Danú, early inhabitants of Ireland who had magical powers, pronounce: day DON-on

Déise: region around Waterford in the southeast, pronounce: DAY-sha

Diarmuid: Dermot, pronounce: DEAR-mid

Dreoilín: wren, pronounce: dro-leen

Dún Ailinne: the centre of power of the kings of Laigin (Leinster), pronounce: doon AW-ling-a

Eibhlín Rua Ní Fhógartaigh: red-haired Eileen Fogarty, pronounce: Eileen or Evelyn ROO-ah nee OH-garthy

Éire, Éirinn: different grammatical forms of the same word, both meaning Ireland, pronounce: AIR-ah, AIR-in

Emhain Macha: Armagh, centre of power of the kings of Uladh (Ulster), pronounce: OW-an MA-cha

Féilim: Phelim, pronounce: FAY-lim

Fiachra: pronounce: FEE-uch-ra

Fianna: warriors, pronounce: FEE-ah-na

Fionn: fair-haired, pronounce: finn or fyunn

Fionnán: derivation of Fionn, pronounce: finn-AWN or fyunn-AWN

Fógartaigh: pronounce: fogarty

Fotharta: pronounce: FUH-har-ta

Gearraí: pronounce: gyar-ee

Gráinne: pronounce: GRAWN-yeh

Laigin: Leinster, eastern province, pronounce: lin

Latharna: pronounce: la-HAR-na

Liath Luachra: pronounce: leah LU-uch-ra

Liath Ní Choinchin: pronounce: leah nee chun-chin

Loígis: A place in the midlands, part of what is currently called Laois, pronounce: leash

Lugh: the god of light and of the harvest, pronounce: loo

Mac Cumhaill: son of Cumhall, pronounce: mc-COOL

Mumhan: Munster, southern province, pronounce: MOO-an

Murtagh: pronounce: Murta

Niamh: pronounce: NEE-av

Nóirín: Noreen

Ó Broinn: O'Brien or O'Byrne, pronounce: o brin

Ó Lochlainn: O'Loughlin

Salach: the most ancient woman in the world, and a sister of the Banshee, pronounce: sal-OCH

Séafra

Seán Óg: young Seán; Seán Óg Ó Hailpín is a well-
n hurler for County Cork, pronounce: shawn·ogue

Sliabh Bladma: Mountains of Bladma, after an early
Silesian invader, on borders of present-day Offaly and
Laois, pronounce: shlieve bloom

Sliabh Laigin: Mount Leinster, in present-day Carlow,
pronounce: shlieve lion

Sliabh na mBan: mountain of the women, in
present-day Tipperary, pronounce: shlieve na monn

Tadhg: pronounce: tige (like tiger, without the r)

Tíreach: pronounce: TEE-roch

Uileog: pronounce: ill-yogue

Uladh: Ulster, northern province, pronounce: ulla